SMASH CUT:

Also by Steven Womack
Murphy's Fault

S·M·A·S·H CUT:

STEVEN WOMACK

ST. MARTIN'S PRESS
NEW YORK

Library of Congress Cataloging-in-Publication Data

Womack, Steven,
    Smash cut: / Steven Womack.
        p.   cm.
    "A Thomas Dunne Book."
    ISBN 0-312-06467-5
    I. Title.
PS3573.0576S62   1991
813'.54—dc20   91-21562
                                                                        CIP

First Edition: October 1991

10 9 8 7 6 5 4 3 2 1

to Michaelangelo

SMASH CUT:

1

DAMN, THE SWELTERING, OVERWEIGHT MAN THOUGHT, THESE ORIEN-
tals just don't sweat.

Robert J. Thibodeaux, the sixty-year-old president of the Louisiana Power Company, leaned to his left as the chopper banked and
headed upriver toward the ghostly white images ahead and below.
The helicopter had lifted off only minutes before, leaving behind the
stifling traffic of the Crescent City as it inched along in its morning
rush-hour crawl.

"This beats driving, don't it!" Thibodeaux yelled. Sweat beaded
on his forehead, above his upper lip, and around the collar of his
short-sleeved polyester dress shirt. Even in the air-conditioned helicopter, the summer heat was tough on a body.

The man next to him, who'd left his suit coat on, turned and
stared. The lack of expression on his face and the absence of visible
moisture anywhere on him quietly astounded Thibodeaux.

Andrew Kwang's mind and voice were calm. He had learned
many years ago not to let his discomfort betray him.

Thibodeaux sweats not only from the heat.

The city was receding behind them now as the pilot slid the
chopper upriver beyond the skyscrapers and the automobiles. Miles
behind them, the Louisiana Superdome faded to golf-ball size, and
the river bridges came to resemble pieces from a child's erector set.
There was some turbulence in the morning air, but Kwang didn't
notice. His mind was centered on what lay ahead of him. Only he
could make the final decision, the result of months of negotiations
and hard, painstaking compromise.

Out of the hazy early-morning blend of humidity and pollution from the upstream refineries, the massive, sprawling facility gradually came into focus.

To the left was an enormous blockhouse of concrete and steel. By itself, it covered an area the size of several football fields, but it was dwarfed by the staggeringly huge cooling unit that stood next to it. The cooling unit looked like an enormous hourglass, Kwang thought, only not so pinched in the middle. It stood hundreds of feet tall and was the biggest single piece of poured concrete he'd ever seen.

Thibodeaux reached in front of him and tapped the pilot on the shoulder. When the young man turned, the older man made a circling motion with his bare forearm, his thumb and index finger held to a point. The pilot nodded; the helicopter began a circling descent.

In seconds, they were hovering over the open throat of the tower. It seemed to go down forever into darkness. Try as he might, Kwang could not see down to the bottom. He had the figures in his head, but they had been meaningless until he'd actually seen the tower. It was titanic, bigger than anything he had imagined. He nodded slightly. The pilot circled again, to within a couple of hundred feet of the tower itself.

Yes, Kwang thought, it would do nicely.

Thibodeaux tapped the pilot's shoulder again and made a thumbs-up gesture. The pilot pushed in the throttle. The whine of the turbine grew as the chopper climbed and headed back toward the city.

"Well, Mr. Kwang, that's it," Thibodeaux shouted over the noise. "The Riverbend Nuclear Power Plant. What do you think?"

Kwang pasted on his inscrutable Oriental smile, his one concession to Occidental expectations.

"I'll take it," he said in a normal voice, confident that the sweating Thibodeaux could read his lips.

2

THE CONFERENCE ROOM DEEP IN THE BOWELS OF THE SUPERDOME WAS
packed with reporters, photographers, and the inevitably blow-dried
television pretty boys with their female counterparts. Thibodeaux,
still sweating in the glare of the lights, made his announcement and
took a seat behind the long conference table.

A man of late middle-age who bore the marks of years of life in
the fast lane stood up. In contrast to the suits and ties around him,
he wore an old pair of khakis and a light-blue sweater that long ago
had seen better years. Brushing his gray hair off his forehead, he
stepped to the podium with a folded sheaf of papers held in his
hands. He cleared his throat with a deep, rolling sound, looked out
over his glasses in a writerly way, then spoke.

"As many of you know, I'm Miller Taylor. I've lived here in
New Orleans for the past five years and am an active member of our
writing community. I'm thrilled that Mr. Kwang has decided to
locate his newest studio here.

"I am equally thrilled," he said, looking up from his notes,
"that Mr. Kwang has hired me as his vice president and creative
director for the studio. . . . I need the work."

Several in the crowd laughed. Those who knew Taylor didn't.

"Mr. Kwang has asked me to read a prepared statement,"
Taylor said, returning to his papers. "After that, he is ready to take
your questions. . . ."

Taylor cleared his throat again, then looked down at his papers.
"Mr. Kwang is pleased to announce, along with Mr. Thibodeaux
and our other honored guests, the agreement in principle to purchase
the Riverbend Nuclear Power Plant facility. Kwang World Pictures

has a long history of utilizing local creative talent, local craftspersons, and local facilities in the production of its movies. With the acquisition of this plant, Kwang World will continue this long tradition. The newest Kwang studio will hold under one roof not only one of the largest indoor production facilities in the world, it will also utilize the plant's cooling tower as the world's largest underwater soundstage."

Taylor heard a murmur of surprise ripple through the audience like a wave. Mixed in with the drawn breaths were what sounded, strangely, like a few chuckles.

In the back of the room, corporate attorney Carlton Smith leaned against a wall. In his sixties and balding, yet still slim, thanks to his lifelong membership in the exclusive New Orleans Athletic Club, Smith had spent his life handling deals like this one for the bank. By successfully arranging financing for the purchase of the nuclear plant, Carlton Smith was proving two things. Not only had the banking authorities and the public been shown that the First Interstate Bank of Louisiana had recovered from its recent trouble, but Carlton Smith had shown himself that he could rebound from the worst professional setback he'd ever endured. There was a great deal at stake here, he thought, and it felt damn good to get back in the game.

"The new Kwang World Pictures studio will mean over three hundred steady jobs for the New Orleans community," Taylor said. "It will also pump an estimated fifty to seventy-five million dollars a year into the local economy. And finally, it will serve as a focal point for a renaissance of the creative community of New Orleans."

Taylor paused for effect, then looked up at his audience. "At this time, Mr. Kwang wishes to announce that the first project for the new underwater soundstage will commence this fall. The film, titled *Gargantua from the Deep 2000 A.D.!!!,* will have an estimated budget of thirty million dollars and a cast of nearly two hundred stars and other actors, plus the crew and local extras. The film will go into major worldwide theatrical release next summer, and we anticipate that it will continue the long tradition of success that Kwang World Pictures enjoys."

Taylor looked up, jogged his stack of papers into a neat pile. "Now, are there any questions?"

There was a rustle of shuffled paper and whirring cameras. A few strobes flashed as the still photographers snapped away. Hands

4

holding pens and pencils went up, the younger ones shooting up, while the older ones took their time. Taylor pointed to an attractive, young red-haired woman holding a narrow reporter's notepad.

"Two questions," she announced. "First, is there going to be any cleanup involved at the nuclear power plant?"

"Let me take that one first," Taylor interrupted. "I want this made perfectly clear. We've been given assurances by the proper state authorities that there is absolutely no threat of contamination or radiation at the plant. As you know, the environmental lawsuits and the cost overruns stopped the project long before it was time to fuel it."

He paused. "The Riverbend Plant is absolutely, undeniably clean."

The reporter scribbled a note on her pad, then looked back up.

"How much is it going to cost to convert the plant into a film studio, Mr. Kwang?"

Kwang leaned forward at the table and spoke into a microphone with an even voice that was devoid of both emotion and accent.

"My accountants tell me the costs will run approximately fifty million dollars."

"So with the purchase price of three hundred million, this will bring your total investment in the studio to around a third of a billion dollars?" the reporter asked on follow-up.

"At least," Kwang answered, as if he were discussing the price of a loaf of bread.

"How can you possibly recoup an investment like that?" the reporter demanded, her head down as she scribbled away.

"I am depending upon my creative people to produce movies that the public will want to see."

Still at the podium, Miller Taylor rolled his eyes in mock horror and stage-whispered, "Now we're in real trouble," to general laughter throughout the room.

"Mr. Kwang," an unusually well-dressed reporter wearing tortoiseshell glasses spoke up. "I'm Greg Anthony, the *Times-Picayune's* movie critic. Can you respond to rumors in the industry that you've been courting Jack Nicholson to star in your first film here, but that he isn't interested because so many of your films have been, shall we say, of questionable taste?"

Taylor looked down uncomfortably as he waited for Kwang to

5

respond. There was a long moment of silence as he wondered whether or not he should speak up for his boss.

"It has always been my contention," Kwang said evenly, "that the true arbiter of taste is the viewing public. To suggest that the moviegoing audience is incapable of determining what is worthwhile is not only disrespectful, but presumptuous as well."

Taylor smiled. He knew Greg Anthony for what he was: a pretentious little snot. Kwang had handled him well.

Suddenly, Taylor felt a tightening below his belt as a tall woman in the middle of the room stood. A full six feet tall and more, the striking dark-haired woman wore glasses, perfect makeup, and a silk dress that Taylor couldn't have afforded to buy anyone in his best years, which were long past him. Her hair was long, yet neatly combed over her shoulders in a businesslike manner. She was still a stunner, Taylor thought, despite the cold in her eyes. This was the moment he'd feared and dreaded.

"I'm Pearl Bergeron," the woman announced, in a voice that was used to being heard. "I am chairperson of the Louisiana Film Commission. You may be here to announce your arrangement, Mr. Kwang, but I am here to go on record in opposition to the proposed sale of the Riverbend facility to you—"

"Sale, Ms. Bergeron," Taylor interrupted. "Sale."

"Proposed sale, Mr. Taylor," the woman snapped. "That sale will not be final for weeks, and no film will be shot there until all the proper permits and zoning variances have been obtained."

"That's true, but—" Taylor began.

"I am also here to announce that the Louisiana Film Commission has unanimously petitioned state and federal authorities to deny permission for Louisiana Power to sell that facility to Mr. Kwang."

A collective gasp rose among the gathered journalists, most of whom seemed to have been caught off guard by the announcement.

"I also wish to announce that the film commission, in conjunction with the Louisiana Citizens for Decency, has filed a lawsuit seeking to cancel the proposed sale as soon as possible."

"On what grounds?" Taylor demanded, before anyone could shut him up.

"On the grounds," Pearl Bergeron said, "that the citizens of this state are not going to stand for the kind of filth that Kwang creates being produced in their community!"

6

The woman turned and walked out, her high heels clicking on the conference room tiles. The staccato tapping gave way to the sound of questions being fired in every direction at once.

Andrew Kwang folded his hands in front of him and stared at the woman as she stormed out of the room. The expression on his face was blank. No one knew what wheels were turning inside him.

In the back of the room, Carlton Smith reached up and rubbed his temples. He, too, had been warned. He wasn't worried about the Louisiana Citizens for Decency; that kind of lunacy could be handled. But Pearl Bergeron was another matter. She swung a lot of weight with the state government.

After all, she was the governor's daughter.

Behind his eyes, a headache was about to flame into life like a glowing ember that the firemen failed to douse. Carlton Smith shook his head slowly, then headed for the nearest telephone.

3

JACK LYNCH LOOKED DOWN AT THE MESS IN HIS SINK AND SHOOK HIS head. How can anybody live like this, he asked himself, staring at the pile of dishes, some of which were beginning to show signs of life.

He turned away to spare himself the agony. Reaching for the dingy glass pot on his coffeemaker, he poured himself one last cup of strong coffee and chicory. He hated the way coffee burned when it had been sitting on a hot plate for too long, but he didn't feel up to making another pot. He sipped the rank liquid and lit another cigarette.

It was 10:00 A.M., and Lynch hadn't left for his office yet. He wasn't likely to be docked for his absence, though, given that he was the sole proprietor of a one-man shop.

Besides, it had been almost two weeks since he'd had a client, and before that, he'd just cranked out a few press releases for a small manufacturing firm in Plaquemines Parish and done a slick but boring sales brochure for a retail computer firm. It had been like that ever since he left the bank; what clients there were brought only boring work, and damned little of that.

He'd been in business now just over three months. It had taken him longer than he'd expected to recover from the savage beating he'd taken in the dark parking lot a year earlier, the same attack that had killed Sally. Afterward, there didn't seem to be much reason to go on. Then, when the authorities came in and took over the bank, Lynch quit before they had a chance to fire him.

Which was fine for a while. He traveled, recovered from his injuries, healed as well as could be expected. But sooner or later he had had to get back to the real world. His savings were nearly gone, and he felt himself becoming stale and weary. He opened up an office, sent out a few feelers, and advertised for public relations clients. He'd hoped that he'd soon be able to take on partners and employees and make a real company out of it. It soon became clear, however, that the kinds of clients he needed in order to prosper just weren't coming to him.

His secretary had walked. He was late on his rent and hadn't had a call in more than a week. He wondered, when he bothered to give a damn, what he would do when the money ran out.

He drew in deeply on his cigarette and thought briefly how he needed to quit smoking. One of these days, when some of this craziness lets up.

Get a job, maybe. He hated the thought of reentering corporate life. The truth was that over his time of recovery and subsequent self-employment, Lynch had become spoiled. He'd had enough of corporate life; the last thing he wanted was to go back to the kind of work he'd done for the bank. He was bored, nearly broke, but still better off than he had been before.

"Maybe I can drive a cab," he said out loud. Talking to himself was another habit he'd picked up over the last few weeks. Lynch was not exactly a hermit these days, but he didn't go out of his way to see people either.

The problem for him, professionally, was that his name in the community had been irrevocably linked with the scandal at the First Interstate Bank of Louisiana. The fact that his name was tied to the trouble because he'd helped expose it was incidental, a bitter and small comfort. The business world had turned its back on Jack Lynch as if he had somehow been rendered unclean by it all.

He sat down at his small kitchen table and unfolded the morning paper. Mixed in with the wire service feeds were a few local stories; the one at bottom right, below the fold, concerned the arrival of millionaire film producer Andrew Kwang in New Orleans. Kwang would hold a press conference that morning to announce his acquisition of the derelict Riverbend Nuclear Power Plant.

Lynch read the article with the trained eye of a former journalist but with little real enthusiasm. Like everything these days, the outside world seemed to bore him more than anything else. As he finished the article, the electronic buzzing of his phone caught his attention.

Lynch looked up with a mixture of irritation and anticipation.

9

Damn telephone, he thought. He hated the thing but felt compelled to jump when it beckoned.

"Hello," Lynch said casually.

"Jack?"

"Carlton? Carlton Smith?" he asked.

"Yes, it's been a while, friend. How are you?"

"Great, just great, Carlton," Lynch lied. "How about you?"

"Pretty well. I tried your office and didn't get an answer."

Dammit, Lynch thought, forgot to set the answering machine.

"Sorry, Carlton. My girl's got the day off and I needed to run back to my apartment for some papers I forgot."

"No matter." Carlton sounded unusually tight to Lynch. But then again, he sounded that way the last time they'd talked at the bank together. Back before the world fell apart. "I've got a little problem here. Of a professional nature. I was wondering how your client load is these days."

"Moderate," Lynch continued with the lie. The last thing one told prospective clients was how badly they were needed. "But I'm always open for interesting offers."

"I may have one for you. Did you see the paper this morning?"

"Yeah."

"The story about Andrew Kwang, the film producer?"

"Still with you."

"I'm afraid he's going to have a bit of trouble negotiating our convoluted little system here. He may be in need of your . . . specialized services."

"All right, I'll talk to him," Lynch said, his voice hiding his rising pulse rate.

"It's rather urgent," Carlton Smith said formally. "Can you make it this morning?"

Lynch looked at his watch. He needed to stop by his office, which was only a few blocks from the bank, and fire up that blasted answering machine again.

"How about eleven?"

"Done," Smith answered. "Have them buzz my office from the lobby."

That's right, Lynch thought as he hung up the phone, I can't just walk in anymore.

10

4

IT WAS THE FIRST TIME IN A YEAR THAT HE'D WALKED THROUGH THE doors of the First Interstate Bank of Louisiana. He'd spent just over a decade of his life here: worked for the Old Man here, fallen in love with Sally here, lost everything but his life here. Lynch had cradled his dying employer's head in his lap as the body of his ex-wife, Katherine, lay sprawled across the floor a few feet away. A security guard had taken her out only a split-second before she could turn the gun on Lynch.

And Lynch had sat in a car outside the bank during the longest night of his life, gun in hand, waiting to kill Sherriff Murphy, the son of a bitch who'd started it all. But at the last minute he'd pulled back, unable to kill in cold blood. Instead, he had watched in a mixture of fatigue and despair as local police and federal agents raided the bank, took control of it, and ended a long chapter in Lynch's life.

Now he stood before the building again, sucking in a deep breath to steady his nerves. The bank hadn't changed a bit from the outside since reopening. Internally, though, it couldn't have been more different, with everyone who was once in top management gone except Carlton Smith. Lynch planted his foot in front of the revolving door, got his timing, and entered as the door spun around in front of him.

Inside, the place seemed to him as cold as a meat locker. Off to his right, the reception desk sat where it always had, with someone Lynch didn't recognize manning it. A security guard stood nearby, again someone Lynch had never seen. He made eye contact with the woman behind the desk and started over in her direction, then stopped next to the guard.

"Excuse me," he asked. "Where's Billy?"

The guard, a young black man who looked every inch a professional, eyed Lynch with practiced suspicion.

"Billy?" he asked.

"The old guy who used to be the security guard out front here."

"Oh, him," the guard said. "He went on medical leave, then took retirement."

"Medical leave?"

"Stress-related." The young man lifted a lip, almost in a sneer, as if stress were something that could never happen to him.

Of course, Lynch thought. Billy was the security guard who had saved his life by blowing the top of Katherine's head off before she could pull the trigger a second time. Billy was an old Cajun boy who'd moved to the city and before that day had never in his entire life had to fire a gun in anger or panic. Lynch hoped he'd gone back to the bayous to find peace and to escape the kinds of visions that still haunted his own dreams.

"Carlton Smith, please. He's expecting me. Jack Lynch." Lynch knew from long-standing practice that anyone wishing to get past the front lobby of the bank had to have a reason for doing so. Still, it felt odd to have to ask permission to enter.

The woman punched four buttons on the phone and spoke into it. Seconds later, she looked up.

"You go up to the—"

"I know where it is," Lynch interrupted her. He walked over to the bank of elevators and pressed the call button. A door opened; he was surprised to see that the elevator was empty inside. The elevators had all been converted to self-service. The long tradition of uniformed elevator operators had died with the Old Man, who had grown up poor and thought pressed, snappy uniforms meant class.

Carlton Smith sat behind his desk as his secretary showed Jack in. He stood with the warm smile of a man who hadn't seen an old friend in a long time.

"Good to see you, Jack. It's been too long."

"Good to be back, Carlton. I guess." Lynch took a chair across from the long desk. He and Carlton simultaneously pulled out cigarette packages. It had once been a shared joke between them that they were the only two left among the bank's top management who still smoked. Everyone else had stopped in an attempt to curry favor

12

with Mr. Jennings, the Old Man, who had loathed cigarettes when he was alive.

"I can see why being back here would be rather bittersweet for you," Carlton said, fitting his cigarette into a polished black cigarette holder.

Lynch stared at his old friend for a blank second. "So tell me about this Mr. Kwang."

"I've got him cooling his heels in the conference room. I'll ask him to join us in a few moments. But first, I wanted to clear up a few things with you. How much do you know about Mr. Kwang and the Riverbend plant?"

"Only what I read in the newspapers."

"That means not much," Carlton said. Their mutual dislike of journalists was another shared attribute. "I've got a file I want you to take with you that will bring you up to date on everything. That is, if you decide to take Mr. Kwang on as a client."

"If he decides to take me on. . . ."

"I think I can handle that," Carlton said. "We have some influence with Mr. Kwang, although I have to be careful not to overestimate it. Mr. Kwang has gotten very rich by building his studios and filming his pictures with O.P.M."

"Other people's money," Lynch said, inhaling deeply on his cigarette.

"Yes. And in this particular case, he happens to be using ours. Tell me, Jack. What do you know about Pearl Bergeron?"

"Pearl Bergeron. Let's see." Lynch's eyebrows flicked up once in surprise, then went back down to neutral. "Governor's daughter. Rich as hell from Mommy's side of the family, I think, plus whatever her father has managed to steal over the decades. I heard Daddy gave her the film commission for Christmas last year. Scuttlebutt in town is she gets off on artist types. Attractive but icy. Intelligent but angry. Frustrated edge to her. She really might have been somebody, if she hadn't been born rich and powerful."

"You seem to know her well," Carlton said.

"I met her a few times. You know how the Old Man felt about the arts. Couldn't figure 'em out, but thought it would buy him some class. He gave money, but he had me handle it. Ballet, visiting opera, cocktail parties, fundraisers. That sort of thing."

"But you don't know her intimately."

Lynch looked over at Carlton and smiled. "I'm not an intimate in that circle. Besides, what's all the interest in Pearl Bergeron?"

"At this morning's press conference, where Kwang announced this film deal worth hundreds of millions, with jobs and prestige and other benefits attached, Pearl Bergeron gets up and yells out she's going to bugger the whole deal. Filed a lawsuit, she says. The film commission's on record as opposing the sale. They'll fight the variance we need."

Jack whistled softly. "She say why?"

"That's what we can't figure out. She ranted and raved on about Mr. Kwang producing smut. But you and I both know, Jack, that if every film producer of questionable taste were to suddenly get ill and die, Hollywood would be a ghost town."

"And the better for it," Lynch commented.

"Agreed," Carlton said. "But my objective here is to see that this deal goes through. Whatever the good Ms. Bergeron's objections to Mr. Kwang are, I want them taken care of. That's where you come in."

"Find out what she wants and see that she gets it."

"In the most discreet way possible," Carlton added. "And as quickly as possible."

"That may take some doing. I hear she's a ticket. Okay, I'll talk to him."

A moment later, the two men stood politely as the secretary led Andrew Kwang in.

"Mr. Kwang, this is Jack Lynch." Carlton extended a hand as he made the introductions. "Jack Lynch, Andrew Kwang."

"Mr. Lynch," Kwang said, extending his hand.

"Mr. Kwang," Lynch said politely, shaking hands. Lynch's eyes ran up and down Kwang in a quick evaluation: wealthy, sophisticated, impeccable taste. Jack reckoned that Kwang was older than he was, although he looked younger. And from the sound of his voice, he was extremely well educated.

So this is the guy who made *Volcano Vixens,* he thought. Jack had seen the film on cable one late night when there was absolutely nothing else to do. Not much story, lots of bad acting by seminaked ex-Playmates of the Month. Not really pornographic, but not likely to wind up being praised by the fundamentalists either.

The only thing uplifting about *Volcano Vixens,* Jack remembered as an afterthought, were the costumes.

14

"I've explained our problem to Mr. Lynch," Carlton said. "He believes he can help."

"I'm so pleased to hear that, Mr. Lynch," Kwang said softly. "Our situation has taken a decidedly negative turn. I'm very concerned."

"Things work a little differently here in New Orleans," Lynch said. "What appears to be a major problem often turns out to be not that big a deal. It's all a matter of knowing how and which wheel to grease."

"And in our case," Kwang said, "Ms. Bergeron is the squeaky one."

Lynch smiled. "It would appear so. Tell me, Mr. Kwang. Have you ever met Ms. Bergeron before?"

The man stared off for a second, as if searching his memory. "No, I do not recall ever meeting her. I don't wish to appear unkind, but after this morning, I hope I never do again."

"You may have to," Lynch said. "But next time, we'll see if we can't improve the circumstances."

"I would be most grateful if that could be arranged. And speaking of arrangements, I have asked Mr. Smith to provide you with whatever you need from my account at this bank."

"We'll put you on retainer, Jack," Carlton said. "Say, five thousand?"

Lynch tried not to gulp. "Yes, that's fine."

"Again," Kwang said, "I am so pleased."

"We'll have a check drawn up for you this afternoon," Carlton said.

"Okay. How can I get in touch with you, Mr. Kwang?"

"For the next two days, I shall be occupying a suite at the Marriott. I would have preferred one of your smaller hotels in the French Quarter, but the needs of my support staff require a larger facility."

"I understand," Lynch said. "I'll call for you there."

Shortly after, Kwang exited Carlton Smith's office. Carlton phoned downstairs to have a cashier's check drawn up for Lynch, then hung up the phone.

"My guess is you needed that check today."

"How'd you ever guess?" Lynch asked sarcastically.

"I know an elevated heartbeat when I see one."

"You know," Lynch said, pacing back and forth in front of

15

Carlton's desk, "he's Asian, yet he speaks with the most homogenized Western accent I've ever heard. He dresses with exquisite taste, yet makes movies that give new depth to the word *trashy*. Interesting."

"Yes," Carlton agreed. "Mr. Kwang is, in many respects, not what he appears."

Jack turned and looked at his old friend. "Yeah. Wonder what he's hiding. . . ."

5

JACK LYNCH SETTLED DEEPLY INTO THE PADDED CHAIR IN ANDREW Kwang's hotel suite. The rooms were in a corner of the hotel near the top floor overlooking the Greater Mississippi River bridge. Across the river, the suburbs of Algiers and Gretna lay sprawled before him. Lynch relaxed in the chair and let his mind wander, as Miller Taylor droned on behind him.

"I don't understand why we can't meet here," Taylor said. His voice, Lynch observed, had a nasal quality to it that bordered on irritating. "Why a restaurant?"

Lynch turned. Andrew Kwang sat across from them, sipping a cup of herbal tea. His eyes were black, penetrating, yet with a serene quality not often found in the high-pressure world of filmmaking.

"That's what she asked for," Lynch explained, more to Kwang than to Taylor. "It was really the only way I could get her to meet us at all. Or you, rather. She was quite insistent that no one else be there. I'll go for the introductions, but once the conversation gets going, I'll disappear while you two work things out."

"If that is possible," Kwang said.

"She was willing to talk," Lynch said. "I take that as a good sign."

"Then so will I, Mr. Lynch."

"Did she tell you what she wanted?" Taylor demanded.

Lynch ignored the question. "I've arranged for a quiet table in the back at Commander's Palace. It's away from the Quarter. You're less likely to get spotted by anyone from the newspapers. I think it's well suited for the kind of talk you'll need to have with her."

Kwang nodded his head agreeably.

"Well?" Taylor asked again. Lynch turned to him, acknowledging him finally.

"No. I don't know what she's got against the project, or against Mr. Kwang."

"Perhaps I can find out," Kwang said, holding his cup calmly in his right hand, "and put an end to this difficulty."

Lynch turned onto Magazine Street at the light and headed toward the restaurant. He'd called in a couple of chips to get a decent table on a Friday night, but it would be worth it. If he handled this properly, it might very well mean a steady contract with Kwang once the studio was underway.

Besides the obvious financial attractions, Lynch also found the man, Kwang, fascinating. For years, he'd worked on the fringes of corporate and political influence, observing the ways in which power flows, the ways fortunes are made and lost, and the sometimes not-so-subtle manipulations of both. Lynch was a skilled observer of the drama with a sharp sense of insight, a keen memory, and a mind that was drawn to see and analyze the things around him in those terms. While he lacked the drive or desire to be a player himself, Jack Lynch was ideally qualified to be what men of power and influence valued above nearly all else: a trusted and capable lieutenant.

Even now, without realizing he was doing it, Lynch was observing, classifying, analyzing the ways in which the world of Andrew Kwang functioned. It was, for him, a delightful and consuming intellectual exercise.

Which had to end at this moment, as the valet parking attendant in front of the restaurant held an arm out waiting for his car keys. Lynch handed the young man the key to his MG and walked quickly through the ornate wood and glass door.

Inside, the early dinner crowd was already seated. Lynch glanced down at his watch: 7:20. Both Kwang and Ms. Bergeron were due to arrive in ten minutes. He hoped one of them would be a few minutes late, the better to avoid confrontations at the door.

His wish came true as he saw Andrew Kwang, accompanied by his chauffeur, enter the front of the restaurant. The maître d' walked up to them and spoke. Kwang looked toward Lynch, made eye contact for a moment, then turned and gave instructions to the uniformed driver, who exited the way they had entered.

At the table, Lynch went over his mental checklist with Kwang.

"Her father's the governor, and she's been around politics and deal making all her life. Very intelligent, well educated, fast on her feet. I know I don't have to tell you this, but the most ineffective way to handle her will be to try and talk down to her."

Kwang glanced quickly at Lynch, then back at the untouched glass of wine he'd ordered. "No, Mr. Lynch. You don't have to tell me that."

"I think she may be looking for assurances that some of her friends, perhaps even herself, can play a part in your local operation. Maybe you could feel her out, see if that's what she's looking for. Then it may be relatively easy to arrange some kind of . . . compromise . . . with her."

"Your delicacy with language is the equal of my own," Kwang said, with just a trace of a smile. "What you're saying is that she wants a piece of the action, and that without it, she can shut down the whole operation, like a union boss who didn't get a big enough payoff."

"After all," Lynch said, smiling, "this is Louisiana. Things work a little differently down here."

"Not really. Your politicians are just more open about the need for graft," Kwang said. "I think we understand each other."

Lynch saw out of the corner of his eye Pearl Bergeron standing at the restaurant's reception desk. Recognizing her, the maître d' snapped to smartly, then turned to lead her to the table.

"She's here," Lynch said.

The two men rose as Pearl Bergeron approached the table. She was dressed in an elegant silk blouse and pin-striped suit—all business, even on Friday night. Her eyes shone brightly through the light tint of her designer glasses. It had been a couple of years since Lynch had run into her socially, and he'd forgotten how tall she was. She stood at least an inch or two taller than his own six feet, with high cheekbones and black hair brushed back over padded shoulders. She was imposing, with a beauty that would frighten most men. Lynch thought she was stunning.

"Ms. Bergeron," he said, offering his hand.

"Mr. Lynch," she said coolly, taking it. "How nice to see you again."

"It's been too long. Andrew Kwang, I'd like you to meet Pearl Bergeron, chairperson of the Louisiana Film Commission."

19

"Ms. Bergeron," Kwang said formally, extending his hand. "It's a pleasure to meet you."

"Yes, well," Pearl Bergeron sniffed, staring down at the shorter man.

Lynch ordered another Perrier while Kwang sipped his cabernet. Pearl Bergeron ordered a vodka martini, very dry. Lynch felt the tension at the table and tried to take some of the rough edges off.

"We're very pleased you agreed to talk with us tonight," he said. "I feel certain that with the kinds of jobs and economic development at stake here, we should be able to iron out our differences."

"Yes," Kwang agreed. "My studio will be a great asset to your state."

"That's still debatable," she glared. "I'm not at all sure it will be such a great asset."

"Perhaps if we could just get to know each other a bit better," Kwang said, "we might find that we don't differ as much as we think. Reasonable people can always find compromise."

"Are you saying our concerns aren't reasonable?"

"No, of course not, Ms. Bergeron," Kwang said. "Your concerns are of great importance to me. I want any fears you have of my activities in your community to be assuaged. It would be helpful to me to know what those fears might be."

Lynch broke in. "Perhaps it would be a good idea for you two to discuss this in private. My feeling is that if you get to know each other, soon this misunderstanding will be cleared up."

Kwang looked at Pearl Bergeron, who lifted a noncommittal eyebrow. "All right, Mr. Lynch," he said. "That might be a good idea."

Lynch stood, and with a nod of his head, left the two sitting over drinks and walked across the dining room to the bar. He glanced over his shoulder before entering and saw Kwang lean toward Pearl Bergeron as she spoke. He knew his absence was for the best. Any deal made would be best done without witnesses.

He felt it was going well. To celebrate, he ordered a scotch and soda, tall, and occupied himself making small talk with the attractive twenty-five-year-old in the tight skirt behind the bar. He lit a cigarette and smiled. Ordinarily, by this time on a Friday night Lynch would have been done with dinner and well into his third or fourth drink. It had been a long day, but a good one.

Perhaps fifteen minutes later, Lynch's private celebration was shattered by the sound of an angry shriek from the next room. His head shot up, and a small voice inside him muttered an obscenity. He threw a twenty on the bar and bolted.

Another angry feminine yell was followed by the subdued protesting of a low, masculine voice.

"Damn you!" the woman yelled again. Lynch turned the corner just in time to see Pearl Bergeron jump to her feet, martini glass in hand. His mouth opened and his right arm came up in a helpless gesture as the glass flew out of her hand, clear, crystalline vodka slinging out in a slow-motion, liquid ballet. The voice in Lynch's head muttered another despairing vulgarity as the scene slipped back into real time.

The glass shattered on the wall behind Kwang's head, just above his raised arms. The drink was dripping off his face now, all over his eight-hundred-dollar suit. His mouth was opened in surprise and horror, as if he were trying to say something and couldn't get it out. It was the first time Lynch had seen a real expression on Kwang's face, and for a cruelly insane moment, he felt like laughing. The scotch buzzed around inside his head as if he'd had a dozen, and he felt control slipping away from him.

"We'll see if you get your damned studio!" Pearl Bergeron screamed again, oblivious to the diners who'd swung around in chairs to watch the scene. "You're out of business in this state, mister! Out of business!"

She jerked around on her heels and was gone. Lynch stood there motionless for a second, and then found himself next to Kwang, down on one knee, before he knew it.

"What in hell happened?" Lynch demanded, reaching for a cloth napkin that had dropped on the floor.

Kwang turned, dazed and wet. "I don't know. One minute we were talking. She gets up, excuses herself to the ladies' room. She comes back. We talk some more. She explodes."

He smiled up at Kwang, embarrassed at the scene. "At least she didn't order a Bloody Mary." The forced smile remained unreturned.

Lynch looked around at the two dozen or so diners in attendance. The room was stone quiet. No one moved. Lynch turned back to Kwang and whispered, "C'mon. Let's get you out of here."

He reached in his back pocket and pulled out his wallet, throwing another bill, this time a fifty, quickly on the table. Kwang regained his sense of what was happening and executed a strategic withdrawal.

"Botched the hell out of that one," Lynch said out loud in the confines of his apartment. He mixed the semiflat soda in with his scotch and swished the two around with ice cubes.

It was after midnight. Even on his fifth scotch, Lynch was nowhere near able to sleep. What started out as a day with so much potential had ended disastrously. Lynch figured it was a good bet that the evening's incident would eventually wind up in the newspapers. He was likely to lose the gig with Kwang as well. He hadn't seemed too angry once they got away from the restaurant, but Lynch already knew that with Kwang it was hard to tell.

Lynch walked into his living room and sat down in the secondhand chair with the one broken spring that was his usual perch. Across the room, a battered orange crate full of old records sat dusty and unused. He thought of putting on an album, of digging something from his long hair days out of the stack. He sipped the drink and reached for his cigarettes; his fingers brushed the television remote control instead. Restlessly, he flipped the set on and began switching channels. Cable was showing old movies, reruns, comedies, obscure sports events, and late-night weirdness. He changed to the local network station and was surprised to find a news program on.

"Local news at midnight?" he asked out loud. He reached for the newspaper and turned to the television section. A West Coast ball game had been on, and obviously had run into overtime. Lynch grabbed the remote and raised the volume.

The sports announcer was finishing his segment, followed by what seemed like a dozen or so commercials. Lynch was scanning the newspaper again, looking for a decent old movie when the news anchor's voice came on again:

"This just in. Police have confirmed that the body found in a French Quarter town house tonight was that of Governor LaMar Bergeron's daughter."

Lynch snapped the paper down in his lap.

"Pearl Bergeron, thirty-eight, daughter of Governor Bergeron and head of the state film commission, was found brutally bludgeoned to death just over an hour ago. We go now to Michelle Conte in the Quarter. Michelle?"

Lynch's jaw settled down an inch or so as a pretty young woman, pad in hand, came on camera.

"Yes, Grant. Neighbors reported hearing screams followed by thumping noises just over an hour ago, but police report there were no witnesses to the murder and no one was seen leaving the scene of the crime."

The newspaper fell out of Lynch's lap. He didn't notice. The report switched to a taped interview.

"We spoke with New Orleans Police Homicide Lieutenant Carl Frontiere a few moments ago."

A plainclothes cop—Dennis Quaid, middle-aged, Lynch thought in his panic—came on, complete with Ninth Ward accent.

"Right now, we're not releasing any details," he said. "All I can tell you right now is that it looks like foul play. We're going to have to wait for the medical examiner to find out the cause of death."

The station switched back to the live remote. "Police are also investigating reports that Ms. Bergeron was involved in some kind of altercation at a local restaurant tonight. We don't know over what, or with whom, and the police stress that as of now, there are no suspects in this case. Back to you, Grant—"

This time, the obscenity was not delivered silently by the tiny voice inside Lynch, but rather from deep within him, a loud and long epithet that threatened to wake up neighbors half a block away.

6

LYNCH'S HAND SHOOK AS HE FUMBLED WITH THE CIGARETTE LIGHTER. Finally he tucked the phone into the crook of his neck and used both hands to get the cigarette lit. A tension knot behind his left ear, next to the receiver, started to throb.

"C'mon, Carlton, answer the damn phone," he said.

The phone rang four more times. Lynch was about to hang up when a sleepy voice answered.

"Carlton?"

"Yes," the voice muttered. "Who is this?"

"It's Jack, Carlton—"

"Do you have any idea what time it is?" Carlton interrupted with a growl.

"It's time to pay attention, Carlton," Lynch snapped. "Listen!"

There was a pause. "Go ahead."

"Have you seen the late news?"

"Of course not, I've been asleep for hours."

Lynch raised the cigarette to his lips and inhaled deeply. "Pearl Bergeron's dead. Apparently murdered."

That brought the older man back to reality. "Oh, hell. This isn't going to be pretty."

"That's not the half of it," Lynch said. "Have you talked to Kwang tonight?"

"No, should I have?"

"Then you haven't heard?"

"Blast it, heard what?" It was Carlton's turn to snap.

"My little arranged get-together tonight didn't go off very well.

In fact, the evening ended with Pearl throwing a drink all over our friend Kwang."

"Oh, God," Carlton said. "In front of how many people?"

"Maybe thirty, thirty-five. . . ."

Jack could hear his old friend draw in a deep breath. There was a moment of silence, broken only by line static on the telephone.

"Jack, let me put you on hold. I'll try to get Kwang, then put you back on for a three-way."

"I'll be here," he said as the line went quiet.

Lynch looked around his cluttered bedroom. Housekeeping had never been one of his strong points, and over the past months, he'd had even less interest in order and cleanliness than usual. A pile of dirty clothes accumulated dust in one corner. A coin-operated laundromat was only a flight of steps down in the basement of his apartment house, yet he hadn't been there in over two weeks. That morning, he'd rummaged through the pile to find a pair of socks that he could live with.

He suddenly felt tired, as if the air had been let out of him. The initial rush of sobriety that had hit with the news of Pearl Bergeron's death was beginning to evaporate, to be replaced by fatigue and the aftereffects of—how many was it now?—scotch and sodas. He snuffed out his cigarette and with his now free right hand rubbed his eyes as he continued holding the phone to his ear. C'mon, Carlton, let's go. Where the hell are you?

One thing's for sure, he thought. When the cops piece together Pearl Bergeron's last night on this side of the veil and find three dozen people who saw her throw both a fit and a dry martini in Andrew Kwang's direction, there were going to be some interesting questions to answer.

"Jack, we can't find him." Carlton's now tense voice came back on the line. "I woke his secretary at the hotel. No one's seen him for hours. Let's meet at the hotel tomorrow morning. Make it eight."

Lynch swallowed. Getting up in six hours after the day he'd had was not a welcome thought.

"Eight o'clock, Carlton. I'll be there."

Andrew Kwang was as frightened as he'd ever been. Somewhere inside him, he carried primordial memories of flight. He remembered the thumping, the terrible bouncing that went on for days until his tiny legs were chafed and raw. He was being carried somewhere, on

25

his father's back, in a burlap bag fastened into a makeshift carrier. There was smoke everywhere, and yelling, and the sound of airplanes flying overhead, terrible wailing, and explosions, then more thick smoke and the incessant bouncing.

Kwang stopped on the sidewalk on Decatur Street, on the edge of the French Quarter, on a Friday night full of sounds and smells that took him back to China in 1946, when his father and mother had carried him over a thousand kilometers on foot to escape the fighting in the Chinese civil war. The smell of burning meat from the barbecue joint two doors down from where he stood was sweet and pungent to the Sybarites around him, but it was driving him in memory to panic and nausea.

He had seen the bodies before, the awkward way their lifeless arms and legs splayed outward in death, the gray pallor of flesh devoid of life energy. He hoped never to see it again.

He had been locked down all his life, shut tight so that no one could see inside. But he felt himself losing control in the swirling flesh and sweat and noise flowing past him on the sidewalk. He'd gone back to the hotel, but the walls were closing in on him. His head spun with panic. He couldn't breathe.

He'd had to get out, right then.

He'd left the Marriott for the second time that night and headed into the French Quarter. He knew what the authorities would think, the connections they'd eventually make. And the disastrous evening in the expensive restaurant, when the bitch had screamed and thrown the drink on him in front of all those people— No one had ever talked to him like that, never even in his childhood back in the Far East, where child and parent alike treated each other with respect and, in the case of his parents, distance.

Then—he felt the flash of anger inside him—there was that incompetent idiot, Lynch, who'd arranged it all. How could he have trusted an unknown quantity to handle such a delicate situation? How could his judgment have been so wrong?

Kwang took a deep breath and walked on, hands in pockets, head down. He had to think, to get away, to figure out what to do next. He felt control slipping away, and there had to be a way to find it again. The faster the better. He felt something hit his left shoulder and lost his footing. He stopped, looked up. Three muscular men with well-trimmed beards and silver chains—the one on the left

26

wearing a spiked dog collar—stood on the sidewalk under a hanging wooden sign that read THE MINE SHAFT.

"Bitch," the thin one on the right said, his shiny, black leather vest falling open to reveal a pierced nipple. "Watch where you're going."

"Sorry," Kwang mumbled, stepping around him. The one on the left, Dog Collar, laughed and raised a can of Dixie beer in his left hand.

"So solly, Chollie," he chimed in falsetto. "Oh, he's so cute!"

"Love your white suit," the middle one called to Kwang's back. "It's *so* Charlene Chan!"

Kwang wandered on past the bars, oblivious to the noise around him. He felt his heart beating inside him, the air rushing past him in currents, the midnight sweat rolling down his sides from his armpits to his belt. He could flee now, be out of the country in a matter of hours. But then they would know for sure, know that whatever had happened—might have happened—in Pearl Bergeron's apartment that night, he was a part of it.

And that was the last thing in the world Andrew King was willing to live with.

A puff of air through Lynch's open bedroom window sent the dirty linen sheers wafting. The gentle brush of the cloth somehow penetrated the sleeping man's consciousness. He twitched, then moaned loudly.

She is back again.

Lynch is naked, lying on an antique brass bed next to Sally. She's nude as well, asleep, and it's dawn. Her brown hair splays across the pillow next to him as Lynch comes to and sees her there. He leans over and gently kisses her. She opens her eyes and smiles, more asleep than awake, then moves closer to him and purrs, rubbing her cheek against his chest like a cat.

He moves to her and hugs her close, then looks up around the room. It's her bedroom all right; he recognizes it, has been there before, but it's different. The edges are gone, all form and no shape, all color and no lines.

He looks back down at her. He brings his free hand around and touches her stomach, flat and tight with still-young muscle, then rubs her harder. She pulls him close, groans. Her breasts are small, the nipples full and pointed and deep crimson and waiting for him. He pulls

27

away from her enough to bring his head down and take her in his mouth. Her head pushes back into the pillow, her neck arches, her jaw clenches, the line between sweet pain and glorious delight dissolving. Lynch brings his hand down between her legs and touches her there, where she's hot and wet and waiting for him. He feels a tightening in his groin and realizes he's erect, achingly hard. His stomach locks in on itself and his breath comes faster. He lets go of her breast and slides, lips still wet, into her neck. He draws his lips back and plants his teeth in her. She shakes like a terrier, bolts of electricity ripping through her.

Sally brings her arms around him and squeezes, locking her hands behind his back and pulling him to her. She opens her legs, ready for him now, and pushes her left leg under him, lifting him off the bed and rolling him into her cradle.

Lynch feels the tightness everywhere now. He arches his back to bring himself into position for her and smiles, burying his face in her hair, as he feels her reach for him. He gulps in a lung full of air as she touches him, then brings him to her. He feels the steam rising off her, just as—

Snap.

Lynch looks around, toward the bedroom window. Sally pulls him wordlessly back, her eyes saying, "Don't go. Not this time. No. . . ."

Snap.

He looks around again. What the hell?

He cranes his neck further, until the bedroom window comes into full frame.

Katherine Herbert, Lynch's dead ex-wife, stares through the window, smiling. The top of her head has exploded, blown open. Blood and brains and goo run down her face, into the dead of her eyes, the crack of her smiling lips. Her long, auburn hair is a tangled, knotted mess of blood and gore and hell.

And in her eyes is light, light from some place Lynch had never seen or known or imagined, and she is looking at him with that light now.

Lynch looks down at Sally, still under him, smiling now in the same way, the life in her eyes gone and replaced by the same hellish light he sees in Katherine's.

The terror leaves him cold, frozen bone cold to the core. He stares back around at the window.

They're all there now: The Old Man, gray and stiff like a manne-

quin, the only movement in his dead face the smile that rises to meet Lynch; Katherine's father, James Herbert, with a neat, round hole in one side of his head, a crater the size of a softball blown out of the other.

Lynch rolls off Sally in horror, feeling the coldness of her hand as she holds on to his erection, still pulling him into her. He feels the tightening in his crotch, the quickening of his breath, the impending crash of the orgasm and the pounding of blood in his head.

They're all smiling at him now. "Go on," they're saying with their eyes, "Have a good time, Jack. Have a good time, Jack. Have a good time. . . ."

He feels her tugging at him. His mouth opens first as if to ask, "What?" and then to—

He turns to her. She's dead now, animate and moving but dead, lying there in a pool of liquid, decaying sludge, the flesh falling back from her bones, the lips drawn back, the hair matted and lifeless and colorless. Her eyelids, now leather in death, pull back to reveal yellowed eyes gaping up at him from a dark and hideous place.

She opens her mouth for a kiss, but inside is only the gray slurry of goop that was once teeth and gums and sweet, sweet, oh God, sweet tongue. A stench so horrible rises from inside her that Lynch's breath is yanked from his body with the force of a mother yanking her baby back from a pot of boiling water.

He tries to pull away, but she won't let go. He looks down; the rotten flesh of her hand, the whiteness of the bones poking through, still holds him. Lynch pulls away. Her hand comes loose from her wrist, still attached to him, like shredded meat at a barbecue from hell.

Lynch tries to scream, his mouth opens in a breathless, silent shriek of pain and fright. The bones of his lower back crack like shotgun pellets on the fly, and he springs out of bed wailing in his own dead silence—

Jack's eyes popped open and his mouth closed to stifle his now real and horribly loud scream. He looked around. A moment later, he realized. . . .

He was back in his bed now, tangled in the dirty sheets, the smell of the night's last cigarette still fresh in his nostrils. He was covered with sweat and panting like an unclipped Saint Bernard in June. He listened for the knocking on his door. A beat.

Nothing. The neighbors were used to his dawn screams. They

29

knew he woke himself up and it stopped; no need to check on him.

"Oh, God," Lynch said out loud. "Jesus. . . ."

It's getting worse, he thought. It's not going to go away. It's getting worse.

7

CARLTON SMITH STOOD IN THE LOBBY OF THE MARRIOTT, FIDGETING AS he looked at his watch for the third time in forty-five seconds: 8:15.

He glanced around again. Could Lynch have gone on up to Kwang's suite? He shouldn't have; Carlton had said they'd meet in the lobby. Then he saw Lynch outside on the sidewalk, moving past the glass and into the lobby. The younger man's clothes were rumpled, and he sweated in the early morning heat like a man with fever.

"You look like hell," Carlton said as Jack approached. "Rough night?"

"The nights are fine," Lynch said, flushed and out of breath. "It's the mornings that are killing me."

"C'mon, let's go. We're late."

The two men walked to the bank of elevators at the rear of the huge lobby. "Sorry I'm late, Carlton," Lynch said.

"No problem. I never did get in touch with Kwang last night so he doesn't even know we're coming."

"You tried back?" Lynch asked.

"About an hour after you called. No one had seen him for quite some time."

"Wonder where he went," Lynch said. He suppressed a wave of nausea that swept over him as as the elevator car began moving. Should have eaten something, he thought. Strong coffee and cigarettes were no way to start a Saturday morning. Then again, Lynch's Saturday mornings rarely started at seven-thirty.

"I don't know," Carlton answered. "And his secretary was very reticent to discuss it."

"You think she knew?"

"He," the old attorney corrected. "A young man named Taplinger. Understand he interned for Kwang one summer while in college."

"Then hit on the guy for a real job after graduation." Lynch finished the sentence for his friend.

The door slid open to reveal a heavily carpeted pastel hallway. The two men stepped out of the elevator, turned right and walked softly past a dozen doors and framed original hotel oil paintings until they reached a suite at the end of the corridor.

"Here we are," Smith said, knocking gently.

The door swung open a moment later, a handsome blond man wearing khaki pants and a safari shirt holding it for them. California straight, Lynch thought, despite the gentle swish of the man's hips as he walked across the room in front of them. Lynch followed Carlton in, entering the living room of an expensive, large hotel suite. A bedroom opened off each side of the room, and a wet bar stood at the right.

"Mr. Kwang's expecting you," the young man said.

"Really?" Carlton asked. "I didn't mention we were coming."

"When I told him you called last night, he assumed you'd be here first thing in the morning."

"I'm Jack Lynch," Lynch said, offering his hand to the man.

"Oh, so you're Lynch," the secretary said with distaste, looking down at Lynch's hand as if it held a pile of dog droppings freshly scooped from the sidewalk. "I'm Mr. Kwang's secretary, Sheldon Taplinger."

"Glad to meet you, Sheldon," Lynch said, dropping his refused hand.

"Where was Mr. Kwang last night?" Carlton asked offhandedly.

"Mr. Kwang was here the entire evening," Taplinger answered.

Jack shot a quick glance at Carlton, who returned it just as briefly before turning back to Kwang's secretary. "You said he was out."

"We apparently miscommunicated. Mr. Kwang was here the entire evening."

"But—" Lynch said.

"Mr. Kwang was here the *entire* evening," Taplinger said, figuring third time was the charm.

32

"Yeah," Lynch muttered. "Gotcha. The whole time, right. . . ."

The bedroom door to the left opened. Kwang stepped into the room wearing a silk bathrobe over pajamas. Lynch suppressed a laugh; the green silk was adorned with a peacock embroidered hem to collar, plumage filling the lower half of the robe like a basket of flowers. What the hell, Lynch thought, the guy probably paid more for that robe than I paid for every stitch I own.

"Good morning, Mr. Kwang," Carlton said. "I hope you don't mind us dropping by like this."

Kwang's face was drawn yet still, as if he'd awakened that morning and put on a mask. He walked across the room to the bar and poured himself a cup of coffee.

"I expected it," he said quietly, blowing gently across the top of his coffee cup, deliberately not looking at any of the three men in the room.

"Can I order you breakfast, Mr. Kwang?" Taplinger asked.

Kwang turned and looked at his assistant, his dark eyes staring right through the young man. Lynch wondered for an instant if their relationship involved anything more than clerical work.

"Not now, Sheldon. Later." Kwang sat on sofa, motioning for his two guests to sit.

"Mr. Kwang," Lynch started, "I didn't really get a chance to tell you how sorry I am that things—"

"Exploded like they did?" Kwang asked.

"Yessir." Lynch looked down at the carpet. His head throbbed and he wished Kwang would offer him a cup of the hot coffee.

Carlton started to speak, but Kwang cut him off.

"Yes, it would appear that the evening went off not quite as you expected. Am I right? And now that Ms. Bergeron has gone on to her final reward—"

"You've seen the papers?" Carlton asked.

"Of course," Kwang snapped. "And this leaves us in a very embarrassing position."

"It may not be all that bad," Carlton said, the level tone of his voice the only soothing noise in the room. Kwang glared at him for a moment, then seemed to clamp himself down once again.

"It's quite bad enough," Kwang said. "I deplore scandal. It is bad for Kwang World Pictures; it is bad for this project."

33

"Mr. Kwang, there's a great deal at stake here. This deal can be saved. If I didn't believe that, I wouldn't be here."

"Mr. Smith, I have no doubt that your intentions are the best. However, with all due respect I must question your judgment in regard to how this matter is being handled."

"What's that supposed to mean?" Lynch asked quietly, the knot in his stomach growing larger.

"You know quite well what I mean, Mr. Lynch. Your incompetence is what caused this—"

"*My* incompetence? How was I supposed to know that crazy woman was going to sling an extra-dry Stoli at you? And if you think I'm going to take—"

"Gentlemen," Carlton interrupted. "This is not going to get us anywhere. Mr. Kwang, I brought Jack Lynch into this because he knows his way around this city. And you need him, no matter what happened last night."

Kwang and Lynch stared at each other for an awkward moment of visual Mexican standoff. "I simply want this taken care of," Kwang said, blinking first. "In the most expeditious way possible."

"That can be done," Lynch said. "I'll make some discreet inquiries Monday morning and find out what the police think about this case, how long it's going to take to get settled, stuff like that. And I'll find out as quickly as possible who'll be replacing Pearl Bergeron at the film commission. Then I'll try to find out if that person is going to have a better, say, attitude toward your project. Which after all, we need pretty badly. This city's taken a beating, economically speaking, over the past decade or so."

"I have heard that," Kwang sniffed.

"If you'll allow me the opportunity to correct my earlier mistakes of judgment," Lynch said, "we'll see if we can't bring this unhappy incident to a happier conclusion."

Carlton smiled faintly. He'd seen Lynch pour it on before. And he'd watched more than one person dismiss the behavior as sycophancy. Carlton knew better.

"Very well, Mr. Lynch. Let's see if we can start over on this, all right? Why don't you call me Monday afternoon here and let me know what you've found out?"

"How long are you going to be in town?" Carlton asked.

"I have meetings in New York on Tuesday," Kwang answered.

"Then I'm on to London. I hadn't planned on being back in New Orleans for at least a month."

"We should have everything under control by then," Lynch said.

"I hope so," Kwang said. Behind his hope, Lynch felt, was a warning. Kwang seemed like the kind of man who usually got what he hoped for.

"For now, we'll leave you to enjoy a weekend in New Orleans," Carlton said. "It can be an experience like no other."

"So I'm told."

Sheldon Taplinger, who'd been standing wordlessly in a corner of the room throughout the discussion, walked over and opened the door to the suite. Lynch and Carlton both nodded good-bye, then stepped through the door. After it closed behind them, Carlton looked at Lynch and smiled.

"Diplomat," he said, as the two walked toward the elevator.

"It was either that or take the guy's head off," Lynch said.

"I'd be careful about taking Mr. Kwang's head off. It may not be such an easy task."

The bank of four elevators stood silent. Then, with a whooshing sound, the doors of the car on the far right opened. Lynch and Carlton stepped in, both fishing for the cigarettes they knew they'd light as soon as they entered the lobby.

Lynch looked at his old friend. "I wonder where Kwang did go last night."

Carlton turned. "I don't know. I hope we never have a need to find out."

As the doors to their car slid shut, the doors two cars over opened. Two men, one in an ill-fitting, off-the-rack, gray suit, the other fitted in custom-tailored pinstripes, quickly stepped out and walked down the hall. The man in front was a police lieutenant, the same one who'd been on the late news the night before, telling a city full of murders that one more had occurred.

Lynch twisted the key in his aging MG, noticing the telltale puff of blue smoke in his rearview mirror. The engine would need an overhaul soon, and he wondered if his five-grand retainer would last long enough to cover it. He'd been lucky that morning in finding a parking spot near the riverfront, especially given that he was running late and fighting a hangover.

35

He'd made the mistake of walking down Canal Street for breakfast. The taste of greasy fried eggs and coffee hung in his mouth like a pall. In a city where food was one of its last real claims to quality, Lynch always seemed to be able to find a bad meal. He lit a cigarette to cover the rancid aftertaste as he studied the oncoming traffic in the mirror. The top was down. The morning was gorgeous, not yet stifling hot, and the throbbing in his head was beginning to dissipate. Spotting a break in the flow, he punched the accelerator, and with a deep-throated rumble, the low convertible darted out into the traffic.

He was headed uptown, toward Audubon Park and the Garden District and the fine old homes of the Rex and Comus gerontocracy. He glanced down at the page he'd ripped out of the phone book as he headed out Magazine Street in the general direction of Lowerline, which ran perpendicular to St. Charles Avenue and the last streetcar line in the city.

He cut through the park, with the overhanging trees draping ghostly fingered Spanish moss. As a younger man, Lynch had spent his college days jogging through the park during the day and parking in its secluded spots at night. He'd stood below the massive concrete wings over the Butterfly Pavilion during the spring of '74, a young newspaper reporter barely two years out of college, and watched the river flow by in torrents during the great flooding. Like everyone, he'd been fearful that the levees might not hold; a local college engineering professor had calculated that if the levee gave way at Audubon Park, it would take less than thirty minutes to inundate most of the city. And people throughout the parish had lined the levees with picnic baskets full of greasy, hot Cajun food and six-packs of Dixie beer and boom boxes and waited for disaster.

The city that care forgot . . .

Lynch felt more and more as if his younger days were long gone. He'd always imagined that he wouldn't mind aging, but now that he was facing forty, it felt like an out-of-control locomotive bearing down on him. He thought back, as he pulled out of the front entrance of the park into the stream of St. Charles Avenue traffic, of the women in his life and the passion he'd had for them.

He wondered if there would ever be anything like that again.

Lynch's reverie was interrupted by an old Volvo jerking out of a side street in front of him. The car was full of laughing young men of fraternity house age, dressed in T-shirts and cutoffs, headed off

36

somewhere for the beginning of a weekend. Lynch slammed on his brakes to avoid hitting them, missing the back bumper by inches and swearing under his breath. He reached for the horn button, but thought to hell with it. Besides, he was outnumbered at least four to one, and in the Deep South, honking a horn at someone can be an invitation for trouble.

He turned onto Freret Street, snaked his way past the illegally parked cars, and headed down the divided boulevard. On both sides of him FOR SALE signs stood out in front of houses, prices reduced, mortgages assumable, God, please somebody take this house off my hands so I can move somewhere and get a job. The oil bust of the 1970s had, for all appearances, permanently crippled the city, the flight of the middle class now a torrent, the tax base—what tax base there ever had been—eroding rapidly.

I'd mourn for this city, Lynch thought as he turned left on Willow Street at the light, but it's too far down the list.

He turned left on Lowerline Street, a narrow, two-way residential street that was barely big enough for one-way traffic. Cars coming toward each other had to play a slow-motion, house-to-house game of chicken. Who would give way first? Somebody always had to pull over to the curb to let the other guy by; there was no other way.

Lynch drove up several blocks, slowly clicking off the house numbers in his mind, until he crossed Burthe Street and found, much to his amazement, that his parking karma was holding. He pulled into a space right in front of Miller Taylor's apartment building.

Taylor lived in apartment C. Lynch walked up to the front door of the three-story, vaguely art deco building. A row of apartment mailboxes and doorbell buttons with every letter but C was laid out in front of him. Lynch frowned, then noticed the taped business card that read MILLER TAYLOR—WRITER/DIRECTOR/CONSULTANT, with the address. Scrawled on the card in broken ink was an arrow pointing to the left. Lynch walked back out of the alcove and around the side of the building. A closed door had another of Taylor's business cards taped up.

Lynch knocked. He hadn't called, had no idea if Taylor was even home. It seemed worth the chance, he thought. He didn't even know what he was going to ask the man, but whatever it turned out to be, Lynch wanted unrehearsed answers.

He heard a shuffling inside, then looked down at his watch:

9:15. A moment later, a sleepy tangle of gray hair and wrinkles came to the door in a pair of cutoffs.

"Yeah?" It was a voice that had seen a lot of smoke and bad booze slide past it.

"Miller Taylor?"

"Yeah."

"I'm Jack Lynch. I've been retained by Andrew Kwang. I'd like to talk with you if I may."

Taylor shook his head, rubbed his eyes. "Kwang sent you here?"

"No," Lynch answered. "I came on my own. I thought maybe you could give me some advice on this little problem we're having now with Mr. Kwang's project."

Taylor looked at him through a pair of bloodshot eyes.

"I'm sorry if I woke you up."

"S'okay," Taylor muttered, opening the door wider and turning his back to Lynch.

Lynch walked through the door and looked around, at the bare, painted concrete floor, at the pale-green cinderblock walls, at the cheap bookcases full of paperbacks and the old Royal portable on a TV tray next to a several-inches-deep stack of manuscript.

Miller Taylor, Lynch realized, lived in a basement.

Lynch followed Taylor in. He saw after a moment that the apartment was actually a small efficiency created out of one side of the basement. A small kitchenette stood off to the right, and beyond that a bathroom with a shower stall and a small walk-in closet. It didn't take long for Lynch to scope out the whole place, and to see that for a man who had to be at least in his middle fifties, Miller Taylor didn't have a lot to show for his time on earth.

"You want coffee?" Taylor asked.

"Yeah, that'd be great."

"Have a seat," Taylor instructed. "I'll get the coffee started, then I got to go clean up."

Despite his obvious penury, Taylor stood straight and tall and rail thin. There wasn't much to identify the apartment as his, Lynch observed. No pictures on the wall, no notes held to the refrigerator by little plastic flower magnets. Nothing besides the books and the typewriter in the one room that served as bedroom, office, living room, and parlor would ever mark this place as Miller Taylor's.

Lynch found himself immersed in sadness for a moment, as if

38

seeing himself in twenty years. He brushed the thought aside, shifted in the cheap vinyl kitchen chair, and looked around for an ashtray. Taylor had the voice and the wrinkles that marked a lifelong smoker, but no evidence of the accessories. He fumbled with the cigarette lighter in his pocket, then let it go.

A moment later, Taylor came back into the kitchen, wearing a pin-striped oxford-cloth shirt with his cutoffs. His teeth scrubbed, hair in place, face washed, he almost looked presentable.

"Again, sorry to wake you up."

"No problem, I had to get up anyway," Taylor said, pouring two cups of coffee. His voice, Lynch thought, had traces of California in it, but its origins were definitely in the Bronx.

"I understand you're the local—what did he call it? Creative director?"

Taylor smiled. "Yeah, that's me. One creative son of a bitch."

Lynch returned the smile. "So tell me, how did you get there? How'd you get the job?"

"I used to work out in L.A., as a writer and director. I even produced a couple of films. Years ago."

Lynch was impressed, and let his voice show it. "How'd you wind up out here in Nyah-luns?"

"You mean New Or—LEENS?" Taylor laughed. "Long story. I sort of . . . retired from life in the fast lane."

"You been out here long?"

"I don't know. Five years or so, I guess. Something like that."

"That's interesting. I'd like to hear more about your work sometime," Lynch said. "But right now, you and I have a problem. You heard about Pearl Bergeron?"

"I figured that was why you were here," Taylor said. "I was watching the news last night. Up late . . ."

"Then you know that Kwang's already so fed up with the problems he's having that he's likely to close this whole project. And I suspect neither of us wants that."

Lynch looked around the room. "My guess is that we both need the money," he added.

Taylor laughed again, his staccato New York voice moving faster now that he was awake.

"Money, Mr. Lynch, is the last thing in the world I'm worried about."

That's apparent, Lynch thought, without saying anything.

"My worry is that we won't get to play in the sandbox any more," Taylor continued. "And this is a very nice sandbox."

"Why do you think Pearl Bergeron was so dead set against Kwang bringing a production facility to New Orleans. It doesn't make any sense. She was the film commissioner; it was her job to get movies made in this city. It would have made her and everybody else look good. What happened?"

The smile disappeared from Taylor's face, an entire row of forehead wrinkles falling with it. Age and self-abuse had given him the appearance of being half human, half shar pei.

"What makes you think I'd know anything about that?"

"I don't know," Lynch hesitated at Taylor's change in tone. "I just thought with you being in the local film community and all— I figured you guys probably all knew each other pretty well."

Taylor stood up and walked over next to the refrigerator, his face to the wall, his back to Lynch. He appeared to be deep in thought, shaking his head and scrunching his shoulders.

Then he turned. "Okay, Jack Lynch, you may as well know. Hell, the police already do. You'll find out sooner or later."

Lynch looked at the man, questions on his face.

"Pearl Bergeron and I were lovers," Taylor said. "Up until about three months ago, we were living together."

8

"YOU GOTTA UNDERSTAND, JACK. PEARL BERGERON WAS A HORSE'S ass."

Lynch sat back in the chair, staring up at the pacing Taylor.

"She had everything in the world going for her. The woman had an IQ that must've been up around 160 or something. She'd been all over the world. Had two college degrees. And what had she done with her life? Bupkiss. . . ."

"But I thought she was, hell, I don't know, a *respected* member of the creative community."

Taylor laughed, a rumbling, rolling laugh from deep within. "Yeah, right, and Ceausescu was a respected member of the Romanian political community. Listen, Lynch, the only thing Pearl had going for her was power and connections. You knew *Daddy* got her the job?"

"Sure," Lynch answered. "But that's just business in Louisiana. I thought she'd done okay with it."

"That's what the newspapers and the other P.R. flacks—no offense intended—"

"None taken."

"—wanted everybody to think. The truth is that Pearl Bergeron was mostly known for her great parties, her terrible temper, especially during blizzards, and for being—how do I say this—a great lay."

"Blizzards?"

"You dumbass," Taylor said after a wicked moment's smile. "Kind of out of touch, aren't you? Pearlie was keister over teakettle in the middle of her blizzard years."

Taylor jabbed the air with a finger, as if trying to win an argument with bravado because logic had failed him. "Coke. Cocaine. Pearl loved the shit. Couldn't get enough of it. The only thing she wanted more than coke was cock, and the two went hand in hand, so to speak."

Lynch noticed the sparkle in Taylor's eyes. It was as if he were telling a dirty joke to a room full of nuns and loving every second of it.

"Was this something you and she shared, these blizzard years?" Lynch asked slowly.

Taylor laughed again. "Oh, hell no. I've had my blizzard years, son. That's why I left LaLa Land. I was executive vice president and creative consultant for ABC's television movie department six years ago. One of about thirty, I might add, but pulling down mid-six figures, driving a Jaguar, living in a three-bedroom bungalow in Malibu that fronted right on the beach."

"Yeah?"

"And one morning I woke up and couldn't remember where I'd been for the past week. Jack Daniels and coke, and I don't mean the sweet, fizzy kind. This shit was coke classic, the real thing. So I bailed out."

Taylor walked into the other room, the one that served as office, bedroom, and living room, and sat in a cheap wooden rocker. Lynch kept his seat in the kitchen, still able to see him in the tiny apartment.

"I drove down to my office, told my secretary good-bye, picked up my last paycheck, fired my agent, cleaned out my bank account, and drove nonstop for six months. When I ran out of money, I was in Destin, Florida. I sold the Jag, bought a bus ticket to New Orleans, and I've been here ever since."

"With Pearl . . ."

"Now don't get me wrong, me and Pearl got along fine for a while. She was a movie-business groupie and knew my stuff."

"But you said she was a horse's ass," Lynch said, standing up and walking into the room where Taylor sat rocking nervously. Lynch couldn't help but notice the man seemed to fidget constantly, as if unable to keep still because of some mysteriously firing neurons deep in his brain.

"She was always destructive when she was mad. Hell, she had the worst temper of any woman I ever met. But after she went to work, it was like she couldn't find nothing nice to say about nobody.

It was 'So-and-so's a dickhead, So-and-so's an asshole' all the time. Never a kind word for anybody."

"Including you."

"Especially me," Taylor laughed. "She kept telling me that I ought to go back to L.A., get back in the business, bring stuff to the city."

"And?"

"I didn't want any of that. Believe me, kid, I had my time in the sun. It's too freaking hot. I want to be head knocker in a tiny, little sandbox."

"Like the one out here."

"Yeah. I wanted it real bad. It felt kind of like my last shot at making a decent living in this business." Taylor looked around the apartment. "It ain't hard to see I've been having trouble lately. Kwang's my way out, without french-frying what's left of my brain."

"And Pearl Bergeron was trying to keep it from happening, wasn't she?" Lynch asked, walking over to the front door.

"Don't get too freaking smug with me, boy. I didn't kill Pearl. Hell, I ain't that creative any more."

There was something about hearing someone try to pronounce his name in real French that drove him crazy. He folded his wallet and badge together and slipped them back into his suit coat pocket.

"That's Frone-tee-AY down here," he corrected, the irritation in his voice apparent. "Carl Frontiere, NOPD Homicide. Not Fronn-tee-air."

Andrew Kwang took the officer's card and stuck it inside his robe pocket. "Excuse me, Lieutenant Frontiere," he said, getting the pronunciation right the second time. "I'm new here."

"Yeah, I know. Listen, sit down, will ya? We got to talk."

"About what?" Kwang asked carefully, taking a seat on the couch. The young lieutenant and his silent, nondescript partner sat in chairs opposite him.

"Now, c'mon, Mr. Kwang, you know what I'm talking about. I'm in charge of the Pearl Bergeron investigation, and I understand you had dinner with her last night. Or at least you tried to."

Kwang shifted and looked at his two guests.

"That is true," he said.

"Well, I'm going to have to ask you about that."

43

The way the young man dropped the ends of his words and pronounced "ask" as "ax" sent silent shivers radiating up the back of Kwang's neck. He sat completely still, hoping no one noticed his hair bristling.

"So what happened last night?"

"To this moment, I am not quite sure. We were sitting, talking, business mostly, when she excused herself and went to the powder room. When she came back, she seemed excited. Tense. I said something—I can't even remember what, exactly—and she started screaming. Then she jumped up and left. I was in such shock, I can't even remember exactly what she yelled at me."

"A couple of witnesses to this little altercation said she slung a drink at you, too."

"Yes. I was shocked at her behavior."

"How shocked were you?" the detective asked.

Kwang looked at him, careful to register nothing on his face. "What is that supposed to mean?"

Frontiere moved forward in the chair, holding an expensive fountain pen over a small notebook.

"Listen, Mr. Kwang, where were you last night?"

Not a muscle in the Oriental man's face moved. Everything about him, Frontiere noticed, was as still as the surface of a bayou at dawn.

"I came back here and cleaned up. Later, I walked around the French Quarter sightseeing. I came back to the hotel sometime around ten. I stayed in for the rest of the night."

"Whereabouts in the Quarter'd you go?" Frontiere asked.

Kwang stared at the lieutenant for a moment. "Excuse me, Lieutenant, but if this line of questioning is going to proceed much further, I believe I shall wish to speak with my attorney."

Frontiere snapped the notebook shut. "Don't get your panties in a wad, Mr. Kwang. You're not under arrest or anything. We're just trying to reconstruct Pearl Bergeron's last night."

"Other than being the last person on earth she publicly threw a drink at, I believe I played no part in her last night."

Frontiere smiled. "At least we think you were the last person she threw a drink at. With her it was kind of hard to tell."

The lieutenant stood up, his movement a cue to his silent partner, who joined him.

"Do me a favor, Mr. Kwang. I hate to sound like one of your movies, but don't leave town for awhile."

"That's quite impossible," Kwang said. "I have a meeting in New York Tuesday."

"Depending on what I find out over the next couple of days, you may have to reschedule your meeting."

"That's equally impossible," Kwang said, his voice stern.

"So do the impossible," Frontiere said, opening the hotel room door. "I hear you guys are good at that."

Kwang stood as the two police officers left the room. As soon as the door closed and he was alone, his hands began to shake, and drops of sweat appeared on his forehead.

9

JACK LYNCH PULLED UP IN FRONT OF THE SMALL SHOTGUN HOUSE JUST off Freret Street and stopped the car. He loosened his tie, sweat running off him in the morning heat. It was nearly noon and the afternoon's simmer would soon be at its worst. He briefly thought of putting the top up on the car; it would make the inside stifling, but at least the seats would be cool enough to touch when he got back. He decided it was too much trouble.

He dreaded this moment, even though he knew he'd feel better once he got it over with. Truthfully, he'd missed her. She was one of the few people he'd been able to tolerate the past few months.

Lynch stood next to his car for a moment, the top of the door not quite as high as his belt. He pulled off his jacket and tossed it haphazardly into the car. He looked over at the house. The front door was open, the glass of the storm door shimmering with reflection. The covered porch kept the worst of the sun away from the front of the house, he remembered. It would be cool in there, even without air conditioning. It was an old house; the ceilings were high, with brass ceiling fans that stirred the air around constantly. Maud Pelletier had lived there most of her life.

He walked the fifteen feet or so up the sidewalk, to the rock wall that ran across the front of what passed as a yard. An old iron gate with spots of rust burning through the gray paint creaked on its hinges as Lynch pushed it open.

He walked past the plastic Madonna holding a baby Jesus that had been set inside a painted, discarded truck tire and up the wooden steps of the porch. The three boards groaned and bent under his weight. He started to knock, but held back as he heard a noise from the backyard.

He stood there a moment. "Here's your chance," he whispered. "Take off, and she'll never know."

A moment of silence followed. "Oh, hell," he whispered again, lifting his chin and drawing a breath. "Get it over with."

He hopped off the porch and started down the concrete walk that ran along the left side of the house. There were only about twenty inches between the wall of the house and the board fence that marked the next-door neighbor's yard. Land had always been scarce in New Orleans, and in days gone by, property taxes were based on the frontage of lots. The wider your house, the more you paid.

Houses were built small and narrow, and ran deep and long, like a shotgun. Few homes had hallways; to get to the back bedrooms, you had to walk past everyone else's bed, which, Lynch remembered with a smile, had made for some pretty interesting situations back when he was an undergraduate and had shared a similar house with two other bachelors.

Lynch stopped at the corner and peeked around. She was there, back to him, bent over from the hip all the way to the ground. She held a running garden hose in her right hand and a trowel in her left. She was digging around in a small plot of dirt cut out of the brick patio while a stream of water ran up in a curve, then down to the bricks and over her bare feet. She wore a faded, once-expensive cotton dress, the kind that rich women passed along to poor women by way of the consignment shops. Trickle-down recycling. . . .

To be in her mid-fifties she sure was limber. She'd been pretty once, too, he thought as he stood there, unnoticed, behind her. But that was before her spirit-killing marriage to an oil worker and twenty-five years or more of office drudgery had taken the glow out of her cheeks. She was still thin, and her gray hair was straight and full. But her eyes hadn't the sparkle they once had, the lines in her face were deep, and the sharp, biting wit that must have been delightful decades ago now had a harsh edge to it.

It had been that harsh edge that set him off two weeks ago, when she said the wrong thing on the wrong day and he blew up at her. He had regretted the words the moment they exploded out of his mouth, but by then she'd picked up her purse and was out the door, gone.

He smiled as he stared at her and fantasized what it would have

47

been like to have had an affair with her back then, in her days as a young girl. There'd been some late and lonely nights recently when he'd wondered what it would be like to have an affair with her now. But there was the little matter of her husband. No matter how big a bastard he was, he was still her husband.

Lynch wet his lips, pursed them, and let out a long, wailing, wolf whistle like something out of a 1940s Abbott and Costello movie.

Maud jerked up like a deer that's heard the hunter crunch a twig behind her. She gasped, dropped the trowel as she whipped around, and brought a hand up to her chest. She frowned, mad as hell, and shot Lynch a look that had some pretty twisted implications to it.

"Durn you," she hissed. "Give me a durn heart attack!"

"You leaning over like that's going to give me one, darlin'," Lynch said. He drawled out the *r* in darling like a long *w,* a joke he and Maud had shared for years over her deep New Orleans accent.

"You wish! What the heck you doing here?"

"C'mon, Maud," Lynch drawled, opening his hands in supplication. "Are you still pissed at me for yelling at you?"

The thin woman reached down and picked up a large dirt clod and lobbed it across the patio at him. Lynch ducked, loose dirt spraying over him as he jumped back two steps.

"Hey, Maud, c'mon darling, you mighta hit me with that!"

"Mighta! You son of a gun, you come a foot or two closer and I'll change that 'mighta' to a 'gonna.' "

Lynch's forced smile disappeared. His shoulders sagged. Damn, he thought, I think she means it.

"Okay, Maud. You want me to go, I'm gone."

He turned and started back up the shadowed walk. Maud cleared her throat, and he heard the faint scraping of her foot on the bricks.

"I oughta go in and get Pelletier's shotgun," she said. Lynch turned and looked at her. " 'Ceptin' he took the keys to the gun case with him."

She dropped the hose into the mud behind her, then walked over to the hydrant and twisted the handle until the water stopped.

She climbed up two of the steps, holding on to the handrail with her left hand, then stopped and turned.

"Well, you coming in or what?"

Lynch smiled, then dropped his head and followed her. A hank

48

of brown hair hung down over his forehead, giving him the appearance of a scolded, regretful schoolboy as he trailed her into the kitchen.

He sat at the kitchen table, the sole remaining piece of what had once been marketed as a top-of-the-line dinette set. The vinyl-covered chairs had long since been replaced by plastic chairs with in-grained flower patterns. It was a mismatch, like most everything else in Maud's kitchen, but it was homey and warm. The room was filled with the smell of strong chicory coffee and the remnants of the morning's breakfast of country sausage and eggs fried in the resulting grease.

"Where's Pelletier?" Lynch asked. As long as he had known Maud's husband, he had been called simply and only by his last name. Lynch wasn't sure if he'd ever even known the man's first name.

"The old bastard left this morning. Two weeks off Grand Isle on an Exxon rig. I can breathe a little easy now."

"Did he leave you any money?"

"Fifty bucks," Maud said, pouring two cups of the strong coffee. "Big spendah. . . ."

"I've missed you, Maud," Lynch said.

She turned at the counter and stared at him. "Yeah, babe, I been missing you, too." She brought the coffee cups over and set them on the table, then reached for an ashtray and handed it to Jack. Maud had never smoked, but her husband had been a lifelong cigar smoker and tobacco chewer. She was used to being up to her bronchial tubes in somebody else's fumes.

Lynch took both the coffee and the ashtray gratefully.

"Why don't you come back to work for me?" He asked.

Maud spewed out a laugh. "What? You crazy? The reason we having to work through this now is me working for you."

"Maud, I was a jerk. I was running out of money. I couldn't pay you. You caught me on a bad day and I blew up at you. I'm sorry."

"And I couldn't even get unemployment because a company as small as yours ain't got to pay the insurance premiums."

"Maud, I picked up a new client Friday. I got a five-thousand dollar retainer."

"Five thousand *American* dollars?" she asked. "Who you got to kill?"

"I ain't got to kill anybody. What I got to do is spend this five grand so they can't fire my ass and take it back. Let me spend some of it on you."

Maud laughed, the crinkles around her eyes deepening. "You a ticket, boy, you know that?"

"C'mon, Maud. Come back to work. I'll pay you as long as I can, then you can take a vacation until I pick up another client."

"You the reason I'm out of work in the first place. You know that, don't you?"

Lynch lit a cigarette and blew the smoke sideways, away from her. "How was I to know the paper was going to fire you for taking a gift or two from me? I didn't mean nothing by it."

"I should've known better. It's just being there for nearly thirty years like that, and losing my pension and all."

"I still think you should've sued the bastards."

Maud sighed and leaned back in her chair, then reached up and adjusted a bra strap. "This ain't exactly the most prolabor state in the country, babe. And I ain't exactly got a ton of dough to be paying no lawyers."

"So c'mon back to work for me, will you?"

"Who's your new client?"

"It's that fellow who's been wanting to start a new film studio in the nuclear plant up the river. Seems he's been having a little trouble getting the necessary permits and things. Carlton Smith brought me in as a troubleshooter."

"Yeah, well, the trouble part's right, anyway."

Lynch smiled. "The trouble's already started. You read the newspaper today?"

"I quit taking that rag when they fired me," Maud sniffed. "I don't want them bastards to ever get another cent out of me."

"You ever heard of Pearl Bergeron?"

"No, she somebody fancy?"

"The governor's daughter."

"Oh, well," Maud laughed, holding her coffee cup between two hands as if trying to warm herself. "You see, me and the governor ain't exactly on speaking terms since I threw him over for Pelletier."

"Maud, she's dead."

"The governor's daughter?"

"Yeah, it's been in all the papers. And on the TV news."

"TV ain't much better than the newspapers," she said absent-

50

mindedly. "Once you get past 'Dallas' and 'Falcon Crest.' And now they took those two off."

"Listen to me, Maud. Pearl Bergeron was head of the film commission, and for some reason or other she was dead-as-hell-set against this film studio."

"Now she's just dead as hell."

"You got it."

"So what's it got to do with you? Your man didn't kill her, did he?"

Jack sat back in his chair, stunned. "Well, hell, I never thought of it. I don't think so. No, of course not. He's not the type."

"What's the type, babe?"

Lynch sat for a second, then shook his head. "If he did kill her, I ain't got nothing to do with it. My job is to try and put together the best campaign we can, so's our man gets his pretty picture in the paper as often as possible until the public is just clamoring to see this project go."

"What's that word? . . . spin-control?"

"Yeah, Maud. That's it. You're learning."

"Well, if I'm going to go back to being the secretary in a P.R. firm, I better learn how to talk the part."

Lynch smiled. He reached across the table and took her hand for a moment, squeezing it gently. It was the first time anyone had taken her hand in months. She blushed.

"Thanks, Leland," Miller Taylor said, pulling a pen out of his shirt pocket. "I'm going to have to sign for it this time."

"You signed for it last time," the older man in the blue work shirt with his name stenciled on the front said.

"I'm good for it, dammit. I got a job," Taylor muttered. "Give me the keys."

The mechanic reached a grimy hand to a wooden pegboard discolored with several decades' worth of grease smears, beer stains, and unidentifiable marks. He pulled down a key ring and handed it to Taylor.

"I got to tell you, Miller, I don't know how many more times I can get that VW running for you."

"If things work out like I want them to," Taylor snapped, "the last thing you'll have to do for me with that piece of shit is haul it off to the junkyard."

"Oh, that's right. I keep forgetting. You're going to get the BMW. Or was it the Jag? I forget."

"Laugh if you want to, smart guy. Whatever I get next time, I'll take it to a real mechanic from then on out."

"Yeah, right," the mechanic laughed. "Like the BMW dealer's going to let you sign for repairs."

Taylor twisted the key in the ignition lock, grimacing as the starter ground and whirred until something in it connected and the engine turned over. An oily smell filled the car as it hollered itself to life, the rotten muffler banging against the undercarriage as the automobile bucked and rumbled.

He pushed in the clutch and ran the stick shift around looking for reverse. Hitting the gear with a whomping noise, he backed out of the garage and headed for the outskirts of New Orleans, to Metairie in Jefferson Parish. The VW was too shot to trust it at highway speeds on the interstate. It would be a long, painful drive out to the Euro-Spa Sports and Fitness Complex. Taylor thought of the 911 he used to drive out in Malibu, and wondered briefly why the hell he had ever left L.A.

An hour later, with his head bursting from the exhaust and the noise, Miller Taylor bounced the car into the parking lot. It bottomed out as he went over a dip, the car's body slamming into its frame. The pounding in his head got worse.

If Taylor had taken a moment to think about it, he would have realized how out of place he looked at the Euro-Spa Sports and Fitness Complex. The parking lot was an expensive brew of the BMWs and Porsches he lusted for, as well as 300 Zs, Miatas, and completely restored mid-sixties Mustangs, with a few more exotic numbers thrown in here and there for good measure.

Inside, the smell of chlorine mixed with perfume and sweat. Grunts of exertion and pain to the point of ecstasy filled his ears as he stepped inside the place. The lights were soft; the rooms were lined with mirrors.

A narcissist's paradise . . .

"Can I help you?" a stunning young woman in a purple spandex bodysuit asked. Taylor stared at her a second and mourned his burnt-out youth.

"Yeah, I'm looking for Teddy. He around today?"

"Chrisman? Oh, yeah. I saw him a few minutes ago. He finished in free weights. He's in the machine room now."

"Mind if I go on back?" he asked.

"You're not a member?"

"No."

"Would you like to be?"

"Oh, honey," Taylor laughed. "I'm way too old for you guys. No, I just got business with Teddy."

The young woman walked off, an eternal smile pasted on her face. "Go on back," she said over her shoulder.

Taylor pushed through a pair of heavy plate-glass doors into the thick air and harsh lights of an Olympic-size swimming pool. The thin, wiry bodies in the pool stroked and burned their way through lap after lap, an occasional splash breaking the cavernous silence.

He carefully made his way back along the wall and through another pair of glass doors. This room was full of high-tech machines designed to sculpt and mold human bodies into the forms of Greek gods and goddesses. The treadmills stood to the left, complete with computerized readouts, and racks of machines that resembled torture cages covered the other three walls.

In the center of the room loomed the tallest machine, with wires and steel beams surrounding a platform fitted below with pistons and air compressors and hissing gauges. A sign on the side of the machine read GRAVITECH—A NEW WAY TO BUILD UPPER BODY!, and below that was a plaque with instructions that would have taken the better part of a half-hour to read.

Sweating bodies in hundred-dollar workout suits groaned and smiled and schmoozed and indulged themselves in their own ultimate masturbatory dreams. It was the sweetness of one's own body that captured the imagination here, as if the only real lust was lust for the self. And strapped into the Gravitech machine in the middle of these artificially tanned, toned, sculpted Adonises and Aphrodites, doing what appeared to be an agonizingly long set of dips, stood Teddy Chrisman. Three women in fluorescent pink, purple, and green exercise leotards, with slinky, black tights to set off the brights, stood around admiringly.

The redhead on the left whooped. "Get it, Teddy!" she yelled, as the veins on Teddy's neck stood out shaking and bulging as he raised himself up.

Taylor walked over and stood next to the redhead. "Jeez, how does this guy do it?"

"Oh, he's just—" the woman chirped as she turned around,

53

then faded into silence as she saw Taylor standing there in a gray sweatshirt and jeans.

"Yeah, I know." Taylor finished the sentence for her.

Chrisman strained and let out a low, guttural roar as he raised himself one last time to full height, then lowered himself, exhaling like a steam engine.

"Hello, Teddy," Taylor said. "How are you?"

Chrisman raised his sweating face from where he'd leaned it against a plastic piece of the machine.

"Oh, great," Chrisman muttered.

"What's the matter, Teddles? Not glad to see me?"

Chrisman pulled a towel off one of the handholds and wiped his face with it, then wrapped it around his neck. He pressed a button on the machine; the red digital readout went dark and the humming of the compressors stopped. Chrisman stepped down, towering over Taylor.

"Computer dips," he said. "Great for the upper body. Ought to try it sometime."

"Yeah, yeah. I'll do that, Teddy. Right now, is there someplace we could talk?"

"Yeah, c'mon. You can buy me a squeegee."

"A what?" Taylor asked, following Chrisman out. He couldn't help but notice that Chrisman was so tall and wide in the shoulders he could see neither in front of nor around the body builder.

"Fruit drink," Chrisman answered.

Taylor reached out and grabbed Chrisman by his left arm, which felt strangely more like holding on to a leg. "I ain't got time for no freaking squeegee."

"So what do you want with me, Taylor?" Chrisman demanded, turning and stopping.

"Where were you last night?"

Chrisman's face turned cold, the muscles in his neck tightening.

"What the fuck business is it of yours?"

Taylor felt a tinge of panic as he realized Chrisman probably could snap his neck like a wooden ruler. No, he thought, too many witnesses.

"Pearl's dead, and I figure there's going to be hell to pay out of it. I just want to make sure the damage is controlled."

"I talked to the cops this morning," Chrisman said. "They're straight."

54

"I didn't ask you their sexual orientation. What did you tell them?"

"I told them the truth about me and Pearl." Chrisman smiled, a sweet yet sad kind of a tender smile at her memory. "I loved her. We was even thinking about getting married. I got nothing to hide."

Taylor leaned against a wall, glaring at the younger man who towered over him. "Get serious, Teddy. You don't think just because Pearl threw me out we never talked, do you?"

"What is that supposed to mean?"

"C'mon, Teddy. We all know where those marvelous cuts of yours come from. Nobody gets muscles like that off a machine."

Chrisman came closer, menacing now. "Watch yourself, old man."

"Pearl wouldn't have talked to me so much if you hadn't left her hungry all those nights. Testosterone cypionate kind of cuts the old sex drive, doesn't it? After you've been on the shit a year or two . . ."

"What did she tell you?"

"The truth, Teddy. When she bought you, she thought she was getting a stud puppy par excellence. Nobody told her the puppy had been fixed."

Chrisman's hands jerked out, grabbing Taylor's sweatshirt on both sides of his neck. He pulled the older man forward about a half inch, then slammed him against the wall, hard enough that Taylor had to stifle a cry.

"I don't know what that bitch told you," Chrisman threatened, "but I fixed all that. Pearl got every bit of me she wanted."

He got down even further in Taylor's face. "More than she deserved."

Taylor looked up at him. "Ain't love grand?"

Chrisman spewed out a long breath of disgust, then let Taylor go. "Get out of here."

Taylor slid down the wall a bit, then caught his footing.

"Did you really think Pearl could pull you out of this toilet you call a career? You spent three years in L.A., and all you got was a few dumb parts in movies they're showing Friday nights on USA. Now you're back here doing freaking car commercials, for God's sake. What the hell did you think Pearl could do for you, besides screw you like a rabbit and pump enough powder up your nose to clog a storm sewer?"

Chrisman stared down at the floor; his vacant, empty gaze was marked only by an occasional side-to-side eye movement.

"Pearl's better off dead," he said under his breath, where no one but Taylor could hear. "I think she wanted it."

"Did you give it to her, Teddy? Did you make her dead?"

Chrisman looked up, the vacant stare melted now into a contemptuous glare. "I didn't kill her. From what she used to tell me, you're the most likely candidate for that."

"Is that what you told the cops?"

"Hell, no. I didn't tell nobody nothing."

"There's a guy looking into this, Teddy. I ain't too worried about the police. Not yet, anyway. But there's a guy named Lynch came around asking me questions this morning."

"So? I never heard of him."

"You never read newspapers, either, Teddy. He's the guy who dug up all that shit on the civil sheriff and the bank. He got a whole freaking bank shut down. And they found the sheriff wearing a shank between his shoulder blades up at Angola."

Chrisman turned and walked off, leaving Taylor standing behind him. "Which is one place I ain't going," he said. "Ever."

"This Lynch guy can be taken care of," he added, yanking the heavy wooden door to the men's locker room open, "if it comes down to that."

10

LYNCH MOANED AND SWEATED IN THE EARLY-MORNING LIGHT. HE tugged at the sheets and rolled; they seemed caught on something. In his dream he was at a long table, and there was a line of people, all of them his mother, passing by and, one at a time, leaning over and slapping him in the face.

With each slap he jerked. With each wicked smile and flash of the hand, he moaned. He pulled on the sheets again. They were hung. He couldn't move. He couldn't roll over in bed. He couldn't get up from the table.

Lynch felt something pushing at his arm, then a voice that cut through the dream-fog, penetrating the surreal blur of the other faces and voices. This one seemed almost real.

"Hey, where y'at?" the voice said. It was a high voice, young, heavy accent.

"Wha—" Lynch moaned and twisted again. One eye came open. There was someone above him, someone with heavily permed hair, blurry eyes. A woman. A nude woman. A *real* nude woman.

"Hey, darlin', where y'at? You having a nightmare or what?"

Lynch's other eye shot open in panic.

"Yeah—" he stammered. "A nightmare."

Where was he? He looked around, then realized he was in his own bedroom. His head was pounding. He was dreadfully sick at his stomach.

"You look awful, Jackie," the woman said. "I'd stay and make you breakfast, but I got to run. Mass's in an hour, and I got to go get changed."

Lynch raised himself up on his elbows. He was twisted around in the sweaty, dirty sheets. The bottom sheet was pulled up off the mattress, crumpled in a corner. Lynch looked down. He was barely covered up, hardly decent.

"Ohhh," he moaned, as the pretty young woman jumped off the bed and seemed to leap across the floor. She was maybe twenty-five, he thought, thin, tight. A dancer's body. He watched as she moved around the bedroom, pulling on a frilly, pink lace bra over tiny, high breasts and a delightfully sexy pair of bikini underwear over long legs. She bent over and fumbled around under the bed for a moment, then came out with a pair of stiletto heels in one hand and a tight, sequined T-shirt in the other. She dropped the shoes on the bed, raised her arms over her head, and slithered into the T-shirt.

Lynch drew in a deep breath as he watched her getting dressed. She was lovely, athletic, a little girl in a woman's body. She sat on the edge of the bed, stuck her legs into a pair of jeans, then rolled onto her back with her legs straight up into the air. Defying gravity and the laws of physics, she managed to pour herself into the jeans as far as the top of her hips. Then she rolled forward and jumped onto the floor, pulling the pants up the last inch or two and zipping them with a flourish.

"Hey, baby," she said, sitting on the side of the bed and placing a hand on each side of his face. "Don't you worry about last night. Everything'll be okay. It happens to all of us sooner or later."

Lynch stared into her face. Her hands were cool and soothing; her touch gentle. Lynch found himself wishing she would stay.

"I got to go now, though, babe. My momma'll kill me if I miss Mass." The woman hopped up and started toward the doorway into the bedroom. At the doorway she stopped, turned, and leaned against the jamb.

"You will call me, though, won't you?" she asked, pouting. "I'll look forward to it."

She turned quickly and started out the door. Lynch could hear her metal heels tapping across his wooden floor. Just as she touched the doorknob, Lynch appeared behind her, wrapped in the sheet, dragging it behind him.

"Let me just ask you one question, okay?"

"Why sure, Jackie," she cooed.

"Just who *are* you?"

* * *

It had been a while since *that* had happened. Lynch poured a cup of coffee out of the old ceramic pot and added a heavy dollop of half-and-half to it. He walked back into the bedroom and looked around. He was still trying to put the last evening together. It was coming back to him, although slowly.

He'd gone to Ray's, his old hangout, which he hadn't visited in months. Things had changed. Ray had remodeled, the place was now called Chez Ray's, and in place of the steaks and fries and muffalettas that had filled the old menu was a lot of stuff Ray said was nouvelle cuisine. Lynch had his dinner—some kind of blackened shit, he neither knew nor cared what—then decided to move to the bar for one last scotch and soda. A basketball game was on the TV above. He got interested. Then she had sat down two chairs over from him. They struck up a conversation. Lynch had never been particularly adept at bar scenes and, in fact, had no intention of picking the girl up. But as the night dragged on and the number of scotches mounted, Lynch found himself deeper and deeper in conversation with her. He had no memory of whose idea it was to go back to his place.

She had scribbled her name and number down on a napkin in the kitchen before leaving. Lynch picked it up with one hand, the cup of coffee an extension of his arm in the other.

"Cindy Langlois," the note read, with a number, then: "Call me."

He had a dim memory of impotence, of wanting to cuddle with the girl, of being held in her thin arms, and of crying in exhausting, overwhelming sadness. Maybe that's why she wanted him to call back, he thought. Maybe she figured he was the sensitive type. Maybe she just liked to see men at their worst.

Lynch knew he wouldn't call her.

He walked back into the bedroom and pushed the power button on the stereo. Lately, he'd found his tastes turning away from the usual jazz and more toward the rock 'n' roll he'd compulsively listened to as a younger man. He'd heard it described as a phenomenon of the baby-boom generation, and one that had created a whole new genre of radio programming: Geezer Rock.

Sting was wailing an old Police tune, "Roxanne." Lynch lit a cigarette and stared out the window, feeling the black dog set upon him like a rock.

I won't share you with another boy. He felt a surge of tension, of anger, as he wondered how many other boys the girl had been with. He erased it all from his mind, relaxing in the insights that came from within: the knowledge that he wasn't going to let this person touch him in the first place, and secondly, that deep down inside him, in his core and in his heart, he didn't give a damn.

He wondered, standing there, when the mourning for Sally would stop.

The phone rang. Lynch turned, unsure of whether to answer it. On the fourth ring, he picked up the phone just as the answering machine was about to grab it.

"Yeah," he said. He wasn't normally a rude telephone answerer, but hell, it was Sunday morning.

"Mr. Lynch?" The voice was an unknown.

"Yes."

"My name is Rowan Wilson," the voice said. "I understand Andrew Kwang has hired your firm to represent his company."

Lynch dipped back into memory. *Wilson.* Where had he heard that name?

"Yes, that's true. How can I help you, Mr. Wilson?"

"I'm a film producer," he said. "An independent like Kwang. I was negotiating to buy the Riverbend facility myself when Kwang stepped in and undercut me. Maybe you read about it in the newspaper."

Lynch remembered the name now. The man had been in the newspapers a few times, but as far as Lynch could tell, Wilson was more skilled at getting his name in the paper than anything else. He'd been in and out of the public eye for several years trying to crank up a homegrown film studio.

"I seem to remember something about that. Yes."

"I think you should know what's really happening here with this business of Kwang's studio and why Pearl Bergeron was so against it. Mr. Kwang's motives aren't as noble as he makes them out to be."

"There aren't many whose are," Lynch said.

"Fair enough. But Kwang hasn't gotten as far as he has by being a nice guy. And I don't think he should be portrayed as some kind of knight on a white horse who's going to come in here and tell us how to run our business."

Lynch was growing impatient and his coffee was getting cold.

"So what are you trying to tell me, Mr. Wilson?"

60

"There's a lot of backstory you should know on this," Wilson said. "Can we do lunch? It'll be worth your while."

Do lunch? Lynch looked over at the clock: 10:30 A.M. "Today?"

"If that's okay."

"Yeah, yeah sure. Where?"

"There's a new place just opened, on the back side of the French Quarter. Chez Ray's. Supposed to have a pretty good blackened seafood menu."

Great, Lynch thought, more carbon.

"Is noon okay?" Wilson asked.

"Yeah," Lynch muttered.

"See you then." There was a click as Wilson hung up.

Lynch walked through the heavy oak-and-frosted-glass doors of his old haunt and looked around, squinting not only from the dim light but to see past the ferns as well. The Sunday brunch crowd was in full regalia, the normals carrying thick copies of the Sunday *Times-Picayune,* while those in need of greater challenge struggled with imported copies of the *New York Times.* Lynch looked around, wondering if Wilson had arrived yet.

His question was answered with a tap on his left shoulder from behind. A puckish-faced man with a roll around his waist and a thick mop of salt-and-pepper hair was reaching through the ferns.

"Jack? Rowan Wilson. Come on around. I've got us a table."

Lynch walked around to the table. Wilson stood behind his chair as Lynch approached. "Glad to meet you, Jack Lynch. I've heard a great deal about you." He stuck out his hand, grabbing Jack's with a hard pump.

"Unfortunately, much of it may have been true," Lynch said dryly. There was something about Wilson that set off his inner guard mechanisms, the P.R. man's version of Hemingway's built-in, shock-proof shit detector. The man was just a little too jovial for strangers, a little too slick for a hungover New Orleans Sunday afternoon.

"Care for a cocktail?" Wilson asked. "Bloody Mary, perhaps?"

"No, just coffee," Lynch answered, shaking his head.

A heavily trussed college-age woman approached the table. "I'm Janie," she said brightly. "And I'll be your server today."

"Well, I'm Rowan and this is Jack. And we'll be your eaters today." Wilson burst out laughing at his joke. Jack looked up at the woman. Their eyes met and communicated the same thought.

"Coffee, please," Lynch said. "Eggs Benedict and the fresh fruit selection."

"Very good, sir. And you, laughing boy?"

Wilson roared again, so loudly the two couples at the next table turned. "Great, don't you love her, Jack? Isn't she great? Let me see, Janie." He picked up the menu and scanned it quickly.

"I'll have the breakfast steak and two, over easy, dry toast. And another Bloody."

"Gotcha," she said, walking off.

"Bitch," Wilson muttered under his breath. "Can't get good help any more these days, can you, Jack?"

"Yeah," Lynch said, in his best patronizing-placating voice. He hadn't been in this business all these years for nothing. "It's tough."

"I asked you to take this meeting with me because I wanted you on background. You need to know what's really going on in this town right now."

" 'Backstory,' I believe you called it."

"Movie term. All the stuff that happens in your characters' lives before the movie starts."

"And when did this movie start?" Lynch asked.

"As far as I'm concerned, it started a year and a half ago, when Andy Kwang decided he was going to yank the Riverbend plant out from under me."

"Tell me something," Lynch said, honestly curious. "What the hell is it about the Riverbend plant that makes it so special to you guys?"

Wilson smiled. "You have to understand, Jack. The days of the great old studios are over. Everybody's an independent now. You produce your own vehicle, you cut a distribution deal with one of the majors, and you're flying."

"That doesn't answer my question, Rowan."

"When every deal's a separate entity, a producer needs something for continuity. Bread and butter. I wanted that tower because it was going to make a great underwater studio, and believe me, babe, underwater flicks are the wave of the future, so to speak."

Wilson laughed at his own joke again. Lynch smiled.

"But there are also a couple thousand pretty useless acres around the tower. I was going to use the soundstage as a way to bankroll the rest of the lot. We were going to wind up with the largest production facility in the world outside of Southern California and Pinewood over in England. We're talking a complete package here—soundstages, postproduction, special effects. The whole shooting match."

"But you said the days of the great studios are over."

"We wouldn't be a studio," Wilson said, leaning over and placing a hand on Jack's arm. "We'd be a production *plant,* and we'd rent out to other filmmakers. That would make our nut and finance the two or three movies a year I want to produce myself."

"Sounds pretty good," Lynch said, pulling his arm back.

"It's great, man. Or it was until Kwang got in on the action. I had two projects in development, one of which was going to be Nicholson's next Oscar. I'm telling you, babe, he loved it."

A plate of eggs Benedict appeared in front of him, and Lynch absentmindedly took a forkful. "So what did Pearl Bergeron have to do with this?"

"Well, I can tell you this, buddy," Wilson said, taking a long slug of his Bloody Mary. "She was on our side. She had sense enough to realize that if we're going to benefit the home folks, it needs to be Americans controlling the operation. Not some foreigner who don't really have any stake in any of this."

"Rowan," Lynch hesitated, choosing his words carefully. "I'm a kind of public relations troubleshooter. As such, my loyalties are to my client. Given the circumstances, I'm not sure there's much I can do to help you. I mean, I'm not a reporter or anything. Not anymore."

"I know that, Jack. I just want you to know that you're not dealing with a man who's completely innocent here. He runs over people to get what he wants. I know. I'm one of them. I wonder if Pearl wasn't one of them, too."

"What does that mean?" Lynch asked.

"I mean that people who mess with Kwang often find themselves out of the loop. Sometimes permanently."

"There's no evidence whatsoever that Andrew Kwang had anything to do with Pearl Bergeron's death. If you start spreading rumors around to the contrary, I can guarantee you're going to have a world of problems on your hands."

"Jack, babe, I got a world of problems on my hands now. But it's going to work out. I just know it is."

Their eyes locked for a moment, then Wilson turned quickly away. He jumped up.

"Lois, hey!" he called, his voice again too loud. "Over here, babe."

Jack looked around to see a woman, half-hidden by the ferns, turn. She looked their way, her face at first tensing, then going blank. Wilson motioned to her, an exaggerated wave of his whole arm, followed by a slight pitch forward in the chair. Is he getting loaded? Lynch wondered.

The woman came over to the table and stood there, arms wrapped around a thick Sunday paper.

"Hello, Row," she said. Her voice was quiet, subdued. She wore a pair of jeans that would have been fashionably tattered if she'd paid more for them; as is, they were just old. A white shirt with fake mother-of-pearl snap buttons fit loosely around her. Her brown hair was straight and hung below her shoulders perhaps two inches. She had brown eyes to match, and a softness to her face that seemed almost unnatural.

"Lois, baby. How are you?" Wilson stood up and leaned across the table toward her. She moved in just close enough for them to brush cheeks, as if it were a chore.

Jack half-stood up, then sat back down as she looked at him and smiled.

"Lois Finlayson," Wilson said, "meet Jack Lynch. Jack, this lady is the finest cinematographer on the Gulf Coast. I've been after her to do a film for me for years."

"Yeah, right, Row," Lois Finlayson said, extending a thin right hand to Lynch. "I'm pleased to meet you, Mr. Lynch."

"My father was Mr. Lynch," he said, shaking her hand. "Call me Jack. Would you care to join us?"

"Well," she hesitated. "I was just going to get a quick bite and—"

"Of course she'll join us. Struggling young camerapersons have always got time for a free meal with a producer."

"Row, I can pay for my own lu—"

"Nonsense," Wilson said, interrupting again without noticing that the woman was genuinely offended. "Sit down."

"All right." She hesitated, then sat.

Rowan Wilson waved for the waitress. "Where is she? I tell you what, I've got to go to the little boys' room. I'll flag her down and send her over on my way."

Wilson got up and walked off. Lynch fingered his cup of coffee almost shyly. Lois Finlayson had none of the flash or seemingly endless pretension that marked every other person he'd met in the movie business so far. If anything, she seemed hesitant and reserved.

"So you make movies, too?" he asked.

She placed her newspaper on the floor next to her, then sat up straight and brushed her brown hair back over her shoulder. "I work a camera, Mr. Lynch—"

"Jack. Please."

"Okay, Jack. I work when I can, which isn't often these days."

"What's a cinematographer doing in New Orleans to begin with?"

"I was born here. Lived much of my life here."

"You don't sound like it."

"Away at schools. Living lots of places away from here. I moved back from Los Angeles about two years ago."

"Got tired of the rat race?"

"How'd you guess? It seems like that's the main reason everybody leaves L.A. these days. That and the fact that no sane animal lives in poison."

"Not that the old Crescent City's much better on that account these days."

"The water tastes terrible here now, doesn't it?" she agreed.

"I wouldn't know. I don't drink it."

"And what do you do?"

"I used to be in the newspaper business, many years ago. Then I got into public relations. I have my own firm now. A small one."

"Are you representing Row?"

"Good heavens, no." Jack laughed. "Even P.R. flacks have their limits."

Lois laughed as well, for the first time, he noticed. "Good, I'm glad to hear that. Any man who refuses to work for Rowan Wilson is a friend of mine."

Lynch smiled again at her. He found his headache subsiding. "Shake, pal," he said, extending his hand. She reached out and took his hand, shaking it and holding it for just a second as Janie, the server, came up behind them.

A half-hour later, the three got up to leave. Rowan Wilson insisted to the point of embarrassment on paying the tab. He signed off the charge slip for his gold American Express card and wrote in

65

a generous tip. He had finished a third Bloody Mary and fancied himself even more amusing now.

As he joked with the waitress, Jack and Lois drifted to the street. "It was good to meet you, Jack," Lois Finlayson said out on the sidewalk. She turned to walk away.

"Do you need a lift anywhere?" Jack called behind her.

"I have a car." She smiled at him.

"See you again sometime?"

She nodded her head, waved and walked off. Wilson grabbed Lynch's right arm. "Pretty girl, huh?"

"Yeah. Real nice."

"Too bad about her, though."

"What do you mean?" Lynch demanded, turning to his obnoxiously jovial host.

"Oh, nothing. It was just that mess she was in a few years back. She got busted filming a porno movie. Lesbian, I heard."

"A lesbian porno movie?"

"Yeah, go figure. Maybe she's a little stiff in the shorts herself. Listen," Wilson said hurriedly, looking at his watch. "I got to go. Another appointment. See you around."

Then, before Lynch could even get a word out, he had turned and walked away. Grateful not to have to make small talk, Lynch slowly walked back to his car.

Inside the restaurant, Janie the server was carrying a tray of empty glasses back to the kitchen when the maître d' motioned her over to a counter.

"Hey, Janie, you run a confirm on that guy at table nine?"

"Line was busy," she said. "I left the receipt by the box and was going to come back for the number."

"This the receipt?" The maître d', an older man with a waxed moustache and a thin layer of rouge asked.

"Yeah."

"I just ran his number. I got a Code 32 from Amex. The guy ain't paid his bill. We're supposed to yank his card."

Janie, already exhausted from the Sunday brunch crowd, looked at the receipt and then at her boss as she realized what he was saying.

"Shit," she hissed, wondering if her tips would cover the bill. "Goddammit!"

11

LAMAR BERGERON'S FATHER FISHED SHRIMP BOATS MOST OF HIS LIFE down in the southern swamplands of Louisiana. Places with names like Terrebonne Bay, Timbalier Bay, Barataria, Bastian, and other sounds derivative of the Acadian French that was centuries old and still spoken as a primary language in those backwater marshes that few outsiders ever visited.

Bergeron had come up out of that place and that era, the Depression of the 1930s, when nobody could buy clothes or cars or even shoes, in some places, but everybody always seemed to eat. There were plenty of crayfish, or as the child Bergeron called them, "mudbugs," and shrimp and even occasionally alligator, which was a delicacy if your mama was one of the few people who knew how to cook it, and dreadful if she wasn't. People raised chickens and vegetables and lived in shacks that had never seen running water or indoor plumbing, and they drank homemade beer and wine and cheap gin and danced on Saturday nights to the tinny sounds of guitar and accordion.

His family had been middling prosperous, and he had been happy as a child. It was only when the war came, and the young LaMar was drafted, that he began to see the outside world and how cruel it could be. He'd proudly called himself Cajun, but now the slick people from the northern part of the state and the bigger cities who were with him in basic training at Fort Polk called him coonass. Years later, he would proudly call himself a coonass as well, and dare anybody not to like it, but then he was young and flammable. More fights than he cared to remember came out of some white trash from Gulfport or Vicksburg or Baton Rouge with a few beers in him making fun of Bergeron's heavy accent and bad English.

He learned then how to scramble for what he could get. And when the war was over, he came back to his small town of Val de Bois, just south of Dulac on the western edge of Lake Boudreaux, determined in an almost clichéd way to make something of himself. He apprenticed to the only lawyer in Dulac while preparing to read for the law, and four years after being mustered out, he passed the Louisiana State Bar exam.

His hair by then had turned prematurely gray, as his father's had been, then snow white. He took to wearing expensively tailored, white double-breasted suits and real Panama hats. He relocated his offices and his life to Houma, to the big city by his standards, where he married Janette Avery, whose family had money from way back. A year later, their daughter Pearl, who thirty-eight years later would be horribly beaten to death in her expensive apartment in the French Quarter, was born.

LaMar Bergeron's practice grew, and he became involved in politics. He was appointed to the Public Service Commission in 1957, elected Mayor of Houma in 1965, and went to Baton Rouge as a state legislator in 1970. In 1974, he fought a hard campaign for the governorship and lost. In 1977, the man who beat him was indicted for accepting kickbacks in a road-paving scheme, yet in typical style, managed to win reelection anyway. In 1982, Bergeron went for the governorship again, this time with a campaign war chest that measured in the millions. He brought together a coalition of upstate rednecks and reactionary zealots with the Cajun farmers and fishermen of his part of the state. He won in one of the largest landslides in Louisiana history. LaMar Bergeron, a man of sophistication and flair, yet who had come from truly humble beginnings, had whipped the fatcats and politicos of the New Orleans–Baton Rouge axis.

His inauguration speech had been delivered first in Cajun French, then in English. He proudly ended his rousing patois with the declaration, *"Laissez le bon temps rouler!"*

Let the good times roll.

And roll they did. Bergeron and his southland buddies filled the halls of the state capitol that Huey built with whoops and hollers and deals that would have done the Kingfish proud. LaMar's gambling junkets to Las Vegas and Atlantic City and Paradise Island became

68

legend, and it was considered the most sublime honor to be invited to accompany the governor himself on the state's private jet.

LaMar had done right by his family and himself. Pearl was educated with the sisters, and when the time came, she was sent to Newcomb, where she mixed with the best of the good girls and the Tulane boys. His wife's alcoholism was a hidden dark spot, cleverly kept from the press by a skillful team of handlers who convinced everybody she was just a shy homebody who preferred to stay out of the limelight. That was fine with LaMar. His wife's sudden and frequent bouts of the vapors gave him more time to pursue his own interests, which were at least five foot ten, no more than 115 pounds soaking wet, and blond if possible.

LaMar convinced himself that the occasional rumors he heard of Pearl's wild parties and binges were just nasty stories being passed around by the opposition. He kept in touch with his baby girl, and she told him that all the tales were just lies. He let himself believe that, for he wanted to believe that whatever she was doing, her heritage as a Bergeron would give her the innate skill to keep her life under control—one genetic predisposition holding another in check.

But something had gone terribly wrong that Friday night at Pearl's apartment. When the news reached them late that night, Janette freaked. Now, having downed enough medication to quiet a foaming-at-the-mouth pit bull, she was too ill to attend the funeral down in Val de Bois. Pearl was to be buried in the family cemetery, two spaces down from her grandfather, the shrimper, and her grandmother, the sweet little old Cajun lady who made the best crayfish bisque anyone had ever laid lips to.

"Hell of a way to start the week," the governor grumbled to Robert Brewster, his chief of staff, as the two climbed into the State of Louisiana's Cessna Citation.

Brewster had been playing catch-up all weekend, trying to get out of the NOPD Homicide office just what had happened down there that Friday night. He thought it strange that the boss seemed more furious than anything else, first at Pearl for getting herself killed and inconveniencing the shit out of him, then at the police for being a bunch of incompetent boobs, and finally at the still-blank face that had yet to be filled in above the caption THE KILLER.

"I want him," Bergeron said. "I want him in the smallest cell at Angola, with the meanest guy with the biggest dick in the entire institution. I mean it, Bob. I want the entire population measured.

69

Line 'em up against the wall for short-arm inspection. The best-hung inmate in the whole place gets carte blanche with the scumbag that killed my daughter."

Brewster opened a notebook as the jet's engines began to whine and the plane jolted forward. He hated to fly and was glad the flight to Houma-Terrebonne would take barely twenty minutes. He jotted down the note "Measure prisoners" on a clean page. He suppressed a laugh at the thought of what would happen if the newspapers got hold of the story that the governor wanted a survey done of the penile-length of the State of Louisiana's prison population.

"The bigger the better," Bergeron yelled as the jet screamed down the runway. "Nothing under seven inches! Don't come back telling me this state can't measure up in the criminal manhood department!"

God, I love this job, Brewster thought as his gut churned with airsickness. Something new every day.

Lynch turned the knob to his office door and was pleased to find it unlocked. He smiled and looked down at his watch: 8:15 A.M.

Maud was back.

Just as he entered, the phone rang. Maud, behind an old wooden desk in the outer office, picked it up.

"Lynch and Associates," she said. Professional, no hint of excess twang. "May I help you?"

Lynch stood next to the desk, briefcase in one hand, a brown bag with a half-dozen warm doughnuts in the other.

"Yes, Mr. Smith, he's right here. Please hold."

Maud punched the hold button and smiled up at Jack. "Carlton Smith. And a Mr. Taplinger called this morning," she said, handing him a pink message slip.

"I'll take it in my office. Here," he said, holding out the brown bag. "Peace offering."

"You don't need to do that, darling," she answered, her voice back to the real Maud. "You trying to make me fat or what?"

Lynch walked into his office, leaving the door open behind him. He was genuinely glad to have the company. The place seemed plain and homely with no one around but him.

"Carlton?"

"Good morning, Jack. What's on your schedule today?"

Lynch opened his briefcase and took out his calendar. It was a

70

practiced move, something he did every day. He knew without looking that he hadn't written anything down there. He loosened his tie and pulled a fresh pack of cigarettes out of the case, then snapped the lid shut and placed it on the floor beside him.

"Let me see," he said. "I actually thought I'd drive down to Houma for Pearl Bergeron's funeral. I'm not exactly sure why. Sort of take the pulse of the living, I guess. I also thought maybe we should send flowers from Kwang World Pictures. Sign of respect if nothing else."

"Good idea," Smith agreed. "Wonder what the governor will say."

"The way I figure it, we'll be able to tell which way the wind's going to blow by any public statements he makes."

"He does seem unable to keep his mouth shut."

"Occupational hazard," Lynch offered. "Maybe even a requirement."

"Sheldon Taplinger called me this morning. He couldn't reach you."

"Oh, and what does Super Secretary want today?"

"Davis over at the *Picayune* called him this morning. Wants an interview with Kwang."

Lynch thought a moment. "The funeral's at eleven. I can be back here by one, maybe one-thirty. Depends on the traffic and how hungry I get."

"Can you set something up around two?"

"Yeah, I'll have Maud call the paper. I'll just go straight back to the hotel. I'll call Taplinger back and have him tell Kwang not to start without me. I also thought maybe I'd try to get a look at the police files on Pearl. Maybe the autopsy report."

"Are we playing detective?" Carlton asked, with a slight hint of mocking in his voice.

"I can't afford it. All I'm trying to do is stay on top of this."

"You knew the police asked Kwang not to leave town?"

Lynch sat forward, ripping the last of the tinfoil triangle off the top of his cigarette pack. "Hell, no. Is he going to do it?"

"He says he has a meeting in New York Tuesday. He's not very happy."

"Neither am I."

Lynch pulled a cigarette out. The smell of the fresh pack was a warm, familiar, toasty smell. He wondered at times if the smell

71

would be so appealing to him when he was hooked up to an oxygen tank.

"Maybe you can take care of that when you talk to the police," Carlton said. "Get them to reconsider. Kwang's not exactly going to take it on the lam."

"I'll handle it today. After the interview."

"Good enough," Carlton said. "Watch yourself down in Houma."

"What's to watch?" Lynch asked, flicking his lighter and holding it to the end of the cigarette.

"Don't forget, my friend. This is a murder case."

"Not to me," Lynch said. "I want nothing to do with that. I'm not a detective, I'm a sewage control officer."

"Call me when you get back."

"I'll stop somewhere and pump a quarter in a pay phone."

"When are you going to get a telephone in your car?" Carlton asked.

"Good God," he sighed. "When hell freezes over?"

Jack stood up and walked into the reception area. Maud was standing next to a table, putting together the makings of a pot of coffee. She turned and smiled when he came in.

"Doughnuts are good," she said. "Try one."

Jack took the cigarette out of his mouth and bit into a doughnut. Tasteless, he thought.

"Seem kind of bland."

"That's cause your taste buds're dead. When are you going to give those durn things up?"

Jack curled his lip at her. *"When are you going to give those durn things up?"* he mocked.

"Okay, you jerk. They're your lungs."

"Hey, c'mon, let's have a little bossly respect around here."

The room was filled with the noise of water dribbling through a plastic funnel and coming out into a glass pot as coffee. It was a familiar noise and smell to Jack. One of the few things about morning he could stand.

"I gave up cigarettes twenty-five years ago," Maud said. "Never missed 'em a day."

"Good for you," he said, starting to turn back into his office, then checking himself. "By the way, dig Pearl Bergeron's obit out of the morning paper and find out what funeral home she's in. Call

72

down to Houma and have a funeral wreath sent over. Sign it Rest in Peace, or some such line, and have it go over from Kwang World Pictures."

"How much?"

"It's billing back as expenses. Go a hundred. And call Davis over at the *Picayune* and tell him—"

"What?" Maud yelled.

"Okay, chill out," Lynch said. "I'll handle that one."

Lynch walked back into his office with the cigarette in one hand and a doughnut in the other. He called the newspaper and left a message for the reporter about the two o'clock interview. He dropped his cigarette in an ashtray and brought the free hand up to his face. He sniffed the inside of his palm, the tobacco smell taking him back almost twenty-five years.

He got up and stood at the window, staring out, and thought of Martin Cromwell, the English boy back in military school who had taught him to smoke.

His mother had sent him there as a young teenage boy when she started seeing the man who became her second husband. He'd hated the school at first, with its rigid strictures and harsh academic demands. The motto of the school had been "In Loco Parentis," a phrase the young Lynch thought meant his mother was crazy, which he already knew. It was only after his first semester of Latin that he found out that it meant "In Place of Parents." And somehow, once he'd settled into the routine of the school, that became a comfort to him. As a middle-aged man now, who'd spent most of his life drifting in and out of bad situations, Lynch missed the safety and comfort of the school, and faithfully sent them money every year.

It was, he remembered, the last time in his life he had felt truly secure and nurtured. And, he thought, while looking down at his hand, he'd almost gotten himself kicked out of school that day in the middle of the hard, bitterly cold winter term of 1967, when Martin Cromwell pulled out a pack of Winstons.

"You'll love it," the English boy said, as the two sat in Cromwell's tiny single dormitory room. It was ten below zero, but Cromwell had opened the window so the smoke could escape. Jack lit the cigarette and started coughing as soon as he put the thing to his mouth. The harsh smoke hurt his nose and burned his eyes and made his lungs ache. But the smell in his palms afterward was a joy, a warm, musty human smell that made him imagine what being a child again in a warm kitchen full of cooking smells would be like.

It was a tough fantasy for Lynch, even then. He had never been a child.

Three days later, the senior prefect caught Cromwell smoking in his room. The next day, the young boy was expelled and tearfully put back on a plane to London to face his furious parents. Lynch had been so terrified of getting caught that he didn't smoke again until he was well into his college years.

"The florist down in Houma says there'll be a twenty-five percent rush charge." Maud's voice brought Jack back from his daydream. "That okay?"

He turned. "Yeah, that's fine. Just make sure it gets there before eleven. I'll be leaving for Houma myself in a few minutes."

"You okay?" Maud asked. "You got that thousand-yard stare again."

Lynch smiled. "Just thinking, babe. I'm okay."

12

LYNCH HAD BEEN TO FUNERALS BEFORE, BUT NEVER ONE WHERE THE governor and half the troopers in the state were in attendance. The traffic jam around the tiny funeral home in Houma rivaled anything he'd ever seen at five o'clock on I-10.

He maneuvered his car, thankful once again he'd had the foresight to buy small, into a parking space that was too short for the Cadillacs and Lincolns that filled the block. He couldn't recall ever seeing that many black limousines in one stretch of a town like Houma ever before. No one else could, either.

Whatever else Pearl Bergeron had been in life, she would be a legend in death. Lynch thought of the things he'd heard about her in the past few days, as well as seen first hand, and tried to form some mental picture of the celebrated murder victim. He had to admit to himself that he was unable to do so. She was a blank. He felt no emotion for her, no sadness at her death, no longing for her to be back among the living.

He was there as a politician, working his way among the other mourners, many of whom were backslapping and joking as if this were a cocktail party or reception rather than a moment of deep and tragic loss. In fact, Lynch realized as he looked around him, most of these people *were* politicians: state legislators, department heads, high civil servants, and political appointees. When the governor's daughter gets herself killed in the wicked and glamorous French Quarter on a Friday night, it behooves everyone to pull it together to show up for the funeral.

A line had formed outside the funeral home, down the long sidewalk that led to the entrance and through the gravel parking lot behind. The building itself was made of concrete blocks painted a pastel green. To the right, a central air-conditioning unit struggled to make the building bearable in the heat.

Lynch walked slowly forward, behind a man and woman who were having a serious argument about the number of mourners.

"There are at least five hundred," the woman insisted, her hair a blaze of artificial orange piled high over too much makeup.

"Shut up, Beatrice," the man hissed, pronouncing his wife's name "Bee-AT-ris." "There ain't anywhere near that many people here."

Ten sweltering minutes later, they entered the building. Sweat ran down Lynch's sides, underneath his shirt and jacket to the waist of his pants. The air inside was thick with heat and humidity and the stale smell of barely masked human perspiration. Occasionally, his head would reel as a cloud of cheap, overdone perfume would drift by. The mourners were packed in like a school of fish, filling every seat and lining the walls.

An enormous bronze-and-gold casket—closed, he noticed—was on a dais in the front of the largest room. All the removable partitions between the individual parlors had been taken down, turning the entire building into a single room for Pearl Bergeron.

Flowers were everywhere; it looked like Derby Day, Lynch thought. An overhead fan spun slowly and helplessly in the heat. Lynch took one of the few remaining empty spots against the back wall and settled against it, feeling fortunate to have a section to lean on. He stared slowly around the dimly lit room as the organist played a slightly off-key dirge. Lynch assumed the people in black in the front four rows were all family and close friends. They looked like a row of dominoes from behind. Lynch smiled to himself as he imagined what it would look like if somebody fell against the person on the far right and, one by one, the black-suited mourners fell against each other until they became a pile of squirming flesh on the floor.

They were all there: the governor without his wife, who Lynch knew was probably back in Baton Rouge either too snockered or too hung over to travel; the lieutenant governor and his wife; the secretary of state; the speaker of the House. If somebody were to open up on this room with an H&K MP5, he thought, the state of Louisiana would be crippled for years.

Lynch recognized the president of the New Orleans Chamber of

Commerce against the wall to the right. The two made eye contact; Lynch nodded respectfully. The president, an insipid-looking man with large bald spot and bad skin, nodded back and brought his hand up to his forehead. He rubbed it across his face as a comment on the heat. Lynch nodded again.

"When are things supposed to start?" the man next to Lynch asked.

"I don't know," Lynch whispered. "Soon, I hope."

"Me, too. God almighty dalmation, I can't stand too much of this heat."

Lynch let his head rest against the wall, feeling the coolness of the concrete, and tried to shift his weight onto the other side of his hips.

He followed the line of faces around the wall one at a time, looking to recognize someone. His eyes stopped suddenly, just as she turned around and saw him.

Lois Finlayson: the cinematographer who had showed up at his brunch yesterday with Rowan Wilson. Lynch wondered if she came down to Houma with him, then found himself hoping she hadn't. Wilson was probably here somewhere, he imagined, but he hoped to heaven she wasn't with him.

She smiled at him and Lynch realized, for the first time, that he had been smiling at her. How strange, he thought, that he would be smiling at this woman without even knowing it.

The preacher, who wore an inappropriately shiny, blue-and-gray polyester suit, got up from the side pew and walked to the podium. He held a large gold-bound Bible in his hand, with a flashy diamond pinky ring on his left little finger and a loud, wide, 1970s tie around his neck. Rural Church of Christ, Lynch speculated. Like one of those guys that come on the public access cable channels late at night screaming about salvation and crying out for money. Your money. It reminded Lynch of why he'd quit going to church twenty-five years ago. Funerals were as close as he ever wanted to get. He imagined what kind of funeral he'd like. Probably none, he thought. Maybe Viking.

That's it, roll me onto a boat, push it out in the middle of Lake Pontchartrain, and set fire to the sucker.

Lois smiled at him again, turning her head first away from him shyly, then looking back. The preacher was beginning his incantation now:

77

"Let us pray," he instructed. Heads bowed as a group. Lynch leaned down slightly, but enough to still watch her if he rolled his eyes up.

Oh, Lord," the preacher bellowed. "Take into your arms the soul of our beloved sister, Pearl!"

Lynch lifted his head slightly. Around him, a few paper hand fans, the age-old types with the wooden stick and the stiff paper printed with Bible verses or a portrait of Jesus, waved.

He found himself fading away as the preacher droned on. At some point, he realized people were singing. A hymn of some kind. He became dizzy and his mind wandered. When would this be over? His head ached and his legs were tired. It was interminably hot. A fat woman three people down to his right wavered and looked as if she might fall over in a faint. The man next to her reached out and touched her arm, and the two began walking silently toward the front door and fresh air.

Finally, it was over. The preacher came forward and bent down in front of the governor, whispering as the funeral directors behind him prepared the casket for the pallbearers. People shuffled around, a few headed out the front door. A double door behind the casket magically opened, letting in a blaze of sunlight that caused Lynch to squint until his head pounded. The yellow rays cut through the dusty air in solid beams, as if God himself had planned to highlight Pearl's final exit from an earthly structure.

The pallbearers lifted the casket and carried it out through the double doors toward a silver hearse outside, its motor running and its doors open. The governor and his staff and family followed the casket out and walked solemnly toward the waiting limousines. The gallery spectators followed.

Lynch watched as Lois Finlayson walked out through the double doors into the gravel parking lot. He speeded up his pace a bit, excused himself a few times, and managed to get through the doors before she left. She was standing outside, in fact, in the shade of a large tree, watching as the funeral director ran around in circles trying to get all the cars in some semblance of an orderly line. This was the biggest funeral he'd ever conducted, probably to be outdone only by the governor himself when he came back home to Houma to get buried.

Lynch walked up behind her, looking past her through the fine brown hair that hung down long and straight over the simple, classic blue dress she wore. He took off his coat and threw it over his right shoulder.

"You can stand here if you want, but you've got to promise not to talk about the heat."

She turned around, smiling. *"Body Heat,* right?"

"What?" he asked.

"That's the opening line Ned Racine uses on Mattie in *Body Heat.* He even had his coat thrown over his shoulder like that."

"That's right. I forgot."

"You're not too smart, you know that. I like that in a man."

"Oh yeah, what else do you like? Lazy? Ugly? I got 'em all."

"Pretty good." She smiled. "Are you the Ned Racine type?"

"Well, Mattie's more my type, actually. I like a woman with larceny in her heart."

A brief smile jumped onto her face, then just as quickly left. "Well, tell me, Mr. Lynch," she said, walking with the crowd into the parking lot. "What brings you down here? To the funeral, I mean."

"Jack, please. Remember, you promised."

"Okay, Jack."

"I'm more curious than anything else," he said, hesitating in order to get his thoughts together. "I didn't know Pearl Bergeron very well, only met her a couple of times. I don't know, maybe I got a thing about funerals. I've been to enough of them the past couple of years."

She stopped and turned. The sun was full in his face and he hadn't put on his sunglasses yet. He squinted as he looked back at her.

"You look like a man who's been to a lot of funerals."

"Thanks a lot." He laughed. "You silver-tongued devil."

"No, I mean it. I pride myself on being able to read faces. You've seen more funerals than a man should see, I suspect."

"Well," Lynch coughed nervously. "What brings you down here? Did you know Pearl?"

"Oh, yes," Lois Finlayson said, taking a step forward and walking again. "I knew Pearl. Better than most, I'm afraid."

"Oh, I didn't know that. I'm sorry for your loss then. It's tough to lose a friend."

"Jack," she said. "I think there's something you should know. It's fairly common knowledge in the business and if you're snooping around like I think you are, you'll find out anyway."

79

"Yeah?"

"I came down here to make sure Pearl Bergeron stayed in that casket. And I'm going out to the cemetery now to make sure she doesn't crawl up out of that hole before they can stomp all the dirt down."

Lynch stopped. She halted a step in front of him, then turned. "Has your car got air-conditioning?"

She looked confused. "Yes, of course."

"I've got a convertible and the air-conditioning's out on it. Can I ride to the cemetery with you?"

Lois Finlayson smiled. "You want to make sure, too?"

"From what I've heard, somebody should."

The air-conditioning in the homicide division of the New Orleans Police Department was on the fritz as well. Lieutenant Carl Frontiere had kicked off his jacket, pulled down his tie, and unbuttoned the top two buttons on his shirt. There was a stack of file folders on his desk that had been there all day, and would have to be taken care of before he went home in order to make room for the next day's inevitable stack of new file folders.

It was already six-thirty on a Monday evening. Damn, he thought, it's been Monday all day. He'd been assigned three other murders that had taken place over the weekend. Combined with Pearl Bergeron's death, that made four new file folders to add to his 73 outstanding ones. And he was only one detective among many. American cities were becoming war zones.

Frontiere looked forward to getting home. He would fire up the minigrill on the balcony of his apartment, which overlooked the swimming pool, then toss on a steak, open a nice Cabernet Sauvignon, and watch the babes taking their late night dips. Maybe he'd even throw on his suit and go down for awhile.

The drive down to Houma that morning had been a long one and cost him a morning's work. That damned funeral home had been choke-to-death hot. Hadn't those people been dragged into the twentieth century yet? Then he thought of the stifling heat of his own office and realized how miserable he'd been all day.

Reality, for Carl Frontiere, was that this day had sucked. He was hot and tired and he wanted to get through these folders as quickly as possible and get home.

The phone behind the stack of folders rang. He was one of the last few guys in the office. No one moved from their desks, so he fumbled behind the pile of manila folders until he found the handset.

"Homicide, Frontiere," he said.

"Lieutenant, this is Sergeant Hernandez on the front desk. I got a guy here says he wants to talk to you about the Bergeron case. Says his name is Lynch. Jack Lynch."

That's interesting, he thought. Frontiere wondered if Lynch had seen him at the funeral home that morning, and if so, if he'd recognized him. Certainly not. It had been a year or more since he'd last seen Lynch, who had not been at his best then.

"Get somebody to show him up, will you, Hernandez?"

"Sure, Lieutenant. He's on his way."

A minute or so later, a uniform from the lobby brought Lynch upstairs. Frontiere examined him as he was led through the maze of desks over to his own. Tall, thin, face beginning to fall with age. Age, hell, Frontiere thought as he remembered the things he'd read about Lynch over the past year or so, it wasn't the age, it was the mileage.

"Lieutenant Frontiere," Lynch said, hand extended.

"Mr. Lynch. Have a seat," he said, motioning to a battered wooden visitor's chair.

"Thanks for seeing me," Lynch said. "Mind if I take off my jacket? It's kind of hot in here."

"Knock yourself out," Frontiere said. "I've had mine off all day."

"Yeah, it's tough, isn't it. I was down at a funeral in Houma today, and believe me, man, it was miserable."

"I know," Frontiere said. "I was there."

Lynch stopped midway through removing his left arm. "Yeah, I guess you would have been. I didn't see you, though."

"I saw you. So how come you were there?"

Lynch finished removing his jacket, then pulled his tie loosely down to his second button. He unbuttoned first the left arm at the wrist, then the right, and began rolling his sleeves up.

"That's kind of why I'm here. My firm has been retained to represent Kwang World Pictures."

"Retained? I didn't know you was a lawyer."

"I'm not. My public relations firm has been retained by Kwang. He's concerned that his problems with the film commission may affect the purchase of the Riverbend facility. There's a lot at stake

81

here. He wants a favorable publicity climate, if you understand what I mean."

"I think I got you."

"He also wants to cooperate with the police department fully. He has no connection with this unfortunate incident last Friday night. But if there's anything he can do to be of help, he's there. He just wants you to know that."

Frontiere sighed and leaned back in his chair. He stared at Lynch for a long moment, just enough to make him uncomfortable. "I love how you guys always use words like 'unfortunate incident.' Kind of like the expression, 'having a dog put to sleep.' Hell, you don't put 'em to sleep, you shoot them full of poison or you put them in a tank and suck all the air out. You don't put them to sleep, Mr. Lynch, you kill them. And that wasn't an unfortunate incident Friday night, it was a murder. A human being had the shit beat out of her so bad she died."

Lynch's face tensed. Below the level of the desk, his right fist knotted.

"You don't have to tell me that, Lieutenant. I just forgot that I don't have to speak in euphemisms to you."

"I know you know that, Mr. Lynch. We've met before, you know."

Frontiere smiled at the puzzled look on Lynch's face. "Only you probably don't remember it. You were a little jacked up."

"When?"

"Last year. You were in the hospital after being—how did you tell us?—'mugged' in that parking lot."

Frontiere watched as Lynch's face fell and his eyes seemed to stare far off for just a split second.

"The hospital . . . " Lynch said.

"Yeah, I was the officer who questioned you about the murder of, what was her name? Sally something?"

"Bateman," Lynch said. "Sally Bateman. She was my secretary."

"Yeah, that's right. She died out in that parking lot if I remember correctly."

Lynch studied the police lieutenant carefully, wondering if this was some kind of game. "You remember correctly," he said.

"Now I got another murder on my hands, and you're connected with it."

"I am not connected with it!" Lynch flared.

"You're here, aren't you?"

"What do you want from me, Lieutenant?"

"What do you want from me?" Frontiere countered.

The police officer paused. He watched as Lynch sat in thought for what seemed like a long time. Finally, he spoke.

"Truth?"

"That's always a good place to start," Frontiere said.

"I want to know what you've got."

Frontiere shifted in his chair and tried not to laugh. "You going after the guy that did this?"

"Kwang blames me for that mess Friday night, in the restaurant," Lynch said. "Listen, Lieutenant, I ain't got a lot going for me these days. My company's not exactly drawing in the clients. I haven't been in the best shape myself the past few months. I need a win in my life. I'm not out to solve your murder, but if I can do a good job by Kwang and see that he gets his film studio set up here, hell, maybe I can get back on my feet.

"It's that simple," Lynch added after a moment. "Basically, I'm desperate."

13

THERE WAS SOMETHING ABOUT A MAN WHO'D SIT IN A STRANGER'S
office and admit desperation that struck Frontiere as strangely ad-
mirable. Honesty was not a quantity he found in great abundance in
his life. It seemed odd to him that someone in public relations—
second only to advertising and politics as a breeding ground for
compulsive liars—could be so painfully candid.

He wondered, in fact, if Lynch was lying. Maybe he was trying
to help his client. But why would his client need help?

"Mr. Lynch," he said. "I can't really open our files to you. It's
against departmental regulations."

"Tell me this, then," Lynch said. "Have you got anything to
connect Kwang to the murder itself?"

Frontiere thought for a moment. "Not really. Only a well-
publicized tossed drink last Friday night."

"How about we trade off here?" Lynch asked. "You know she
was a cokehead, right? The night she threw the drink in Kwang's
face, she had just gone to the ladies' room. When she came back, she
was kind of wild. Like maybe she'd tooted up in the loo."

"You think that's why she threw the tantrum?"

"Maybe. In any case, why keep Kwang here? The guy's not
really a flight risk. I mean, hell, if he wanted to run, he could. But
where would he go? He's famous. Sooner or later, he'd show up
somewhere and you could just have him extradited."

"I don't know. He's a material witness, at least. As far as I'm
concerned . . ."

"Is there anything else you need to know from him? Can he
answer any more questions?"

"Not right now. No, I don't think so."

"Then let him go," Lynch said. "If you really need him back here for anything, he'll show up. It's a good enough risk. He's got quite an investment here. Besides, from what little I can tell, you're not going to find any shortage of people with motivation."

Frontiere looked hard at the man across his desk. "What do you mean by that?"

"I've talked with a few people, just to find out a little about Pearl Bergeron. She wasn't very popular. Even her ex-lover, that Taylor guy, told me she was a horse's ass."

"There seemed to be problems in that area, yes."

"Now it's you that's slinging bull, Lieutenant. You and I both know if you want a list of people who didn't like her, all you got to do is go to the phone book."

"You know," Frontiere said, "I popped a guy last year for icing his sweetie's ex. The ex-husband would get drunk and come around and start beating up on his used-to-be old lady. One night, the guy comes over when she's entertaining a gentleman caller, who proceeds to whack him to death with a broom handle.

"I been in this business a while," he continued, "and I tell you, you got to work hard to beat somebody to death with a broom handle. Hell, that's work. And when I asked him why he did it, he just looked at me and said, 'The guy needed killing.' He *needed* killing. . . ."

"Just like Pearl, huh?"

"That's what some of these people are saying to me. Of course, they're all denying they did it. But nobody seems brokenhearted over it."

"Was she raped, Lieutenant? I mean, could this be random violence? We got a fair amount of that in this city, you know."

"Not likely. Pearl lived in the Quarter, but she had money and she had access to the best security. The state police had the alarms installed in her apartment. And they weren't tripped or anything. No, the way we figure it, whoever whacked her got in because she knew 'em.

"And no," he said after a moment, "she wasn't raped. She had a couple hairline skull fractures, one depressed skull fracture, the usual contusions and abrasions, some bruising around the throat, and a broken arm."

"Jesus," Lynch sighed.

85

"The way we piece it together, the assault started on the second floor of the apartment, on a landing above the main entrance foyer. Somebody threw her down a flight of stairs. Then when that didn't kill her, they rolled her over in front of the door, sat on her chest, and beat on her some more."

Lynch winced. "Sounds nasty."

"It wasn't a pretty sight," Frontiere said. "You want to see?"

"You mean?"

"I can't show you the whole file, but you can see the crime scene photos. What the hell? Maybe you can tell me something."

Frontiere reached across his desk to a pile of folders and flipped through them. He pulled a thin one out, one that was sure to grow thicker over the next few weeks, and opened it.

An eight-by-ten glassine sleeve inside held a series of color photographs. Frontiere handed them across the desk to Lynch.

Pearl Bergeron lay at the bottom of a flight of steps, her arms twisted out grotesquely from her sides, her dress pushed up vulgarly to the middle of her thighs. One leg was cocked out at an unnatural angle, with the other jammed into the corner where two walls met. Her face was still and cold, even in the photograph, with a patch of bloody hair down on her forehead. Her eyes were open in slits, staring straight up in death, with her teeth bared as if her last thoughts were of pain and hate. Lynch could see in the photograph what he'd seen before: that people in death cease to be people anymore even in appearance. They look more like mannequins— large, contorted, gruesome dolls.

He thumbed through the remaining pictures: Pearl photographed from every side, from farther up the stairs on the landing, from floor level; then the entire apartment, the doors, the outside entrance. The collection of shots was standard police abstract compendium, perhaps in a little more detail because of the importance of the victim, but still a technical rendering of a very personal and final type of horror.

Not a pretty death, Lynch thought. And from what he could tell, not a particularly quick or painless one either.

"Any ideas what kind of person could have done this?"

"Strong," Frontiere said. "But not necessarily an Olympic athlete. Maybe young and agile. You got to be in pretty good shape to beat somebody to death with your bare hands, but you ain't got to be Arnold Schwarzenegger."

86

"Any idea of a weapon?"

"We found a glass flower vase broken on the landing. Cheap, very thick and heavy. Probably the only cheap thing in Pearl's apartment. Bits of glass embedded in her scalp, the skin covering her jaw. Few other places. Coroner says from the angle, the killer was probably left-handed and taller than Pearl."

"I've seen enough," Lynch said, handing the photos back across the desk.

"Yeah, it comes on you kind of quick, don't it?" Frontiere asked, eyeing Lynch's pallor. "You okay?"

"Yes," Lynch said, rising from the chair. "Thanks for your help. If I find out anything that I even think can help you, I'll call."

"Yeah, you do that, Mr. Lynch," Frontiere said, standing up.

"By the way, what about Kwang?"

Frontiere thought for a second. "Kwang can leave town if he has to. But he has to let somebody in this department know of his whereabouts for the time being. That okay with you guys?"

"I'm sure it will be," Lynch said, offering his hand. "I'll be sure he keeps in touch with me, and I'll keep in touch with you."

"Great," Frontiere said. "That way we all keep in touch. Wonderful day in the neighborhood, right?"

Marco Cerasini discreetly looked at his watch as he stood at the podium: 9:45. Thank God his lecture would be over soon. His mouth was dry, and he was exhausted.

"Scene endings include the terms 'Cut To' and 'Dissolve To,' as well as a few others that you won't see very often," he said to the class of seventeen adults. "They go at space sixty-three, a line below your last line of scene direction, with an extra line space separating the scene ending and your next slug line."

It was week two of Cerasini's basic screenwriting course at New Orleans Community College. Tonight was the lecture on formatting screenplays, which was widely regarded as one of the most boring lectures given on the entire campus. The class was noncredit and administered through the continuing education department of the school. His students were all aspiring screenwriters, but beyond that they had little in common. He'd had housewives, doctors, business executives, pilots, architects—anyone who thought they had a movie in them, and all blissfully unaware of the odds against them. No matter. As long as they had the two-hundred-dollar course fee,

Cerasini was glad to have them. There were no course requirements, no grades, no credit given. It didn't make a hoot in hell to him if anyone ever did the work; he stood up there week after week, delivering the same lecture notes over and over until it all became rote.

He'd tried to have the course converted from noncredit to credit, but the English department had very little regard for him or his subject. He'd never bothered to finish his master's degree, though it was listed on his curriculum vitae, and most of those stuffed-shirt assholes considered writing for the screen blatant hackery.

"Okay, group," Cerasini said. "I think it's close enough to ten to call it an evening. Any questions?"

A hand at the back of the room and to Cerasini's left shot up. It was a hand he'd seen many times before and belonged to a long-haired aspiring songwriter with no visible means of support.

"Yes," he said amiably, trying to remember the guy's name while thinking what a jerk he was.

"What about the term 'Smash Cut'?" he asked. "I've seen that in a couple of scripts."

"Smash Cut," Cerasini said. "A scene-ending term. You won't see it very often, and when you do, it's usually in murder mysteries or suspense/adventure films. It indicates a particularly abrupt and violent ending."

The young man's head went down as he copied every word.

Jesus, Cerasini thought, lighten up. Who gives a shit?

"Anything else?"

This time, no arms went up. It was late; the class was tired. These late Monday nights went on forever. Cerasini hoped they'd move the class to a later day next semester. It was too hard to keep people's attention on Monday.

"Okay, guys," he said. "See you next week."

Immediately, people jumped up and began loading books into bags and briefcases, shuffling papers, coughing, milling about for a few minutes longer. The continuing education classes had a reputation as being great places to latch on to someone. It seemed as if at least half his class each semester were more interested in checking each other out than in listening to anything he had to say.

A fat woman with bad skin and ill-fitting clothes approached the lectern where Cerasini was stacking homework assignments—the few that had actually been turned in, that is. Marco could never remember her name, but he had the vague impression that she knew what she was talking about. She'd turned in a scene a week earlier that was actually semiliterate. The shock set him back a week.

"Professor Cerasini," she began, "I'm having some trouble with this script of mine that's just not coming together like I blah, blah, blah, blah, blahblahblahblahblaaaaahhhhh . . ."

Cerasini stared past the woman, off into the far corner, where *she* was just getting up out of her chair.

Cerasini had watched her for weeks. He found her tremendously attractive. It seemed as if there were at least one in every class, one woman that made him want to get down on all fours and chew the carpet and bark at the moon like a demented mongrel. Usually, he could brush it off. At his age, he had no business lusting after women he couldn't have and wouldn't have the energy to do much with if he could.

She made it hard for him to stop thinking about her. She kept coming up after class and talking to him. He'd been trying for the past three weeks to screw up his courage enough to ask her out for a drink after class. He could remember what she wore each night since the semester started. He found himself thinking of her during the week, which was something he never did for any of his other students. She had an aura about her, he thought. Her brown hair was unfashionably long and would have been drop-dead gorgeous with the right kind of perm. Somehow the fact that she wore it natural, though, made it all that much more attractive.

"Can I see you after class?" she mouthed from across the room, pointing at him. Cerasini nodded his head yes, he hoped not too eagerly, and held back the urge to jump up and yell.

". . . So, anyway, Professor, I was wondering if you'd have time . . ."

Oh, God, Cerasini thought, this woman is still talking to me. He jumped back into the conversation and tried to figure out how much he'd missed.

". . . to look at this rewrite and tell me what you think. I know it's a bother, but I figure if I can just get my protagonist's goals outlined a little more clearly, then I can justify having my Act I climax on page thirty-eight rather than on page thirty or so."

What in the hell is this woman talking about?

"Sure, no problem," Cerasini said, furrowing his brow to indicate his pondering/reflective mode. "I think what you're talking about here may very well work, but let me take the script home and look it over and talk to you next Monday night."

"You could call me at home," the woman said hopefully.

If I can remember who the hell you are, I will.

"I've got your number written down somewhere," he said. "But why don't you give it to me again just to make sure. Oh, and be sure and put your name on the paper as well."

The woman practically panted herself breathless with delight. "That's wonderful." She hesitated. ". . . Marco."

The woman in the back of the room approached the teacher's desk, standing back a few feet waiting for Cerasini to finish with the fat, and now blushing, lady. She straightened up, the bags of flesh under her arms quivering loosely, and handed Cerasini the slip of paper with her name and phone number on it.

"I think you have a wonderful story to tell here," he said, laying it on thick to get rid of the woman. "It's sensitive and caring and I want to see more of it. I want to see where you go with this. I really do."

She held her notebook and textbooks crossed in her arms like a schoolgirl. As she turned, he took her right arm lightly with his left hand and steered her toward the door. He felt her tremble beneath his touch.

Gag me with a Barbie leg.

"I thought I'd never get rid of her," he said, closing the door and turning back to his desk.

"I think she's in love with you," she said.

"Just my luck. Now, what can I do for you, Lois?"

Lois Finlayson set her briefcase down on the teacher's desk and leaned against a student desk in the front row. She wore a pair of tight, faded jeans and a blue oxford-cloth button-down shirt.

"I just wondered if you'd heard anything about the murder of Pearl Bergeron," she said.

Cerasini walked over to his desk and leaned against it, his hips resting at the point where the top of the desk meets the front. He hoped the thing didn't start sliding around on him. Physical grace was an attribute he'd yet to acquire, and he'd learned over the years that it was one of the few things he couldn't fake.

"I thought that was terrible," he said, looking directly into her eyes, the brownest pair of eyes, he was sure, that he'd ever seen.

"So did I. I just wondered, because I knew you had at least a couple of scripts in to the Kwang people, and what with her trying to stop the project and all . . ."

"How did you know I'd submitted anything to them?" Cerasini asked, genuinely curious.

"Miller Taylor's a friend of mine," she said. "I was talking to him a few days ago."

"Have you submitted anything?"

"I'm not a writer, you know that." She smiled demurely. Cerasini's heart ached. "But I did let Miller know that I was interested in any film work that came up. It's been a while for me, but I still know my way around a set."

Cerasini remembered the rumors he'd heard about Lois Finlayson and her work. He fantasized about getting her in front of the camera, rather than behind it.

"Miller wants to direct," she added. "I think that's the angle he's pursuing with Kwang. And if he gets to, then I think I'll probably be his cinematographer. If we could just find the right script."

Marco Cerasini reached up and stroked his chin. He'd been trying to grow a beard lately, but it just wouldn't come in thick enough. He'd been thinking that if he could just look a bit more Mephistophelian, then perhaps those jerks in the NOCC English department would take him seriously. Maybe if he could put on a little weight.

"I've sent in a couple that I think might work," he said. "I've got one that won first place in the Albuquerque International Film Festival screenwriting contest last year. Robert Redford was supposed to show up to present the award, but he couldn't make it. I don't know, Earth Day or something."

Lois Finlayson looked at Cerasini and smiled. The guy was pushing forty-five at least, she figured, and had yet to actually sell any of his writing. She'd seen guys like that before: hopelessly burnt-out wannabes who lacked either the talent or the determination or the luck to actually make it as writers, yet who refused to just hang it up and get a life. She'd met more of them than she cared to remember; thank heavens she hadn't fallen for too many of them. But she knew all the signs: the puppy-dog looks, a toss-up between the incessant self-centered braggadocio or the endlessly nauseating self-pity. Either it was "I won second place last year in the Appalachian Poetry Contest," or "Poor me, all I want to do is write for a living and no one will give me a chance."

She'd heard it all before, and Cerasini had all the signs of having it bad. He'd probably ask her out for a drink before she could get out of there.

"Say," Cerasini said brightly, "how'd you like to drop by the Napoleon House for a drink."

And listen to you pontificate about story structure for the next hour or about how you worked with DeNiro in New York? she thought. No, thanks.

"I really can't," she said, as sweetly as she could muster. "I have to get up early tomorrow. I just wondered if you'd heard anything about what was going to happen at the film commission with Pearl gone."

"In fact, I know that my name has been tossed around in some circles," Cerasini said. "I don't know if I'd take it or not, though. It might interfere with my writing."

Lois looked at him and imagined him slitting his own mother's throat to get the job. It was an easy fantasy to create.

"Oh, come on. If you got offered it, you'd probably take it, wouldn't you?" she asked.

"Yeah," he said flatly. "I probably would."

"I heard she was beaten pretty badly," Lois said. "It must have been a lousy way to die. I went down to her funeral this morning. Out of respect, you know."

"Was her funeral this morning?" Cerasini asked, desperate that he might have missed something.

"Yes, the governor and everyone was there."

Cerasini's brow furrowed, this time for real. "Oh, hell," he said. "Were you good friends?"

"Yes," he answered, distracted. "I thought a lot of her."

"So did I. A lot of us in the community did."

Cerasini looked at her, confused. "I thought, after what she did to you, that—"

"Oh, no," Lois said. "That's history. We'd worked through all that. One has to forgive in this life, right? My bitterness toward her did nothing but knock me off center. I got over it and got my life back on track."

" 'You're a better man than I, Gunga Din,' " Cerasini intoned.

"We do what we have to, Marco," she said. "We do what we have to."

14

KWANG PACED NERVOUSLY BACK AND FORTH ACROSS THE SUITE. HIS plane was due to leave in less than an hour and there was no sign of Lynch or Carlton Smith. *Where were they?*

"Sheldon, what's holding them up?" he asked as his secretary entered the room with a garment bag over one arm and a suitcase hanging from the other.

"They called ten minutes ago and said they'd be right over," Taplinger said. "Just relax."

"Damn," Kwang muttered. He was more tense than usual today, so much so that he was having trouble maintaining his usual calm. Kwang's mental solitaire was broken by the sound of the doorbell. Sheldon stepped over and opened the door. Lynch and Carlton Smith stepped in quickly.

"I'm so sorry we're running late," Smith said. "Our contracts department had some problem with their word processors this morning."

"Strange how computers have made us *their* slaves, isn't it?" Kwang said, his cool returning. "Gentlemen, I suggest we conduct this business on the way to the airport. My limousine is downstairs and there's enough room for all of us. I'll see that you're delivered either back here or to your offices after our plane departs."

"Jack tells me your interview with the newspaper went well yesterday," Carlton said as the four stepped on to the elevator. The bellman had taken the bags to the sidewalk earlier, and they were already loaded in the limousine.

Kwang stared straight ahead at the door of the elevator. He found the sinking sensation associated with elevators unpleasant.

"Yes. I was impressed with Mr. Lynch's ability to guide the interviewer in appropriate directions."

Carlton looked over at Lynch. The two made eye contact momentarily. Impressed, Lynch thought. Hell, I was brilliant: right reporter, right questions, and in a week or so, the right story.

Kwang turned around as the elevator door opened. "I also want to thank you for arranging things with the local authorities."

"No problem," Lynch said. "All part of the package."

"I think I may have underestimated you," Kwang said. "If I offended you in any way, please accept my apologies."

"Happens all the time," Lynch said. "Don't worry about it."

In the lobby of the Marriott, a group of reporters and a television news crew waited. Kwang exited the elevator first, in his white silk double-breasted suit, followed by Carlton Smith, Lynch, and finally, Taplinger. Kwang's secretary carried two cases, one a large attorney's contracts case, the other a standard-issue executive's leather briefcase.

The newshounds rushed the four. "Mr. Kwang, how has the murder of Pearl Bergeron affected your investment in the Riverbend facility."

Lynch stepped forward. "Mr. Kwang has no comment at this time on the ongoing investigation into the Bergeron tragedy. However, the plans for the Riverbend project are proceeding."

"Mr. Kwang, has your visit to New Orleans been difficult?" It was the same attractive redhead who'd been at Kwang's press conference a few days earlier.

"Your city has expressed its hospitality to me in a unique and unforgettable way. I look forward to returning as soon as possible."

"What about the rumors that the police wanted you held as a material witness?"

"Those are rumors," Lynch interrupted. "Don't believe everything you hear, especially on television."

"Ladies and gentlemen," he continued, to laughter, "Mr. Kwang has a plane to catch. And you know how the traffic is here."

"Hope your plane's not 'til tonight," a cameraman muttered next to Jack.

The four jostled through the crowd toward the revolving doors of the hotel lobby. One by one, they escaped into the sunlight and piled into the limousine, Jack, Carlton, and Kwang sharing the large backseat, Taplinger up front with the driver.

Carlton opened his briefcase and took out a stack of papers. He closed the briefcase, set it across his lap and placed the papers on top. "These are ready for your signature, Mr. Kwang."

"I trust the changes my attorneys requested have been incorporated," Kwang said.

"Yes," Carlton answered. "It was difficult to get the board to go along with the release clause, but they have agreed."

"Until our offices here are completed, your office will continue to act as our liaison with the state authorities. If the necessary permits and licenses do not come through," Kwang said, "then the entire escrow will be refunded."

"Minus the loan fee," Carlton added. "If you don't get your film studio, Mr. Kwang, you're only out roughly four hundred thousand dollars."

Lynch's head reeled. These guys were talking six figures like it was milk money. To someone like Kwang, four hundred grand was considered a "service charge." Lynch figured he could retire on it and spend the rest of his life listening to Stan Kenton and reading trashy paperbacks.

The limousine sped through the thick traffic, then onto the freeway enroute to the airport. "Sheldon, hand me that itinerary you drew up."

A hand with a manila envelope came up over the front seat. Taplinger handed the envelope to Jack without turning around. Twenty-five minutes' worth of small talk later, the limo pulled up in front of the departing-flight area and illegally double parked. The chauffeur held the door for the three in the back seat.

Twenty minutes later, Kwang and Taplinger were in the middle of the first-class section of a Pan Am flight to JFK. Another limousine would meet them there, and Kwang would be on his way to the second of six meetings he would have that day.

As the 747 went down Runway 28 and started its takeoff roll to the south-southwest, Kwang looked to his left, where his secretary sat in the aisle seat.

"I hate to fly," he said, just loud enough to be heard over the engines.

"You'd never know it by looking at you," Taplinger said. "You're always so cool about it."

"Nothing is ever what it seems," Kwang said. As the nose gear

95

of the aircraft lifted, Kwang imperceptibly slid his hand over and touched Sheldon Taplinger's leg.

Taplinger smiled to himself and discreetly looked around. Everyone, including the flight attendants, was safely strapped away, out of sight until the plane leveled off. He brought his hand down over the seat divider, then forward a bit.

He reached over and took Kwang's hand in his own, then squeezed it and held it tightly as the plane became airborne.

The limousine pulled up in front of Lynch's office. The black-capped chauffeur again dutifully came around to open the door. Lynch stepped out, stuck his head back in the car to say goodbye to Carlton, then thanked the driver with a five-dollar bill.

Upstairs, Maud was reading a paperback, waiting for something to happen.

"Hey, Maud, where y'at? What's happening?" Jack asked as he came in the door.

"What's it look like's happening? I'm getting older and tireder by the minute."

"Aren't we all, babe. Any calls?"

"Just one." She handed him a pink slip. Jack's eyes brightened: Lois Finlayson.

"You must be glad to get that one," Maud said. "You get the Chinese guy on the plane?"

"That 'Chinese guy,' as you call him, just had me delivered back here in a white stretch limo at least a block long. Jeez, the damn thing had to cost a fortune even to rent."

"He's got it. So what's next?"

Lynch sat on the used sofa he'd picked up at an office-furniture repo auction. It was cracked on one end, but it was real leather, like in a lawyer's office.

"I'm looking forward to an extended low-stress period. All I have to do is make a few phone calls and see that that newspaper story gets printed, then get the word out that you and I are sources for Kwang stories from now on out. I may even try to hustle up a few clients."

"Good idea," Maud said. "That five grand ain't going to last forever, you know."

"After I pay my back office rent, I'll do good to make it last the month."

"Oh, great. That means I can look forward to being stuck at home with Pelletier again."

"Now, now, darling," Lynch said, standing up and turning toward his office. "Something will come up."

"Yeah, like death and taxes," she said behind him. "And you can't afford neither one of them."

Lynch sat at his desk and dialed the number in front of him.

"Portable Productions," a female voice said. He wasn't sure—it could be her.

"Lois Finlayson, please."

"Speaking. This you, Jack Lynch?"

"You got him. Where y'at, Lois?"

"Right cheer, dawlin'," she said. It was a favorite game of hers, practicing her native New Orleans accent even though she'd long since educated it out of her system.

"Returning your call. What can I do for you?"

"You could buy me lunch. Or I could buy you lunch. Whatever."

"Love to. When and where?"

"Could you stand Ray's again?"

"Yeah," Lynch said. "Maybe we could get rid of the bad memories associated with our last time there. That is, unless you're inviting Rowan."

"Get real," she said, following it with a child's giggle.

"Noon?" he asked.

"Sure. I look forward to it, Jack."

Well, thought Lynch, life's getting better after all.

Lynch fingered a gin and tonic and debated lighting a cigarette. Lois Finlayson sat across the table from him, a glass of white wine in front of her. The restaurant was packed with local business people escaping both their offices and the hot sun, but he had managed to get a quiet table in the corner.

"So what's Portable Productions?" he asked.

"It's my company. I run it out of my house. That's why I have to be portable." She was wearing a pair of blue pleated pants with cuffed legs and what looked like a pair of man's wingtips. A paisley scarf was pulled around her neck and tied loosely over a beige silk blouse. Despite himself, Lynch felt his attraction to her growing. It made something gnaw at him inside. She was the first woman he'd

97

felt this for in a long time. Since Sally, in fact. He remembered that he'd wondered over the last few months if he had it in him anymore. Then he smiled to himself. Hell, he thought, it's only lunch.

"What are you smiling at?" she asked, smiling back.

"Oh, I was just thinking."

She settled back in her chair and fingered her wine glass. "What were you thinking, if I'm not prying."

"I was wondering why you asked me to lunch," he said. "And I was smiling at my own surprise at being attracted to you."

She looked down at her glass for a moment, then back to him with the smile still on her face.

"Why should that surprise you, that two people would be attracted to each other?"

"We don't know each other," he said.

"People never do at first. That's usually why they become attracted in the first place."

It was Lynch's turn to smile again. "Right. It's only when they get to know each other that the attraction goes away."

"You are cynical, aren't you?"

"Just careful."

"Tell me, Jack Lynch, what is it in your life that's made you so suspicious of women?"

"Works better the other way around," he said. "What is it in my women that's made me so suspicious of life?"

"I'll be happy with answers to either one."

Jack picked up his gin and tonic. The tall, frosted glass was covered with condensation, cold and slippery. He took a long sip of the drink, savoring the bitterness of the tonic and the iciness of the gin. The smell of gin was one of the memories of his childhood, some long-forgotten primordial sensory exchange with his father.

"I'm not sure I have any answers," he said, putting the glass back down.

"They're hard to come by anyway," Lois said. She sipped her wine, closed her eyes, and moaned. "That's delightful. But I'm not used to drinking in the middle of the day."

"Neither am I," Lynch said. "I do most of my drinking in the evening. When the day is over and the work is done."

"Sort of a reward?"

Lynch thought for a second. "No, not really. More to just relax and go to sleep than anything else."

"Are you one of these tortured people who never sleeps well?" she asked.

Lynch wondered if she was getting giddy. Her hair was flipped back over her shoulders, but a strand had fallen down across her forehead. It gave her a certain mid-1940s, Bacall look, especially with the pleated pants, and Lynch had a sudden urge to try and remember if he could whistle.

"This conversation is taking a decidedly heavy turn," he commented.

"Sorry. Didn't mean to get too close. It's just that—"

"It's not a matter of getting too close," Lynch interrupted. "I just still haven't quite figured how I got here."

"I asked you," Lois said, "and you said yes."

He felt the first sensations of the gin going to his head. He shouldn't have ordered the drink. This was more than he felt like handling.

"This is a new one on me."

Lois shifted, aware that he was becoming uncomfortable. "There are other things we can talk about as well," she said. "Like the movie business. I'll bet you don't know much about it, do you?"

"Not really."

"Well, let me tell you, Jack. The first thing you do is automatically assume that everything you hear is a lie. No matter what anybody tells you, until they prove otherwise, they're lying. I learned that a long time ago."

"The P.R. business is pretty much the same way."

"Not at all," Lois said, a new sternness in her voice. "There's nothing like the movie business at all. In other forms of business, the lies are at least grounded in reality."

Lynch pushed his empty plate around in front of him. He hadn't tasted his meal as he ate it, and now he couldn't even remember what it was.

"And in the movie business?"

"No connection whatsoever. There are people around here who will lie when it's easier to tell the truth. There are people in this business who'll lie when it's to their benefit to tell the truth. I can't figure it out. I've never seen anything like it."

"You're the one that sounds cynical now."

"Only about that. There really is nothing in the world like it. And it's rampant. Even Andrew Kwang, who's made a fortune and has everything in the world he needs, and fears nobody, would lie if it suited him."

"You think he's lying now? Lying to me?"

"Well, let me ask you and you tell me if he's lying. Has he told you about Harry McMillan."

"No, who's he?"

Lois smiled. "So he hasn't been completely truthful with you."

"Who's Harry McMillan?"

She picked up her wine glass and swished around the last sip in the bottom of the glass. She held it in her hand and stared through it.

"Harry McMillan was a great director, but he was a lush and his career was on the skids. Then he made the mistake of signing on with Kwang to do a film. Kwang interfered with him, kept meddling with the film. Harry'd been assured he'd have artistic control. This was supposed to be Kwang's first attempt at quality filmmaking. They were on location in Australia, doing the screen adaptation of a book, some obscure novel called *The Rain and the Window*. Harry and Kwang locked horns. Harry got drunk and popped him one, right in the kisser. Two days later, Harry's body was found just off the Great Barrier Reef by a couple of scuba divers."

"Murdered?" Jack asked.

"Exquisitely," Lois answered.

"So what does that have to do with Kwang and all this mess?"

"Jack," she said, swallowing her last dollop of wine. "Harry McMillan was Pearl Bergeron's ex-husband."

15

LYNCH'S GLASS STOPPED IN MIDAIR. "SAY WHAT?"

"Harry McMillan and Pearl Bergeron were married. They divorced a few months before his death."

"And he worked for Kwang?"

"On this one film only. His last."

Jack placed his glass back on the table, the wetness plopping on the wood and sliding a bit. He stared at his hand for a moment.

"How long ago was this?"

"I don't know. I just read about it in the trades. *Hollywood Reporter*, I think. I was living in L.A. Maybe six, seven years ago."

"How come nobody back here picked that up? You'd think the newspapers would've caught on."

"Maybe it's your job to see that they don't," she answered. "The murder occurred in Australia. Pearl and Harry had been living in some hotshot L.A. suburb. Sherman Oaks, I think. Why would the papers back here make a big deal out of it?"

"Besides," she added. "You know the news business. You surprised they didn't dig?"

"Not really. I hope nobody—" Lynch shook his head and faded out for a second. "I wish Kwang had told me about this."

"Maybe he didn't connect the two. Pearl was in Australia when Harry was killed, but that doesn't mean she actually met Kwang."

"Yeah, but it might explain why she hated him so much."

Lois reached across the table and took his hand. He tensed, surprised at the move, and fought the urge to pull back. "Maybe it would. Listen, Jack, I'm not usually this forward, but I'd like to see you again. You want to go out sometime?"

Lynch smiled. "Sure. I'd love to." He felt like a sixteen-year-old.

"What kind of music do you like?"

"What the hell, I'm easy," he said. "I'm a little old for heavy metal, but if that's what you like, I'll give it a try."

She laughed, her eyes darting from one side to another. The glass of wine had made her giddy.

"Let's hit one of the jazz clubs," she suggested. "Maybe see what's coming up with the symphony."

"Sure," Lynch said. "I'll call you and we'll set something up."

Lynch pulled out his wallet to pay the check.

"Wait," Lois said, pulling her purse off the floor. "I asked you out. My treat." She'd pulled out her wallet and snapped a credit card smartly on the table next to the check. "Don't tell me you're one of these macho types that can't stand to have a woman pick up the check."

"No, it's just that I—"

"Then put your wallet up." Lynch thought for a second, then did as he was told.

"Very good," she said, taking his hand again. "You know how to get over those kinds of feelings, don't you?"

"How?" he asked suspiciously.

"Invite me out to lunch," she said. "Then you can pick up the check."

"I'll do you one better," he said, holding her hand tighter. "What are you doing for dinner tonight?"

Lynch could hear the clacking of manual typewriter keys from inside the apartment. As he strode up the concrete walk toward the building, he noticed that Taylor's one window was open.

He stepped off the walk and into the grass, over to the window. He looked in to see Miller Taylor at a folding chair, shirtless, in cutoff jeans, pounding away on his old Royal portable. Sweat poured off the older man in the heat.

"Kind of hot for having the windows open, isn't it?" Lynch said through the window.

Taylor jumped, the metal chair legs scraping metallically across the painted concrete floor. "Damn," he said, "sneak up on a guy!"

Lynch smiled. "Sorry. I just wanted to stop by, check on a couple of things. You got a minute?"

Taylor straightened his chair up. "Sure, c'mon in."

Lynch walked around the corner of the house and pulled the screen door open. He walked in, expecting the tiny apartment to be a sweatbox. Instead it was cool, despite Taylor's sweating intensity.

"Hey, it's not bad in here."

"Concrete slab construction right on the ground," Taylor said, wiping his face off with a wadded T-shirt. "Sucks the heat right out of the place."

"So how come you're sweating like that?"

"I always sweat when I write," Taylor said. "I usually bleed, too."

Lynch walked over, looked down at the half-inch-thick stack of papers. "What're you working on?"

Taylor opened the refrigerator door, pulled out a cold beer. "Want one?" he called from the kitchen.

"No, thanks," Lynch said, remembering what the gin and tonic did to him over lunch.

"Screenplay," Taylor said, popping the metal top and stepping back into the room. "I got inspired. First time I've tackled anything like this in a long time."

"You going to show it to Kwang?"

"Eventually."

Lynch sat down in the rocker. "I've been looking around. Nothing heavy. Just trying to learn more about Pearl. The people around her."

"Yeah?" Taylor asked cautiously.

"Tell me about this guy she was living with when she died," Lynch said. "After you moved out. His name was in the paper. Chrisman, right?"

"Teddy Chrisman," Taylor said.

"Yeah. What was he like?"

"Have you tried to talk to him?" Taylor asked.

"No. Shouldn't be hard, though. Unless he's moved away, which the cops aren't likely to let him do."

"No, he's still living in the apartment. Knowing Teddy, he'll stay there as long as he can. Until they chase him off." Taylor took a long pull on the cold can of Dixie.

"So what's he like? The paper said he's an actor."

"And all actors are alike," Taylor said. "Assholes."

Lynch smiled. "So give me a distinguishing characteristic."

Taylor leaned back in the metal chair, contemplated his beer can. "Teddy's a mediocre actor. But he's got an incredible body and an ego to match. He might make it someday. Good-looking guys with no talent have done it before."

The older man came forward, put his elbows on his knees. "I'd be careful, though, if I were you. Teddy's got a bad temper. He's real volatile. I think it's all those steroids he's been on. Guy's got some incredible muscle cuts. You can bulk up on free weights, but I've never seen anybody get as well defined as he is without some chemical help."

Lynch studied the man in front of him for a moment. "So he's got a bad temper, huh? Flies off the handle easy?"

"For some reason or other," Taylor said, "and I'm not sure why, I don't think he killed Pearl. Maybe he did."

"What makes you think he didn't do it?"

"The problem with Teddy is that he's got this incredible body but not much to go along with it upstairs. If he killed Pearl, he'd do it in a stupid enough way to get caught. Beating her to death would be too obvious."

"Maybe I should find time to go talk to him."

Taylor raised the beer to his lips, drained the last third, crushed the can in his right hand.

"Like I said, I'd watch myself if I were you," he said. "Teddy can be dangerous when he's provoked."

Lynch managed to raise a faint smile. "I'll be careful. I'm one of these people who depend on innate cowardice for protection."

He stood up, the chair rolling gently back and forth behind him. "I've got to go," Lynch said. "I just wanted to stop by. I'm on my way to the library. Trying to check out a guy, maybe you heard of him. Harry McMillan. . . ."

Taylor looked up at him from the metal chair, his face carved wrinkles set in stone. His chest heaved slightly as he burped some of the beer's carbonation.

"You have been digging," he said.

"So you know him," Lynch said. "Do the police know yet about McMillan?"

"If they do, I didn't tell them." Lynch remembered Lois's warning about the film business being full of compulsive liars. Maybe Taylor was telling the truth, though, he speculated. It wasn't going to help him any to have the cops suspect Kwang of Pearl's murder.

104

"You ever met Harry McMillan?" he asked.

"Coupla' times," Taylor said. "Back in the L.A. days. Don't remember much about him. About any of it, in fact."

Lynch opened the screen door. "Must have been some life," he said.

"A laugh a minute," Taylor said. But he wasn't smiling. He stooped to watch through the window as Lynch walked out to his car. When he heard the motor start, he breathed a deep sigh.

"Shit," he said out loud. He reached over to his desk, picked up the telephone, punched seven numbers. The phone rang once, twice, then Taylor smiled to himself.

"Hell, no," he said, placing the receiver back on the hook. "It ain't my problem."

Teddy Chrisman turned to his left and cranked his right forearm arm up into a ninety-degree angle with his upper arm. That right bicep was coming along nicely, he thought. Being a southpaw, he'd always had trouble keeping the right up with the left.

And that damned D-Ball—Dyanabol—had just quit working after a few months. He'd been warned that he was just about maxing out on the dosage. He'd been through the testosterone cypionate cycle until it had done its best as well.

But this new stuff was incredible: HGH—Human Growth Hormone.

The fitness center had gotten it for him—standard operating procedure. Every health club he'd ever belonged to had been able to get steroids for its best and brightest. It made the club look good to have the new buddies walking in and seeing the animals prancing around in body gloves, greased down in front of the mirrors, benching three or four times their own weight. The grunting and groaning and preening was just plain good for business.

He'd heard of HGH before. The East Germans were supposed to have been using it for years on their women swimmers. It was lean and mean and left your pee clean. Good stuff.

Only drawback was, Randy, the owner of the fitness club, had warned him, that you absolutely could not exceed the standard time:dosage curve. There was no outside envelope to push here. It was a wall.

"I mean it, Ted," he'd said that first time, as Teddy pulled the straps on his one-piece neon-green lycra bodysuit over his shoulder

105

and down, "don't come in here a month from now wanting me to double your hit."

They were in Randy's office. Teddy trusted the guy; after all, he'd been on the stuff himself for two cycles in the past year. The shit was incredibly expensive. An eight-week series of injections was just over twelve hundred dollars, money he'd had a tough time getting out of Pearl.

"This juice'll turn you into a fucking ape, man," he warned, as Teddy pulled the suit down to his knees and bent over. Assuming the position, he looked behind him to make sure Randy was ripping the paper off a new disposable needle. That was the only thing about crunching 'roids that worried him: that someday, somebody would hit him with a used needle.

There was something not-so-vaguely erotic about bending over in front of Randy, who'd won at least a dozen body-building titles before he retired and opened up the club. Teddy suppressed the electric chills that ran through him as he stood there. Goose bumps came up on his legs, which were greased for his workout and shaved from the last competition.

"This stuff'll elongate your jaw, make your feet grow, change the shape of your forehead. All kinds of shit if you abuse it," Randy said matter-of-factly, as he poured alcohol on a cotton ball, then rubbed a three-inch-wide circle of wetness on Teddy's left buttock. "This stuff'll even restore your sex drive. You're going to want to fuck like a racehorse. You'll want to fight with every son of a bitch that looks at you funny. This is some powerful shit, man."

He held the needle up, thumped it and pressed the plunger to get the air bubbles out, then sank it in Teddy as deep as it would go.

As Randy pressed the plunger, Teddy felt the familiar, deep-within burning of the hot liquid going into him. His heart beat faster, and he felt the beginnings of an erection. HGH worked fast, he'd been told. In a matter of days, Randy said, he'd feel the weight coming on, the cuts of his already developed muscles becoming even more defined. He'd feel new strength surging through him, new energy, new power. He'd feel his control coming back, his virility renewed. Pearl would have no reason to complain ever again. He'd split her in half like a side of beef. He'd pound her into jelly.

After that first injection, Randy pulled the needle out, then came up behind Teddy and rubbed his bottom. "You'll be kind of sore tomorrow," he said, rubbing slowly in ever-widening circles.

"But it'll be worth it, boy. You're fixing to take the ride of your life."

That was two months ago, and Randy had been right. Teddy Chrisman had put on thirty pounds of pure muscle mass in those eight weeks. His body fat percentage had gone down to two and a half. He'd broken his own, and the club's, record in power lift. He was benching almost six hundred pounds. Pearl Bergeron had been getting laid like she'd never been laid before, all the way up until the night she was killed, the night Teddy Chrisman took his last shot in the cycle.

Now he was ready for L.A. again. This time, they'd listen to him. This time, they'd take him seriously. Teddy Chrisman was going to be the next Ferrigno, the next Schwarzenegger.

The next Mr. Universe.

Maud Pelletier looked around the empty office and wondered what to do next. She'd opened the mail, drunk her coffee and eaten her beignets, gone to the bathroom, and listened to that fellow who reads the books out loud on the public radio station every morning. Finally, she'd gotten so bored she even dusted all the furniture.

"If that durn Jack Lynch doesn't get into this office and give me something to do *soon,* I'm going to go nuts," she said out loud.

It was three in the afternoon and she had yet to hear from him. No call, no note. Where was he? No wonder the business was going down the toilet. Yesterday afternoon, she sat at her desk and read every magazine in the place. The phone didn't ring once, not one single, solitary, blessed time. Where was all this great business he'd been talking about?

There was a jolting, loud creak as the wooden door with the frosted glass panel swung inward so fast that Maud jumped. Lynch power-walked in, obviously in a hurry, head down, looking intense. He walked right past her and into his office without a word.

She got up from her chair slowly, wondering if now was a bad time to talk to him. She decided to chance it, and peeked gingerly around the corner.

"Well," she said lightly, "fancy you coming in today."

Lynch looked up at her, his forehead a mass of wrinkles. "Oh, hi, Maud," he said sorrowfully. "I'm sorry. I should have called. I've been busy today."

"Thank heavens somebody has, babe," she said. "Coffee?"

"Hey, that'd be great," Lynch answered as he fumbled through his cluttered Rolodex. Unstapled business cards dropped out of the file as he flipped through it. "Dammit," he muttered. "I've lost a card out of my file here, Maud. Would you get me the number of the *Los Angeles Times* please?"

"Sure." Maud turned to her desk.

"Make it the toll-free number if they've got one," Lynch called after her.

Maud laughed. *Tightass,* she thought, as she dialed 1-800-555-1212 and waited for the operator.

"Yeah, good morning, darling, you got a toll-free number for the *Los Angeles Times?*" Maud reached for a pen and scribbled down the number, then got up and poured Lynch a cup of coffee. She carried the slip of paper and the steaming mug of coffee in to him.

"What, you looking for a subscription or what?"

"No, I've been to the public library. You ever heard of a man named Harry McMillan?" he asked.

"No. What, he famous or something?"

"Not any more," Lynch answered. "He be dead. Murdered."

"Lots of people be dead, murdered. What makes him so special?"

"He used to be married to Pearl Bergeron. He was a film director, and he used to work for Andrew Kwang."

Maud whistled.

Lynch held the cup of coffee to his lips and blew across it. "No kidding."

"The cops know about it?" Maud asked, pulling the visitor's chair close to his desk and settling into it.

"Good heavens, I hope not," Lynch sighed, dialing the 800 number. "I've been over at the main branch of the public library going through newspaper microfilm. The *New York Times* had a brief obit. The *Picayune* didn't have anything."

"Surprise, surprise," Maud said. "So you got to go to the library, now you ain't got a contact down in the newspaper morgue."

Lynch smiled. "Yeah, funny how that works, ain't it?"

His expression changed as a voice on the other end answered. "Hi, *Los Angeles Times?* Hank Haley, please."

Lynch held his hand over the mouthpiece as the operator put him on hold. "Old friend of mine from college. Used to edit the

108

school newspaper, then went out to the West Coast and got a job. Now he's in management, pulling down six figures. Jeez . . ."

"In the newspaper business?" Maud asked, aghast. "Nobody makes that kind of money in the newspaper business."

"You do if you go to a real newspaper."

"Lord a'mighty," she sighed. "I ain't never seen no real newspaper, then."

"Guess you ain't. Hank? Hey, bro', what it is! Jack Lynch in New Orleans." Lynch smiled for a long pause. "Yeah, I'm still down here. Can't bear to be away. Gets in your blood, or in your pants, wherever. Kind of like a fungus that won't go away. Yeah. How's Jan?"

Lynch's face dropped. "Oh, no, I'm sorry. When? Aw, jeez. That's tough, buddy. I'm sorry. Hey, listen, it happens to the best of us. Katherine and I been divorced years now. Oh? Yeah, you heard about that, huh? Yeah, it's been tough, but I'm okay now. Listen, buddy, I know you're busy. I'm trying to find out some information on a director out in Hollywood. Harry McMillan's his name. Guy was murdered a few years ago. I'm working on a little something back here and I'm trying to make a few connections."

Lynch was silent for a long moment. He reached into his pocket and pulled out his cigarettes, drew one from the pack, and lit it. "Yeah. In Australia, I heard. Anyway, his ex-wife, it turns out, was murdered here in New Orleans last week. I'm kind of working the fringes of it and I'm trying to get a little background. Can I what? Okay, sure I'll call your stringer if it turns out to be worth a story. What's her name? Here, let me get a pen."

Lynch fumbled for a moment, then Maud handed him a pen. He wrote down a name and number as the voice on the other end of the line dictated. "Sure, it turns out to be worth something, I'll call her first. Let you guys beat the local papers, which won't be hard."

He smiled. "Okay. I sure appreciate it. Anything you got. You want to what?"

Lynch's smile faded quickly. "Fax it? Well, I haven't gotten around to getting a—"

Maud waved for him to stop, then grabbed his Rolodex and flipped through the cards, until she pulled out a First Interstate Bank of Louisiana card with Carlton Smith's name on it. Below his office number was another number, with the word *Facsimile* next to it in parentheses.

"Oh, wait, here it is," Lynch said. "I can never remember the damn number. You know how it is."

Lynch read off the number. "Later today? Hey, great, Hank. Owe you one, buddy. Ray's? Oh, God, Hank, you wouldn't recognize it. It's a freaking fern bar now."

He laughed out loud. "Yeah, nothing good lasts forever, does it? Listen, see you around, guy. Give me a call sometime."

Lynch hung up the phone. "Thanks. You're fast on your feet."

"This guy going to be able to help you?"

"I don't know. We were pretty good friends, once. Years ago. People come, they go. You know how it is."

"Sure. Okay, you got anything for me to do? I'm going stir crazy around here. Don't the phone ever ring?"

"It's been that quiet, huh?" Lynch polished off the last of his coffee.

"Heck, yeah. Like a tomb."

"Great. Well, you've been wanting a little vacation soon, right?"

Maud stood up. "I'd love one, but first I got to keep a paycheck long enough to pay for it."

She walked out of the office. "Maud," Lynch said from behind her. She stopped.

"Yeah?" She turned. He was smiling, almost sheepishly. When he smiled like that, she thought, it took ten years off him. He ought to do it more often.

"I had lunch with somebody," he said, softly.

She felt a pang in her stomach. You crazy old thing, she thought. What you think, he's going to want you?

"Yeah, who?"

"Her name's Lois," he said. "Lois Finlayson. She's a cinematographer."

"She work for that Kwang fellow?"

"Trying to."

"You like her?"

"Yeah, I think I do. A lot. I don't know."

Maud looked across the room at him. She'd known him for years, and she believed this was the one area of his life he was completely incapable of handling. When it came to women, that boy was about as crazy as a shithouse rat.

110

"You watch those movie people," she said. "They ain't like the rest of us."

"C'mon, Maud, they put their pants on the same way we do."

"Yeah," she said, turning back toward the reception area, "but it's what they wear under them, boy. It's what they wear under them."

Lynch stared into space as she disappeared. What was that supposed to mean?

"Sometimes, Maud," he whispered. "I just can't figure you out."

16

"SO WHAT'S HE LIKE?" LYNCH ASKED, RAISING A SNIFTER WITH AN INCH of Courvoisier left in it to his lips.

"He's a wannabe," Lois Finlayson said, holding a glass of red in her right hand. The restaurant was dark, quiet, deep in the Quarter's residential section. Away from the tourists. Lynch brought her there because it was one of his favorites, a special place he didn't come to very often. The restaurant was rarely full. In fact, Lynch often wondered how it made enough money to stay open. He leaned on the back two legs of his chair and let his head rest against the cool stone walls behind him.

"A wannabe?" Lynch asked. "So Marco Cerasini wants to be in the movies, too."

"He thinks he can write movies," Lois said. "You ask me, he's living in his own private Idaho."

"Everybody wants to be in the movies," he commented.

"Seems that way. Like everybody thinks he's a writer." Lois smiled at him. She wore a blue chiffon dress with shoulder pads that was cinched at the waist with a thin leather belt. She looked business, but with just a hint of sex and charm thrown in as well.

"The few real writers I've met," she continued, "I couldn't touch them. I mean, every bozo with a word processor thinks he's a potential Nobel Prize winner or an Oscar-winning screenwriter. Truth is, not one in five hundred can sustain it to the end."

"I've written a slew of press releases and articles in my life," Lynch said. "I'd never try anything like a novel."

"Maybe you should." She smiled at him across the table. They had been talking for almost an hour after their meal.

"So you met him in that class?"

"I wanted to get a better understanding of how this stuff is structured, you know. I wasn't going to write anything. Anyway, he started hitting on me, especially when he found out I'd done a few movies. I don't know whether it was business or pleasure or what. I just know I wasn't interested."

"Did he know Pearl?"

"What is it with you?" she kidded. "Always about Pearl. You have a crush on her or what?"

"Just my undying curiosity," Lynch said. He threw his arms out wide, like a nightclub singer.

"You better be careful," she laughed. "Your undying curiosity may get you killed."

Lynch went cold. "Meaning what?"

"Just teasing," she said defensively. "I mean you're going to fall out of that chair and break your skull if you're not careful."

Lynch smiled again. "Sorry. Hey, listen, you want to get out of here?"

"Sure, I'm stuffed, for now. Maybe another glass of wine later."

Lynch waved for the waiter and pulled out his wallet. "I got an idea. It's too early to call it an evening. Let's take a drive. Go out to the lake or something."

"Sounds wonderful. Let's do it."

The two fell into an easy, relaxed walk down the dimly lit streets of the Quarter. The cracked sidewalk under their feet rippled and dipped. The streets were nearly deserted in the quiet, cool summer evening. It was the time that Lynch had always loved the best, away from the craziness of the day and the business district, the pounding of the docks, the tacky freneticism of the tourist traps. It was the kind of night that reminded him of why, with all its problems, his love affair with the city continued despite everything.

That affair was sorely tested in the next moment, as the two rounded the corner. Lois was telling him that she thought Cerasini's degree was either completely faked or the product of a diploma mill when Lynch saw it.

The MG was up on blocks, its wheels gone, its ragtop slashed open like a rape victim's dress.

"Oh, shit," he sputtered as he saw the car, or what was left of it. Lois stopped in midsentence, held his hand tighter, and said "Wha—?" before she also saw the car.

Lynch ran quickly down the sidewalk and across the street.

"Dammit," he yelled. His coattails flew as he jumped up and stamped his foot down on the sidewalk. "Son of a bitch!"

Lois came up behind him. "Ohmigod," she said.

The steering wheel was gone, along with both seats, the radio, the carpet, the gearshift knob. The bonnet of the car was up, with an empty space where the battery used to be. Both headlights were gone. The boot of the car was open as well, and twisted on its hinges so that it would never close properly again. The spare tire, the jack, the tire tools, and a small tool box were missing.

A deep scratch, all the way down to bare metal, ran the length of the car.

"Jesus." Lois's voice was low, as if she were frightened. She held Jack's arm tightly.

She looked around. The doors of the buildings around them were all closed, the windows all shuttered. As she looked up, she noticed the heavy, moisture-laden air was settling down on them as fog through the dim yellow of the street lights.

"Jack, it's awfully quiet around here. You think it's safe?"

He looked around as well. Suddenly, he felt naked and vulnerable. Like most people, Lynch had grown attached to his car in an almost emotional way. Sometimes he felt like he lived out of it. Now here it was, stripped and ravaged, possibly beyond saving.

"We better get to a phone," he said. "Call the police."

Two hours later, Jack stood next to an NOPD blue-and-white with the crescent on the door and watched as a tow truck hauled the MG off to the garage. The reports had been filed. Lois had stayed there with him the whole time. The policeman had warned them not to hang around on the streets; it was getting late, and this *was* New Orleans, after all. Just as the cop pulled away, a cab braked to a stop next to them.

"C'mon," Lynch said, as he held the door for her. "I'll take you home."

Lois Finlayson's apartment was in the back of a house off South Claiborne Avenue, near where the streetcar line ended and the real traffic began. It was a well-lit street, with sidewalks that were in good repair and homes that showed signs of life. The cab pulled up in front.

"I'll see you soon," Lynch said, wanting to kiss her good night but afraid that the evening, like his car, might be beyond salvaging.

114

"You look like you could use a drink," Lois said. "C'mon in. It's not even midnight yet. I'll take you home later."

"That's an awful bother," he said. She took his hand.

"C'mon," she said, pulling his arm. "Pay the guy."

"You hoid the lady," the driver said from the front seat. "Pay da guy and go get yaself a drink."

He'd been telling them how he'd moved to New Orleans from Brooklyn because the cab driving was safer. The accents were so similar he felt right at home, but he'd been robbed twice in the last month.

Lynch paid up and climbed out of the cab. "C'mon," Lois said, taking his arm and walking up the narrow driveway. "The entrance to my apartment is in the back."

The two walked into a small, brick courtyard in back of the house. A wrought-iron staircase led up to the second story.

"Shhh, my landlady's asleep. She doesn't mind my having company. Just don't wake her up."

They climbed the stairs quietly, and opened the door into a small kitchen with windows all the way around the back wall. Lois turned the overhead on to reveal white porcelain and tile everywhere. Her dishes were washed and stacked neatly in the sink.

God, Lynch thought, I hope she never sees my place.

"Here," Lois said, pointing in front of her. "Go on in and sit down. Turn the stereo on if you want, but not too loud. I'll make us a couple of drinks. Gin and tonic okay?"

"Perfect," Lynch said. "Just the night for it."

Lynch had just settled on the couch when she appeared with two tall glasses. A slice of lime and a tiny sprig of fresh mint hung off the side of each glass.

"Here, hope you don't mind the mint. We grow it in the back yard."

"No, it's a nice touch," Lynch said, aware of his own nervousness. The front windows were open to the street, with a slight breeze blowing in. The orange halo of the streetlights radiated out in a wide arc in the humid night.

"Do you mind if I put on a pair of jeans?" she asked. "You can take off your tie if you want. We'll call it a trade."

Lynch smiled. "Sure, go ahead." He loosened his tie, then stretched to pull off his coat behind him.

Jack could hear her fumbling on the other side of the wall

115

behind his head. Then he heard the sound of a zipper being pulled down, and the gentle thud of feet hitting the floor after stepping out of a dress.

The sofa was off-white, a tasteful Haitian cotton, and the table in front of the sofa was teak, in a plain and simple Scandinavian style. A framed, apparently original movie poster from *The Maltese Falcon* hung on one wall, with a Monet print in the hallway. Lots of earth tones, shades of Santa Fe. Taken altogether, he guessed that here was a lady with taste, a lady who was usually in control, a lady who probably would know just what to do with a lot of money. If she had it, that is.

He heard the light in the bedroom click off and looked away just as she came back into the living room. She sat down next to him and reached for her glass.

"That's much better. I don't mind dressing up, but you can go too far with that sort of thing."

Lynch turned. She wore the same pair of tight, faded jeans he'd seen before and a man's white shirt, a button-down oxford cloth. He found himself wondering who it had belonged to. Maybe she bought it for herself.

"I'm really sorry about your car," she said.

"Me, too. But this is New Orleans, you know. I guess I should be glad it hasn't happened before now."

"Isn't it tough to keep a convertible from getting ripped off?"

"I never lock mine," he said. "That way the top never gets slashed."

"But it was slashed tonight."

Lynch smiled at her. "Car thief in a bad mood?"

She laughed back. "At least you haven't lost your sense of humor."

Lynch settled back on the couch. "I used to get crazy when stuff like that happened. I've mellowed out over the past couple of years. If getting my car trashed is the worst thing that happens to me today, I'll be fine."

"You are philosophical, aren't you?"

"I still take things too seriously sometimes."

"Like this business with Pearl Bergeron?" Lois asked, crossing her legs and running a thin finger around the wet top of her glass.

"Don't you think that's serious?"

"Of course it's serious, but it's also history," she said, leaning forward and placing her glass on a copy of *Vanity Fair* that was lying on the table.

"Jack, the truth is that Pearl is dead and we're alive, and nothing can change that. If you ask me whether I'm sorry she's dead, and you ask me to be truthful about it, I won't lie. I'm not at all sorry she's dead. She wasn't a very nice person. I won't miss her. On the other hand, I'm grateful to her. It was only her death that put me in the position of being able to spend the evening with a very nice man. One that I find very attractive."

Lynch smiled, again as nervous as a teenager. "I guess I kind of owe old Pearl one, too."

She smiled. "Can I ask you something, Jack?"

"Sure, Lois. Anything."

"Will you put down that drink and kiss me?"

Lynch's head swam. He stared at her for a second to make sure he'd understood what she'd said. He finally decided that he'd heard right.

He leaned forward and placed his glass on the magazine next to hers. He laid his right arm across the back of the sofa and turned to face her. She smiled and scooted over next to him.

"Why am I so nervous about this?" he asked.

"Me, too."

Her eyes were open wide, staring back at him through the deep brown of her irises. "Well?" she asked.

He leaned over and touched her lips with his. She held there softly, not pushing, not pulling away. Their lips remained touching for a few seconds, not opening further, but not closing completely. His eyes were half-closed, hers still wide open.

Finally, he felt it welling up inside him. He held it tightly locked down for as long as he could stand it, then he had to let go.

Lynch sputtered at first, then let loose with as deep a belly laugh as he'd felt in a long time.

Lois sat there, lips still pursed as he pulled away.

"I'm sorry," he choked, still laughing. "I couldn't help it."

She smiled as well, then giggled brightly, her cheeks twisting upward in a huge smile, the light bouncing off her eyes.

"Oh, hell," she laughed. "We're a pair, aren't we?"

Lynch was practically doubled up by now. His eyes watered, and he pulled his right arm off the couch to brush his cheeks.

"Let's try not to get too carried away with this passion stuff, okay?"

She reached across the table and picked up her glass. "What? Did the sexual revolution leave us by the wayside or what?"

"I don't know," he said, his breath coming normally now, the fit of laughter nearly passed. "I haven't laughed like that in a long time, though. Thank you."

"That's the first time I've ever seen you laugh like that. You're welcome," she said. "I think you're a very sweet man, Jack Lynch. Maybe a bit too controlled, though."

"And I think you're a very sweet lady, Lois Finlayson." He paused for a moment. "Maybe I am too tight. I've always been like that. It has its good points, though. I always fill the ice trays when I take the last cube, and I always put the seat down on the toilet."

"A rare man indeed."

"I think I'm just a little scared of you," he said.

"Why should you be scared of me?" she asked seriously. "I won't hurt you."

He pulled his tie a little looser. "Famous last words."

"C'mon, really," she said. "Why would you be afraid of me?"

Jack looked at her. "Because."

"Because why?"

He took a deep breath and let it out slowly. "Because I haven't been this attracted to anyone in a long time, and this is happening very fast. Too fast . . ."

"And you feel guilty about it, don't you?"

"What do you mean?" he asked after a moment.

"Because your fiancée was murdered what, a year ago? You're not supposed to ever be touched again or feel anything again or ever be happy again. Right?"

"I didn't know you knew about that," he said.

"I read the paper," she said. "I talk to people."

"The paper never reported that Sally was my fiancée."

"But they reported what happened when you found out she was dead. There was an interview with the doctor. A man doesn't go off the deep end like that because a casual acquaintance was killed.

"I took a guess, and I was right. Wasn't I?" she asked.

Lynch stared at her. "What do I do with all this stuff?" He felt himself choking inside, the pressure inside his head growing, his eyes filling. "I don't know where to put it all. This shit feels like it's never going to go away."

She reached out and took his hand. "It's never going to go away until you put it behind you and go on with your life."

"How do I do that?" he asked. Despite himself, a trickle ran down the side of his face. "I don't know how, dammit."

"You open yourself up to the possibilities," Lois said. "By letting yourself feel again, the good stuff and the bad, until it all gets used up. Some of it won't ever go away. You'll always have this little lump inside you. But the worst of it will. We've all suffered, Jack. Some of us not as much as you. Some of us more."

Her hair hung down long over her shoulders. She looked younger than her age in the faded denims and the man's white shirt with the tail out. She was thin and slight, and Lynch found himself aching for her despite his every effort not to. Slowly, he reached over and touched her shoulder, feeling her beneath the shirt. She was warm, her skin moist in the hot night. In the dim light of a lamp next to the couch, she seemed to glow.

He drew her to him, sliding over on the sofa to meet her. He kissed her, with a passion and intensity he hadn't felt since Sally's death.

He buried his face in her hair, nuzzling her, the toasty smell of her hair a warm, almost pungent aroma in his nostrils. He felt his own responses, the sensations of another person's closeness to him strange and foreign. He felt silly, as if he'd been scripted into a bad soap opera. Man loses fiancée, then feels guilty a year later when he winds up wrapped around somebody else.

Hell, he thought, she's gone. Forever. And I'm still here. And this world is a bitch to go through alone. If Sally were there somewhere watching him, he hoped she'd understand.

He had always figured he'd never feel anything for anybody again. That was then, this is now. Who said that? he asked himself as he saw Lois's eyes drift downward in front of him. He pulled her closer. God, she felt good. Yogi Berra? No, he was the one that said the opera's not over 'til the fat lady sings. The soap opera, that is.

Lois pulled him close as well, then moaned as he kissed her and his hands ran up and down her back. He brought his face down into the crook of her neck and found himself raking his teeth across her skin. Her head went back, her back arched, she pulled herself up onto his lap and ran her fingers into his hair. He raised his face up to her. She leaned down and planted a kiss on his open mouth, her mouth open as well. Her legs wrapped around him as his arms pulled her closer.

That was then, this is now . . . Nixon? he thought. Nineteen sixty-eight?

She pulled his head to one side and burrowed into the nape of his neck, kissing and biting him at the same time. Jolts shot through him and, for the first time in long memory, Jack Lynch finally stopped thinking.

Maud Pelletier looked behind her when she heard the doorknob turn. She smiled as Lynch walked in, his jacket and shirt looking as if he'd slept in them.

"I wondered if you was coming in today."

"Oh, yeah, Maud. I was just kind of tired. Slept in."

"Yeah, but obviously not at your own house," she said, offering him a cup of coffee. "I been calling you there for the last hour."

Lynch grinned. "Yeah? How'd you know I didn't just have the phone unplugged?"

"Because I left four messages on your answering machine." Maud walked over to the desk and sat down. She picked up one of the three letters that had come in the morning mail and slit it open. "I haven't had much to do here this morning except answer phone calls from the police and your insurance agent."

"My car," Lynch said, pulling off his jacket and looping the collar around the top hook on a coat rack. "Got trashed last night in the Quarter. I don't even know if it's worth saving."

"Aw, babe, I'm sorry to hear that."

"Yeah, me too. Pissed me off something fierce." He lit a cigarette and picked up the Styrofoam cup of steaming coffee. "If the insurance company doesn't total the car, then I get a rental until the MG's fixed. If they decide it's totaled, then I get a check today and have to go hassle with buying new wheels."

"That must be what the cops called about, then," she said, holding out a pink message slip. "A Lieutenant Frontiere . . ."

Lynch took the slip of paper and looked at it. "You sure?"

"What? I can't handle a phone message now? Is that it?"

"Chill out, Maud. It's just that Lieutenant Frontiere is NOPD Homicide. Why would he be calling me about the car?"

Maud picked up a heavily powdered beignet from a paper plate to her left and bit into it. "You could call him and find out," she suggested, her voice muffled by the cake doughnut. Little flecks of powdered sugar floated down.

Lynch peered at her, confused. "What the hell's going on?"

The afternoon sun was at its peak as Lynch peeled off a ten-dollar bill and handed it to the cab driver.

"Want me to stick around?"

Lynch looked down at the woman taxi driver. She was easily fifty, had chained smoked the whole way out River Road, and told him her entire life story, including the tale of her recently deceased husband of thirty-five years, who had been the finest man she ever met, complete with a AAAAA+ credit rating. She had a son who'd been to Vietnam and now drank too much and couldn't hold down a job, and that would be breaking her heart except for her daughter, who did everything to help her and worried about her driving a cab, which she just did to make extra money, not that she really needed it, you understand. She prayed every day that her son would come around, but she didn't think it was doing any good.

"No, thanks," Lynch said. He just couldn't take any more.

The cab pulled out of the gravel parking lot, spraying gray dust that hung in the still, heavy air like a pall. Lynch turned around and walked toward the open garage that was the Jefferson Parish MG dealer's body shop. A large white Ford sedan sat out front, one that practically had UNMARKED COP CAR painted on it in broad letters. Lynch thought maybe his next car would be a white, unadorned, behemoth LTD or something like that, so the traffic flow would slow down every time he entered it.

As he approached the garage, he heard the jerking whine of air-powered tools and the clanging of hammers. The place was fat with the smell of paint and chemicals. Over to one side, a well-dressed man had his back to the open door.

"Lieutenant Frontiere?" Lynch asked, then louder. "Lieutenant?"

The man turned. Lynch was continually amazed at how dapper and young the man looked. He was well-groomed, well-dressed, well-carried. Lynch suppressed the urge to slap him.

"Mr. Lynch," Lieutenant Frontiere said, his heavy accent even harsher in the loud voice he had to use to get over the roar of power tools. "Thanks for coming by."

"How'd you get involved in this?" Lynch shouted. "Since when does Homicide cover car stripping?"

"Since this morning," Frontiere said, turning and motioning for Lynch to follow. "Since the investigators went through your car."

Still confused, Lynch followed the policeman through a door into an institutional linoleum hallway leading past a customer lounge. He struggled to keep up as Frontiere walked rapid-fire toward a door at the end of the hallway.

"Loud as hell back there, ain't it?" Frontiere asked, looking back.

The two came to the door, pushed it open, and walked back out into the hot sun and a large lot full of trashed automobiles. Lynch guessed this was where the dead ones came to lie in state before they could be hauled off to the junkyards and the compactors. They stepped over rusted auto parts, between the abandoned, damaged hulks of the cars until they came to Lynch's naked, ravaged MG at the end of a long line. Lynch winced again, seeing it.

"The officers came out this morning to take a look at your car, Mr. Lynch," Frontiere said, taking out a notebook and pen, scribbling something in it, then replacing it in his pocket. "And while they were examining it, they found this."

Frontiere was pointing down inside the car to a space under the dashboard just in front of the gearshift lever and the transmission hump. A tan shoebox with the lid still on was wedged in the small space.

"Did you see that last night?" Frontiere asked.

"No, it was dark. I didn't pay any attention. I mean, the car was so trashed and all."

"Well, hold on to your cookies, Mr. Lynch," Frontiere said, bending over from the waist to pull the box out of the car. He held it gingerly, with both hands, and placed it on the hot metal of the hood. Lynch stepped closer as Frontiere pulled the lid off the box.

"Oh, Jesus," Lynch yelped. Inside the box was a dead wharf rat fully a foot long. It was about the dimensions of a good-size cat, with a hunk of thick wire twisted around its neck. The creature's paws were curled up under it as it lay on its side in death. A small trickle of blood ran out of its nose just under its bulging, still-open eyes.

Lynch turned away in disgust and nausea. "You know anything about this," Frontiere asked.

"Oh sure," Lynch snapped, "I always carry dead fucking sewer rats around in my car. It was a gift for my date and I didn't get the chance to give it to her!"

Frontiere reached inside his pocket and took out a plastic envelope. Inside was a slip of paper. "The animal was strangled. Probably the wire was looped on the end of a stick or something. And they left this tied around its neck.

"Hold the note by the corner," Frontiere instructed. "We're still going to try and dust it."

"Stop asking questions about Pearl Bergeron," the typewritten note said, "or you'll wind up like Mickey here."

"Somebody went to a lot of trouble to scare you," Frontiere said.

Lynch looked from the note back to Frontiere.

"It worked."

17

ROWAN WILSON'S DREAM OF HAVING HIS OWN INDEPENDENT FILM STU-
dio in New Orleans was badly stalled. It had been over two years
since he'd announced at a press conference his intention of purchasing the Riverbend facility. The accompanying press, he had hoped,
would help him draw in the last few investors he would need to get
the deal underway.

Even if he never bought the place, he would have been happy
to put together enough seed money to put a project into development, that never-never land for movie ideas that allowed men like
himself to make a damn good living without ever having to do any
real work or produce any real films. Get a few films into the black
hole of development, and a guy could live pretty well indefinitely.
The costs could legitimately eat up hundreds of thousands of investors' money, with no return expected, intended, or required. Eventually, he might actually have to begin filming something.

But even then, there were ways to get around that.

The problem was that except for a few old people who sank just
short of seventy-five grand into the studio, the investors dried up
after Kwang moved in. Rowan Wilson was, for all intents and
purposes, flat broke. He'd been living off credit cards, dodging bill
collectors, and sponging off girlfriends for nearly a year. He'd given
an engineering firm a fifteen-thousand-dollar retainer fee to do a site
inspection of the facility, but he never really intended for the bastards to go ahead with it. Now they were suing him for nearly a
hundred grand.

And now Pearl Bergeron was dead.

Not that Pearl Bergeron was all that great an ally. A reporter from the *Times-Picayune* had interviewed her last winter about the prospects for Wilson Films International, Ltd., and she said something snotty like, "While I have no personal knowledge of Mr. Wilson's credentials or project, we wish him the best of luck."

Well, have personal knowledge of this, bitch! Wilson had thought that day with a raised finger in the air. He'd been trying to get in to see her for weeks; she refused to meet with him. Even after he was interviewed by the local CBS affiliate and profiled in the local business newspaper—that had a circulation of what, maybe three thousand?—she wouldn't see him.

Yeah, the bitch had it coming, he thought as he read the article about her funeral. I'm not going to feel bad about it. She had it coming.

But what to do next? He flipped through his battered Rolodex to find the number of that fat guy who was news director at the television station—the one who looked like Pavarotti with a painful case of hemorrhoids.

"There you are," he said aloud, dialing the number. There was a pause as the phone rang on the other end, followed by the nasal voice of a switchboard operator. "John Griffin, please. Yeah, Rowan Wilson calling."

Wilson leaned back in his chair and looked out the glass front panel of his office. He'd rented a cubicle in an office condo, the kind with eight or ten guys in one-room offices sharing a common secretary. As long as the secretary remembered to answer his line with the right company name, it worked out fine. Once, one of his investors called for Wilson International Films, Ltd., and the secretary had answered, "Waste Recyclers, Inc.," the name the guy down the hall who ran a two-truck garbage pickup operation had chosen for his company. Wilson had a tough time explaining that one.

She was cute, though. A well-built redhead with long fingernails. Yeah, his favorite kind.

"Hello," a gruff voice on the other side of the phone said.

"John, hello buddy!" Wilson was feeling very jovial.

"Hello, Rowan. What can I do for you?"

"Hope I didn't catch you at a bad time, buddy. Just wanted to catch the latest on the Pearl Bergeron murder."

The voice harrumphed loudly, the sound of either exasperation or bad sinuses. Rowan Wilson chose not to notice.

"It's a bad time, Rowan. We're twenty minutes short of deadline here."

"I'll make it quick, Griff. Just tell me the latest."

"Not much. We hear the governor's been all over NOPD Homicide. Understandably so."

"Any indication who he'll appoint to head the film commission?"

"Nothing right now."

"Well, Griff," Wilson began, "in view of the mysterious circumstances of Pearl Bergeron's death and its obvious connection to Andrew Kwang, I think it's time for me to start a push again to beat him out of the Riverbend facility."

"I thought you were out of that one for good, Rowan."

"I was, until I saw how Pearl Bergeron was trying to protect the morals of the citizens of Louisiana, and what it cost her. I think we owe it to her memory not to let this guy come in here."

"The question is can you stop him?"

"I think we can. I'm in what I believe to be final negotiations with some very heavy hitters. We're also about to sign a major Hollywood star to our first project. This is going to give us the guns to make our final push."

The news director hesitated. "C'mon, Rowan. We've heard this kind of thing before."

"All right, Griff, I'll admit my last deal kind of fell apart at the end. I thought I was dealing with somebody who had stones. The guy wimped out on me at the last minute. But this time, it's solid. You can take it to the bank."

"Okay, Rowan. Who is it?"

"Deep background, buddy?"

"Yeah, Row. Deep background. Who's the heavy hitter and who's the big Hollywood star?"

"Deep background. Off the record. I just returned last week from Paris, where I was in final negotiations with the Aristotle Onassis Trust. They're serious, Griff. They don't want the publicity of negotiating with a major. They're too low profile. They buy into an independent, though, they've got an automatic foot in the door. All the Europeans want to get into American movies, man. It's the best investment in the world. The only place a movie ever loses money is on the books. I can't give you all the details, but we're very close on this one."

"So I've heard. All right, I'll buy it for now. Who's the star?"

"Seriously, Griff? You want to know."

"Don't prick-tease me, Rowan. Who the hell is it?"

"It's Cruise, man. Tom."

"Get out of here."

"No, man, shit, listen. Two years ago, I bought the movie rights to this obscure historical romance called *Love's Lonely Laughter*. What the hey, call me sentimental. The book went nowhere and the author needed the bucks. I felt sorry for him. I picked it up for bupkiss, and whaddaya know? Turns out it's Tom's favorite book. Six months, maybe nine ago his agent calls me, says Tom's wanted to play the drunken artist ever since he read it. We been in negotiations. He's doing it for scale, man!

"Of course," Wilson added, "he's taking points."

"Net or gross?" Griffin asked, laughing.

"Gross, of course. Tom didn't just fall off the turnip truck."

The fat news director was laughing steadily now. "God, I hope you're not bullshitting me. You got to promise to introduce me to him if he ever comes to town."

"We're due to start location shooting in October. I'll get you a set pass."

"Great."

"Besides, we owe it to the memory of Pearl Bergeron. Why don't you send around a reporter? I'll give you a good interview. Make you look good."

"Where?" Griffin asked. "Your office?"

"Sure," Wilson said. It would be easy enough to manipulate the jerk once he got there.

"Okay. Around three?"

"I'll be here."

"So long, Cecil B. DeMille," Griffin said, hanging up.

Rowan Wilson hung up the phone and smiled. It was an easy game when you knew how to play it.

"So long, you fat suckhead," he muttered.

In her apartment Lois Finlayson pulled back the sheer curtains on the windows facing the street. She'd been in most of the day. She'd made a few phone calls here and there, but found herself feeling terribly unmotivated to do anything. She was waiting to hear

127

from Miller Taylor, to find out what Kwang was going to do about those test shots of the Riverbend facility.

She needed the job badly. She'd put an ad in one of the trade papers to sell off her equipment, but she was holding on to what really valuable stuff she had left. There had been a few phone calls for the lights and the filters, but no follow-up.

Ten years in the business, and she wasn't any better off now than she was when she started. Cinematography had always been a tough field for women to break into, but the advances for women in other professions, other industries, seemed to have passed the technical end of the movie business by. Women could work wardrobe, makeup, script girl, assistant, all the traditional roles. But if you were a woman and you wanted to be a grip or an electrician or a sound man, it was about as difficult to find those jobs as it was back when Jack Warner thought women were either actresses, housewives, or whores. For a woman who wanted to stand behind the camera, it seemed to Lois Finlayson, you had to add one other requisite to all the usual ones: lunatic.

The jobs just weren't there. They were hard enough for men to get.

It was all she'd ever wanted to be, to do. Other little girls would try on Mommy's makeup and dance around in front of the mirror, little Marilyn Monroes, little Elizabeth Taylors. While the other little girls were playing dress-up, Lois was washing dishes to earn enough quarters to buy a roll of film for her daddy's Super 8 home movie camera.

Her frustration had grown proportionately over the years. She wanted this so bad she'd sacrificed relationships, money, jobs, even a chance at marriage with an OB/GYN from Shreveport who wasn't such a bad guy, at least not for a doctor. Now she was in her early thirties, not old by anyone's standards except her own and those who didn't know any better, and all she'd had to show for it was a resume full of hit-or-miss projects, a few industrial films, and a bad case of burnout. Then, of course, there were the films with Darlane.

She could have stayed with Darlane Robinson out in L.A. Darlane had told her she could work for her any time she wanted. Her work was good; she was dependable. The money was terrible, but even the actors didn't pick up much in that line of work. It was the kind of work you had to do for love, so to speak.

Occasionally, she'd go to the local video store during the day, when there were few customers, and go into the separate, closed-off room where the adult films were kept just to see what Darlane had been up to lately. Darlane Robinson's *Exquisite Love* films were part of a new trend in X-rated movies: dirty movies made from a woman's point of view. No denigration of women, no rape, no violence, no humiliating shots of men squirting all over their partners. These were different—romantic fantasies where the people actually took off their clothes and *made love*. Darlane used to tell the crew she didn't make films of people fucking. She made movies of people loving.

Lois snickered as she thought of Darlane, who was notorious among the crew for being completely asexual. Nobody ever saw her with a man; nobody ever saw her with a woman. She went home alone each night. Lois always attributed it to the Golden Arches Theorem: If you worked behind the counter all day asking, "You want fries with that?", you sure as hell didn't want hamburgers when you got home.

"I'm bored," she said aloud, plopping on the couch. She wished Jack would call. They'd had a wonderful night together. She'd seen him off that morning with the promise to call later in the day. So far, no call. Maybe she'd misread him.

But she doubted it.

She pulled a strand of long, brown hair from behind her shoulder and nervously wrapped it around her finger. There was the sound of a car passing by outside. Lois ignored it until she recognized the sound of it pulling to a stop.

A car door opened, then slammed back shut. She jumped off the couch and was at the window in two steps. She smiled down just as Jack Lynch looked up. He was in a black sedan, probably a rental from his insurance company.

He was coming up the back stairs by the time she could get to the kitchen door. She opened it smiling, then stopped when she saw his face.

"What's wrong?" she asked. He was ashen, gray, tired. Dark circles had formed under his eyes. They hadn't gotten much sleep the night before, and she had gone back to sleep after he left, but Lois didn't remember him looking that bad.

"Rough day," he said. Lynch took her in his arms and gave her a hug, then pushed her back just far enough to get to her lips. His

129

breath smelled of coffee and stale cigarettes. Lois made a mental note to buy him a toothbrush to keep at her place.

He pulled away. "You look great. I'm glad to see you."

"For God's sake, c'mon in. What's happened?"

He walked by her, through the kitchen, and directly into the living room. He pulled off his jacket and tossed it aside, then turned to her, sweating, and loosened his tie.

"My car getting trashed was not random crime," he said.

"What do you mean?"

"The cops called me this morning. Not the car stripping detail but Homicide."

"Homicide?" Lois asked, shocked. Her hand involuntarily went to her mouth.

"There was a note in the car, warning me to stop asking questions about the Pearl Bergeron murder."

"My God, what kind of note?" She walked past him, over to the chair opposite the couch and sat down.

"The note said that if I didn't stop poking around, I was going to wind up like the—"

"Like the what?"

"Lois, the note was in a shoebox, crammed in there with a dead, strangled bloody rat about as long as my forearm."

She gasped, both hands covering her face, all but her eyes. "Jesus—"

"Yeah, right," Lynch said, sitting down on the couch.

"But what were you doing? I mean, what kinds of questions have you been asking?"

"I didn't *think* I'd been poking around that much," he said. "Obviously, I stumbled onto something and don't even know what it was. But it got somebody's attention, and they decided to do something to scare the hell out of me."

"It worked."

Lynch laughed. "Funny, that was my reaction, too."

18

"I NEED A DRINK," LYNCH SAID.

Lois looked past him, to the wall in the kitchen. The clock read ten after five. She stood and walked toward the door. "Me too," she said.

"Let me see," she said, opening a cabinet door. "I picked you up some Scotch."

"Anything," Lynch said behind her. "Whatever. Make it light."

She mixed the drinks and handed him a tall glass, the ice inside clinking, the glass sweating. "So what are you going to do?"

Lynch stared down at the drink. "Hell if I know."

He turned and walked back into the living room, settling down on the couch like a man twice his age. He looked up at her as she walked past the coffee table, glass of red wine in hand.

"All I'm trying to do is make a lousy living. Next thing you know, some bastard trashes my car and leaves me dead rats as a calling card."

Lois looked out the window, to the black Ford outside. "Where'd you get the car?"

"Insurance got me a rental. My agent says he thinks they'll declare the MG totaled. It'll take a couple of days to get the check cut."

He got up from the couch and walked over to stand behind her, looking out the window. He put a hand on each of her shoulders, massaging the knots of muscle that had gathered just above her collarbone.

"Is that good or bad?" she asked.

"It would be great if I had the money to pay for a new car," he answered. "I don't. I'll have to take blue book on the MG and try to find something used. Pain in the neck."

He leaned down and nestled his face in the crook of her neck, breathing the smell of her hair deeply. "You feel awfully good."

Lois cocked her head a little, pressing into him. She was silent for a moment. "Tell me about her," she said finally.

Lynch was quiet for a long moment as well. Then he stood up straight and wrapped his arms around her shoulders, his head propped against the nape of her neck. "I feel like a widower sometimes," he said.

"In a way, you are."

Lynch turned and walked over to the coffee table, picked up his drink. "She was funny," he said. "Wicked sense of humor. Real dry, almost sardonic at times. There was a hard edge to her. She'd had her share of bad times, I think. With men . . ."

"Did Sally have any children?"

"No," Lynch answered. "We talked about it a few times. Real vaguely. You see, we'd both been married before, and it ended badly for both of us. I didn't even date for a long time. You know, the usual stuff when you're divorced. You figure, 'Hot damn, hooray, I'm out of that shit,' and you hit the singles bars and party and get laid as much as you can as fast as you can to prove to yourself you're still able to find somebody, anybody. Hell, it almost doesn't matter at first."

"Then it starts to," Lois said.

Lynch sat on the couch. He looked tired, distracted. "Yeah. Real quick. And you realize there isn't any way you're going to reconnect with anybody, not *really* connect, anyway. And I just kind of faded away for a long time. I worked every day, most days, anyway. I had a lot of freedom to come and go as I pleased back when I worked at the bank."

"And you guys worked together, right?"

Jack held his drink in his hand for a moment, then took a long slug of it before speaking. "It's funny, I saw her every day for years. We picked at each other, zinged each other all the time, like an old married couple. Only we weren't going home together at night. Then one day, it's like I'd never seen her before. And she was all new."

"That's what happens when you fall in love."

He looked up at her, then smiled in a way she couldn't quite understand. "Yeah, that's what happens. I felt alive again. Suddenly, it's like I could get up in the morning. And my gut would knot up whenever I got around her. And then we became lovers and things got real serious real fast."

Lois grinned. "That's hard to handle for you, isn't it?"

"I've always been a little slow on the uptake," he said. "Takes me a while to catch on. But after a while, I did. In spades. I got real crazy about her, and the deeper into it I got at the bank, the more I wanted out. The more I wanted to get away from all that craziness and just go somewhere with Sally."

"Which is what we were getting ready to do the night she was killed," he added after a few long seconds.

"How did it happen?" Lois asked, then sighed and looked away as if she'd just caught herself saying something she really hadn't meant to. "Listen, you don't have to answer that if you don't want—"

"It's okay," Lynch interrupted. "Really. You mind if I smoke?" He reached into his shirt pocket and pulled out the pack.

"I wish you didn't," she answered. "But since you do, I guess it's all right."

"I'm going to give these goddamn things up one of these days," he said, almost meanly.

"Right."

Jack lit the cigarette and inhaled deeply, then took a sip of the drink. "It was late at night," he began. "We were going to sneak by the office and pick up a package, then deliver it to a friend of mine in the district attorney's office. Somebody we could trust. Then we were going to get out of town fast. We were leaving New Orleans for good."

Lois pushed open the casement window a crack, then cranked the handle to open it all the way. Dusk was in full bloom now, and off beyond the rooftops of the houses across the street she could see the deep-blue and orange splash of a glorious, sulfurous New Orleans sunset. It had been one of the reasons she took the apartment. She'd first looked at the apartment late one day, with the incredible explosion of colors through the living room window, and it had set the camera in her soul on fire.

"Only there were a couple of goons following us," Lynch continued, the smoke from his cigarette drawn toward the now open window. "Real tough guys. They grabbed us when we got out of the car and started beating the ever-loving dog shit out of me. They were

133

just holding Sally quiet, but she started fighting them. She didn't take crap off anybody. And it got her killed."

"One of life's lessons," Lynch said, smiling bitterly. "You want to stay alive, you learn to take the crap."

"My God," Lois whispered.

"When I came to in the hospital and found out she was dead, I went completely bananas. I don't even remember most of it. But something in me's never been the same again. I mean, I wasn't exactly all that tightly wrapped before. After that, though, after they buried her . . ."

"How long ago was that?" she asked.

"A year or so, maybe longer. Since then, I just feel like I'm walking through sludge all the time. Going through the motions, as if . . . Oh, hell, I don't know."

"As if you're carrying all this weight around, and it never lets up," Lois said. "It stays with you constantly. You can't get away from it. You can't deny it. You can't accept it. Suddenly, the rules don't count anymore. Nothing works like it's supposed to."

"You sound like you've been there," Jack said.

"I've had my share of disappointments in life. Most people spend their entire lives trying to figure out what they want to be when they grow up." She walked around the table and sat down on the couch next to Jack. "Since I was a girl, I've known what I wanted to do, what I wanted to be. I just wasn't blessed with the skills necessary to circumvent a shitty system designed to keep me from doing it."

"It sounds to me like you've done okay," Lynch said.

"I've managed to keep myself working, most of the time, but that's about all. I once dreamed of doing something great one day. Now I'd be content to make a halfway decent living. I'd like to live a normal life. Have a real love life, a future. Maybe even a family. I've made mistakes. Bad ones. They'll probably keep me from ever having the things I want."

"What mistakes?" Lynch asked. "You mean the adult movies?"

"You knew about that?" she asked, her jaw dropping just a bit.

"Rowan Wilson made some crack about it. That day at Chez Ray's. The day I met you. I didn't listen to him much. He's a sleazeball."

"Damn straight. And a pathological liar at that. The only way

134

I'd ever work for him is if he paid me in cash. I wouldn't even trust him with a cashier's check. He's too slick."

Jack leaned to his left and threw his left arm around the back of the couch. "So how did you get involved with . . . that?"

She looked at him, hard. "You mean fuck films?"

"Whatever you want to call it?"

She sighed and leaned back, staring off at the filtered dusk colors blending into a puddle of light on the ceiling.

"I went out to L.A. after I got out of college. I went to Sophie Newcomb on an art scholarship. I didn't have much money. But I went out there all bright and eager and ready to make it. What I wound up doing was living out of my car, working temp. Getting lots of offers for lackey work, plenty of which I took, and fighting off jerks who kept thinking the casting couch applied to tech people as well as actors."

She shifted a little on the couch and settled in toward him. "Who knows? Maybe that would have helped. As you well know, I'm no virgin—"

Lynch tried, without much success, to suppress a laugh.

"—but I also wasn't interested in sleeping with every guy who came along and said he could get me a job. I was out there six years, I guess, and had done well enough after all that time to actually get an apartment with a roommate in one of the dirtier sections of town. Then I met Darlane."

"Darlane?"

"Darlane Robinson. You ever heard of her?"

"No, can't say as I have."

Lois smiled. "You're obviously not an aficionado of erotica." She let the "aficionado" and "erotica" roll off her tongue with an exaggerated lilt.

"Well, I've seen my share. But I haven't made an academic study of them."

She reached over and took his hand. Her gentle squeeze felt good to Lynch, in both a comforting and an arousing way. He felt himself stirring, as if some mysterious reservoir of hormones within him had refilled after being emptied rather abruptly.

"Sometime we'll have to take a look." Her voice had a teasing quality to it. "Not that you seem to need any prompting. Anyway, Darlane Robinson is a maverick producer/director, even in the

135

world of adult films. She makes a line of movies aimed at women. *Exquisite Love,* they're called.

"They're really very sweet," she continued. "The characters in the films are always in a relationship. Most are married. There's no violence, no perverted stuff. No rape, no cum shots."

"What?"

"You know, where the guy pulls out of the woman to have his orgasm and then makes a big mess all over her. For some reason or other, traditional sleaze films always show that."

"Guess to prove that they're watching the real thing. No simulations."

"Either that, or all men are closet homosexuals and only in love with their own pricks."

"You think that's it?" Lynch asked, grinning.

"Sure, why not? So I went to work for Darlane Robinson. I answered an ad—she was looking for a woman shooter. I figured anybody that specifically wants a woman cameraperson must be okay. Turned out the whole crew were women."

"You're kidding? A bunch of women making fuck films. What a hoot."

"Only in L.A.," Lois agreed. "The only guys on the set were the actors, and they were all carefully screened. None of the traditional stars of adult films. What we were mostly looking for was reasonably good-looking, ordinary people."

"So what was that like?" he asked. "Being on the set of an adult film?"

The edges of her lips curled upward. "My, my. Curious, aren't we?"

"Can't help it. I'm secretly a sex maniac."

"Right. That's why you went a year without a date."

"I went a year without getting involved with anybody. That doesn't mean I didn't have a date."

She looked at him funny. "I don't think I want you to elaborate on that."

"Okay. But what was it like? On the set, I mean."

"Oh, at first you're nervous as hell. There's something about seeing naked people just walking around so matter-of-factly, then seeing them do stuff in a room full of people that most of us are too shy to do alone, that strikes you as, well, so—"

"Naughty?"

"Yeah," she giggled. "That's it. Naughty. In a childlike, voyeuristic kind of way. Like catching your parents making love or something. It's weird. And I hate to admit it, but there's something about it that's kind of, well, arousing."

"It's designed to be that way, isn't it?"

"Yeah, but you think, well, I'm educated and I have good taste and I'm just plain better than that. That kind of cheap physical stuff isn't going to work on me."

"Then it does."

"Damn right," she snickered. "I wasn't even seeing anybody at the time, so it was kind of rough the first few days. I mean these people who are in these things are young and beautiful and very, very skilled. But then the strangest thing happens."

"What?"

"After about the first three days, you don't even notice. You're totally insulated from it."

"Just a job?"

"And not a very well-paying one at that."

"I'm surprised."

"You remember me telling you that the first thing you learn in the film business is that everybody's a liar?"

"Yeah."

"Well the thing they lie most about is the numbers."

"So a lot of money comes out of those kinds of films—"

"And disappears down the black hole. Nobody but the very top guys see any of it. Even the actors get paid badly. The top-notch porno stars will get a couple of grand a day. Beginners are lucky to get a few hundred."

Jack grinned broadly. "So you really got to love your work?"

"It's a dirty job, but somebody's got to do it."

Jack brought his arm down around her shoulder and pulled her in toward him. He was hugging her outright now, warmly, feeling her breathe next to him. "So what made you get out?"

"Several things. First, you run into a lot of not very nice people in the adult film business. Guys who always have some bruiser next to them with a bulge under his left armpit. They figure they can have their way with anybody they want. After all, they're the money guys behind the picture. The actors usually get hit on first, but occasionally one would decide he wanted to take me home. And I wasn't going."

"Good for you."

"Also lots of drugs. I hate cocaine. I've seen what it does to too many people. It makes them crazy. The lifestyle in general got to me. But also, the thing that finally got it for me was how detached I began to feel about it all."

Lynch moved his face into the loose net of her hair, the ends brushing gently against his cheeks, dragging across his senses. He had the urge to close his eyes and drift, to leave conscious thought behind.

"The worst part of all, for me, was this sense that I was somehow becoming detached from my self, my body," she said. "That the physical act of love had become so mechanical that on the few occasions when I'd allow myself to be touched, it was as if I couldn't *feel* it anymore. That was when I knew I had to get out."

She turned and looked at him. Her face was blank for a second, as if she were trying to figure out the look on his face, his half-closed eyes, the dreamy expression.

"You're either incredibly relaxed," Lois said, "or you've got the worst case of bedroom eyes I've ever seen."

Lynch smiled at her, a smile that was, thankfully, returned. "I just haven't allowed myself the luxury of feeling this good in a long time."

She settled into the crook of his arm and let her head fall back. He shifted slightly, was above her now, then slowly lowered his lips to hers. He held himself there, barely touching her, hardly moving, then let the weight of his head down slowly, the pressure on her lips increasing. She took in a deep breath through her nose, let it out softly as her mouth opened just enough to take him in.

He tightened his arms around her; she brought her arm up and pulled him close to her, tilted a bit now, almost on top of her. She was holding him, opening up to him, wanting him. Lynch found himself wanting her more and more as well, as if the months and years of being locked down and controlled were finally giving way. He thought briefly of Sally, then pushed her from the front of his mind. She was still there, would be there always. But he was, little by little, becoming determined to get on with his life.

He brought up his right hand and touched a breast, his hand unfolding like a blossoming flower to take it in. She moaned, shifted a bit, the pressure inside her building. He felt the thick cloth beneath her blouse, the strap, the heat rising from her. He raised his lips from her, and her eyes gradually, sleepily opened halfway.

"Are you feeling detached now?" he asked.

She laughed softly. "Oh, no. I'm very much in touch with my body right now. And yours . . ."

Lois reached up and unbuttoned the top two buttons of his shirt, then pulled his tie further down and kissed the light down that covered his chest. He held on to her, his hand drifting about, feeling how slowly they were going in contrast to their first nervous, almost hurried love. It had been an axiom in Lynch's life that the first time was always the roughest. Unlike many men, he had never had much desire, or much skill, for acquiring quick, casual partners. He had discovered early in life that without some element of feeling for the person he was with, sex held about as much pleasure, and significance, as any other bodily function.

His hand pressed on her stomach now, an abdomen that was flat and hard and unmarked by excess or childbirth or age. She was thin and tight, her hips barely the width of her shoulders, her breasts small. Lynch took in the smell of her hair and the sweet, almost musky odor of a human body in a state of late-afternoon arousal. He felt his heart beat faster, his breath come quicker.

Her movements became more hurried as well. She pulled his shirt tail out of his waist and ran her left hand across his stomach, a belly that was becoming increasingly flabby as age and the years of excess began to catch up with him. Self-consciously, he sucked in his gut and hardened his abdominal muscles, as if she cared at that point, and if she did, as if his exertions would keep her from noticing that his body was not what it had once been.

Her right hand was behind him, rubbing the small of his back. Her left hand ran up his chest slowly, to trace a circle around his nipple. She exhaled a long breath. "God, you feel good."

He leaned into her neck and opened his mouth, getting a fold of skin between his teeth and gently nibbling, then gnawing on her. The jolts shot through her with each movement of his jaw. She inhaled sharply and twitched, the shock throughout her body delightfully unexpected.

"I want you," she whispered.

Jack noticed that he had become uncomfortably hard, the pressure inside causing a burning sensation deep within.

139

"I want you, too," he whispered into her ear, then taking the lobe gently between his front teeth, he rolled it back and forth.

"What are you doing?" she asked, with a barely implicit request to keep doing it.

"Just playing," he said.

She turned and smiled at him. "You're learning."

19

LYNCH WALKED OUT OF HIS OFFICE BUILDING INTO THE WHITE-HOT SUN of a summer afternoon. He instantly broke a sweat, pulled off his jacket and threw it over his shoulder like a sack. The rental was parked farther down the street at a meter that had long since run out of time. He approached the car and saw the ticket folded neatly under the windshield wiper on the driver's side. He tossed the ticket into a wire wastebasket a few feet away.

The vinyl bench seat of the boxy car was hot as a Pyrex casserole dish fresh out of the oven. He winced as he sat down, then pulled his hand back sharply when he touched the steering wheel. The car was too hot to drive the few blocks he needed to go. He climbed back out of the car and locked the door, then dug the ticket out of the wastebasket and put it back under the wiper. He turned and began walking down the street, turned right onto Poydras a few blocks from the Superdome, and walked toward the river.

By the time he turned on to Carondelet and began walking in the shadows of the tall buildings, he was soaking wet and panting. He regretted not calling Carlton on the phone, but he needed the walk. He was itchy, the walls of his office closing in on him.

The bank was still several long blocks off, almost to Canal Street. The smell of car exhaust combined with the stench of overheated air and curbside garbage to make his head swim as he walked. It seemed as if he would never get there.

The guard inside the door looked at him suspiciously. The blast of cold air from the bank lobby had caused Lynch's face to splotch as his reddened face began returning to its natural color. His shirt was plastered against him; his hair was wild, windblown. He did not look like a good customer.

He walked up to the reception desk. A different woman was there this time, a young red-haired women with thick lips and too much makeup. She gave him a look that said she had him pegged. Whatever he was up to, she was on to him. And there was no way he was going to get away with it. Lynch found himself staring at her intently, glad to be back in a place of cold air and afraid that if he lifted his arms to straighten his hair, he'd knock the whole place out.

"I'd like to see Carlton Smith."

"Oh?" she asked snidely. "And who may I say is calling?"

"You may say Jack Lynch is calling." Lynch pulled a hand across his forehead. A drop of sweat fell onto the front of her desk and splattered into a spot about the size of a dime. The receptionist looked at the spot, then back at Lynch.

Silently, she punched the buttons on the telephone. After a moment, "A Mr. Lynch to see Mr. Smith." Another long pause, then the woman placed the phone back on its hook.

"You can go on up," she said, jaw tight as she pulled a tissue from a box and rubbed it across the front of her desk.

"Sorry about the wet spot," Lynch said, smiling. "Seems like it's always the guy's fault, right?" The woman wrinkled her face in distaste.

He managed to get his coat back on to cover up his wet shirt by the time he got up to Carlton's office, but the old lawyer was observant enough to notice the steam still rising off him.

"A real scorcher out there today," he commented.

"You got it," Lynch said. "I walked here from my office."

"What in heaven's name for?"

"It was too hot to fight the traffic."

"Call a cab to get back," he suggested.

"Think I will. I also think I'm on to something that may cause us problems. I've been real low-key about it so far, but it may come out anyway. I've got a friend in Los Angeles working on it for me. He was supposed to fax it to your office."

"I don't think it's come yet," Carlton said, pouring Jack a glass of water from a pitcher that sat on his desk on a black lacquered tray. "What's this all about?"

Lynch told him the story of Harry McMillan's death, as much

142

of it as he knew, anyway. "And it probably doesn't mean anything," he concluded. "But it's a connection and I don't like it."

Carlton Smith leaned back in his chair and entwined his fingers behind his head. "I don't either. This is getting more and more complicated every day."

"Nothing's ever easy, right?" Lynch sipped the water, feeling the iciness in his throat like cold steel.

The two men heard a buzz in the outer office, then a voice answering the phone. A moment later, the intercom line buzzed.

"Yes?" Carlton said, pushing a button.

"Sheldon Taplinger on line one."

"Kwang's secretary?" Lynch asked.

Carlton shook his head, punched another button and picked up the phone. "Carlton Smith."

A long pause. "Yes? I see. I can understand that. Of course, he's upset. When will—"

Carlton scribbled a few notes down on a pad next to the phone. "Yes, that's fine. Call me then. All right. Good-bye."

He placed the phone back in the hook. "It would seem," he said in response to Lynch's inquiring look, "that things are moving faster than we expected. Andrew Kwang has been asked to return to the city for further questioning. It seems the police already know about Harry McMillan."

"Damn," Lynch muttered. "Damn, damn, damn."

"You don't really think Kwang had anything to do with this, do you?" Lynch felt like he was almost begging.

He flopped into a chair in front of Frontiere's desk. It had taken him twenty minutes to find a parking space near the police station; the air-conditioning in the rental car had taken a sudden turn for the worse. All in all, it was turning into a lousy day.

Carl Frontiere paced back and forth in front of the chair. "What happened to all this damned honesty you were talking about?" he demanded. "You tell me what you know, I keep you informed."

"I wasn't holding anything back from you," Lynch semi-lied. "At least not anything I thought was important."

"You didn't think it was important that Pearl Bergeron's ex-husband was killed on the set of a Kwang movie?"

"I heard that as a rumor," Lynch protested. "You want me to

143

come to you with rumors? I was checking it out when I found out you already knew. I came here as soon as I could."

"What were you checking out?" Frontiere said, sitting back down behind his desk. He hadn't had the greatest of days himself.

"This," Lynch said, reaching into his pocket and taking out a folded set of shiny fax-paper sheets. Frontiere reached across the desk and took the papers.

"I've got a friend on the *Los Angeles Times*," Lynch explained. "He faxed me those stories from their morgue."

Frontiere unfolded the slick sheets: three news stories, the fuzzy, black copies made harder to read by the optical scanning of the fax machine. The headline of the first story read: DIRECTOR FOUND DEAD AT AUSTRALIAN FILM SITE. The second, a bit longer, included a photo of McMillan and was headlined: MCMILLAN'S DEATH RULED HOMICIDE; AUTHORITIES SEEK CLUES.

A headline on the third read: AUSTRALIAN AUTHORITIES CALL REPORTS OF MCMILLAN FIGHT "INSIGNIFICANT." Frontiere bent the sheet back to straighten out its crease. His eyes, tired from the long day and burning from the overwhelming pall of cigarette smoke in the squad room, focused on the copy.

Australian authorities called reports that murdered film director Harry McMillan fought with his producer the night before his death "insignificant."

Several witnesses testified at an inquest yesterday that McMillan and independent film producer Andrew Kwang brawled over the final cut of the Kwang World Pictures release *The Rain and the Window.*

According to one witness, Kwang was so dissatisfied with the film that he ordered it shelved permanently. At a meeting the night before his death, the allegedly intoxicated director argued violently with Kwang, then slugged him when Kwang fired him and ordered him removed from his office.

The next day, January 19th, McMillan's body was found washed ashore on a deserted stretch of beach barely a mile from the film location. An autopsy revealed that he died of a cerebral hemorrhage that accompanied a skull fracture. There were numerous other bruises and injuries as well.

At the time of his death, the autopsy also revealed,

144

McMillan had a blood alcohol level of .23 per cent, more than twice the level of legal intoxication.

The film *The Rain and the Window* will not be released. A Kwang World Pictures spokesman said recently that the last remaining print of the film had been destroyed.

Australian authorities report no progress in their investigation of the homicide.

"Seven years ago," Frontiere said, looking at the date on the fax. "Anything else?"

"That was the last story reported in the *Times*," Lynch said. "Harry McMillan was shipped home and buried in Florida, I believe. That's the last of it."

"Except for the murder of his ex-wife . . ."

"You think any of this is reason enough to drag Kwang back here and get the news jerks all hot and bothered again? I swear, those guys are like bitches in heat."

Frontiere stared Lynch down. "You know how much crap we're taking from Baton Rouge on this? I got the state police, the LBI, the governor's office calling down here every damn day on this. It's not like I ain't got other things to do, you know. And the more I find out about this Pearl Bergeron, the more I think maybe she set herself up for this. I ain't going to say anybody that gets murdered deserves what they got, but Pearl Bergeron was not the kind of girl I personally would have taken home to mother."

Lynch smiled, shook his cigarette package open, then extended it toward Frontiere. "Life's a bitch, then you die," he said. "You smoke?"

"Only secondhand," Frontiere griped. "Occupational hazard around this place."

"Did the coroner's report on Pearl Bergeron come back?"

Frontiere eyed Lynch suspiciously. "Why?"

"Just curious," Lynch said. "I wondered how loaded she was when she bought it."

Frontiere cracked a smile as well, one of only a few that day. "Not as bad as her ex. Her blood alcohol level was only .08 per cent. She wasn't even legally loaded."

"I'm surprised."

"Don't be. Her tastes just lay in other areas. Her blood had a

145

whopping level of cocaine, along with your garden variety drugstore items. Valium, Xanax, Prozac."

Lynch whistled. "This was a lady with a very high level of anxiety in her life. What you suppose she was so nervous about?"

Frontiere laced his fingers behind his head. "I'd like to know, myself. Speaking of anxiety, you got any ideas who left the organic fur coat in your car?"

Lynch stood up. It was nearly six, and for the first time in a long time, he had a dinner date in the middle of the week. No more Budget Gourmets and a six-pack in front of the tube, he hoped.

"Yeah, somebody with one lousy sense of humor."

"You sound pretty cavalier about it," Frontiere observed.

Lynch ground his cigarette out in an ashtray on the next desk. He looked back at Frontiere, his voice tightening.

"I'm scared to fucking death."

20

MILLER TAYLOR STOMPED THE FRAIL ACCELERATOR ON THE OLD VOLKS-
wagen, the chattering roar of the engine growing in response. He hit
a bump, a deep, hard pothole that shook the whole car. He looked
between his knees just as another few inches of rusted, thin floor-
board fell through onto the pavement of North Rampart Street. He
could see the street whizzing by below him in a black, blue, and gray
asphalt blur now.

To his left the Municipal Auditorium went by and then the
shaded, crowded, multihued blast of colors that was Louis Arm-
strong Park. He slowed, pumping the brakes to make sure the car
was actually going to make the turn, and maneuvered into the old
quarter at St. Philip Street. A block down, the blue-and-white saw-
horse of a New Orleans Police Department barricade blocked the
street. Taylor squealed the car to a stop, double-parked it next to
somebody's Lincoln, and got out.

A small crowd of people gathered in front of the barrier, while
two sweaty, rumpled uniformed cops kept everyone sufficiently
back. Over the heads of the mostly young, mostly black crowd,
Miller saw two microphone booms raised at odd angles to one
another, and a bank of lights off to the right adding, despite the early
hour of the morning, to the day's sweltering heat.

He walked up to the mass of people, then gently pushed his way
into the crowd. A tall black kid maybe twelve years old with a
basketball and a hundred-dollar pair of sneakers blocked his way.

"Excuse me," he said, easing around him.

"Excuse yo' mama," the kid threatened.

"Right," Taylor muttered, motioning for one of the policemen to move over his way.

"Yeah?" the cop demanded. Crowd control was considered shit detail in a city known for the size and behavior of its crowds. The officer was sweating dark-blue streaks down his uniform, and he wanted nothing to do with being friendly to a civilian.

"I got a message for a guy on the crew," he lied. "Can I cross?"

The cop looked at him. He didn't look any weirder than anybody else, but then again.

"Look, there's the director," Taylor pointed. "Ask him."

An enormous gray-haired man with a ruddy face and a T-shirt two sizes too small spotted them and smiled.

"Charlie," Taylor called out, "I got to see Chrisman. Okay?"

The man shook his head. He looked exhausted, weary beyond his many years of filming commercials in the heat. "Yeah, we're on five. Make it quick."

Taylor looked at the cop, nodded, then ducked under the wooden barricade and came up on the other side.

"He's over by the makeup truck. Probably getting his biceps oiled," the director said, nodding and dipping his head as he walked away. "Got to do something to sell these piece-of-shit American cars."

Miller stepped over a wrapped set of power cables, then turned behind a large white van. Three women in bikinis and plastic high heels stood in the shade, sweating their makeup off, sipping cold drinks out of paper cups. One smoked a pink cigarette. All were gorgeous, all excited about being in a major local commercial.

"I'm looking for Chrisman," he announced. "Any of you girls seen him?"

"He's over there." The blondest of the three girls pointed. She was wearing a lime-green bikini with black polka dots. What there was of it was barely staying on. Miller felt himself salivating, and found himself speculating on how much surgery she'd had.

He headed in the direction she'd indicated, then turned behind a short semi and spotted Chrisman about ten feet away. He carried a jar of Gatorade in his left hand and wore a muscle shirt with a tight pair of khaki pants. He did indeed look as if his biceps had been oiled.

"Teddy," Miller called.

Chrisman's massive shoulders swiveled around. He wore thick

148

pancake makeup, and his hair was moussed into a solid mass. He
looked at Miller and his jaw clamped shut. He stopped in front of
a large RV that was parked with its motor running and set the jar
down on the steps in front of a closed door.

"A word with you, Teddy," the older man said, quickstepping
to catch up to him.

"I got nothing to say to you, man," Chrisman said.

"You asshole," Taylor hissed. "Did you think you'd get away
with that?"

Chrisman turned. "Get away with what?"

"Trashing Lynch's car. That was awfully stupid."

In a quick New York heartbeat, Taylor found himself slammed
against the hot, metal side of the RV, a line of rivets digging into his
back.

"Every time I see you lately, you aggravate me," Chrisman said,
his eyes glowing darkly beneath the makeup. "That's not very
smart."

Taylor tried shifting to the side, but was unable to move be-
neath Chrisman's tight, knotted hands. "Chemicals getting to you,
Teddy? You been pumping those 'roids so long you feel like Sergeant
Rock, right?"

Chrisman's hands clamped even tighter. The front of Taylor's
white, button-down oxford-cloth shirt was wound as tight as a clock
spring. "What do you want from me?"

"You're going to bugger this whole deal if you don't lighten up,
son. None of us wants to see this project go down the toilet."

"What makes you think I give a damn about your project?"
Chrisman asked.

"Maybe you *don't* give a damn about it. Maybe you'd rather
spend the rest of your life sweating your balls off making used-car
commercials in the hot sun. Then again, maybe that's a better trade-
off than spending the rest of your life playing patty-cake with the
boys up at Angola. . . ."

Chrisman pressed his face closer. His breath was hot and unpleasant to Taylor. "What do you mean? I didn't do anything to
wind up there."

"Pearl was a bitch, son. No getting around it. Maybe she
pushed you too hard. You blew up, couldn't handle it anymore. Big,
strong guy with a temper like yours wouldn't have much trouble
beating a woman to death, now, would he?"

149

Behind the two of them, a voice on a megaphone yelled, "Actors! Places! Where the hell is Chrisman?"

Teddy eased his grip on Taylor's shirt. "He wouldn't have much trouble doing the same to an old man, either."

Taylor walked into the lobby of the hotel and stopped cold. Outside, just up from Canal Street, where he'd been lucky enough to find a parking space, two carloads of teenaged kids with speakers the size of garbage-can lids were having a full competition in the lunchtime traffic. The noise of some rap that struck Taylor as mildly obscene shook off the walls, the air around the two cars literally vibrating with thunderous sound and bouncing on shot-to-hell shocks as the kids danced inside the cars.

Holy cow, he thought as he scrunched his shoulders up toward his ears in passing the cars, those poor bastards will be deaf before they're thirty.

Amazingly enough, it was quiet inside the Marriott, relatively speaking, of course. There was the usual music from the bar, the sounds of talking and laughter muffled by the cavernous lobby. Thankfully, the architects had built some soundproofing into the place. Urban life, he thought. We all need soundproofing.

He walked toward the registration desk, only to stop cold at the sight of Sheldon Taplinger standing at the high counter, obviously agitated, straining to see over it. A crumpled hanger bag leaned against his left leg; his right leg helped hold up an overstuffed, scuffed lawyer's briefcase.

"Sheldon, what's the matter?" Taylor asked.

The young man turned around. A shock of dark-blond hair hung down over his forehead. His eyes were bloodshot, with great black half-moons riding high on his cheekbones below the eye sockets. He obviously was piqued.

"The damn suite's not ready," he yelped, a bit too loudly. The elderly couple in the line next to him turned to stare. "Kwang's in the coffee shop, steamed as hell at me, and there's not a damn thing I can do about it. And these idiots tell me there's nothing they can do about it either!"

Taylor suppressed a laugh at the normally controlled young man's display of temper. It had taken Taylor a long time to learn that minor discomforts like this were rarely worth the damage to your heart that came from ranting and raving. Besides, he remem-

150

bered, you usually wind up having to apologize to someone for making a horse's ass out of yourself.

"I'll tell you what, Sheldon. You handle it. I'll go see if I can help take the rough edges off Andy."

Taylor turned and walked away just in time to keep from hearing Taplinger say, "You keep calling him Andy, he'll take some rough edges off of you."

Miller Taylor spotted Kwang in a corner of the coffee shop, a *USA Today* unfolded in front of him and a cup of hot tea on the shiny fake-marble tabletop. He walked up to the table and cleared his throat, a sound that got no response from the man who was now his boss.

"Mr. Kwang?" he said. Kwang looked up at him from a front-page article about the mating habits of today's teenagers.

"Mr. Taylor. Please sit down."

Taylor sat as Kwang's eyes returned to the newspaper for a few moments. He finished the article, or as much as he wanted to read of it, then folded the paper neatly back together.

"I understand there's a problem with your suite," Taylor offered.

"Yes, but I'm sure Sheldon will be able to handle it."

"When did you get back in?"

"Approximately two hours ago," Kwang answered.

"I'm sorry you had to come back here before you were ready."

"It is of no real consequence. There is business we can transact while I'm down here. You can review your projects with me. Perhaps even now, if you like."

Taylor blanched. He hadn't expected to be put on the spot like that. As the creative director for the local office, it was his job to review and develop film projects to submit to Kwang. So far, he hadn't found any.

"I've reviewed a number of queries from agents and writers," he began. "I've read a few scripts, and assigned several to readers for formal coverage. I have to tell you, though, sir, there hasn't been much I've been terribly interested in."

"Finding the right kinds of properties is the truly difficult part of this business," Kwang said. "Actors, directors, craftspersons all can be had. It's that right script that so often turns out to be nearly impossible."

"I couldn't agree more with you, but I think there are some

151

talented writers out there. I feel like we're going to get something that will be uniquely suited to the new Riverbend studio."

"If there ever is a new Riverbend studio," Kwang said, raising his cup for a sip of hot tea. "I'm expecting Mr. Carlton Smith here within the hour with a progress report on our licensing situation."

"Will he be bringing Lynch with him?" Taylor asked, trying to make the question sound as offhanded as possible. Kwang looked at him.

"I'm not sure. There are some things I need to discuss with Mr. Lynch, certainly. But I don't know when we'll meet."

"Yeah. I see."

Kwang's voice changed from that of a man making conversation to a man giving orders. "You will have your report into the New York office by the end of next week. I want to know the status of all your creative projects. Send your expense and hour sheets, and a memo detailing your progress in compiling a list of useful nonunion craftspeople. If our licensing goes through, I want a crew out there within ten days to begin shooting the promotional spots."

"Okay, no problem." Taylor's heartbeat rose and sweat formed in his palms at the lie. Truth was, he hadn't done any of that.

"Also," Kwang continued, "I'll need to have your final script for the promotional film. I trust you've had time to make the changes."

Taylor swallowed. He hadn't touched the thing since it was Express Mailed back to him a week earlier.

"Just a few final things to check on," he said.

"The Independent Filmmaker's Association convention is in Chicago in two months. I want a work print ready to show by then."

"Two months, huh?" Taylor felt the beginnings of a killer headache growing behind his left eye. "Sure, no problem."

He knew that on the remotest chance the script and budget could be approved, the location shooting done, and the postproduction work completed in time, the final lab work would probably drive them over the deadline. If the short film made it to the convention at all, it would still be dripping wet when it arrived.

Taylor heard footsteps behind him, and turned to see Carlton Smith and Jack Lynch approaching the table. Taylor studied Lynch closely, wondering if a man who'd been severely threatened walked or talked any differently than anyone else.

"Hello, Andrew," the distinguished, polished, older attorney

152

said, extending a hand. Kwang shook the hand and smiled. "It's good to see you back. Sorry it's not under better circumstances."

"We cannot always choose our circumstances, can we?" Kwang said graciously, rising from his chair and motioning for the two to take seats.

"Certainly not," Carlton agreed. "But we can make the best of them. And I believe we have the opportunity to do that here."

"Hello, Mr. Lynch," Kwang said, in a surprisingly kind manner, given the unevenness of their past dealings.

"Hello, Mr. Kwang," Lynch said. He extended his hand, surprised at the warmth of Kwang's handshake as all three sat. "I'm sorry about your room."

"We can discuss our business down here as well as we can anywhere else," Kwang said as a waiter approached the table. The group ordered coffees, then Carlton Smith placed his briefcase on the table. He opened it and pulled out a pile of formal-looking typed papers.

"I believe we can expedite this last stage of the purchasing process relatively quickly," he explained. "Since the threat by both Louisiana Power Company and Kwang World Pictures to sue the Louisiana Regulatory Commission if they blocked the sale was taken seriously, the commission has indeed backed off. The Industrial Revenue Commission has approved our bond issue, and the First Interstate Bank of Louisiana has processed its paperwork and established procedures for underwriting the issue. A number of companies, funds, and well-placed individuals have expressed strong interest in the bond issue. I don't expect the initial public offering to last very long. What doesn't go first round will be picked up quickly on the secondary market."

Kwang smiled faintly. Carlton Smith held the pile of documents between his two hands, then snapped them smartly on the tabletop. He handed them over to Kwang, then reached inside his suit coat pocket. He took out a shiny, black Mont Blanc fountain pen, removed the cap, and handed the pen, barrel first, over to Kwang.

"In short, sir," he announced, "with your signature on this last series of documents, you've bought yourself a nuclear power plant."

"Imagine, gentleman," Kwang said, a lilt of excitement in his voice, "signing away a half billion dollars in the coffee shop of a hotel."

Kwang held the pen between his thumb and the first two fingers of his left hand, then signed the top document with a flourish. One by one, he fingered the sheets of paper, reviewing each one, then appended either his signature or his initials at the bottom of every page.

"You'll see that my Hong Kong office receives the appropriate copies of each of these forms," Kwang said.

"I'll have them messengered out this evening," Carlton said. "They should arrive in Hong Kong within twenty-four hours."

"And in Sunday morning's newspaper," Lynch added, "there will be a very nice page-one spread in the Living Section on the studio. I think you'll be very impressed."

"Good, that's very good." Kwang said. Sheldon Taplinger, minus the garment bag and overstuffed briefcase, appeared at the table.

"Everything's okay with the suite," he said, handing Andrew Kwang a key. Traces of exasperation remained in his voice. "The bags are up there now, and the manager said he'd have a complimentary bottle of champagne sent up, for what that's worth."

Kwang smiled broadly, as wide a smile as any of them at the table had ever seen on him. "It would appear, gentleman, that our circumstances are improving. I suggest we adjourn to my suite, where perhaps we might put that bottle of champagne to good use."

The five men walked out of the coffee shop and toward the bank of elevators. Lynch stayed well behind; the cool air of the lobby and the thick carpet under his feet a delight. He was moving slowly. He felt good. There was a new interest in his life, he felt new energy. The sweet smell of success was in the air all around him.

From behind, he spotted a familiar face moving past him, and it took a moment for him to make the connection. Another man followed. The first man forced his way between Taplinger and Carlton Smith, then tapped Kwang on the shoulder just as the elevator door opened and three well-dressed older women walked out.

"Mr. Kwang," the familiar voice said. Kwang turned to face the man who'd had the gall to touch him in that way. "Lieutenant Frontiere, New Orleans Police Department, Homicide. I have a warrant for your arrest. Please come with me."

"On what charge?" Carlton Smith snapped.

Frontiere pulled a folded warrant out of his inside coat pocket. "Murder, Mr. Smith. The murder of Pearl Bergeron . . ."

21

LYNCH FELT HIMSELF BLOCKED, CLOGGED UP, AS IF HE WANTED TO scream and couldn't get the sound out. This was disaster of the worst sort, the kind of horrible mistake that only gets neatly straightened out and resolved in half-hour television shows, or in the ninety minutes or so allotted to a modern feature film. In real life, he knew too well, justice is more a function of resources and timing than of guilt or innocence, and nothing ever got wrapped up neatly or easily or quickly. Nothing.

But in his profound and deep cynicism or, as he preferred to think of it, realism, Lynch knew that things could be worse. Andrew Kwang could afford the best lawyers money could buy. Carlton Smith was already on the way to the bank to arrange the blank cashier's check for Kwang's bond. It didn't matter if the judge made it fifty million; Kwang probably could raise the cash or a guarantee in a matter of hours. And the bank would be happy to back him up in whatever it took.

Kwang would, Lynch felt, be all right in the end. If it took an infantry division–size batch of attorneys and a hundred years' worth of appeals, Kwang would eventually be cleared. He had too much money not to be. As for tonight, Lynch anticipated that he, Carlton, and Kwang would have a late dinner together, followed by an extended strategy session.

Lynch despaired at the thought of missing dinner with Lois. But the kind of catastrophe they faced now was a public relations one, and it was in this kind of damage control that Lynch's hard-learned and hard-earned skills rose to the challenge. At this level of disaster, things could easily get out of hand. What had started out as a business deal, albeit a huge one, could rapidly take on the character-istics of a typically calamitous Democratic presidential campaign.

He called Lois from his office and told her the news of Kwang's arrest.

"I've already heard," she said. "It's on the radio. Arraignment's set for three, right?"

"That's what they tell me."

"The courtroom should be packed. Save me a seat."

"I'll try, lady. Take care," he said, hanging up.

Lynch sweated rain-shower torrents as he maneuvered the rental car, its air-conditioning now completely shot, down Tulane Avenue away from downtown and toward the courthouse. A police officer started the engine of his cruiser just as Lynch rounded the corner in front of the courthouse. Lynch pulled to a stop behind the police car to claim its parking space, then swore out loud in frustra-tion and impatience as the driver behind him laid on his horn. He looked into his rearview mirror and made eye contact with the guy behind him, who was now blocking the lane-and-a-half-wide boule-vard completely.

"Screw you, ace," Lynch mouthed. "You just want the freaking parking space, and you ain't getting it."

Finally, the blue-and-white pulled out and Lynch squeezed in. He stepped out of the car, after the jerk behind him had passed, and crossed around front onto the sidewalk.

Above him, what seemed like hundreds of feet in the air, Lynch saw the words carved in the harsh stone of the Orleans Parish Court House, the same ones he'd seen for years as a newspaper reporter and citizen. Only this time they brought a chill to his soul:

THIS IS A GOVERNMENT OF LAWS, NOT OF MEN.

Lynch stopped, staring, and wondered about that. Ahead of him, halfway up the steps to the entrance of the huge building, a television news crew lay in wait. A fat cameraman with a Betacam in his shoulder sling leaned against a towering Greek column. Obvi-ously bored, he fidgeted with the power cord as the sweat poured off him and soaked through his dingy pullover shirt.

Lynch bowed his head slightly, hoping he wouldn't be recog-nized as he ascended the shallow-pitched stairs. His luck didn't hold out, however. The same young woman whom Lynch had seen on television the night of Pearl's murder approached him.

"Mr. Lynch," she said loudly, as she came to within a dozen steps of him, "can we talk to you?"

He raised his head wearily, sensing that, like all reporters' requests for interviews, this one was more of a demand performance. This was a *journalist,* dammit, on a *story,* and woe betide anyone who didn't cooperate.

He nodded his head yes.

"Michelle Conte, Mr. Lynch," she said brightly, "Channel 7 News. Can we do an interview with you on the arrest of Andrew Kwang?"

"Why me?" he asked, futilely.

"I know your firm represents him, Mr. Lynch," she said. "I read your press releases." Michelle Conte smiled sweetly at him. Butter, he thought, wouldn't melt in this woman's mouth.

Lynch straightened his jacket and buttoned the middle button, largely to cover up the front of his white shirt, which was now two shades darker from sweat.

"Okay," he agreed.

"Harold," the woman ordered the fat cameraman, now stooping against the column with his camera at half-mast, "c'mon down here. We'll get him on the steps."

"Is this an interview or an assassination?" Lynch joked.

"What?" The young woman turned on him, serious and dark now. "What did you say?"

"Just a joke," Lynch muttered.

"I'm sorry, I didn't hear you," she said. "The traffic noise is high out here."

"Nothing."

"I'm speaking with Jack Lynch," the woman began as the tiny red light above the camera lens glowed, "whose local public relations firm has been retained by Kwang World Pictures. Mr. Lynch, what is your reaction to the arrest of multimillionaire film producer Andrew Kwang?"

The woman stuck her microphone in Lynch's face. "My reaction, I think, is one of shock and concern. Other than that, and stating that Mr. Kwang is entirely innocent of the charges and allegations made against him, we'll have no comment at this time."

"Have you spoken with Mr. Kwang?"

157

"Not since the arrest," Lynch answered, lying.

"Was he surprised to be arrested?"

Lynch smiled pleasantly. "I believe you could say that. Especially given that he's innocent."

"Are you aware of the evidence against him?"

"No comment at this time, please. And I've really got to get inside the courthouse, Ms. Conte. The arraignment starts in a few minutes."

The attractive young woman turned away from him as if he were an image on a screen that had just been turned off. He walked carefully up the granite steps as her voice-over continued behind him.

"Prosecutors say witnesses spotted Andrew Kwang leaving Pearl Bergeron's apartment the night of the murder—" were the last words he heard as he stepped through the imposing wooden doors of the courthouse and into a blast of cool, musty air.

"Good God," he said out loud. "It's going to be a long night."

Judge Alvin Diliberto's courtroom was packed with reporters, spectators, courthouse hangers-on, film freaks, and people with little else to do besides watch other lives dangle helplessly before a "government of laws, not of men."

The judge sat at his elevated bench. He jogged a stack of papers together, looked out over his jammed courtroom with something resembling distaste, and mumbled to his bailiff. Then he peered out over his wire-rim glasses at a helpless-looking black man in his early twenties, who stood next to an equally helpless-looking young attorney. The black man wore a full-length orange jumpsuit with the letters OPSD—Orleans Parish Sheriff's Department—stenciled in black spray paint on the back.

Lynch hoped to hell they wouldn't drag Kwang in wearing one of those.

"Mr. Pouissant," the judge intoned, "it is the opinion of this court that sufficient evidence exists for you to be bound over for trial. Defendant to be held in the parish jail. Court date to be set within thirty days. Bond set at ten thousand dollars."

God, Lynch thought, thirty days in that rathole of a jail before you even find out how long you'll have to rot there before trial. And it was clear from the look on the guy's face that the ten thousand may as well have been ten million.

Some system, he thought. With a little luck, he'd get through his entire lifetime without needing that kind of justice.

Lynch's mental wandering was interrupted by the judge's order to call the next case.

"People of the State of Louisiana versus Andrew Kwang," the bailiff called. A door to the judge's left opened, and Kwang was led in, handcuffed, but at least still in his suit. He was marched over to the defendant's table, where Carlton Smith appeared a moment later by his side. A deputy removed the handcuffs and stood at attention behind the table.

A man opposite the defense table stood. "District Attorney-General Lanzo for the state, Your Honor. Mr. Kwang is charged with a violation of Louisiana Code—"

Lynch looked around, the sound of the D.A.G.'s voice fading as he concentrated on the people around him. Sheldon Taplinger sat in the row behind the defendant's table, his head held rock still.

Two seats over, Miller Taylor sat. His hair was pushed straight back, as though he might have combed it with his fingers. Behind him, wearing a gray suit, sat Rowan Wilson. Great, Lynch thought, I can see this guy shooting his mouth off to the news freaks outside; that is if he hasn't already managed to get himself interviewed.

Lynch felt someone's eyes on him. He looked around the courtroom and saw a young man to his left and a few rows back, with chiseled features and a body that took up two places.

Teddy Chrisman. Wonder what he was doing here? Lynch thought.

The door to the courtroom opened. A blast of cool air from the hallway entered the stuffy, overcrowded courtroom. Lynch turned, saw Lois, smiled. He motioned with his arm to get her attention.

Lynch bent to whisper to the guy next to him. "Can we squeeze one more in here?"

The man obligingly scooted over as far as he could. Lois came up the aisle, crossed over Lynch's pulled-back legs, and pressed herself into the seat.

"Hi," she whispered, taking his hand. "What's going on?"

Lynch held her hand tightly. Despite the circumstances, he was excited to see her. "Nothing yet," he whispered back.

"Is he okay?"

"I think so."

159

"I missed you today," she said out of the side of her mouth, without looking at him.

"I missed you, too," he answered low. He felt her heat next to him, her skin still hot from the outside air. She shivered as her body adjusted to the coolness of the courtroom.

"What are they going to do with him?"

Lynch brought her hand up and laid their clasped hands on his left leg. "I think the D.A. will give just enough evidence to bind Kwang over for trial. I'm not sure what happens after that."

"Will he get bail?" Lois asked.

"Good God, I hope so," he sighed. Lynch felt a clamping in his chest at the thought that bail might be denied. From what he could tell, though, the charge wasn't going to be premeditated, capital murder. Not the kind of problem that would keep him from getting bail.

The sound of the bailiff's voice booming across the courtroom brought Lynch back to reality.

"Call Lieutenant Carl Frontiere."

A door to the left of the jury box opened and Frontiere walked in. He looked cool, confident, less harried than Lynch remembered him. He'd been here before, Lynch thought. He knew the routine. He had his hand up, ready to be sworn in, even before the bailiff crossed over to him.

The district attorney approached him. "State your name for the court reporter, please."

"Lieutenant Carl Frontiere, Homicide Division, New Orleans Police Department."

"Where were you the night of August 17th, Lieutenant Frontiere?"

"That's Frone-tee-AY," the police lieutenant instructed, his Ninth Ward accent emphasizing the third syllable. Lynch suppressed a laugh.

"Sorry, Lieutenant."

"No problem. On the night of August 17th, I was called to the scene of a suspected homicide at 1824 Dauphine Street, in the French Quarter, near the intersection of Governor Nicholls."

"And what did you find there?"

"We found the body of one Pearl Bergeron, who had been pronounced dead at the scene by paramedics. There was some dis-

160

array in her apartment. It was apparent from the scene that a struggle had occurred."

"I want to show you some photographs, Lieutenant." Attorney-General Lanzo approached the stand with a glassine envelope holding eight-by-tens. "Photographs previously registered with the court, Your Honor."

He handed the envelope to Frontiere, who carefully slid the photographs out and looked at them.

"These have my seal on the back," Frontiere said. "They are photographs of the crime scene."

"Is the deceased in that photograph Pearl Bergeron?"

"Yessir, it is."

"Submitted into evidence, Your Honor," Lanzo announced.

"So ordered," Judge Diliberto intoned.

"Now, Lieutenant, have you conducted an investigation into this homicide?"

"Yes, Mr. Lanzo. We have followed all standard procedures in pursuing this matter."

"And what have been the results of that investigation?" Lanzo asked, as if reading from a script.

"During the course of our investigation, we discovered certain items of circumstantial evidence that indicate the accused had motive and opportunity, and was indeed present at the scene. We also have numerous witnesses who witnessed a violent altercation at a public restaurant between the accused and the deceased the night of the murder. We also have witnesses who place the accused at the scene of the crime the night of the crime."

"Is the accused in this courtroom?"

"Yessir, he is."

"Would you state his name for the record?"

"Yessir. Andrew Kwang."

"That's all, Lieutenant. Your Honor, witness names and affidavits will be provided during pretrial discovery. The state maintains that sufficient proof exists both that a crime was committed and that the man charged with the crime at this time is the likely perpetrator. At this time, the state rests."

"Cross for the defense at this time?" Judge Diliberto asked quickly. They've all been through this before, Lynch thought. They're just checking off the items on the list, one at a time, until they can go home.

161

Carlton Smith stood. "Carlton Smith for Mr. Kwang, Your Honor. I am temporary counsel for Mr. Kwang pending his retention of full-time counsel for this matter. At this time, we have no questions for the witness."

"Witness is dismissed," the judge ordered.

"Defense moves that all charges be dropped with prejudice for lack of evidence, Your Honor. Everything the state has given us at this time is entirely circumstantial."

"Motion denied."

"Request for bond, Your Honor."

Lanzo stood. "Your Honor, the state requests bond be denied. The defendant, as you know, is quite wealthy and a foreign national. We feel there is sufficient flight risk to justify denial of bond."

"Your Honor, that's ridiculous," Smith shot back, obviously disgusted. "The very reasons the district attorney states for denying bond are good reasons to grant it. Mr. Kwang is so widely known that it would be virtually impossible for him to hide anywhere on this earth. We request release on recognizance."

"Your Honor—" Lanzo called. Judge Diliberto cut him off.

"General Lanzo, sit down. I'm not going to deny bond to this man simply because he's a foreign national and a prominent personality. What I am going to do is set a sufficiently high bond to guarantee appearance, and I'm going to confiscate Mr. Kwang's passport for the time being. Just to remove any temptation. Is that agreeable to the defense?"

"Your Honor, there's no need to confiscate Mr. Kwang's passport. I'm not even sure applicable law allows you—"

"Applicable law in this courtroom is what I say it is, Mr. Smith," Diliberto interrupted. "And those are my terms. As they say, gentlemen, take it or leave it. . . ."

Carlton Smith leaned down and whispered something to Kwang, who sat there without a trace of expression on his face. Behind them, Lynch was startled at the calmness Kwang displayed in the face of what felt like an assault. Carlton stood back up and faced the judge.

"The terms are acceptable, Your Honor."

"Stand up, Mr. Kwang," the judge ordered. Kwang stood.

"Do you understand, Mr. Kwang, that you are to surrender your passport immediately upon payment of bail and your release? And that you are not to leave this state until this matter is settled?

162

And that you are to keep the local police apprised of your where-abouts at all times?"

Kwang stood still for a moment, then said in a low, steady voice, "I do, sir."

"Bail is set at $2,500,000, ten percent guaranty bond acceptable, under the terms described. Trial date to be set by the criminal court clerk's office. Gentlemen, I believe our business is concluded. Next case, please."

Lynch bent slightly and whispered to Lois, "I'll be right back."

He stood and walked up the aisle quickly, to where Carlton and Kwang were standing behind the table. As the bailiff called out the next case, the deputy came over and took Kwang's arm.

"He has to go back to a holding cell until we can make bail," Carlton whispered.

"What can I do?" Lynch asked in a normal voice.

Carlton thought for a second. "Have you still got your rental car?" Lynch nodded.

"Good. Bring it around to the back of the courthouse. We're going to try and get Kwang out of here without appearing in front of any cameras."

Lynch turned and scurried down the aisle. As he passed the row where he'd been sitting, he noticed that Lois Finlayson had disappeared.

22

LYNCH HAD TO ADMIT IT: KWANG WAS THE COOLEST GUY HE'D EVER met in his life. Here he was, facing an indictment that could put him in a place where educated, genteel people *really* don't belong; in charge of a worldwide film operation that he couldn't control because he couldn't leave New Orleans; and with a half a Big One committed to a project that he now wished he'd never heard of.

To add insult to injury, he was stuck in traffic in the backseat of a rented Chrysler during one of the hottest weeks of the year with no air-conditioning. Lynch was nearly screaming hysterical obscenities himself; how Kwang managed to stay in control was beyond him.

"Jack, I hate to ask you," Carlton asked from the backseat, where he and Kwang had finally given in to the climate by loosening their ties, "but this heat is taking its toll on me. Would you mind tossing the cigarette?"

Lynch scowled. Great, he thought. Just freaking great.

"No problem, Carlton. Listen, fellows, I'm sorry about the AC up here. I've been meaning to take the car back to the rental place and get another one."

He drew deeply from the cigarette and then, holding it cocked between the thumb and bird finger of his left hand, sent it sailing out into traffic.

"What is the next step?" Kwang asked. "Where do we go from here?"

"I think the first thing is to get you quietly back to the hotel," Carlton said above the noise of roaring engines and blaring horns and radios cranked up to roughly the level of an F-18 on takeoff.

"Then we have to arrange for the best criminal attorney we can find."

"You won't take the case yourself?" Kwang asked.

Carlton smiled at him. "I appreciate the sentiment, friend. But I've never tried a criminal case, let alone one of this magnitude. Besides, I work for the bank. I don't mind subbing to help out a valued client, but you'll be much better off with someone else."

"Then I shall want the best," Kwang admitted softly. "I'll have my corporate attorneys in New York get in touch with James Neal or F. Lee Bailey. Perhaps that fellow in Wyoming—"

"Spence," Carlton said. "Gerry Spence. Yes, they're all good. And if they're available, they'd make great advocates. I think, however, that you may want someone on the team who's familiar with the ins and outs of the local system."

"Like with my public relations problem?" Kwang asked, looking toward the front seat. Lynch's eyes met Kwang's in the rearview mirror for a moment. He tried to read his passenger, without success.

Lynch wondered again if Kwang was going to wind up blaming this mess on him. If he had not arranged the dinner with Pearl, then she might have been murdered anyway. But she would have been murdered without a room full of people seeing her sling a drink at Kwang beforehand.

He slammed on the brakes in the middle of a right-hand turn onto Canal Street. The car skidded to a stop just as some idiot in a battered, decades-old red Ford ran the red light and nearly wiped them out. Lynch swore to himself, trying to keep the violence level as low as possible, then completed his turn onto Canal. It was rush hour now, and ahead of him lay twenty-five or thirty blocks of automotive hell. It would take an hour to get down to the Marriott.

Lynch settled back into the steaming hot vinyl of the Chrysler and wished for a cigarette, a scotch and soda, Lois. And mostly, to get away from where he was.

"I recommended you to the director Kwang's got in mind," Miller Taylor said, lifting up his sweaty wax paper cup full of flat soda. The smell of frying burgers and pungent barbecue sauce wafted over to the table like a cloud of grease-laden toxic gas.

Lois Finlayson bit into her sandwich, a Billy's Broiler #3 with cheese—no tomato, and chewed quickly. The smile that came to her face leaked red sauce out the right side.

"And?" she asked, her voice muffled by the fluffy hamburger bun.

"I don't think we're going to have any problems," Taylor answered. "I've got the script, what there is of it, finished. I don't think we'll have any problem getting it by Kwang. He's got other things on his mind."

Taylor smiled at that, as if enjoying some private joke. Lois obligingly smiled back at him.

"So I figure," Taylor continued, "we'll start filming late next week. I've arranged to have all the film stock and equipment sent up to Riverbend a few days before so everything'll be ready."

"Great," Lois said. "I know you probably don't have storyboards or a shooting schedule yet, but can you give me some idea of what kind of shots you're going to be looking for?"

"We probably won't get storyboards, if we get them at all, until the last minute. This is only a quickie promo film. You might just have to wing it."

"That's okay. I've never worked with the director, but that won't be a problem. It never has been before. You're not having a director of photography, right?"

Taylor reached across the table and took one of her french fries, then popped it in his mouth. "Maybe you can get the credit. I'll talk to Kwang. You done much aerial work?" Taylor asked. He leaned back and stared at the younger woman, letting his mind wander briefly, wondering what she would look like out of those tight jeans and the man's oxford-cloth shirt.

"You saw my demo reel," she said, aware that she was being mentally undressed. Like most women, though, she had become used to it over the years. She shifted in the metal folding chair, trying to relax, trying to remember how badly she needed this job. "I've done a bit. I know my way around a Tyler mount."

"That's what we'll have on the chopper, I'm sure," Taylor said, looking away. It had taken him a few seconds, but he had finally realized that he'd been leering at her. Even at his age and with his burnout statistics, the urge to merge still sneaked up on him occasionally.

"So what, like I'll just leave my schedule open next week and wait for you to get back to me?" Lois put that trace of sugar in her voice that she knew from years of experience would cut the harshness of words that were essentially a demand.

166

"I'll get back to you by next Friday. Is one day's notice okay?"

"Oh, yes. That'll be fine."

"What equipment will you be bringing?"

"What'll you be shooting with?"

"An Arri BL3, I think," Taylor replied.

"You doing sound?" she asked. "Why a sound-sync camera for stock shots?"

"The director's decision," Taylor replied, "not mine. What have you got?"

"I've got an Arri 2C, but it's hot-rodded to fit a Steadicam."

"You got a Steadicam?" Taylor asked, impressed that she would have so sophisticated a piece of equipment.

"Actually," Lois smiled, "the bank owns most of it. I'm making the payments, when I can."

Taylor whistled. "How much you got in it?"

"About sixty-five grand, all total," Lois replied. She fidgeted with the remains of her hamburger and looked around the restaurant. She was uncomfortable talking money to a relative stranger.

"Damn," Taylor said. "No wonder you need work so bad."

"Okay," Lois sighed, "I admit it. I'm desperate. What can I say?"

"Aren't we all. I did everything short of offering Kwang a blow job to get this job. And if I'd thought it would have helped, I'd have done that."

She smiled, as he expected. She also thought Taylor was a revolting old man, but she'd be damned if she'd let him know that.

"You must have been cheering like hell when Pearl bought it," Taylor commented.

"Weren't we all?" Lois asked, pasting on her sweet smile again. God, what you have to go through to find work in this business.

"Good heavens, you look terrible," Maud said, starting to laugh but then realizing that that was not such a good idea.

The dark splotches of sweat were visible now even through the jacket. That Lynch's entire ensemble for the day would have to be trashed was a distinct possibility. He fell against the wall, his legs nearly giving way under him as he stood against a ventilation register through which tepid air struggled into the room.

"I don't feel well," he muttered.

"You don't look well," Maud agreed.

167

He looked at her, trying to focus. "Where the heck have you been?" she asked. He tried to focus again.

"In traffic," he sighed. "For nearly two hours. I helped sneak Kwang out of the courthouse, then we went straight into Friday rush hour traffic. It took over an hour to get down to Canal Street, then I had to drop Carlton off at the bank, then find a parking space down here."

"Holy cow," Maud snapped. "Ain't you ever heard of taxis?"

Lynch pushed himself back up the wall and stared at her through bloodshot eyes. "Not now, Maud. I'm not in the mood to kid around."

"So what happened in court?" she asked, following him into his office.

Lynch related the details of the afternoon's proceedings. He rolled up a damp shirtsleeve and caught a glimpse of his watch as he did so.

"Jesus, Maud, it's after six on a Friday. What're you still doing here?"

"Figured the Friday crowds on the streetcar would be a pain. Besides, I haven't talked to you since early this morning. Just wanted to see if you were coming back, or if you needed anything."

Lynch laid his head back on his thickly padded rented executive chair. "You're sweet, Maud. I wish I could afford you."

She smiled back at him. "I wish you could, too. But for the time being, you can't. So let me get out of here, okay?"

Maud turned and started into the outer office. "Oh, by the way," she said, looking back over her shoulder, "you had one message. Your lady called."

Maud couldn't help but notice the smile that came to his face, the first one she'd seen in a day or two. "Lois Finlayson, right? That the name you told me?"

"Yeah, Maud. That's her."

Maud grabbed her purse, a ragged, scuffed, gray leather bag with a thin leather thong acting as a strap, and pulled it over her right shoulder in a secure, clamped-down, beat-the-purse-snatchers manner.

"I guess I don't need to tell you to have a good weekend."

"I hope you don't," Lynch said as she turned away. "Hey, Maud?"

"Yeah?"

"You having a good one?"

"Yeah, great," she sputtered. "Pelletier's coming home. We prob'ly go dancing or something."

Lynch leaned back on the sofa and settled into the soft pillow as far as he could go. He was finally cooling off after asking her to crank up the air conditioner.

"How much?" she asked.

"Set it on 'meat locker.' " he requested. "Thank God, there was no meeting."

"Meeting?"

"I thought for sure I'd be stuck with Kwang and Carlton all night."

He'd gone by his apartment, found it profoundly depressing, and packed a bag with a change of clothes and his junk out of the bathroom. He was finding it harder and harder each day to hang around his own space. The walls seem to shrink, concentrating the dirt and the disorder and the chaos. There was a time in Lynch's life when he kept his surroundings reasonably presentable. In fact, during his corporate years and the years of his marriage, he often felt so out of control of his life that the only way he could gain control was to clean compulsively.

I can't control my life, by God, but I can control my stuff.

Those days were gone, however. Now that he'd gained some hard-won control over his life, he often felt that he'd earned a worthless prize, that he was letting himself go to hell. To make matters worse, he mostly seemed not to care. At least not until he'd met Lois. He was still reluctant to have her over to his place. Maybe he'd clean up this weekend. Maybe not.

"Hope this is okay," Lois called from the kitchen.

Lynch's head felt too heavy to raise from the pillow. "I'm sure it'll be fine."

Lois walked in carrying a loaded tray. She bent carefully from the waist, then set it down on the coffee table in front of the sofa. Lynch looked over; two tall drinks in frosted glasses, a plate of cheese and crackers, another bowl of sliced fruit.

"Wow," he said.

"You finished the scotch last night and I didn't have time to buy any more. Hope a gin and tonic is all right."

169

Lynch pulled himself up into a sitting position. "It's great, babe. Long as it's cold."

He reached for the drink and raised it to his lips. It felt like heaven pouring down the back of his throat.

"I don't mean to sit here like a slug," he said, after lowering his arm to the side of the sofa. "It's just been a long day."

Lois came around the table and sat next to him. "It's okay. I'm glad to see you."

"It's great to see you, too. This one's been a killer."

They sipped drinks, noshed on the fruit and cheese. "What do you want to do tonight?" Lois asked.

Lynch thought for a moment. "Want to stay in?"

She smiled. He reached over and took a strand of her hair, wrapped it around his finger, stared at it a long time. "Yeah. This is weird for me. I'm usually trying to get away from stuff like this."

Lois leaned forward, kissed him lightly on his cheek. He turned, kissed her back for a long time, pulled her closer to him.

"You mind if I take a shower?" he asked. "I've sweated so much today, I feel like I've been rolling in Vaseline."

Her lip curled. "Yuck. Please do. I'll get a clean towel for you."

Lynch stood and stretched. A cold shower would clear the cobwebs, make him functional for the evening. He walked into the bathroom behind Lois, who handed him a thick towel, kissed him, then left him alone.

The white tile felt cool to his bare feet. He pulled off his pants, feeling the cool air blowing over his legs from a wall register next to the bathroom closet. He removed the last of his clothes and stepped into the shower, waiting until he'd pulled the translucent plastic shower curtain to before turning on the water.

The cold water and the pressure shocked him. He sucked in a quick, deep breath and felt his skin break out in goose bumps. Like most people who spend their days dressed in business suits, he was often surprised how wonderful it felt to be standing naked under a shower at the end of the day.

Why do people even wear clothes? he wondered. His interior monologue was interrupted by the sound of the door opening.

He looked up. "Lois?" he asked. "That you, babe?"

There was no sound, but he could see through the filmy layer of shower curtain a form moving on the other side. He was about to say something again when a hand reached up and pulled the curtain back a couple of feet.

Lois bent over slightly from the waist, nude. Her long, brown hair draped her breasts, and her thin arms held the curtain back.

"I thought you might want some company," she said over the hiss of the shower.

Lynch smiled and felt himself young again. He unconsciously contracted his abdominal muscles, wanting to look as young and tight as she was.

"Great."

She stepped in carefully, one leg at a time, toes pointed like a dancer. Lynch thought briefly of the last time he'd been in a bathtub with a woman, with Sally, and felt a pang somewhere deep inside him that he made some effort to ignore. Lois was there, and she was real, and his life had changed again for the better. This time he hoped to hold on to it.

She squealed when the water hit her. "God, it's cold. How do you stand it!" He reached behind him and cranked up the hot water. The room began to fill with steam.

Lynch wrapped his arms around her, guilty at his own delight, amazed that he could continue to feel this good. She was wet and slippery, eager to hold him, her face on his, her eyes closed under the blast of the shower head. He held her tighter; she moaned as he kissed her neck, gnawed on her shoulders, ran his hands over her with a passion and intensity he'd forgotten he could muster. She fell back against the wall, letting herself go limp in his arms. He held her up against the hot, dripping tile, the fog of the shower enveloping them, smearing them in moisture, rattling their senses with the searing heat and the strain of standing up and the incredible, unfathomable bliss of their lovemaking.

She had her arms around his neck now, her legs spread around him, her feet planted on the wall of the bathtub behind him. He leaned down, with his hands around her waist to help hold her up, and took first one, then the other of her nipples in his mouth, kissing and tugging in a frenzy until she moaned and grunted and found herself nearly howling for him. He stood up, moved his hands down behind her to form a seat for her; she pulled her feet up off the porcelain wall of the tub and planted them in the small of his back. Then he was in her, grinding against her, her back sliding up and down the soaked, sloppy wall of tile behind them. The steam became thicker, until they could barely see the walls around them. They pumped away at each other, surrounded by a great blazing glorious sunlit cloud until they exploded together, crying and squealing and sliding down the wall until they were lying exhausted in the bathtub, panting, with the hot water pouring down on them, drenching them until they were red as beets and wrinkled as prunes.

The orange glow of the alarm clock's face penetrated his closed eyelids. He came back to consciousness slowly now. Carefully, he opened an eye: nine-thirty. There was no light save the dim glow of the streetlights coming through the sheers pulled to in the window. He rolled over a bit, the stiff, cool white sheets crumpling under him. He felt for her; she was still there, breathing deeply in sleep.

Lynch thought back over the evening. They'd climbed out of the bathtub when the water heater went dry and started spraying cold water over them, then had a glass of wine with the intention of making dinner. But they had touched each other only briefly in the act of getting dressed, and in the thick, heavy air-conditioned air of her apartment had found themselves excited again. And Lynch had done something he hadn't been able to do—even, to the best of his recollection, with Sally—in many years. He'd made love to a woman twice in the space of one evening.

Before, when he was a young man, he'd found that, as in trashy novels, once had never been enough. But those years were long behind him, and now once was usually plenty. Not tonight, however. The dreadfulness of the day, the tension and the frustration and the heat and the traffic had left him with an excess of suppressed energy that surprised him. He felt old most of the time, considered himself old most of the time, but there was something about Lois that dispelled that awful feeling of life having passed him by. He had always been a gentle lover, but with Lois it was different. He had wanted her, felt almost as if he'd taken her, but she wanted him, too. And for the first time since Sally (and, before that, for many years), he felt completely and blindly wanted and accepted. It was, for him, a matter of faith as much as love.

When they had lain there after making love a second time, they surprised each other by going once again. That time had been the slowest, the longest, in some ways the sweetest. Then they had dropped off to sleep in each other's arms, the near-silence of the room like a blanket over them. Only the low whisper of air moving

172

in and out of the vents and the deep, relaxed breathing of the two disturbed the quiet.

She stirred now, her breathing changing as she shifted in the bed. It was dark and cool in the bedroom. Lynch realized as he came up from the black well of his sleep that he hadn't had the dreams again. The horrible dreams that had tortured and plagued him since Sally's death had finally quit.

His grieving was over.

23

"SO LET ME ASK YOU," LYNCH SAID, "HOW DO YOU DO THAT?"

"Do what?" Lois asked, as a long, stringy piece of cheese from a bite of omelet hung out of her mouth, stretching and refusing to let go of the gooey mass on her plate.

Lynch, his elbow bent and planted on the table, propped his chin on his hand, and cocked his head sideways. "You know . . ."

She fumbled with the cheese, trying unsuccessfully to bite it in two, and finally resorted to pulling it loose between her fingers. Lynch thought at that moment that she was as beautiful a sight as he'd ever seen in his life, sitting there at the small table dressed only in a long, white shirt that hung almost to her knees, her hair barely combed and thrown back over her still-sweaty shoulders. Both inhaled the musty smell of lovemaking, the air-dried scent of two bodies tussling together in the heat of both passion and climate.

She laughed at him, her mouth still half full, playing with him. "No, I don't know. What?"

Lynch felt himself blush. He raised his glass and took a sip of wine, then put it down.

"It's just that I've never made love with a contortionist."

Lois giggled. "A what?"

"I mean, I've never seen anybody who could pull both their feet behind their head. Especially when they're . . . preoccupied like that."

It was her turn to blush. She swallowed the rest of her bite and stretched in her chair, her arms over her head, shaking her hair down off her shoulders.

"It was the Steadicam," she said.

"What?" he asked.

"Two years ago," Lois explained, "when I bought the Steadi-cam. The thing weighs between forty and sixty-five pounds, depending on what kind of rig you've got it set up for. It's a lot of weight for someone my size. Compresses the spine, you see. So I had to work to get in shape to handle it. I started taking yoga classes and one thing led to another."

Lynch moaned. "It sure did."

"That's not what I mean, doofus," she kidded. "I started having back problems almost from the beginning. I was spending more time at my chiropractor's than I was on location. When I took up yoga, it helped a lot."

"I'll say," Lynch said. He smiled at her, raised his glass as if offering a toast to her flexibility and skills.

"You have a one-track mind."

"And you are definitely the track I want to take," he said.

She went dark for a moment, then smiled again. "Hey, you want to see it?"

"I thought I'd already seen it all."

She shook her head, smiling down at the floor. "You're terrible. Really, you are on your way to becoming a dirty old man."

"I am not dirty," he insisted.

"I meant the Steadicam."

"You mean," he asked in mock horror, "the Inner Sanctum?"

In the short time they'd been seeing each other, Lois had never invited him into the back bedroom. She explained that it was her combination office/storeroom and was in a constant state of chaos. He hadn't pressed it, but confessed to a certain curiosity about it.

"Sure," she said. She picked up her wineglass and stood, pushing the chair back across the floor with a flourish. "Let's go. I think once a woman's been intimate enough with a man to show him her yoga tricks, he deserves to see her office."

"Be still, my beating heart," Lynch said lightly as he followed her down the hallway.

Lois opened the door to the bedroom and flicked on a light. The place was bare of furniture, except for a wooden workbench she'd had built against the wall. The room was packed with equipment, though: great, black cases holding lenses, camera magazines, camera bodies, cables, meters, battery packs.

In one corner stood a weight bench and a set of free weights.

175

Lynch noticed there was no dust on it; it was obviously used regularly. In the opposite corner, mounted on a heavy, metal stand, was a contraption that looked like something out of "Lost in Space."

"Where did you get all this stuff?" Lynch asked in awe.

"Picked it up over the years," she said. She walked over, placed her glass on the workbench, and turned. "Here it is. My life as a cinematographer. Only things haven't been so good lately. The jobs are hard to come by.

"Even the Steadicam jobs," she continued, pointing toward the metal stand, "have been slow in coming. And there aren't that many people out there who even know how to use the thing."

Lynch walked over to the corner. The metal stand had several stout arms coming out from its main post. On one arm hung what looked like an ultra–high-tech life preserver, jet black with pockets, Velcro straps, loops, and hooks.

On another extension, a complicated array of black robotic arms and chromed metal joints, rollers, and attachments hung. Below the lowest free arm, another arm with a rack full of equipment swayed perilously in midair. Lynch recognized what looked like a battery pack and a meter, with several dials and lights next to it, and, a little further up on the rack, what looked like a government-surplus oscilloscope.

"How does this thing work? he asked.

Lois sighed. "I'll show you. But I won't be able to keep the thing on very long. You've kind of worn me out tonight."

"Right," Lynch jibed, "like you're so old and out of shape."

"Well, I can't help it. It's late and I'm tired."

"My, getting grumpy, aren't we? Can I help you with that thing?" he offered.

"Oh, no," she said quickly, as she pulled the vest off the metal arm. "If you don't know what you're doing, which, my dear, you don't, then you'd only cause problems."

Lynch smiled. "Well, *excuse* me."

Lois pulled the black vest on and fastened it in front with a wide Velcro belt. She pulled a strap to tighten it, then shook it around on her shoulders, beneath thick pads, to make sure it was secure and in place. She fastened another safety strap, then turned and backed up next to the arm holding the robotic piece.

"First you put on the vest," she explained as she moved. "When it's on tight, you hook up the sled."

Her fingers worked intently yet securely as she fastened the maze of tubes, racks, and equipment to the vest. Then she pulled a lever on the stand to free the apparatus and, with a smooth movement, backed away from it. Lynch's mouth fell open. She looked like she was strapped inside some kind of orthopedic robot. "Good heavens," he whispered.

"It's something, isn't it. See how this rotates." She turned, dipped, knelt halfway to the floor, then rose back to a standing position. The end of the main extension arm and camera mount hung stationary in midair, as if it were magically balanced, suspended out there with no connection to her body or gravity.

"How does it work? I mean, where are the gyros?"

"The amazing thing is there are no gyros," she said. "It's a series of gimbals and high-tech bearings. The whole thing works on Newton's whatever-the-hell-it-is Law of Physics."

"What?" he asked, physics not being one of Lynch's strong points.

"You know, the one that states that a body in motion tends to remain in motion until another force acts on it, and a stationary body will remain stationary until something moves it."

"Inertia?"

"Yeah. That's it."

Lynch laughed quietly to himself. He was well aware of the inertia he'd encountered in his own life; he was unaware that it had been summarized as a law of physics.

"Now watch. It's even more impressive when you get it *all* hooked up."

Lois pulled the arm of the Steadicam out in front of her, then dipped and pulled it up under the camera that was mounted on the top part of the vertical stand. She hooked the arm to the camera mount, unfastened the whole apparatus from the stand, and stepped back two feet.

The camera seemed to hang out to her side precariously, as if it might fall over on a moment's notice and most likely take her with it. She had to bend slightly from the back, with one arm holding on to the camera mount, so that from the side her legs, torso, and the Steadicam made a Tinkertoy Y.

She guided the camera around expertly with her left hand, then switched with equal ease to the right. She had become part of the machine, working both sides of her body without favoring one side or the other. The camera swiveled from left to right, smoothly and evenly, as if on a high-tech dolly.

"Damn," Lynch said. "Robocamera . . ."

Lois giggled. "Yeah, nice toy, huh? This is my baby."

"What kind of camera is that?"

"It's an Arri 2C, the standard 35 millimeter camera for wild shots."

"Wild—"

"Shots where you don't have to worry about synching sound. It's not a quiet camera. It's not self-blimped."

"Okay. I'm following you, I think."

Lois reached down to her side, to the rack that was slightly behind her and turned a few knobs. A green glow came from the four-inch screen on the rack.

"When the camera's out there in position," she said, walking around confidently without even looking where she was going, "you can't see through the eyepiece. So you rig up a video connection and you watch what you're framing through the scope."

"How do you focus the thing?"

She looked up, surprised. "Good question. You're not a complete bimbo after all, you know that?"

"I guess that means I'll have to be happy with being an incomplete bimbo. So answer the question."

She swung the Steadicam rig around again, demonstrating how, in effect, it turned the human body into an incredibly versatile camera dolly.

"Your first A.C.—first assistant cameraman, for the uninitiated—has to pull focus for you," she explained. "You're a little bit limited in the lenses you can use. You want to go for as much depth of field as possible."

She stood next to Lynch. "See? Check out the scope."

Lynch stared into the green monitor. "It's so bright," she added, "because we shoot a lot outside. A standard black-and-white monitor would be drowned out by the sunlight. You have to have a high-intensity rig."

It almost hurt his eyes to look at the image in the scope, but in the glass he could see the rest of the room through the camera's eye. A grid of vertical lines divided a lined box with a cross hair in the middle like a gunsight.

"What are the lines for?"

"Framing. Helps you keep everything tight and level."

Lynch backed away so she could move. "Babe, this is great. I'm really impressed. Where do you use this thing?"

"The Steadicam is probably the neatest innovation to come along in years," she said, walking over to the stand and hooking the camera back to the stand and letting go of the rig. "It's revolutionized camera work. The whole thing's expensive as hell, but it saves a fortune in production costs. You could actually shoot a whole movie without ever using a camera dolly.

"And since there are so few Steadicam operators out there," she added, hooking up the sled to the stand and pulling herself free of it, "or at least so few really good ones—"

"Of course," Lynch interrupted.

"Of course. There are so few good ones that you can charge a whole lot more than for standard camera work."

She pulled the vest off and hung it up. Lynch noticed a line of sweat around her waist and neck, and dark areas of damp shirt all over her torso. Despite the ease with which she carried the camera and its rig, and the short time she'd had it on, it was obviously harder than it looked.

"You okay?" he asked.

Now that she was free of the weight, she let her shoulders sag. Her weariness showed through her smile.

"Just tired."

Lynch walked over to her, took her shoulders and turned her around. He planted a hand on either side of her neck and began massaging her, slowly and deeply.

"That's wonderful," she said, her voice soft and tired.

"We can do more of this if you want. Want to go sit down on the couch? I'll bring the wine in."

"Sounds wonderful," Lois said, reaching up with her right hand and touching his hand on her shoulder. "I want to go to bed soon."

He squeezed her, then reached down to her waist and tickled her. "Bed again? Just can't get enough, can you?"

She jerked away from him, laughing. "To sleep this time, you joker."

Her head was against the back of the couch, her eyes half closed when he returned with the cold bottle of wine. He poured them each a nightcap and handed a glass to her.

179

"Lois, if there's so much demand for Steadicam operators, how come you've had so much trouble getting work?"

She turned away from him, her eyes darkening. "I told you why," she said, grumpy with fatigue and reluctant to talk.

"I just don't understand, that's all. You're obviously talented."

"Talent doesn't mean anything in this business, dammit," she snapped. "There are lots of talented people out there who never get anywhere."

"It's just that—"

"Oh, damn," she interrupted. "I knew this evening was too good to be true. Why can't you just leave it alone? I told you all that stuff about me, and I don't want to talk about it any more. If you don't like it, you know where the door is."

"Hey," Lynch said, trying to soothe her. "Chill out, darling. I was just asking. Didn't mean to upset you. It's just that I'd like to see you work again."

"You'll get the chance. Next week. I talked to Miller Taylor today. I got the job doing the Riverbend facility promo shoot. We start principal shooting Friday. Should only take a day, maybe two at the most."

Lynch straightened. "What?"

"I'm going to be the shooter for Kwang's promotional film on the Riverbend facility."

"Wait a minute," Lynch said. He spoke too quickly, without waiting for his brain to fully engage. "I don't like you getting involved in this mess."

"So who appointed you my father?" she demanded. "Who the hell do you think you are? I haven't worked in two months and now you're telling me to turn down a job with the most successful independent studio in the world? Screw you, buddy. I like you, Jack. But I don't like you *that* much."

Hell, Lynch thought, this evening is turning sour quickly. Maybe he should go home, cut and run. That would have been his usual solution, but he held back this time.

"I'm sorry. It's just that this mess with Kwang and Pearl Bergeron had got me in a knot. I care about you a lot, Lois. Maybe too much. And the thought of you working with someone who might be a murderer is a little tough for me."

"I can take care of myself," she said. "Besides, I thought you were convinced Kwang was innocent."

"I don't know now," he said. "After what I heard in court today, I'm just not sure."

She took his hand and held it firmly in hers. "Jack, I don't want to talk about Pearl Bergeron anymore. I don't ever want to hear her name mentioned."

"Lois, that's going to—"

"Ssshhh, Jack. Listen to me. This is important to me. I want to get on with my life. I want to forget Pearl Bergeron ever existed. Will you help me do that?"

"Lois, I—"

"Will you, Jack?" she demanded, harsher now. "If we're going to be together, you're going to have to do that for me. It's the only way, Jack. Do you understand?"

He was silent for a moment, staring into the brown of her eyes, his thoughts melting away inside him. "Yes, darling. Of course. Let's forget it."

She smiled. "Thank you, Jack Lynch. I appreciate that. And I'll try to make sure it's worth your while."

Lois inclined toward him on the couch, the tail of her shirt pulling up as she came closer. Lynch put his arms around her, felt her lips on his, his hands running down her back, beneath the shirt, to her bare skin.

I'm too old for this, he thought, as his eyes closed. He slid down on the couch as she pulled herself on top of him.

24

TEDDY CHRISMAN STILL FOUND IT HARD TO BELIEVE SHE WASN'T GOING to be around anymore. It's not that he'd had all that much time to get used to her; they'd only lived together a short time before her murder. Between the fights, though, he and Pearl had had a few good times together.

He lay back on what had once been their bed, wondering what he was going to do at the end of the month. He sure as hell didn't have rent money for another place; in fact, he wasn't even sure where he was going to come up with the money to move, let alone a deposit on another place.

If he'd been a little quicker, he would have grabbed more of Pearl's jewelry and hocked it before the governor had the chance to send his assistant down from Baton Rouge to inventory her belongings. Chrisman put his hands behind his head, letting the weight push him even deeper into the soft pillows, and stared at the ceiling, trying to think of the guy's name. What was it?

"Brewster, Robert Brewster," he said out loud.

Brewster had worn a jet-black suit that day, with tiny, almost invisible gray pinstripes woven through the cloth. He wore a vest, something that Chrisman knew from his compulsive reading of *Gentleman's Quarterly* was considered outdated, and talked as if he were trying to keep from screaming.

He'd gone through the closets, her jewelry boxes, her bureau, counting in embarrassing detail every item of clothing, every piece of jewelry, each personal item recorded so that the governor's wife, or whoever, could get down here as quickly as possible to box it all up. It was amazing the sheer amount of petty detail that had to be taken care of when one was snatched away from this vale of tears on such short notice.

Brewster told him he could stay in the apartment until the end of the month, as long as he kept his mouth shut about it; but after that, the free ride was over. And everything on this sheet better be there when the packers came, or Teddy would have to answer to the governor himself.

Screw the governor, he thought. No more free ride, hell. If I could find those papers, the free ride would be just beginning.

He'd looked everywhere. The problem was that he really didn't know what he was looking for. One night, after three martinis, a couple of lines of the finest Peruvian olfactory dust, and four Xanaxes, Pearl had drunkenly, sleepily told him of the papers she'd copied up in Baton Rouge. Her father had been furious when he found out about it, and he made her promise never to tell anyone about what had happened on that land all those years ago.

In return for that promise, he had made Pearl a promise of his own: the Louisiana Film Commission, which meant the chance to meet stars, mingle with the shakers and movers, and maybe even a shot at a gig in the movie biz after he left office.

But Teddy Chrisman had vacuumed up a few that night him-self—he didn't drink; it put on weight he couldn't afford—and now he couldn't remember what she was talking about. That is, if she had ever really explained it to him. All he could remember was her blathering on and on at what by the end of the evening felt like a million miles an hour about her father and what the press would do to him if it ever got out.

And he remembered her saying, over and over, that it "wasn't even his fault! He wasn't even governor then!" He'd inherited the whole mess from past governors. And that it had all been sheer idiocy; nobody knew how dangerous it was back then. Nobody cared.

Pearl ranted on for hours that night, until Teddy couldn't take it anymore and finally told her to shut the fuck up, he'd had enough. She threw a lamp at him and told him to get out. He held her down while she screamed and cried and twisted, until she finally calmed down. He'd leaned down to kiss her and she bit him, hard, on the cheek, and they wound up balling away half the night, fueled by anger and passion and coke, until their heads hung over the side of

183

the great brass bed, sweaty and exhausted and finally, mercifully, burned out.

So what if Teddy played in both sides of the garden? Pearl knew it. They even did a threesome one night, a reverse twist on the standard ménage à trois. Teddy danced in the middle that night, the cream filling in the Oreo cookie. Oh, the nights they had spent together . . .

What the hell was she talking about?! a voice inside his head yelled.

He jumped up off the bed in a fluid, arcing motion. He landed on the floor on the balls of his feet, far more supple than his muscle-bound appearance would suggest.

He walked across the room and into her large walk-in closet. Pearl's clothes still hung there, neat and pressed and expensive. Everything from eighty-dollar pairs of jeans to designer labels Teddy'd never heard of. He shuffled through the dresses, looking for anything that might be unusual but feeling for anything out of place as well.

Nothing.

He thumped the back wall of the closet. The building had been renovated in the last few years, and sheets of drywall had been mounted over the century-old original brick. The place was as solid as Pearl had been volatile.

Teddy banged the walls all the way around the closet. If there were a hollowed-out place anywhere in the apartment, it wasn't there. He stepped out of the closet and back into the bedroom.

It was a useless exercise, he felt. The night before, he'd been over every square inch of the apartment, even brought a tire iron up out of his Trans Am and tapped the floors. If Pearl had hidden anything, it would take a better thief than Chrisman to find it.

Finally, he gave up and decided to take a shower. He walked into the kitchen first and poured a diet soda. He carried it into the bathroom and set it down on the vanity. Teddy Chrisman stopped for a moment in front of the mirror, admiring himself; the square set of his jaw, the deep blue of his eyes, the hard ripple of his muscles beneath the white knit shirt.

Damn, he thought, I'm good.

He pushed the sliding glass mirror to one side, revealing the medicine cabinet. All of Pearl's illegal recreational drugs had been carefully removed and disposed of by the police and the state troopers, probably at a cops-only party later that weekend. But her prescription drugs had been left behind. Teddy opened up a small, amber-plastic pill bottle and dropped two five-milligram valiums into the palm of his right hand, then popped them in his mouth and chased them down with soda.

Suddenly, he felt a flash of anger that Pearl was gone. It's not that he missed her or anything, at least not for herself. He'd leave missing Pearl to someone who had a better heart than his. But it truly and genuinely pissed him off to lose a meal ticket.

He slammed the prescription bottle onto the glass shelf so hard that the glass cracked into three or four large pieces, all of which dropped into the sink and exploded in a spray of glittery fragments.

"Damn," he snapped, holding up his hand to make sure he hadn't been cut. His anger spiked again, and he slammed the inside back wall of the medicine cabinet with his closed fist. A fine cloud of white powdered sheetrock dusted his hand.

He pulled back, muttering another obscenity, then caught himself. Drywall dust inside the medicine cabinet? he thought.

Teddy looked closer. There was a tiny slit in the metal, and below that were embossed the words USED BLADES. He smiled. His father had put blades into a slot in the metal like that when Teddy was a kid, and he always wondered where they went. The black hole of razor blade hell?

What concerned him now, though, was why he'd never noticed the slit before. The inside of the cabinet was painted white; the darkness behind the wall should have made the disposal slit look like a black gash. Only it wasn't black.

Teddy looked closer. *It wasn't black.*

"What the hell?" he said out loud.

He reached into his pocket and took out a small fingernail clipper. Unfolding the file, he carefully raised it to the slot and pushed it in.

Something gave way.

"Well, well, well," he hummed. He looked closer. He'd never noticed it because whatever was behind the used razor blade slot in the metal medicine cabinet was as white as the paint on the cabinet itself.

Maybe even as white as paper . . .

Teddy stared inside the cabinet. A smile came to his tight lips as he thought about what he'd found. He slid the mirrored door

185

shut, then spread his arms wide and grabbed each side of the cabinet. There was barely a half-inch or so of metal lip protruding from the wall of the bathroom, but when you can bench press three times your body weight, you don't need much grip on a five-pound medicine cabinet.

Teddy noticed as he dug his fingers in that the caulk around the cabinet was still soft. He grunted, squeezed his hands, and heaved.

Definite overkill. The whole medicine cabinet snapped out of the wall like it had been held in with children's paper paste. The bottles of shampoo, the tube of toothpaste, Teddy's acne cleanser all bounced around inside the cabinet like ball bearings in a metal can.

It was all Teddy could do to keep his own bearings. He fell back against the opposite wall of the bathroom, cursed under his breath, then regained his footing. He held the medicine cabinet to his chest and peered carefully over the edge behind it, like an acrophobic mountain climber looking carefully over a precipice.

A white eight-by-ten envelope stuffed with papers was taped securely to the backside of the medicine cabinet. If he had moved out without finding it, a hundred years might have passed before it was seen again.

"What the—" Teddy Chrisman muttered. He had no idea what was in the envelope, but he had a feeling his karma had taken a very abrupt and sudden shift for the better.

Quickly, he set the cabinet on the bathroom floor. He knelt down beside it, his telephone-pole thighs stretching the fabric of his white pants tight across his skin, and pried a finger under one side of the envelope. Carefully he peeled the tape off, then pulled the envelope free.

"Rock and roll," he whispered to himself, Johnny Winter–style, as he tore open the envelope flap. The papers inside were all dull, gray copies of old documents, some more than thirty-five years old. The paper was slick, felt almost wet, like the kind of shiny toilet paper you get in cheap hotels.

Teddy separated the top sheet from the rest and looked at it. It was on letterhead that read STATE OF LOUISIANA at the top, with the state seal, and below that DEPARTMENT OF THE INTERIOR.

The document was dated July 31, 1952.

Teddy read the memo as best he could, but truthfully, he had little grasp of its contents. It was written primarily in the bureaucratic legalese that was as prevalent forty years ago as it is today.

186

He flipped through the rest of the documents. There were maybe thirty-five or forty pages of similar sheets. Teddy tried to establish a thread, pull together a search string in what passed for his brain, all unsuccessfully. If you couldn't lift it, press it, fuck it, or beat it to death, Teddy Chrisman didn't know what to do with it.

He stood up and walked into the bedroom, carrying the documents at his side like an overdue homework assignment. He slapped them down, frustrated, on the bed and pulled out his wallet. In the section that held his folding money, a tiny slip of paper, dulled with age and body moisture, lay hidden. He unfolded the piece of paper to reveal a phone number, then picked up the phone next to what had been Pearl Bergeron's side of the bed.

"Hello?" he asked after a voice answered the phone. "Hey, this is Chrisman. Can you come over here? I think I've found something."

"I've filed a discovery motion," the gray-haired attorney in the pin-striped suit pronounced. "We should know what they've got officially in the next day or so. But I spoke with the district attorney on an informal basis, and while what they have is largely circumstantial, they can place you at the scene the night of the murder. And within a few hours of the murder, I'm afraid."

Charles Horn, the sixty-seven-year-old dean of New Orleans criminal lawyers, dropped his glasses down to the end of his nose and looked over them at his client.

"Frankly, Mr. Kwang, that scares the hell out of me. Especially since you've denied ever being at her apartment that night."

Andrew Kwang looked out the window of Carlton Smith's office into the bright Louisiana sun. His shirt was still clammy beneath his silk jacket; the heat seemed to penetrate all the way to his core. He was sick of New Orleans, tired of the heat, the overwhelmingly oppressive humidity, the sense that you were somehow trapped inside a rotting, decaying jungle that just happened to have a lot of concrete and grass growing in the middle of it.

Kwang wanted to go home, wherever home was.

He looked up slowly at the new attorney, then over to Carlton Smith behind his desk and then to the forever-rumpled Jack Lynch in the other visitor's chair.

"All right, gentlemen," he said slowly, his eyes dipping to the hunter-green carpet of the elderly Smith's office, "I was there."

He heard Lynch suck in a quick, deep breath behind him.

Charles Horn drew in a breath that was equally deep, but slower in coming. "Well," the man who would defend him against a murder charge said, "now that we've got that out of the way."

"Before we go any further," Carlton Smith interrupted, "I want to know if it represents any risk to Mr. Kwang to have Jack in on this conversation. Obviously, Mr. Kwang can say anything to his attorneys, but—"

"Who's paying him?" Horn demanded, looking up from his legal pad to peer once again over his eyeglasses.

"His first check came by way of the bank," Carlton answered, "but the money ultimately came from Kwang World Pictures."

"But you hired him?" Horn asked.

"Yes."

"Then he was hired as an operative by Mr. Kwang's attorney," Horn said. "We're covered, if you want him to stay."

Kwang looked at Carlton Smith, the obvious question on his face.

"I'd like to help, if I can," Lynch said.

"I can vouch for Mr. Lynch's discretion completely," Carlton Smith said.

Kwang turned and stared directly into the face of the man who, on the surface, had already brought him more bad luck than he'd ever had.

"Please stay, Mr. Lynch. I would appreciate your input in this matter."

Jack knew better than to break a smile. Nevertheless, he let a small nod of the head slip by.

"Back to business, gentlemen," Horn continued. "Mr. Kwang, tell me just what you were doing going to Pearl Bergeron's apartment that Friday night."

Marco Cerasini walked the two blocks from his car to Pearl Bergeron's apartment as quickly and as inconspicuously as possible. It wasn't that he had trouble finding a parking space—the usual French Quarter excuse for walking extra blocks—it was more that he didn't want his car anywhere near the place.

He pressed the buzzer. That overgrown, second-rate Schwarzenegger better bloody be here, he thought. They were both already in over their heads. If not for the cops finding a witness who saw

188

Kwang that night, their own two heads might be on the chopping block now.

Steps—hard, fast steps—banged down the stairway. Marco waited while Chrisman fumbled with the lock, opened the front door, then fiddled with the lock on the wrought-iron gate until he got it open.

"Hurry up," he hissed.

"I'm hurrying," Chrisman said, as he finally got the right key in the lock. The gate swung open and Marco stepped in. Chrisman shut the door behind him and locked it. The two stood there on the stairway leading up to the entrance foyer of the apartment.

Suddenly, Teddy threw his arms around Marco's shoulders and kissed him. Cerasini stiffened as the young bodybuilder's wet lips mashed his own. Teddy pulled back, a frown of disappointment on his face.

"I thought we weren't going to see each other for a while," Cerasini said, his voice low and threatening.

"I had to call you. I found something," Teddy explained.

"It better be important," Cerasini said.

The young man took Cerasini's hand, his grip intense and strong.

"C'mon."

The two men quickly climbed the hard wooden stairs to the thick carpet and plush furniture that had once belonged to Pearl. A layer of dust had settled over everything because the cleaning lady was no longer coming twice a week, but Cerasini wouldn't have noticed. Compared to his side of a shotgun duplex off South Claiborne Avenue, this was a rich lady's digs.

"So get me a drink and tell me what you've found," Cerasini said, his voice softening as he glanced around the apartment. "Preferably in that order."

"Here's what I found," Teddy said, handing Marco the envelope. "What you want? Wine spritzer?"

Marco took the envelope and sighed. "If that's all you got."

"Pearl had some vodka in the freezer."

"Stoli?" Marco asked, eyes brightening.

"I think so."

"Oh, good, it's probably as thick as mud. About two fingers in a martini glass, if she's got it."

Chrisman walked toward the kitchen. "Actually," he said over his shoulder, "Pearl don't got shit anymore."

"Yeah," Cerasini muttered, opening the envelope and pulling out the waxy sheets of paper. "Ain't that a fact."

By the time Teddy returned with the glass of chilled vodka, Cerasini was deep in thought. He read quickly, his eyes by turns opening wider, then closing to slits.

"So that's it . . ." he muttered.

Cerasini read for five more minutes, through fifteen or so pages of documents. Unlike Chrisman, he understood, with a blend of native intelligence and years of education combined with a lifetime of slinging bullshit, exactly what he was reading.

"Well," he said, as he placed the last sheet next to the untouched glass, "at least we finally know why Pearl Bergeron didn't want Kwang to put a studio up there."

Chrisman looked at his teacher, his friend, his sometime lover questioningly. "Yeah, I figured there was some reason Pearl had that stuff hidden. I figure it must be big stuff."

Marco laughed loudly, falling back on the couch and drawing his knees up to his belly. "Well, baby, you figured right."

"But what is it? I don't understand."

Cerasini slid deeper into the couch, giggling uncontrollably. "It's Governor Bergeron covering up a cover-up of a cover-up, on and on, all the way back to when you were a little boy!"

Marco got his breath back, then sat up on the couch, struggling to keep a straight face. He placed a hand on each of Teddy's knees and rubbed softly, lasciviously.

"And dear, sweet Pearl was trying to help keep it covered up, so her daddy and all his buddies wouldn't wind up on the fucking 'CBS Evening News' with fucking Dan Rather trying to ream them a new one.

"Chrisman, you gorilla tubesteak," Marco continued, grinning, taking Teddy's face in his hands and pulling it to within an inch of his own, "listen closely. You and I are two very rich sons of bitches."

Teddy's face brightened. "Oh," he drawled, "I don't get it."

As he felt Marco Cerasini fumbling for his zipper, Teddy Chrisman's face brightened even more.

25

LYNCH HEARD A NOISE IN THE OTHER ROOM. HE AWOKE IN AN INSTANT to find himself surrounded by darkness. He squinted, trying to adjust. He rolled over looking for the clock by his bed.

It wasn't there. The sheets were cold next to him. Where was he? Then he remembered. He was at her place. He shook his head, turned, looked to her side of the bed. Orange numbers glowed 3:52 in the blackness. He noticed that his head wasn't hurting. Then he remembered again: he hadn't had anything to drink the night before. The first night in years, as long as he could remember.

Her side of the bed was empty. It was dreadfully quiet. Had she left in the middle of the night? Lynch was up on his elbows now, straining to see more. The heavy drapes of the bedroom kept the streetlight's ambient shine out. Where was she?

"Lois?" he called out softly, the sound of his voice cutting through his consciousness. He was surprised to find himself so coherent at this time of the night.

No answer. "Lois?" he called out a bit louder.

He was pulling the covers from his right side when the door opened and a blaze of hallway light burst in.

"Ow," he muttered, squinting at the black form standing above him, surrounded by a bright corona of painful white.

"I'm sorry," she said, her voice sweet and low in the night. "I didn't mean to wake you up."

"You didn't," he said, reaching for her as she sat on the bed. "I just woke up. You were gone."

"I was getting dressed."

"Why so early?"

"Call's at five-thirty and it's almost an hour's drive out to Riverbend."

"Jesus, I forgot. You're making a movie today."

She rubbed her palm down his bare back. He brushed his hand against her leg. She was dressed already, in a rough pair of jeans and a workshirt.

"Go back to sleep," she said.

"I want to go with you."

"Are you sure?" she asked. "I know you said you wanted to, but I just figured you were trying to be nice."

"I was," he said. "But I also told Carlton Smith I'd be there. Several reporters have been invited and I'm getting to play P.R. flack."

"I hate that word," she said. "Why do you call yourself a flack?"

Lynch rubbed his head against her shirt. "What would you call it?"

Lois leaned down until the tips of her hair were dangling in his face. One caught the end of his nose, sending a violent tickling sensation deep into his face. He forced back a sneeze and brought his hand up to rub himself.

"If you're going to go, you better get up. But we're going to take two cars, right?"

Lynch pulled himself up on the bed and pushed his bare feet over the side and onto the floor. "That seems silly," he said. "Why don't we just go in the same car?"

She pulled away from him and stood up, standing over his naked body with her hands planted on her hips.

"No, I won't have that. I won't have the crew and Kwang and who the hell knows else gossiping about us. It's tough enough for a woman to make it in this business without everybody thinking she got her job by sleeping with somebody.

"Besides," she continued, her face breaking into a smile. "Four-teen-hour days on location are no place for the weak at heart. It's a pretty good bet you'll be ready to leave long before I do."

Lynch stood up and wrapped his arms around her. "Well, la-de-dah, Miss—excuse me, *Ms.*—hotshot filmmaker."

He felt her warmth next to him, her softness through the rough work clothes. "We got time to jump back in bed for a little while?"

She pushed him away. "No," she said. "It's work today. That's

192

all. Work. Nothing else. We're talking nose-to-the-grindstone stuff here."

"I get the point," he said, heading for the bathroom and a hot shower. It had been his experience over years of sexual frustration that cold showers were tremendously overrated. After all, he thought, why be freezing to death and aroused?

The sun was a good half hour away as Lynch followed Lois's car out River Road, still driving the rental with the bad air-conditioning. The insurance company had paid off the MG and given him two more days to find another car before cutting him off. He'd heard about a 1973 Fiat 124 Spyder with only eighty-six thousand miles on it out in Jefferson Parish with an asking price of twelve-hundred dollars, but he was still waiting for the guy to call him.

Lynch drove with the windows down, the wind whipping past him at sixty miles an hour in the semicool morning. Even with the windows cranked open, the first hints of the day's ensuing heat were approaching. Another scorcher was on the way.

As they left the stink of the city behind, the dank, heavy smell of the river filled his nostrils. His left arm hung bent over the door, his elbow out in the still, humid air of the thick night. Lois drove fast in front of him; he strained to keep up with her.

He lit a cigarette and fiddled with the radio. The AM static crackled and popped and spit out muffled voices first, then country music, then tacky commercials. Nothing of real interest. Lynch was looking for one of the religious programs. The howling of a screaming fundamentalist was just what he needed to keep going on so little sleep.

They drove for nearly an hour, the sun coming up directly behind them, the glare in Lynch's rearview mirror germinating a small headache until it occurred to him to twist the thing out of the way. They left River Road near LaPlace, crossed the Mississippi northwest of Norco and looped back through Reserve, with the sun in their eyes this time, on Louisiana 18, a two-lane battered state highway populated mostly by locals and huge, dirty tanker trucks heading back and forth to the refineries. Somewhere a few miles farther on, in a part of the state that even today was largely deserted, they began seeing the signs.

LOUISIANA POWER COMPANY the first sign read, and below that, centered, RIVERBEND NUCLEAR POWER FACILITY.

Lynch slowed the car as Lois, in front of him, began searching for the turnoff. It wasn't hard to find; as they turned a bend in the highway, the massive concrete cooling tower seemed to rise out of the swamps like a monster in an early 1960s Japanese nuclear-paranoia film. It dwarfed the other buildings easily, carelessly. It feared no evil, Lynch thought, for it was the biggest, meanest son of a bitch in the valley.

A chain-link fence ten feet high and topped by concertina wire snaked around the perimeter of the property. Lynch continued following Lois's car for perhaps another half mile, when she slowed to turn left.

A guardhouse and gate blocked their entrance. A hand-painted sign that read KWANG WORLD PICTURES had been nailed to the eaves of the small blockhouse. Lynch braked to a stop as the uniformed guard approached them. He went first to Lois, spoke a few words, checked his clipboard, then pointed down the road, with a twist of his wrist to indicate she should bear to the right.

Lynch rolled up to the guard after Lois had pulled away. "Yessir," the man said, leaning toward the car window.

"Jack Lynch. My name should be on your list."

The man fumbled with the clipboard, turning a page. "Cast or crew?" he asked.

"Neither. I'm the public relations coordinator."

"Oh, yeah, here you are. You're on the producer's list. Down this road until you see a split. Bear to the left and follow the signs to G Building. They'll be a security guard there. Just ask for directions to the office."

"Thanks," Lynch said. His voice was heavy with fatigue and smoke. He drove down the shell-and-gravel road, through the high grass and soft marsh that bordered either side, until he came to a split. He was surprised that the land was so undeveloped. Great clouds of white crushed-rock dust sprayed behind him as he drove toward a group of concrete buildings that seemed to be scattered randomly across the landscape.

A rectangular parking lot had been cut into the grass, with perhaps a dozen expensive cars slotted neatly together. Lynch squeezed in next to a silver Mercedes and got out. His feet crunched across the gravel as he walked to the building. He guessed that one of the first things Kwang would have done here would be some serious road mending.

Behind him, in a grove of trees a quarter of a mile away, he heard shrieking and the fluttering of wings as a flock of large birds took off away from the sun and the buildings. It was strangely quiet here, he thought. The towering gray-and-white concrete buildings rose out of the swampland, some of their bases still enshrouded in low-lying fog, giving the place an eerie feeling. He half expected some radioactive, albino alligator to come crawling up out of the bog with a knife in its teeth.

Lynch noticed for the first time that none of the buildings, as far as he could see, had windows. They were all concrete blockhouses, like those in the wartime pictures of the buildings he'd seen of the Manhattan Project facility.

The building immediately to his left had the letter *G* painted above the doorway. He opened the trunk of the car and took out a large cardboard box. Lynch had spent a good part of the last week preparing press kits for the days of shooting. There was a promotional brochure on Kwang World Pictures and neatly trimmed copies of both the interview with the *Picayune* and the local weekly entertainment tabloid, *Dos Gris.* He'd included as well a map of the facility, a schedule for the day, and an introductory letter from Kwang on company stationery, which, of course, Lynch had penned himself.

He walked to the building, balanced the box in one hand, and pulled the latch on the steel door with his free hand. It gave way and slowly opened, its heaviness assisted by a gas compressor at the top. The security guard at the desk inside was barely out of her teenage years, with a shiny complexion and the remnants of acne scars clear on her face. She looked uncomfortable in her polyester uniform, and nearly as sleepy as Lynch.

"Jack Lynch," he said, standing at the counter. Behind the young woman, a bank of television monitors showed monochrome views of different areas of the building and the outside area. The only thing the different views had in common was a complete lack of any living thing in motion.

This place is a freaking ghost town, he thought.

"Down the hall, sir, to your left. Room Fifteen. There's coffee and doughnuts set up and a producer's meeting set for five-fifteen." Lynch looked at the clock on the wall. He had ten minutes.

Inside the room, four other people in work clothes and two in suits stood around drinking the hot coffee, munching the sickeningly sweet doughnuts, smoking cigarettes until the room had a gray pallor to it.

He introduced himself around, then grabbed a Styrofoam cup and retired into a corner as quickly as possible. For a public relations executive, Lynch had discovered within himself a surprising distaste for small talk with strangers.

Promptly at five-fifteen, the door to the room opened and Miller Taylor walked in, followed by Kwang, Sheldon Taplinger, and an enormous man with a huge potbelly and a great shock of thinning blond hair hanging down in his face. He wore jeans and had a director's eyepiece on a lanyard around his neck.

"Gentlemen," Taylor announced from the middle of the room, "welcome to the first day of shooting at Kwang World Pictures' Riverbend Studio. We're glad you could make it. As you know, I'm Miller Taylor. This is Andrew Kwang. And the gentleman to my left is Jerry Hagan, the director of the promotional film we'll be shooting today."

"Good morning, people," Hagan boomed, in a voice that seemed to echo around inside his body as if it were an empty cavern.

"Mr. Lynch has prepared press kits for today. Sheldon Taplinger will be handing them out," Taylor continued. "The press will begin arriving here at about eight, with shooting to begin at nine. Right now, the shooting crew is preparing its equipment, the actors are being made up, and all other preparations are being made. The only thing I want to remind you of is that you must read the instructions inside the press kit that's being handed out now. Stay out of the areas indicated, and stay out of the crew and cast's way. That way, there won't be any problems."

"Yeah," the director interrupted. "That's the big one. I find anybody stepping into my field of view or getting in my way today, we're going to have you airlifted to the top of the cooling tower and dropped in. Where's this fellow Lynch?"

Lynch's head snapped up from the back of the room. He nodded acknowledgment and raised his right index finger.

"When the press gets here," the director's commanding voice continued, "I want them kept back. I hate reporters. They get in my way, I'll give them something to write about."

Lynch decided immediately that he would comply with the director's wishes. He had no desire to tangle with him on as little sleep as he'd had. Or at any other time.

196

"Until the press arrives," Taylor said—Lynch raised an eyebrow and his attention level at the same time—"you gentlemen can have the run of the facility within the bounds described in your packages. Have a good one. See me with any questions. That's all for now."

Lynch read the rest of the information in the package quickly. As he finished the last page, he realized he was alone in the room. He'd wanted to talk briefly to Kwang. Nothing important, really. He just felt the need to say hello.

Instead, he walked down the hall and out into the heavy, rapidly warming air. A hundred yards or so ahead of him, Kwang and Taylor were walking with the director and another group of men. He decided to follow at a distance, just to get a feel for the place and slowly catch up to them.

The shells crunched beneath his feet. As they neared the center of the complex, the number and density of the buildings increased. They were identified only by letter, and though they were of different sizes, each had the same design.

The first reporters arrived shortly after eight, and for the next four hours Lynch acted as a guide while running interference with the journalists who'd really showed up only on the hope of getting an interview with Kwang. He handled them skillfully, his years as a reporter giving him just the insight necessary to head them off. He controlled them, manipulated them, channeled them, until by lunchtime the ones who had stayed were as docile as sheep.

In a large building that was literally in the shadow of the cooling tower, a catering crew served up shrimp and crab, steaks, and fresh gumbo for the guests and press. Lynch discovered that he'd worked up quite an appetite, as well as a pretty good sweat, walking around the facility in the hot sun. There had been little in the way of real activity that anyone could see. Most of the reporters wondered when the action would start, unaware that working on a film crew was largely the same as being in the military. Most of the time, you waited for something to happen.

He hadn't seen Lois. The crew's lunch had been catered in another building. After lunch, the press would be routed over to an actual shooting, and Lynch would be able to see her at work.

In fact, according to the schedule he'd been handed that morning, Kwang himself was to appear in the film to talk about the new facility. The early part of the promotional film would be a simulation of a soundstage shoot, hence the need for actors. But after lunch, the actors would be done, Kwang would do his lines, then the rest of the day would be taken up shooting stock shots of the studio, including, the printout noted, some aerial shots.

He was excited at the prospect of seeing Lois Finlayson work, his curiosity about the process of filmmaking heightened by his personal interest in her. Since they'd become lovers, he'd felt alive again; a prospect that, when he was honest with himself, scared the hell out of him.

"Mr. Lynch," a voice called. "Over here."

Lynch walked across the lot to the building labeled *R*. A young woman with a clipboard and a pencil in one hand and a spare tucked behind her ear crossed to meet him.

"Mr. Hagan says filming starts in ten minutes. If your reporters want to see the shoot, they better get over there now."

Lynch walked back across to the half-dozen reporters and photographers who remained. Two of the local television stations had sent crews earlier, but they were long gone, as were the reporters who were working on tight deadlines. A free-lance video cameraman who had, at the last minute, managed to worm a pass out of somebody— Lynch wondered who—was the only one with a television camera left.

He gathered the group together, then led them about a quarter-mile to the main reactor building. This was the largest building besides the cooling tower itself, the primary building where the entire facility was controlled. Lynch had no idea what usually went on inside a main reactor building; his ignorance of nuclear power was rivaled only by his lack of interest. But he was impressed by the sprawling building, with its maze of control rooms and panels and underground tunnels. Lynch had checked out the building earlier that morning, briefly, so he knew where the filming was to take place.

Just inside the building, Lynch spotted Miller Taylor standing in front of a doorway with a pad of paper in his hand. He was talking to Teddy Chrisman, who still wore traces of makeup, khaki pleated pants, and a white Izod LaCoste shirt that could have been a size or two too small for him. His chest muscles strained against the fabric.

Lynch wondered how Teddy could have gotten a job on the shoot, given the circumstances. He also wondered who the man was standing next to him, the thin man with the curly, jet black hair and the distinct five o'clock shadow. Italian, Lynch thought, but who?

198

A crowd gathered in the main control room, which was still full of equipment and panels and massive electronic control boards from the days when the plant was simply a nuclear plant, in addition to the jam of lights, deflectors, mike booms, and cables that now constituted a movie set. The people of Louisiana, Lynch remembered, through their taxes and their underwriting of what were now practically worthless bonds, had paid for all this stuff. If they knew how it had been left to rot, then sold to someone for approximately ten cents on the dollar, they'd probably want to see someone executed.

Then again, maybe not, he thought. Sometimes people just didn't give a damn.

"Your attention, please!" Lynch's thoughts were interrupted by the thunder of the director's voice. "I'm Jerry Hagan and I'm the director on this set. I'd like to welcome our visitors to the set, especially the press, and let you know that the crew has set aside an area where you may watch the shooting. Please stay inside that area and remain very quiet. Thanks a lot. Enjoy yourselves."

Andrew Kwang appeared to the right of the set, in a freshly pressed suit and makeup. Lynch watched him out of the corner of his eye while straining to see Lois through the crowded room. He had neither seen nor spoken to her all day. He bent down to look between two people who'd just walked away from each other.

There she was. Her hair hung limply down her back. She sat in a chair on a dolly, the camera set in front of her. Sweat showed through her shirt. None of the shooting had been outside yet, but she'd hauled and set up equipment with the rest of the crew, Lynch was sure. He could tell from her movements that she was tired. He felt bad; he should have gone home last night and not kept her up so late.

About five minutes later, the director yelled "Action!" Kwang was standing with his back to the largest, most complicated looking panel of gauges, knobs, and switches. It looked as high-tech as the space shuttle, Lynch thought, and would be impressive in a promotional film.

He couldn't hear what Kwang was saying, but knew that it would be a calm, probably ad-libbed speech about the studio, its facilities, and his plans for the future.

Hagan yelled "Cut" at an appropriate place, then leaned down and whispered to Lois. She turned some knobs on the camera, spoke some instructions to her assistant, then bent back down to the camera's eyepiece. After two more takes, Hagan yelled, "Great, Mr. Kwang, that's wonderful!" Then he looked across the room and yelled, "Print it."

Lois punched a few more buttons, none of which Lynch understood, then removed the film magazine and gave it to her assistant. The assistant deferentially handed her what Lynch assumed was a fresh film magazine, then stood by as she loaded it quickly and easily. The crew began moving around, shutting down lights, hauling cables and equipment; their day had been a beehive of manic activity punctuated by long periods of dull waiting.

Lynch felt a tap on his back. He turned to face a young woman reporter who, he remembered, was working her first job out of college. It's the new ones trying to make a mark for themselves, Lynch knew, who usually stayed the longest on what were essentially fluff feature pieces like this one. It wouldn't take her long to learn that this kind of story had no hard news value whatsoever and was hardly worth the six hours she'd already spent on it today.

"What's next?" she asked.

"Now we go outside." Lynch smiled at her. "Back out into the heat. We're doing one more shot with Mr. Kwang, then stock shots, and sometime around three, I believe, the helicopter is supposed to arrive for the aerial shots."

"Can I go on the helicopter with the film crew?" the woman asked eagerly. Lynch tried unsuccessfully to remember her name. It hadn't registered when she introduced herself that morning.

"I'll be glad to check," he lied amiably, "but I doubt that will be possible."

The woman turned away, disappointed. Lynch grinned and shook his head. He pushed his way through a crowd of technicians as unobtrusively as possible until he was right behind Lois.

"Ms. Finlayson," he said, "how nice to see you again."

She turned to him. "Well, Mr. Lynch, how are you? Enjoying the filming?"

"I'd enjoy this day a whole lot more if I were lying in bed next to you," he whispered.

"I couldn't agree with you more," she laughed. "It's very hot outside, and the worst is yet to come."

"You look exhausted," he said, his voice at a normal level.

She looked around, figured there was no one within earshot. "I am. I didn't get a whole lot of sleep last night."

200

"I'm really impressed with all this."

"Just another day at the office. What I'm dreading is the next series outside. I'm on the Steadicam, doing a walk-and-talk with Kwang around the grounds." Her voice trailed off. "It's got to be ninety-five out there."

"Can't you tell them you're too tired?"

The edges of her mouth turned upward in a weak approximation of a smirk. "Yeah, sure. They'll understand. It only costs about five grand an hour to keep the crew going. I'm sure Hagan will cut me some slack."

"How about I give you the longest back rub you've ever had tonight?"

She reached down and picked up a tool tray. "Sure, if I can stay awake. Listen, I got to go now."

"See you later," he said, then he lowered his voice. "I wish I could kiss you."

"Later."

A half-hour in the hot sun later, Lynch stood, jacket off, shirt wringing wet, sleeves rolled up, watching as Lois pulled the scene off beautifully. Kwang, in the same suit, still as pressed as a board, somehow without a drop of sweat anywhere on him, marched through the scene in three takes.

Looking like a cross between a robot and a high-tech, multi-armed Hindu goddess, Lois walked ahead of Kwang, the camera out to her side and pointed behind her. Lois's head was bent down, studying the monitor. She kept her balance beautifully, as graceful as a dancer, as poised as a veteran actor. Lynch watched in awe as she enacted before him what he'd always considered the definition of a professional: somebody who took the toughest jobs and made them look easy. He was proud of her.

As the crew broke the set, Lynch managed to get a chance to maneuver himself close to her again. It was only when he got to within a few feet of her and she pulled off the black vest to reveal a workshirt soaked through with sweat, that he realized what a hellish time she'd had with the scene.

"You okay?" he asked.

She didn't answer. She fastened the vest to its mount and walked over to the shade of a parked Winnebago, then sat in the grass and leaned against the hot metal, her head hung between her knees, her arms wrapped loosely around her legs.

201

"Can I get you something?" Lynch asked. He was trying to maintain a little detachment here when, in fact, he was terribly worried about her. "You need some water or something. You're not careful, you'll have a heat stroke."

"I'm okay," she said, raising her head. There were large circles under her eyes and her brown hair was matted with sweat. "I'll get something in a minute."

The assistant director, the woman with the clipboard who had talked to Jack earlier that morning, approached them.

"Ms. Finlayson, one of the crew is bringing you some ice water."

"Great, thanks, Ricky."

She reached up and took Jack's hand. He pulled her to her feet. "I've got to go," she said. "We've still got the ground stock shots to shoot."

"This is too much," Lynch said. "They can't expect you to work like this in this heat."

"Making movies is hard work, babe," she said. "Even little ones like this."

The sun seemed now to burn off the sides of the concrete buildings like flame off a deflector. Waves of heated air danced and wavered above the gravel. Dust hung in the air like the residue of a fire.

"Why in the hell would anybody want to see this place on film in the first place?" Lynch snapped, frustrated and tired himself.

"Just business, Jack. Chill out," she said as she walked away from him, back to her equipment.

"I wish I could," he muttered. He headed back to the building where the last of the reporters would be waiting in line for cold drinks and soaking up the frigid air of the heavily air-conditioned buildings.

Two hours later, the stock shots were completed. Lynch noticed his forehead and his arms were turning red. They were all going to suffer tonight for their day in the sun. But the day was nearly over; it had to be. The only shots remaining were the aerial ones, then cleanup. Fourteen-hour shooting days, he'd been told, were standard on a movie set.

Lynch was struggling through small talk with the four reporters who were left. The freelance video cameraman had remained as well, still lugging his broadcast-quality Betacam around as if it were light

202

as a loaf of bread. Behind the group, from the direction of the river, they heard the chopping noise of blades splitting the air and the high-pitched whine of an engine far above them.

"That must be the helicopter," Lynch said. He pulled out his map of the Riverbend Studio and located the helipad. It was a couple hundred yards down from where they stood, near where the river took its long, lazy bend.

"Anyone want to go watch this?" he asked.

"Sure," the cameraman said. "I could use a shot of a chopper."

"Yeah, let's go," the novice reporter said, some eagerness taken out of her voice by the brutal heat. "It beats standing around here."

The ten-minute walk felt like an hour. By the time they got to the helipad, the chopper, a slick Bell Jet Ranger in a metallic-blue-and-silver paint scheme, was on final. The pilot skillfully maneuvered the helicopter to within a few feet of the pad, dust and gravel flying out for yards around, then settled it down with the gentleness of a mother's nudge. The screaming of the engines, even at idle as the helicopter blades wound down, drowned out all conversation and most thought. Finally, the pilot cut the engines and the noise settled into a combination of turbos winding down and the slowing whop-whop-whop of the blades as they came to a halt.

When the chopper was quiet, the technical crew gathered around it, preparing to load equipment and film. The pilot got out of the aircraft and walked over to the director. The two men leaned over a map of the area, their heads close together, wrapped in intense conversation.

Lynch made small talk out of the side of his mouth, by this time bored to death with the few reporters who'd stayed and wishing they would all leave so he could. His real attention again was focused on Lois, as she carried a camera up to the helipad, then stopped.

Her assistant opened the side door of the Jet Ranger for her, then stepped aside as she placed the camera inside the helicopter. She stood there for a second, half in and half out of the aircraft, then stood straight up quickly. Her expression was grim and angry; even from a distance, Lynch could see she was upset.

"Excuse me, please," Lynch said quickly to the nattering woman standing next to him. "I'll be right back."

He disengaged himself from the crowd and walked toward the table where the director and the pilot were poring over charts and making notes. Lois walked quickly up to the group and angrily shoved aside a crew member who happened to find himself in her way.

"Goddammit," Lynch heard her say. "There's no Tyler mount in the helicopter!"

The director shot straight up. "What the hell you mean, no Tyler mount in the helicopter?"

"Just what I said," Lois snapped, her hands out to her sides in frustration. "There's no mount in the chopper. No place to put the camera."

Hagan grabbed the pilot's lapels. "Okay, Bruce, what happened?"

"Mr. Hagan," the pilot stammered. "Connie had me take it out. She said someone from your office called and said you wouldn't need it. Said you were going to go with a Steadicam."

"Jesus Christ!" the director roared. "What idiot did that?"

"Oh, that's just great!" Lois yelled, anger and weariness in her voice. It was obvious to Lynch that the whole crew was exhausted, nerves were frayed, tensions high and climbing.

Hagan grabbed an assistant and practically yanked the man off his feet. "Find out who called the charter service this morning. I want somebody's head, dammit! Now!"

The hapless gofer disappeared as quickly as possible.

Miller Taylor walked up to Lynch. "What's wrong?" he asked.

"Something about a Tyler mount not being in the helicopter?"

"Oh shit," Taylor sighed, raising his hand and massaging his forehead. "Just what we need."

"What's a Tyler mount?" Lynch asked.

"It's a standard camera mount for a helicopter. Used all over. I don't know how it works, but I know if you ain't got one, you're going to have a rough time getting decent shots out of a chopper."

"The pilot said something about Lois going up with the Steadicam."

"Yeah," Taylor said, bringing his head up and rubbing his eyes, "yeah. You can do that. It's hell on the camera operator, though. I tell you, that's one tough little lady over there. She's already done as much work in one day as most men do in a week."

The yelling over, the director, pilot, and Lois were struggling for a way to get the shots to work. Finally, Lois separated from the group and walked over to Jack and Taylor. The pilot headed over to the helicopter and pulled out a small toolbox from under the pilot's seat.

"What's going on?"

"I'm going up with the Steadicam," Lois said, her voice barely audible. "Man, what a long day."

"No shit, babe," Taylor said, putting his arms around her shoulder. "C'mon, you can do it. Think how good this is going to look to Kwang."

She looked at Jack, smiled wanly, then over at Taylor. "Yeah, sure. Listen, I've got to go get my gear."

The pilot asked for a volunteer to help him remove the backseat from the helicopter. Teddy Chrisman stepped forward, along with his dark-haired friend, and the three men set to work.

Forty-five minutes later, Lynch was backing away from the helicopter with the rest of the crowd as the engines began roaring with their ever-increasing pitch. The screaming whine filled all ears, again rendering conversation impossible. The side door of the chopper had been slid shut, but Lynch caught a glimpse of Lois on the floor, in the back, strapped into the Steadicam, surrounded by equipment, held in by a safety harness.

He waved. She smiled back weakly.

The blades changed angles, grabbing the air and lifting the chopper off the pad and into the sky. The young woman tabloid reporter pulled on Lynch's shirtsleeve.

"What's the plan?"

"They'll climb about two thousand feet," he answered, "then fly about a half-mile away for a long shot. Then they'll come in for a close-up of the tower itself, where the underwater soundstage will be built."

"How long?"

"I don't know. I doubt very long. The magazines in those cameras only hold four minutes of film and I'm not sure she can change magazines on board the helicopter."

The young woman craned her head, her flattened hand held to her forehead to shield her eyes, and stared toward the sun.

"I really don't know," Lynch said again, squinting into the sun himself.

The chopper climbed slowly in the hot, thin air, then picked up speed as it approached altitude and headed away from the cooling tower. The sound of the engines dissipated into a soft, receding whine. Across the river, Lynch strained to watch as the chopper hovered motionless and the back door slid open on its rails.

He could see her in the distance, on her knees in the back of the helicopter, weighted down with the rig. She finished the long shot, then reached away from the camera with her right arm and pulled the door shut as the copter began moving back toward the plant.

The noise grew again, but not enough that Lynch couldn't hear Hagan shouting instructions into a walkie-talkie.

"Okay, Lois, looking good!" he yelled. "Now bring us in for a close flyby, around the tower just a few feet off it. Get as close as you can and still keep the whole shot in frame! Then it's Miller time, baby!"

The chopper banked to the right and crossed the river quickly on a close approach to the tower. The front part lifted up slightly as it slowed, an airborne horse being reined to a stop. The crowd below craned necks, shielded eyes from the sun, and hoped to get some of the breeze from the helicopter's whirling blades.

The door slid open again, with Lois plainly visible. She pulled her windblown hair behind her and tucked it under the back of the vest, then rested her hands on the Steadicam. As the pilot manipulated the controls of the chopper to slide it by the tower at just the right angle, she began filming.

The chopper gathered speed and began a slow, banking descent. The drone of the engine became louder. All eyes focused upward as the helicopter expertly and quickly slipped by the tower, barely fifteen hundred feet above their heads, and began climbing to set up for another approach.

"Oh, that sun hurts my eyes," the reporter complained. "I think I'm getting a sunburn."

"Yeah," the videocamera operator behind Lynch said. "This camera's almost too hot to touch. I think I'm going to shut her down and call it a day."

Lynch stared at the helicopter as it flew levelly and slowly toward the top of the tower, where Lois would get her straight shot right down into the gaping concrete mouth.

"Listen," he said, dropping his hand from his eyes and turning around. The camera operator had eased the Betacam down from his shoulders and was holding it only a few inches off the ground. "I'd like to thank you for being here," he said in his smoothest P.R. tones, "let you know you're welcome back any—"

His sentence was interrupted by a shrill, horrible scream from the young reporter. Lynch, in his heat- and fatigue-fogged brain, let loose a curse. His ears hurt. He stared ahead as the videocam operator jerked his head up with his mouth open, then yanked the camera back to his shoulder.

Lynch whipped around to see what everyone was looking at. Fifty arms were pointed straight up, mouths hanging open, screams and groans breaking loose from constricted throats. He felt a terrible, sharp, stabbing pain in his chest as he stared in horror toward the top of the tower.

Lois Finlayson hung out of the helicopter, legs dangling helplessly in midair, the weight of the camera rig still on her back, pulling her down, as she held onto the one thin safety strap that was the only thing keeping her from disappearing into death down the throat of the tower.

26

LYNCH BARKED AN OBSCENITY AND BOLTED FOR THE HELIPAD. HE HAD no conscious thought of action; indeed, there was nothing he could do. So he ran straight for the place he thought she'd be when the chopper got down.

If she could hang on that long.

He craned his neck upward as he ran. The pilot seemed to be lowering the massive helicopter slowly, as if nothing unusual were going on, no tiny woman holding herself and sixty pounds of camera equipment by a strap so thin it was barely visible from the ground.

Off to the left, a couple of hundred yards away, the vast expanse of concrete tower reached into the sky. A tiny staircase ran from the base, around the circumference of the cone, rising in a shallow spiral all the way to the top. Perhaps, Lynch thought in desperation, the pilot could edge in close to the tower stairs and put her off there.

No, too close to the tower. A gust of wind would blow the helicopter into it. . . .

Damn you, Lynch's mind raced along with his feet, *hurry up!* And he thought, in the split seconds between footsteps, that if her grip gave way and she fell, he'd strangle the guy flying that thing and take about an hour to do it.

Lynch was the first to get to the concrete pad, his heart pounding, his middle-aged smoker's lungs snatching desperately at gulps of air. He was directly under the helicopter now, as it settled down toward the ground. He bent his head back as far as it would go.

She was hanging on, just barely, but still there, kicking her legs toward the skids of the aircraft, trying to get a foothold to support some of her weight. She swung out, the Steadicam sled and the camera flopping around behind her, and touched the skid with her right foot. It held for a second, then gave way, her body swinging like a pendulum as the helicopter continued downward for what seemed like an eternity.

"Hold on!" Lynch yelled as loudly as he could, in spite of a dim recognition that there was no way she could hear him. Lynch heard the pounding of footsteps and yells behind him, over the roar of the chopper, and looked over his shoulders to see the crowd surging toward him.

"Back up!" a voice yelled. Lynch turned.

"We've got to catch her!" he yelled. "If she lets go at the last minute!"

"Be careful!" someone else yelled.

Jerry Hagan jumped up on the pad next to him. He held the walkie-talkie in one hand and was waving frantically with the other. "C'mon," he yelled into the radio. "Bring her down."

"Why's he coming down so goddamn slow?" Lynch yelled. The blast of the rotors was tearing at his face now, blowing tears across his cheeks and instantly drying them.

"I don't know," Hagan yelled back.

Lynch looked up. The aircraft was barely fifty feet above them now. Lois still kicked and clawed with her feet at the sled, but her grip looked firm.

Only a few more seconds, Lynch thought. For God's sake, hold on.

Her feet were right above him now; Lynch jumped up, as the helicopter continued settling even more slowly now, and brushed the bottom of her running shoe with his hand. The helicopter settled another foot. Hagan and Lynch had a leg in each arm now. They pulled her body outward at an angle, away from the body of the aircraft now, so that the chopper could put down on the pad without crushing her legs under it.

The roar of the turbine engine changed pitch, and the rotors shifted to grab less air. Lynch strained to hold on to her, dodging the camera and equipment as it swung crazily about.

The chopper skids touched the concrete, and the pilot pulled power immediately. The engine went silent as the spinning rotors buffeted them with a few final blasts of air.

Lynch opened his eyes, which he hadn't realized he'd shut, and

209

tried to focus. His face was flushed, and his first heart attack felt like it was knocking on the door to his chest cavity.

But Lois was alive.

He could feel her shaking, her muscles still locked tight in her legs. He set her down gently on the pad. He heard a noise, turned, and realized the crowd behind them was cheering.

Lynch pulled himself up and over the edge of the open door. He caught a glimpse of Lois's face and felt, for a moment, as if he were going to break out crying.

Her jaw was locked tight as a vault, her teeth bared, her lips pulled back as if in an awful death. Her face was frozen, but her eyes were alive, darting back and forth, unable to comprehend what had happened to her.

"My God," he yelled as the rotors quieted down. "Are you all right? Lois!"

She couldn't move. Every muscle, every ligament, every nerve in her body was locked down tight. Lynch grabbed her hands on the blue nylon seatbelt strap. Her knuckles were bone white under her skin, her fingers still clamped onto the belt.

"Let go, baby," he said, trying to make his voice as soothing as possible. "Let go. You're okay now."

He pulled at her fingers. It was like trying to pull a padlock off a door.

"You've got to let go, Lois," he said. "Please."

Something in her eyes changed. She looked up and seemed to recognize him. Her lips relaxed; her mouth closed for a moment.

"I can't," she gasped. "They're stuck."

"Be careful," Hagan said. "You'll break her fingers."

Lynch shifted himself into a standing position. He carefully stuck two of his fingers under one of hers, then pulled as gently as possible. It was like prying a stubborn lid off a jar. Finally, one finger gave way, and Lynch could see something red under her hand and all over the belt.

Blood.

She had held onto the rough belt so tightly that she'd stripped skin off her palm as she fell out of the helicopter.

Lynch winced. When she got feeling back in her hand, that was really going to hurt.

He carefully rubbed her hands to loosen them, then pried her fingers from the belt. Her hands were still frozen, like claws, in

210

midair. He pulled her arms down into his lap and began rubbing them.

Behind them, a pickup truck pulled up. The driver turned and backed it toward the helipad. In the bed of the truck, an unrolled mat lay waiting.

Lois stared wide-eyed at Jack. "You're okay," he whispered. "You're okay."

She began to shake hard suddenly, all over. Lynch felt something wet on her arms and pulled them up; the backs of her forearms were scraped and bleeding where she'd gone over the side of the chopper.

"I'm co-co-cold," she stammered, her teeth chattering.

"She's heatstroking, going into shock," Hagan said. "We better get her inside fast."

Two crewmen approached. Lynch motioned them out of the way. Hagan reached down and removed the bulky camera from the sled, then unhooked the sled from the vest.

"My camera," Lois whispered, as if the effort to say anything else were too much. Her eyes were half-closed.

Jack peeled the Velcro cummerbund apart, then unhooked the rest of the jet-black vest. He pulled it open; her chest was soaked with sweat.

Together, he and Hagan gingerly lifted her out of the vest and onto the bed of the pickup truck. The pilot was standing next to the truck. Lynch spotted him and a sudden flash of rage shot from him before he could stop it.

"You son of a bitch!" he screamed. He jumped down from the truck and grabbed the guy's lapels. "What took you so long to get her down?"

The pilot's eyes darkened and he placed a hand on each of Lynch's. "If I'd come down any faster, I would have jerked her loose when I slowed for final. She'd have fallen the last couple of hundred feet.

"And if you don't want both your arms broken," he continued, "you'd better let go of me."

Lynch's hands relaxed, his expression softening as he loosened his grip on the pilot's shirt. "Sorry. I didn't know."

"Forget it," he said. "Get her over to the infirmary. I believe that's the bravest lady I've ever met."

The driver started the truck, then kicked it into gear. Lynch climbed aboard and the truck bounced over the rough gravel road all the way across the complex to a building marked with a red cross. Lynch sat cross-legged in the bed of the truck, cradling her head in his lap, whispering to her to hold on. She lay quietly, smiled at him for a moment, then seemed almost to drift in and out of sleep.

"There's a nurse back at the infirmary," Hagan said from the back of the truck. "Kwang requires it at every shoot, even the nonunion ones."

The nurse was outside the building waiting for them. She was an older woman, a tough local who'd seen everything from gunshots to car wrecks to degloving injuries at drilling sites. She looked into the bed of the pickup.

"Inside," she ordered. "Now."

The two men lifted Lois and carefully eased her to the edge of the truckbed. Then Lynch, with strength he didn't know he had left, lifted her and carried her inside like a child. Awake but drowsy, she nestled her head in the crook of his neck.

An examining room opened off one side of the hall. The nurse stood at the entrance, holding the door open.

"Put her on the table." Lynch painstakingly set her on the padded table. "Now get out," the nurse instructed.

"Can I stay?" Lynch asked, trying not to plead.

"Out," the woman barked.

"Will you need a doctor?" Lynch asked again as he backed out of the room.

"I'll *tell* you if I need a doctor. Now get out of here."

Lynch walked back outside the room. He felt nauseated, exhausted, chilled himself. He'd been out in the sun too long. His strength, his reserves were sapped. He had nothing left to give anyone, could feel nothing save his own relief that Lois Finlayson was still alive.

Hagan stood next to the fountain, splashing cold water on his face. He stood up, got a look at Lynch.

"You look gray as a channel cat, boy," he said in the softest voice he'd used all day. "Get over here and splash some water on your face."

The thought was a welcome one. Lynch walked over, and as Hagan held the handle for him, he laid his head in the cold metal of the water fountain and let the icy water pour over him.

"Damn, boy," Hagan said, the boom returning to his voice. "I

212

ain't never seen anybody react to anything like you did to that little girl almost getting herself killed. You her boyfriend or what?"

Lynch stood up, not bothering to wipe the dripping water from his face. His eyes narrowed. He barely knew this man, let alone trusted him.

"Why do you care?"

Hagan smiled, then broke into a laugh. "Damn, son, you have got it bad."

Lynch realized they were alone in the waiting room. He walked over, sat down on the couch and put his head back. It was as if someone had punctured his inner tube and all the air had escaped from him at last.

The door opened. Andrew Kwang stepped in quickly, a light sheen of perspiration now visible even on him, with a panting Sheldon Taplinger lugging the inevitable overstuffed briefcase behind.

"I heard what happened," Kwang said, concerned. "Is the young woman going to be all right?"

Lynch stood up. "She's in with the nurse. I don't know—"

"Aw, hell, Mr. Kwang," Hagan said. "She'll be fine. To be so small, she's one tough lady. I'll say that for her. One tough lady . . ."

"What happened?" Kwang said, his voice stern and directed at Lynch.

"I don't know. She was in the helicopter and suddenly she fell out of it. There was no one in the back with her to help pull her in. The pilot got down as quickly as he could."

"Why was she up there with that apparatus? I understand a Tyler mount was ordered."

"Somebody canceled it," Hagan said. "We decided to go with the Steadicam."

Kwang turned to Hagan, who stood perhaps a foot taller than his boss. Kwang looked up at the director as if he didn't give a rat's rusty goddamn how big the other man was.

"I will not have lives risked on my sets," he said. "That scene could have waited until the Tyler mount could be secured."

"Not and stay within budget we couldn't have—"

"Budgets are secondary, you idiot," Kwang said, his voice low. He was not about to scream and yell. His natural reluctance to humiliate a subordinate, however, was overshadowed by his anger. "I won't have anyone killed on my set."

213

Kwang turned away from the man. "That's the last thing I need."

Oh, Lynch thought, the last thing *you* need. Forget there was a woman lying in the back room who was nearly killed by both altitude and fright. The last thing *you* need.

Lynch suppressed the urge to explode.

The men heard the sound of a car approaching at high speed. The noise outside became louder as the car got closer. Hagan and Lynch stared at each other, unspeaking, as the car outside locked its brakes at the last minute. The sound of gravel splattering off the concrete walls filled the room.

The door burst open and the pilot came in, followed a half-step behind by Miller Taylor and the young woman reporter.

"All right, I told you there wasn't anything wrong with my bird!" The pilot held a blue strap—half of a seat belt that he'd unbolted from the floor—in his left hand.

"Look at this," he said, holding it out toward Lynch. "Just look at this." The man was nearly in tears.

Kwang took the belt from him. "What am I looking at?"

The pilot yanked the belt back, unaware that the man in front of him was one of the top independent film producers in the world.

"Look at it," he pleaded. "Look at that end."

He held the belt up. The end of it was frayed, like a ripped piece of nylon, but only for about quarter of an inch. The rest of the end had been sheared off neatly, without shredding any of the fibers.

"See," the pilot said. "The belt didn't give way. Somebody cut it."

Lynch felt light-headed, the way he had the last time he'd had laughing gas at the dentist's office. The smell of alcohol filled his nostrils, his head spun. His peripheral vision faded into a maze of sparkles and stars, and he felt his heart beating in his ears.

"Somebody tried to kill that girl," the pilot said.

And suddenly, as if it were yesterday, Lynch flashed on the image of Sally lying in the parking lot that dark night when her blood had run down the asphalt until she was dead. He had helplessly crawled next to her, laid an arm across her, felt somewhere in the black pool of his unconsciousness that her life was slipping away.

The pilot spoke again, this time from the far end of a long, dark tunnel, a tunnel whose end Lynch could barely see because it was closing off so fast. A fierce whooshing sound filled his ears, and the voices around him grew distant and far away. He felt himself sway back and forth, then hands were on him, and he let go of everything.

Maud Pelletier was so bored she simply couldn't take it any more. Jack was out at the Riverbend Studio all day and the phone hadn't rung once.

It was an easy job, and Jack was good to work for when he could afford to sign the paychecks. But she didn't see how the boy was going to be able to do that much longer. Kwang was still his only client, and Jack didn't seem that concerned about getting any more. The retainer Kwang had paid was dribbling away fast. Maud figured privately that he had another three weeks, maybe a month if he were lucky, before he had to shut down the office.

Thank God, she thought, the boy hasn't got any children.

Maud was so bored, in fact, that she'd gone home at lunchtime, picked up her small portable television set, and lugged it back to the office on the streetcar. She'd sweated like a linebacker carrying the damn thing in the heat, but it beat sitting there in the silence. She knew Jack wouldn't be back, and she'd already read every *Reader's Digest* and *National Enquirer* she could lay her hands on. She had to do something or she was going to go nuts.

When she got back to the office, the red light on the answering machine was a solid, unblinking red. No messages.

"Figures," she said out loud to the empty office.

There was a new soap opera on that had started just the week before, a blue-collar soap called "Life's Hard Sweetness." None of this crap about some yuppie doctor or lawyer worrying about whether his wife really loves the new BMW he bought her, and is she having an affair with his business partner, and all that. There were real people, oil drillers and 7-Eleven cashiers and gas station attendants and people who had to work a second night job at the Winn-Dixie to make ends meet. People she could identify with. People who didn't worry so much about their husbands having affairs as they did their husbands coming home drunk with loving on their minds.

Maud lifted the television up onto her desk, then pulled an extension cord out of the bottom desk drawer. She wound the cord between the two visitor's chairs and over to the wall.

The old black-and-white came to life, its bent antenna struggling to pull the signal inside the office building. Maud fiddled with it, trying the antenna in every position possible until she could finally see what looked like a picture.

The sound was good, though, and she could follow what was going on. In the show, as far as Maud could tell, a trucker whose name was Vince had gotten home from a two-week road trip. He wanted to stay home with his wife that night, have a few cold ones and grill some steaks, but it was her bowling night and her team was up for the league championship. Maud bent over in her chair, pulled her knees up to her chest, and watched intently as the engrossing story unfolded.

The damn phone rang.

Vince had his wife wrapped in his arms. He was about to kiss her. The music was rising.

The damn phone rang again.

"Oh, heck," Maud said, reaching over to turn the sound down. She picked up the phone.

"Lynch and Associates, Public Relations. May I help you?"

"Maud?"

"Yes."

"This is Carrie, over at Carlton Smith's office. You guys got a fax waiting over here."

Maud stared at the TV. Boy, these soaps were getting risqué. "Okay, Carrie. I'll pick it up in about an hour."

The woman on the other end sounded irritated.

"Maud, I really wish you'd come pick it up now. After all, you guys shouldn't be using our fax anyway."

"Mr. Smith said it was okay," Maud said defensively.

"For that one call. He didn't say make a habit out of it."

"All right," Maud sighed. "I'm on my way."

Maud hung up the phone, reached over and turned off the television. "Stinker," she whispered.

She didn't have cab fare and the streetcar was nowhere in sight. Maud set out walking. Same on the way back: no sign of the trolley. By the time she returned to the office, she was soaking wet. And all for a silly fax from the newspaper friend of Jack's out in Los Angeles. Another article on Harry McMillan's death. A short one, in fact, just on the funeral. Hardly worth the walk.

Maud got back to the office in time to catch "The Love Connection." The phone didn't ring again for the rest of the day.

27

SHE RATTLED ON ENDLESSLY, AS IF UNABLE TO STOP TALKING, AS SHE lay soaking in a tub full of vinegar and tepid water to ease the sunburn. For the first time since he'd known Lois Finlayson, Jack wasn't listening to her.

"I've never been so scared in my life," she said, with more than a note of cheerfulness in her voice. At first, Lynch was surprised to hear her in such good spirits. He lifted his third scotch and soda to his mouth and let the icy shine of the glass rake across his lips. He'd finally attributed her exuberance to a combination of exhaustion, a Darvocet with codeine, the frosty Cuba Libre she'd let Lynch fix for her, and the giddy realization that she was alive.

She chattered on in the background as Lynch stood in the hallway outside the bathroom, leaning against the wall with the drink in one hand, a lit cigarette in the other. His brow tightened. He'd felt the elation himself when they first got back to her apartment, but it had dried up during his reflections on what had happened that day. Despite the scotch and his own exhaustion, Jack Lynch was as sober as he'd been the day he was born.

Someone had tried to *kill* her. Why? Was Lois Finlayson somehow involved in this on some level that he didn't understand? Maybe she knew something she didn't even know she knew. Had she seen something?

Lynch racked his brain, trying to make sense of the day's events. Was all this tied together? he asked himself. Pearl's murder, the trashing of his car, the attempt on Lois's life?

Maybe it was the scotch and the fatigue and just not being able to give a damn anymore, but Lynch felt little in the way of fear, which he would have readily admitted was not at all like him. If anything, growing within him were the beginnings of a pretty good-sized rage. He studied the wall barely two feet or so across the hall, eyeballing it so intently that the color began to run and swirl, as if the paint were still wet and thick and fresh off the brush.

Up until now, Lynch had only a passing interest in who killed Pearl Bergeron. For him, it had been more of a challenge to keep Kwang's business, to play the public-relations game of putting the best face possible on an ever-deteriorating position.

Spin control.

But this was different. The longer he thought about it, the more he figured it was all tied together. Someone out there was trying to hurt him, and hurt one of the few people alive that he gave a damn about.

Somebody out there figured Jack Lynch was looking for a murderer, an assumption that up until that very moment had been wrong.

There was a coldness in him, a coldness he hadn't felt since the night he had laid on an examining table in the emergency room, knowing somewhere inside himself, even though he hadn't been told yet, that Sally was gone and he was once again alone. Inside, he felt that cold like a hard lump. His mind was suddenly clear; he knew what he had to do.

"So, anyway, I just figured what the hey, she wasn't going to fire me, right?" Lois's voice from inside the bathroom was still going full tilt. He couldn't summon much in the way of tenderness for her right now; there was no room. And he sure as hell didn't know what she was talking about.

Lynch straightened and pushed himself away from the wall with his elbows. His cigarette had burned, unsmoked, down to his fingers, and the ash lay dead and gray on the hardwood floor. He walked into the bathroom, flicked the butt into the toilet. Lois was lying back in the bathtub, the cool water covering her sunburned neck and arms. Her face was lobster red as well. Her left hand, the palm still bandaged, hung over the side of the tub. She was going to be sore for a few days.

She was drifting now, sleepy with fatigue and medication. The drink sat half-finished on the edge of the bathtub. She looked at Jack as he came into the bathroom, then smiled dreamily.

"I'm sorry," she said. "I'm rambling."

Lynch's eyes rested on her body, so lean and strong and young. The water was just high enough to cover her stomach and parts of her breasts; her nipples were wet and hard in the cool air. Despite the streak of coldheartedness he'd felt in the hall, he found himself warming to her. Her hair floated lazily in the water, over her arms and shoulders.

"You okay?" he asked.

"Oh, yeah," she answered, yawning. "I'm fine. Tired. I could use a good night's sleep."

"I'm going to make sure you get one," Lynch said. "I'm taking off in a few minutes."

Her expression darkened. "You're leaving me alone. Why?"

"So you can get some rest."

"Jack, somebody tried to kill me today. You're going to leave me alone and expect me to *sleep?*"

Jack slid down the wall of the tub. His knees were on the floor now, his elbows resting on the cold porcelain. "Is there any reason somebody would want to kill you?"

She frowned at him. "That's ridiculous. Why would anybody want to kill me?"

"That's what I'd like to know," Lynch said. He paused for a moment. "Lois, how did Teddy Chrisman get a job on that set today?"

"How should I know? I didn't do the casting." She slid down in the water a little further, the water touching her jaw line as she pouted.

"Who was that guy with him?"

"Which guy?"

"The dark-haired one. Little guy, looked kind of weaselly."

"That was Marco Cerasini," she laughed. "He teaches the screenwriting class I'm taking. Or was. I'm not sure I'll go back. Remember, I told you how he tried to get me to go out with him?"

"And you wouldn't, right?"

"Obviously," she kidded, smiling. Then her face lost its smile. "You don't think Marco—"

"He and Teddy Chrisman were helping the pilot pull the backseat out of the helicopter."

"My God, Jack," she said. "But why would he want to kill me? He's a writer. He's used to rejection."

219

"Maybe he got tired of it," Lynch speculated. "Some people can only take so much, then they blow."

"But how could he have planned to do it then? He didn't know I was going to be there, did he? How could he have known the Tyler mount wasn't going to be in the helicopter?"

"I don't know, Lois. I'm not even saying he did it. I'm just saying that all of this stuff, my car getting trashed, the cut seat belt, all of it goes back to one person. I think it's the person that killed Pearl."

"But why involve us in it?" Her voice was high, almost a squeal.

"I was asking around a bit, poking my nose in maybe where I shouldn't have. I was only trying to protect my client. I wasn't seriously looking to find Pearl's murderer."

He reached into his shirt pocket and took out a cigarette, stuck it in his mouth, then squinted as the lighter flared at its tip.

"But, by God, I am now."

She was still for a moment, breaking the silence when she'd gathered her thoughts. "If you have to go, I understand. I'll be okay. Just tell me you'll be careful." She stood up out of the water and motioned for Jack to hand her a towel. "I'll lock the doors tight and take the phone off the hook and do the best I can to get to sleep."

"Yeah," Lynch said, preparing himself mentally to go. "That's the best thing you can do."

Lois wrapped the thick pink towel around herself tightly, then stepped out of the tub. She threw her hair behind her, shook her head, and stood on tiptoe to kiss Lynch softly, longingly, as if she weren't at all sure she wanted to let him go.

"Do be careful," she whispered. "Will you?"

"Sure." He smiled at her, his arms wrapped around her. He squeezed.

"Oh, not too tight. I'm still sore."

She led him to the door and kissed him again on the way out. He stood at the landing until he heard her lock the door and bolt it. He walked down the wrought-iron stairs and onto the concrete driveway, then around front to where the car was parked.

Behind him, Lois Finlayson stared at the spot on the wall where he'd leaned for a long time. For the first time in her life, she was truly frightened.

Everything, she decided, was going wrong.

* * *

Lynch's apartment was not only cluttered and badly in need of a good cleaning, it was now showing signs of having been abandoned. He came in through the back door and flicked on the light. A battalion of New Orleans cockroaches scattered across his kitchen table.

"Jesus," he muttered, angry at himself for having left a half-eaten blueberry bagel with cream cheese sitting on the bare wood. The bugs had carried off most of it; what was left was beginning to show signs of hair growth. Lynch pulled the garbage pail next to the table, swept all the remains safely into the plastic bag, then ripped open another roach motel and tossed it on the table on his way into the bedroom.

Thankfully, no insects were visible in his bedroom. Either there weren't any, or they'd all heard him coming. Lynch was disgusted with himself and with the place. Good thing he wasn't planning on hanging around.

He showered quickly, then changed into a clean white shirt and a pair of jeans. Then he opened up the hall door and stood on a stepstool to reach a box hidden in the highest, most remote part of the closet. He fumbled with several boxes, finally locating the one he needed. He carefully withdrew it and stepped down onto the floor.

Lynch carried the box into the bedroom, sat on the edge of the bed, and pulled the lid off. A curious smile crossed his face; he hadn't seen the thing in months, not since he had settled back into his apartment and tried for a while to get his life in order.

He pulled the Smith & Wesson .38 revolver out of the box. Inside the shoebox was a smaller box of cartridges. He took them out and loaded the gun.

The problem was how to carry it. It was altogether too hot to wear a jacket. There was a holster around somewhere, but he wasn't sure where. Besides, without a jacket the gun would still be visible.

Lynch looked across the room, wishing for a moment that men could carry purses without getting strange looks and inappropriate assumptions.

"Wait a minute," he said out loud. "They can . . ."

Lynch put the gun in his briefcase, exited the apartment, and headed for his car. Once in the car, he started it and pointed it down Elysian Fields Avenue. A few blocks down he would turn left into the old, residential part of the French Quarter, the part of the French Quarter where Pearl Bergeron had once lived.

Sometimes, Eddie Bell felt like this late-night work was killing him. Fortunately, he didn't need much sleep. Sometimes he wished he needed more; that way, he wouldn't spend so much of his off time swilling Pabst Blue Ribbon and hanging out in the bars. At least working nights meant that he missed most of the Atlanta traffic.

The truth was, Eddie's job as a technician at the Filmcrafters Lab was perfect for him. Eddie was a small man, with slightly hunched shoulders, a growing, jellylike paunch, and chronic bad breath. For the past fifteen years, much of his work had been performed at night, either in the dark or under faint safelights, which gave him an unusual aversion to sunlight and a certain bug-eyed appearance. He was forty-two and balding, an unattractive man still living with his aging mother, who was growing more senile every day.

The job had moments of high stress but was mostly routine. Filmcrafters was probably the biggest movie lab in the South, and its location near Hartsfield International Airport in Atlanta meant jobs got in and out with good turnaround. Film came in from around the country. Eddie performed the initial step of developing the negative, which was then passed along to someone else who pulled the slop, or work prints for rushes and editing.

Most of the job was automated. Once everything was working, you could pretty well settle back. Eddie had little interest in the contents of what he was developing. As long as everything came out of the soup clean and dry and ready to pass on to the next guy, he was doing his job.

This particular night a lot of small jobs had come in. A half-hour documentary, a few student films, and a couple of other jobs that he didn't know or care about.

The last one was rolling out of the tank now. Eddie performed his usual cursory examination of the film stock under safelight as it came out of the drier, before fastening it to the takeup reel and sending it on to Butch Weaver in the next department.

Eddie squinted in the dim light. Something was wrong.

"Damn," he muttered. "Just what I need." Eddie Bell hated when things went wrong. He shrugged his bent shoulders, the cheap polyester of his discount dress shirt riding up on his back.

He started the takeup and processed the rest of the job: six magazines on one reel. When all of the job was out of the soup, he

222

reached over and killed the safelight, then slowly turned the dimmer up on the overhead. Eddie had installed the dimmer himself because the shock of a light coming on after hours in near darkness was too much for his sensitive eyes.

He pulled twenty or thirty feet off the reel and examined it under white light.

"Oh, no," he said. "What the—?"

He reached for his phone and punched in a three-digit extension.

"Yeah, what is it, Eddie?" Eddie didn't care much for Butch Weaver. His voice to Eddie, was like broken glass in a wooden box.

"Butch, you better get in here. I got a problem."

"In a minute."

Butch Weaver, despite his name, was a standard-issue gearhead nerd, complete with pocket protector jammed with pens and a clip-on tie.

"What is it, Eddie?" Butch demanded. "I'm busy." His nasal voice grated worse in person than over the phone. Eddie pulled out a length of film.

"Look."

Butch took the length of reddish film stock negative, held it close under the the thick lenses of his glasses, then pointed the film and his head toward the light.

"Jeez, Eddie, what'd you do? Mr. Turner's going to be awful pissed."

"I didn't do anything, Butch," Eddie said, angry himself.

The negative film was full of faint streaks, probably invisible, or at least mostly unnoticeable, to the untrained eye. But for Eddie and Butch, the tiny imperfections in the film meant the job had been botched, that either the customer or the lab had screwed up. The film was unusable, ruined. Eddie reviewed in his own mind the procedures he'd taken. He couldn't have done anything wrong; for one thing, the rest of the jobs that night had come out just fine.

"Looks kind of like a light leak," Butch whined.

"That's no light leak," Eddie snapped, feeling the polyester shirt holding in his armpit sweat. "I ain't never seen a light leak like that."

"Me either," Butch said. "It's weird. We'll have to wake up Mr. Turner."

"Like hell we will," Eddie said.

223

"Where's the paperwork on the job?"

Eddie reached for the file folder. Who was the customer?

"Kwang World Pictures," Eddie said.

"Aw, jeez," Butch sniveled. "That's a big one."

Eddie Bell reached for the phone. He would have to call Mr. Turner, who did not like to be awakened at home with problems.

"Somebody," he said to Butch as the phone rang, "is in deep doodoo."

A mélange of sounds filled the air as Lynch left his parked car and headed up the rippled cobblestone sidewalk toward Pearl's apartment. From his left, through an open window, came the sweet trumpet and trombone combinations of traditional New Orleans jazz, the kind you heard in the movies. It had become a tourist's stereotype, the kind of stuff many musicians hated playing even to the point of, like the Preservation Hall Jazz Band, charging the suckers twenty-five dollars to play "When the Saints Go Marching In." But to his right, farther up the street, a group of black teenagers in sneakers you had to pump up were threatening the civilized world with the urban-warfare rap of 2 Live Crew and NWA, sounds that Lynch neither recognized nor had much potential for understanding.

To him, it was just the city's noisy assault on his senses. He struggled to maintain his train of thought, to figure out what he was going to say, what he would ask, where he was going in this sudden inquiry. There was so much to think about, so little he really understood.

As he sat in his parked car, he debated with himself fully ten minutes over whether to carry the pistol with him. In retrospect, he wasn't exactly sure why he'd dug it out, except that some pervasive and intense dread had filled him. He didn't know if he could use the pistol if he had to, was, in fact, fairly sure that, more than anything else it was likely to get him in trouble.

He left the pistol locked in the briefcase and stuffed the case as far under the dashboard as it would go. It was there if he needed it.

He was hot and weary and frightened and mad as hell. Whatever it was that was driving him on, he thought, as he climbed the two levels of brick steps and pressed the doorbell, it was powerful stuff.

He heard steps coming down the stairs. He had driven by the building the day after Pearl's murder, later in the afternoon, when the police were still blocking the sidewalk with the yellow tape that read CRIME SCENE—DO NOT CROSS, but he hadn't stopped. The white-washed building with the wrought-iron flower boxes below the windows (high enough to be out of reach and safe from vandals), looked as he had always expected an apartment building in France would look, although Lynch's knowledge of French architecture was limited to the articles he'd read in *National Geographic*.

The door behind the wrought-iron security gate opened. Teddy Chrisman stood looking at him in the syrupy orange haze of the streetlight trying to figure out who he was.

"Teddy Chrisman, I'm Jack—"

"I know who you are," Chrisman interrupted. "What do you want?"

"I came by to ask you a few questions."

He could see over Chrisman's shoulders a stairway that led up to Pearl's second-floor apartment and, at the top of the stairs, the same fellow who'd been at the Riverbend Studio earlier that day. Marco Cerasini, Lois had said his name was, and Lynch wondered what he was doing there in what used to be Pearl's apartment.

"You a cop or what?" Chrisman demanded, his voice deepening.

"No, I'm not a cop," Lynch said, "and you know that. You going to let me up or what?"

"Why should I?"

"Because I saw you and that fellow at the top of the stairs helping out in the back of that helicopter today. And fifteen minutes later, Lois Finlayson nearly gets herself killed because somebody cut the safety belt. Now, maybe the Norco cops couldn't draw any conclusions from that. But I wonder if NOPD Homicide would have the same problem."

Chrisman looked up and down the street, as if half expecting a fleet of blue-and-whites with crescent insignia on their sides to pull up with sirens screaming and lights blazing.

"Let him up, Teddy," Cerasini called from the top of the stairs.

Chrisman stepped out of the way. Lynch eased past the dark glare of the bodybuilder and quickly climbed the stairs. He followed Cerasini into the apartment and looked around in awe.

Pearl had class, he thought, real class. The place was decorated stylishly, with subdued and intellectual taste. The sunken living room was covered with thick off-white carpet that set off the expensive furniture. Definitely not veneered particle board that came with a set of assembly instructions, Lynch speculated.

"Have a seat, Mr. Lynch," Cerasini said. He seemed casual, completely at home in Pearl's apartment.

"Thanks," Lynch said, taking a seat on the sofa. Marco sat across from him in a bentwood rocker. Chrisman sat in an overstuffed chair that matched the sofa.

"That was quite a little bit of heroics you pulled off today, Mr. Lynch," the thin, dark man said. "The way you stood there with that helicopter bearing down on you, waiting to catch Ms. Finlayson if she fell. One has to wonder what you would have been willing to risk to save her."

"Just trying to help out," Lynch said. "No heroics involved."

"All the same, it was impressive. You expect that sort of thing from a macho man like Jerry Hagan, but we all thought you were just another one of the suits."

"Tell me, Marco," Lynch said, "how did you wind up on the set today?"

"Teddy invited me."

Lynch looked over at Chrisman. "Miller Taylor said it was all right."

"How did you get on the set?" Lynch asked.

"I auditioned for a part, just like everybody else," Chrisman said, his voice a low, threatening growl. "And I got one."

Lynch took a deep breath. "What are you two up to?"

Chrisman moved forward in his chair. Marco Cerasini held up his hand. "What do you mean?"

"You don't think that just because charges have been filed against Kwang that the police aren't still looking for Pearl's killer, do you?"

"I rather suspect that's exactly what's happened," Cerasini said. "After all, the police have their killer. He'll soon go to trial and that will be it."

"Kwang's hired himself a damn good lawyer. All the evidence against him is circumstantial. And here in front of me are two guys, both of whom have a real strong vested interest in the movie business, both of whom knew Pearl and knew she wanted to stop the studio. And both of whom apparently are living in Pearl's apartment.

"Now you tell me," Lynch continued, "who are the cops going

226

to come after when the charges against Kwang are dropped for lack of evidence? Or when he goes to trial and gets acquitted?"

Chrisman stood up. "We ain't doing a thing wrong, man, and you got no business—"

"All right, Ted, I'm leaving. I've said what I wanted to say. Both you guys had a reason to want Pearl out of the way. And both of you had the chance to do it. I'm just telling you what it looks like, that's all."

"You don't know what you're talking about, Lynch," Cerasini said, smiling at him and gently rocking in the chair. "We didn't have anything to do with poor Pearl's murder. We both miss her a lot, although I must admit I didn't know her anywhere near as well as Teddy did. I do know, though, that you're being very nosy. And that nosy people sometimes wind up making fools out of themselves. Or worse."

Lynch moved toward the door. Chrisman stepped in front of him, as if to stop him. Then he reached for the handle with his left hand, turned it, and held the door open for him.

His *left* hand, Lynch thought. "Teddy," he said casually, "I didn't know you were a southpaw."

"So what," Chrisman said, his voice low. To Lynch, he seemed to take on an almost simian appearance.

"Nothing. Nothing at all. One other thing I am curious about, though," Lynch said, standing in the doorway and addressing Cerasini, "given that I know Teddy used to live with Pearl and that you've been spotted in the company of women from time to time—"

"Yes?" Cerasini asked.

"How long have you two been seeing each other?"

Chrisman's jaw set hard. Marco Cerasini smiled. "You *are* nosy, Jack Lynch."

"Okay, I confess. I'm nosy."

Cerasini stood up, his thin frame rising out of the chair smoothly. "We're all made up of many parts, Jack. Some of those parts like to bat from both sides of the plate. You should try it some time. It's only natural."

Lynch smiled. "Remember Katharine Hepburn in *The African Queen?*"

"Of course."

"Nature is what we were put on earth to rise above," Lynch said, grinning.

Lynch descended the stairs with Chrisman behind him, bracing himself against the chance that the larger man might try to shove him down the steps.

Once his visitor was outside, Chrisman pulled the gate to, then slammed the door behind Lynch. He trotted back up the stairs to the foyer quickly. Marco was standing there, glaring darkly.

"Ted," he said. "I don't like this. Not a damn bit. I have a feeling we should make our move as quickly as possible. Then it might be a good idea for us to disappear for a while. How'd you like a long vacation?"

Chrisman smiled. "I have been kind of tired lately."

"Good. Hand me the telephone."

Outside, Lynch walked down the steps and back to his car with the distinct feeling that he'd wasted his time. He had no idea what had just been thrown into the game.

28

GOVERNOR LAMAR BERGERON WAS IN HIS PRIVATE SITTING ROOM, THE hidden one behind the governor's office in the state capitol building. It had been a long day, what with those blasted picketers out front screaming and yelling. He couldn't hear them from his office, but he could by God look out the window and see them, along with the camera crews from the three networks. Once again, the people of the State of Louisiana were being paraded across the nation's television screens during prime time, portrayed as a bunch of boobs. This was the second year in a row that those right-wing wackos down on the floor had pushed through a bill outlawing abortion for any reason whatsoever, even to save the mother's life. Hell, they figured let the mother die if the fetus can survive. The bill would be in his office by 8:00 A.M. tomorrow; he would veto it, of course, but he was wary of the consequences.

One group of ultra–right-wingers even favored giving the death penalty to doctors who performed abortions. Thank heavens that wasn't written into the bill, although it wouldn't have made any difference to him. Bergeron had always wondered, without ever saying anything to anyone except his closest group of advisers, how a group of people could be convinced on the one hand that human life was the most sacred thing in the universe, and on the other hand willing to execute anyone who didn't agree with them.

Didn't make any damn sense to him, although he had to admit there was a great deal that didn't make sense to him anymore. Sometimes he hated this job. Lately, especially since Pearl's death, retirement was starting to look better and better. He was tired of the fights and the threats and the recriminations that were so much a part of politics these days. In the old days, politics had centered on the art of consensus. Nowadays, it mainly involved not pissing off any one special-interest group so badly that they'd turn it into a personal crusade to nail your hide to the wall.

There was a knock at the door. Dammit, he thought, I told you people to let me alone. He wasn't even in the mood for female company tonight.

"Yeah," he said. Robert Brewster stuck his head in the door.

"Sorry, Chief," he said. "I know you didn't want to be disturbed, but I figured I'd better call you."

Governor Bergeron raised his glass of Jim Beam with a dash of spring water to his lips and took a long pull. The brown liquid burned under his tongue, along his throat, all the way down his gullet.

"What is it?" he demanded, setting the glass down. Brewster was a good man, one of the few that could be trusted. But sometimes he was a bit too timid. If it were important enough to bother him this time of night, it was important enough for him to spit it out.

Brewster looked behind him nervously, then stepped into the sanctuary and closed the door behind him. A television with the sound turned down danced blues, reds, and greens off the ceiling. The air felt cool, but heavy and thick with the smell of the governor's cigar smoke.

"We got a call a few minutes ago. Guy insisted on speaking with you. Said it had something to do with Pearl's—"

"Murder," the governor finished the sentence.

"Yessir, murder. Switchboard refused to send it up here, beeped me down on the House floor, and had me take it in the caucus room."

"Bob, get to the point. I don't care where you took the goddamn call."

Brewster flushed. The boss was in a bad mood. He subconsciously found himself slipping into his own form of verbal shorthand, a quirk of his that appeared when the stress levels got too high. "Guy wouldn't identify himself. Said he'd found papers that had been in Pearl's possession. Knew about the problems at Riverbend. Said if we paid him a quarter of a million, he'd destroy the papers and disappear. Wants cash. Calling back tomorrow."

There was a long moment of silence. Governor LaMar Bergeron's face was as set in stone as the statue he hoped would someday

230

be erected in his honor. "The Riverbend problems? You mean some fucking civilian knows about the Riverbend problems?"

"It would seem so, sir."

Bergeron was angry now, exasperated. He mocked his right-hand man: " 'It would seem so, sir.' What are you, Brewster, an English butler? Hell, he do or he don't."

"He do, Chief. He cited dates, memos, the whole ball of wax. Either he found Pearl's papers or she had copies and gave them to him."

"We searched that place upside down, rightside up, right? Those papers weren't in that apartment!"

"Not that we could find, Chief."

"Damn straight, not that we could find!"

Brewster stepped forward, closer to his boss. He was caught up in the situation now, his anxiety over delivering bad news to the Governor dissipating. "Could they have come out of here? Out of this office?"

"No way. The Riverbend file doesn't exist. Not anymore. I made sure of that myself."

"But sir, it does exist. And we're getting a phone call tomorrow with an offer to sell."

"Well, we'll take this guy's offer," the governor said, easing back in his chair and raising his glass again. "Only not in the way he thinks we will. Get a trace on the line when he calls. Get hold of Captain Springer, tell him to be in my office at eight."

"Yessir," Brewster said. Springer was the closest thing the state police had to a genuine covert-operations specialist. A former DEA operative, he had left the agency five years earlier in the middle of some controversy over the treatment of suspects. If the boss was calling in Springer, Brewster thought, I'd hate to be in that poor ignorant fellow's shoes tomorrow. If he had any sense, he wouldn't even call back.

"Okay, Chief," Brewster said after a moment's silence. "Anything else?"

LaMar Bergeron glared at the television over the top of his whiskey glass. "Bob," he said, "I won't go down as the governor who presided over the worst environmental scandal in the history of this country. If I have to shoot those sons of bitches myself, that Riverbend file is going to remain buried. I'm not the man who caused that mess. I'll be damned if I'll take the blame for it."

231

* * *

Jack Lynch opened the door of his office at nine-ten Monday morning and walked in, pleased with himself at having gotten there within a reasonable approximation of the morning business hours. Maud Pelletier was behind her desk, watching a game show on a small black-and-white television, the sound turned down, her back to the door.

"Oh, hi," she said, embarrassed. "I didn't have anything else to do. I even dusted the furniture. Hope you don't mind."

Lynch pulled off his jacket. It was already nearly ninety outside, with the humidity turned up today like the flame under a deep-fat fryer.

"Of course not," he said. "Anything going on?"

"You got a fax Friday. It's on your desk. And there's a fellow in your office waiting for you." She lowered her voice. "I put him in your office because I didn't like being in the same room with him. Name's Rowan Wilson. Sleazy guy."

"Yes," Lynch whispered back. "A sleazy guy. You did good."

"And your insurance agent called. Wants to know when you're taking that rental car back. He said it was supposed to be returned last Thursday. You get it in by lunchtime, they'll cut you some slack. Otherwise, their daily rate is sixty-five dollars."

"Doesn't make any difference anyway," Lynch said, disgusted. "The credit card I gave 'em is maxed out."

"Oh, good," Maud cooed, "then they'll just come take you to jail. Say, by the way, I heard about your girlfriend. It was on the news Friday night. She okay?"

"Yeah, she's all right. Tired. A little bunged up. But okay."

"You see her this weekend?"

"My, aren't we nosy?"

Maud turned around, sat back down in her chair. "Just curious, that's all. Excuse me for caring."

Lynch reached out and put his hand on her right shoulder. She tightened under his touch. "I'm sorry," he said. "Thanks for caring. And yes, I saw her this weekend."

Maud turned back around, stared at him a moment. "She a nice girl? Really?"

"Yeah, babe. She's a nice girl. Want you to meet her soon."

"Don't be bringing her home to me. I ain't your momma."

"Right," Lynch said. He walked over and opened the door to

232

his office quickly, half-expecting to see Rowan Wilson standing over his desk, going through his things.

If he had, he'd already finished. Wilson was sitting patiently on the scuffed leather couch, reading a three-month-old *People* magazine.

"What can I do for you, Rowan?" Lynch said, walking around his desk and easing into his chair. Behind the desk, he was ready to play whatever power games Wilson was interested in. It may be small turf, Lynch thought, but it's *my* turf.

"Hello, Jack," he said, as he bounded up off the couch and stood over Lynch's desk with his hand out. Lynch reached up as if it were a terrible effort and shook Wilson's hand.

"Good to see you again," Wilson piped up, parking himself in the chair across from Jack.

"Yes, Rowan, it's been a while. How can I help you?"

"I came to see you because I want to arrange a meeting with Kwang. My financing has finally come through on the Riverbend facility. With Kwang's legal problems and the other challenges facing him, I thought perhaps he might reconsider letting a local take over the studio."

"Why come to me, Rowan? Just call and make an appointment with him. Hell, he can't even leave town."

"I tried that," Wilson said, his head melodramatically dipping. "I called his lawyer and his secretary and he refuses to see me."

Lynch suppressed a smile at the theatrics. "I would take that as a pretty good indication of how willing he is to sell."

"You and I both know Kwang will never run that place successfully. He doesn't know his way around this state."

"You mean he's not as crooked as a water moccasin wrapped around a swamp stump?"

"Now listen, Jack," Wilson said, genuine exasperation in his voice now. "Who would you rather work with? Me or that foreigner?"

Lynch stood up, his eyes on fire and a thin sheen of sweat breaking out on his forehead. The coat of perspiration gave him the look of someone slightly mad, although it mostly came from the old air-conditioning system's inability to fight the heat.

"I'd rather spend the rest of my life hosing the pigeon shit off Jackson Square, you sleazebucket. For the last couple of weeks, I've been putting up with you out of a sense of business propriety and common decency, but no more. My answer to you is the same as Carlton Smith's and Kwang's and Sheldon Taplinger's and the last dozen women you've dated: No."

Wilson's mouth hung open. That crack about the last dozen women he'd dated was below the belt and uncalled for, even if a quick mental audit on Wilson's part uncovered the fact that it was true. He had been in a long dry spell, in more ways than one.

"You're making a mistake, Jack," Wilson finally managed to get out. "I may not be pulling down the kind of bucks Kwang is, but I know more about the way business is done down here, and that, buddy, puts us on a level playing field." Wilson pointed a finger up at him from his perch on the edge of the visitor's chair. "And you signed on with the wrong team."

"I'm shaking, Rowan. I really am. Right now, I'm busy. So would you mind getting out?"

Wilson's face, beneath his pallor and the head of well-sprayed salt-and-pepper hair, turned deep red. He stood up, searching unsuccessfully for some rapid-fire comeback, then gave up.

"You'll be sorry, Jack," he said. "Before I'm through with you, you'll wish you'd pulled out of this."

"No, Rowan," Lynch said loudly, his heart racing. "I wish your *father* had pulled out!"

There was a loud slam as Wilson bolted out the front door of the office. Lynch sat back down in his chair, jerking his tie loose and running his fingers through his hair to get it off his forehead.

Maud stuck her head in the door. "What was that all about?"

Lynch grinned at her. "Nothing much, I just had to get the trash out of here."

Maud sniggered. "Looks like you did a pretty good job."

It had been a long time since Lynch had gone off on someone like that. Funny thing, it felt kind of good. He didn't know he had it in him.

Lynch walked into the screening room and eyed the tense crowd. Kwang was there, with Taplinger in attendance as always. Miller Taylor stood at a podium in front of the small room looking uncomfortable and restricted. Jerry Hagan had walked in in front of Lynch, still sweating through his red knit shirt in the unbearable heat. He'd just come in from Dallas, he said, and had rushed out to the editing room in a cab.

234

Standing behind Taylor, off to one side, Lois Finlayson looked exhausted. It was bad enough what she'd been through while making the film, but finding out barely seventy-two hours later that it was all in vain was nearly too much for her. She'd called Lynch in tears, and he'd dutifully offered to come pick her up and drive her out to the screening, and to do anything else he could to help her out. Once again, she'd insisted, she would handle it herself. But could he be there? She would probably need a drink and a shoulder to cry on afterward.

"We're all here now," Taylor announced. Lois sat in the front row, next to the young man who had been her first assistant cameraman. Everyone else was slowly taking seats as well. Lynch sat in the back row, by himself. He spread his arms out across two chairs on either side and tried to get comfortable.

"We'll roll in a minute," Taylor continued. "But first I want to tell you that at this point, we're not trying to affix blame to anyone. None of us has seen the film yet. Nobody knows what went wrong. But, as I'm sure Mr. Kwang will agree, this is not the way we'd hoped to get the Riverbend Studio off the ground."

Taylor's comments were met with silence. This isn't a screening room, Lynch thought, it's a freaking funeral parlor.

Taylor sat in a chair in the front row just in front of Kwang. The people in the room had spread out, as if getting as far from each other as possible might dissipate the fallout.

The room went dark. Immediately, Lynch heard the smooth clicking of a projector behind and above him, and the cool blackness was cut by a shaft of bright, blue light. Images began dancing in front of the crowd on the white screen. This was raw footage—no sound, no edits, no continuity. Just straight from Lois's camera to the lab and onto the screen.

The soundstage shots came on first. Actors pretending to be actors making a movie did their pretend acting on the fake soundstage, which itself was a phony, two-dimensional neighborhood. The film looked okay to Jack. He studied it closely, as best he knew how with his untrained eye, but so far he hadn't found—

Dammit, there it was! He sat up straight in his chair, stared hard at the screen. Discolored streaks appeared in the images. Nothing glaring. Nothing a completely ignorant eye would notice, but still there nevertheless. The bad parts changed from frame to frame,

235

bouncing across the screen in a twenty-four-frames-per-second ghost dance.

What was it? Lynch wondered. He'd botched camera film before, like most people. You open the camera without remembering to wind the film back into the canister. Or you leave it in the car for too long in the hot New Orleans summer and the edges of the film melt together inside the can. But those kinds of mistakes were minor foul-ups compared to this. In a home movie or with a roll of snapshots of the pooch, it wasn't worth worrying about. But when you strive for perfection and spend a fortune in the process—

Lynch's thoughts were interrupted by growling. The huge, hulking, frustrated, hot Jerry Hagan, seated three rows in front of Lynch, was growling like a threatened junkyard dog. The seat was vibrating with the movement of air in and out of his chest. Lynch took his eyes off the screen for a moment and realized that his was not the only head in the theater that had turned to face Hagan.

The scene on the screen shifted again. There was Kwang, in the control room, speaking silently into the camera, with little flashes of silver and blue fox-trotting across his face.

"Aaarrrgghhhh," the director howled. "Jeezuusss. . . ."

Lynch thought for a moment that only someone from Texas could howl the name Jesus and make five syllables out of it.

The animal sounds coming from the director drowned out the rattle from the projection booth. If this were an omen of what was to come with Kwang World Pictures, Miller Taylor had the distinct wish that he'd kept his last job tending bar at that frat hangout over on Maple Street.

Kwang's portion of the promotional film was over now. Lynch watched the airborne shots in awe, until the chopper shifted a certain way and suddenly, the images tripped over themselves and outside the aircraft, bouncing up and down in a crazy-quilt array of blues and grays and earth tones and snatches of Lois as she dangled out the side of the helicopter with the camera still running. At one point, Lynch sat transfixed by his own image, reaching up to the helicopter as if he could pull it out of the sky and set it down on the ground like a falling baby. Finally, as the images on the ground began to grow in size, the magazine had gone dry. Now the film stopped, the blue-steel shaft of light from the projector turning to blazing, painful white.

The projector stopped and the house lights came up slowly.

236

Hagan was on his feet, jumping up and down in a temper tantrum that would have been hilarious if a very agitated, probably dangerous three hundred-pound man weren't having it.

Kwang stood, held up his hand for quiet. The room was suddenly still. Even Hagan stopped jumping.

"Does anyone have any idea what happened?" he asked quietly.

Lynch watched the crowd as heads turned this way and that. Finally, Lois spoke up from the corner.

"Mr. Kwang, I've had light leaks before, but never one like that. I've checked my equipment and the whole camera crew checked procedures. Honestly, sir, I don't think we did it."

Nicely handled, Lynch thought.

Hagan stood crouched with a fistful of hair pulled down in his face. "For twenty-five cents, I'd go over there and strangle the whole camera crew just to see how it felt. But she's right. I ain't never seen a light leak like that. It had to be either the lab or the stock."

"Maybe an X-ray fog," Lois's assistant spoke up.

"X ray, hell!" Hagan boomed. "That film never went through an X-ray machine!"

"Do we know that for sure?" Kwang asked, still standing. The sound of his voice seemed to instantly restore calm. "With the security measures on airliners these days, with shipping companies, could the material have been X-rayed by accident? Was the film stock box plainly marked?"

"We had it shipped in by air freight the week before," Taylor said. "If they X-rayed it, then we've got a helluva claim against them."

"I'd double-check the lab as well," Lois said.

"I'm going to leave Mr. Taylor and Mr. Hagan in charge of discovering where our problems lie." Kwang spoke up again. "For now, we're going to account for this episode by calling it a 'burn-in' experience. I don't want it to be repeated."

"It won't be," Taylor said.

"Damn straight," Hagan agreed.

"I would like to see the cast and crew reassembled for another day's shooting, preferably by this weekend."

Lynch shot a glance in Lois's direction, wondering what her reaction to having to go through a repeat of last Friday would be. She remained the professional, which Lynch knew meant that her distress was hidden.

237

"People," Kwang said, motioning to his secretary that it was time to leave, "we are going to make this operation successful. That is as clear to me today as when I first began looking at the site. Whether or not each of you remains a part of this will be determined by how quickly we fix these problems. Good day."

It seemed to Lynch that the entire room was at attention as Kwang walked up the aisle to the exit. As he passed the last row, next to where Lynch stood as well, he stopped.

"Mr. Lynch," he said.

"Mr. Kwang."

"I am surprised to see you here. It's not necessarily part of your contract."

"I don't always limit my work to the strict terms of a contract," Lynch said. "When I set out to protect someone's interests, I do whatever is necessary."

Kwang eyed him coldly. "Good. I hope you don't lose sight of what your client's interests are. Has Mr. Wilson spoken with you?"

"Yes," Lynch answered, wondering if Kwang was having him watched.

"And?"

"I threw him out of my office."

Kwang almost cracked a smile. "As usual, I have underestimated you."

"Happens all the time," Lynch said dryly.

Kwang turned and left. As soon as he went out the door, voices rose again. Lois skirted up the side of the small theater and crossed the row of seats in front of Jack to face him.

"I didn't do anything wrong, Jack," she said, determined. "Not a thing."

"Lois, how long had that film been sitting out at the Riverbend plant?"

She thought for a moment. "I don't know. Day or two maybe. I could check with Miller."

"No, don't. Just curious, that's all. You going to be around tonight?"

"You asking for a date?" She smiled at him, her face relaxing for the first time that day.

"Of course. I'm a glutton for punishment."

"Oh, really?" she said. "A side of you I haven't seen. I'll have the whips and chains ready."

238

"I'll hold you to it," Lynch said, turning to leave. He had a few things he wanted to check out before the day was over.

"Oh, no," she whispered. "I wanted to do the holding."

On his way out of the building Lynch had a mental image of the two of them tying each other up. Sometimes, he speculated, it was hard to tell when she was kidding.

29

"MOST OF THE EVIDENCE YOU'VE GOT ON KWANG IS CIRCUMSTANTIAL, right?"

Carl Frontiere clasped his hands behind his head and leaned back in his barely padded chair. "You know, Lynch," he said, "you keep this up, I'm going to make you apply for a P.I.'s license."

"I'm not interested in a P.I.'s license. It's just that having a murder charge hanging around my client's neck makes it tough to give him the image I want."

"Has Kwang told you why he went to Pearl Bergeron's apartment that night?"

Lynch shifted uneasily in the chair. "I haven't pressed him on it. No."

"Has he told his lawyer?"

"Even if I knew that," Lynch said, "I couldn't tell you."

"We've got a witness in the neighborhood who saw him knock on the door, then the door opened, and he went in. We found his fingerprints on the stair rail leading upstairs, and even, my friend, on the body."

Lynch's mouth opened. "You guys can do that? Off a body, I mean?"

"New technology, buddy. I don't know how it works, but Forensics can pick 'em up. They found them on her neck."

"But she wasn't strangled."

"No, he must have been feeling for a pulse after he killed her."

"Wait a minute," Lynch said. "If he was smart enough to wipe the upstairs clean, why did he screw up on the stair rail?"

"Panic, maybe," Frontiere answered, putting his feet up on his desk in a distinctly unprofessional manner. "He screwed up. Besides, we didn't check every bloody surface in the apartment. That's just about impossible."

"But it's not impossible for you guys to charge him with murder on so little evidence?" Lynch asked angrily.

"Hey, let's not get confrontational here," Frontiere said. He was taking a course at New Orleans Community College called "Therapeutic Approaches to the Criminal Justice System." Confrontational was a word that got tossed around a lot.

"I'm not getting confrontational. I just don't understand how you guys think you've got a case. What does Kwang say?"

"You know better than that. On our first interview, when he wasn't a suspect, he just played it real cool. Now his lawyer won't let us talk to him."

"Did you guys get any physical evidence from him?"

"We took hair and skin samples from him, but they didn't match anything on the scene. But we got the clothes he was wearing that night; found blood on his pants leg. Just a spot, but it matches the smear on the wall."

"That only puts him at the scene," Lynch insisted. "You already knew that."

Frontiere pulled his hands down and scooted forward in his chair. He placed his elbows flat on the desk; his jaw jutted forward as he spoke.

"I'm not going to pretend we've got an airtight case against Kwang. I'll tell you privately, and if you let this get out I'll make you regret the day you ever met me, that we're still keeping our eyes open. I think there's a lot we haven't figured out yet.

"But," he added, "we had to charge *somebody*. That came down all the way from the top."

"And Kwang's the foreigner, the outsider," Lynch said, his jaw locking in a mean grin, "the Chink. . . ."

Frontiere's eyes darkened. "Are you calling me a racist, Lynch?"

"If you were a racist, you wouldn't be the only one around here."

"Let me tell you something, buddy," the sweating, tired, irritated homicide lieutenant said. "You say what you want to about the rest of these people. But I'm no racist, goddammit. I hate everybody equally."

241

Lynch broke out laughing, despite himself. "I'm sorry, Lieutenant," he said between bursts. He laughed so hard his eyes teared. He reached up with one hand to wipe them. "It's just that I've never heard such unbridled honesty come out of the mouth of a public official."

"Well, you just watch that racist shit around me. I don't like to be called something I ain't."

Lynch gathered his wits. "You told me the coroner said the killer was left-handed."

"And Kwang's left-handed."

"Right," Lynch said. "But so's Teddy Chrisman, Pearl's boyfriend from the steroid highway. I hear that stuff gives you a bad temper."

Frontiere reached across his desk for the now several-inches-thick file on Pearl Bergeron's murder. He flipped through a pile of papers, finally stopping at one particular sheet.

Frontiere whistled. "Man, how could we miss that? I don't know if it means anything. Chrisman had an airtight alibi. But it's worth keeping in mind."

"What was Chrisman's alibi?"

"He was out at a bar with a buddy. Some guy that teaches a writing class over at the college."

"Ahhh," Lynch said. "Then let me tell you this, my friend."

Jack Lynch was not a great believer in hunches, even though there were times in his life when he had tapped into some mysterious stream of unconscious thought or insight, some dark pool of subliminal energy. But he had never labeled it anything like a hunch or intuition.

But there was something bothering him, something about the way the last few days' events had gone from a confusing bad to a baffling worse. There was a root cause, he felt, something that tied all the transpirations of the last couple of weeks together: Pearl's murder, the trashing of his car, the attempt on Lois's life, the screwup with the promotional film for the Riverbend Studio. Maybe, he thought, things had happened before Pearl's murder that were also pieces of this mess.

What tied it all together? What person was at the center of this?

"Something just ain't right," he said aloud to his empty car. Lynch was stopped at a red light on Tulane Avenue, the late-after-

242

noon sun bearing down on the black hood of his car, glaring off the paint like crystalline ice. His windows were down; he'd long since given up hope of relief coming from the car's air conditioner. Lynch noticed with each push of the accelerator the heaving of the small engine. The temperature needle climbed higher as the car sat there in traffic. He was on his way back to the rental agency, to thankfully be rid of the damned thing.

The problem, of course, was that he didn't have another car. He thought of just pulling into a new car lot and buying the first thing that caught his eye. The car dealers, especially the ones who sold American cars, were so desperate for business that they were now offering no-qualifying financing—the kind Lynch would need—and no down payment. Some were even offering a sizable-enough cash rebate that he would be able to pay next month's office rent when the check came in.

The light finally changed. Lynch pulled ahead with the traffic as it moved slowly, painfully down the avenue. The rental lot was out in Metairie; he'd have to hit the interstate and get out there quick before they closed. They were going to be hacked off enough at him for getting the car back so late. He wondered, as he pulled into the entrance ramp to I-10, how the buses were running these days. Would he be able to get a bus back into town? For that matter, he thought, as the traffic slowed to a stop on the concrete ramp, did he even have any cash on him?

He fumbled with his wallet and finally got it out of his back pants pocket without undoing the seat belt. He had seven dollars in cash. That would get him back into town, even if he had to switch buses a few times.

The guy in back of him honked his horn. Lynch looked up to see the traffic pulling away in front of him. He waved an apology out the rear window and pressed on the gas. The car pulled up the ramp, onto the highway. Lynch found himself surrounded by concrete, the poured concrete of the ramp, the highway, the raised abutments of the elevated highway. The searing light of the low sun hit the white concrete and reflected back in an almost blinding brilliance, even from behind his dark sunglasses and the tinted windows of the car.

Concrete, Lynch thought, I'm surrounded by concrete. If hell exists in an urban setting, it's made out of concrete.

Concrete. . . . Suddenly, Lynch thought back a few days, to that Friday when he'd nearly heatstroked walking around the Riverbend facility, surrounded by the feverish, blistering white concrete buildings. It was a white like nothing he'd ever seen, not the chalky, rough white of unworked ivory, the blanched white of bones drying in the sun, but rather the exploding white of stars going off in your skull after someone had laid a pipe to the side of your head, or the flashing white of an atomic fireball explosion.

His mind wandered. The Riverbend Nuclear Power Plant . . . Kwang World Pictures . . . newsreels flashing white atomic explosion . . . mushroom cloud . . .

X-rays . . .

Fogged film. His heart jumped.

Fogged film.

Fogged film. Fogged— No, he thought, the place was never—

"X ray, hell!" Hagan had yelled.

X ray hell. . . .

The traffic slowed quickly into a jam caused by construction. Lynch didn't notice in time. Lost in thought, he slammed on his brakes; the sedan skidded in a rubberized scream across a lane of traffic, causing the oncoming car to lock its brakes as well. Obscenities were audible above the blaring of horns and the attack of the jackhammers.

Lynch jerked his head around. There had to be a way to get off this thing. The car stalled; he twisted the key. The overheated engine struggled to catch.

"C'mon, baby," Lynch said, remembering his adolescent years when he talked to cars to get them started. "C'mon. . . ."

The engine ground and twisted, finally sparking to life. Lynch looked over his shoulder: the driver behind was shaking a fist out the window. Going to be trouble here soon. Trouble on the highway.

"Dammit," he yelled at the car in front, "get out of the way!"

The car moved, finally. Lynch pulled in front of the angry driver behind him and yanked himself and the car into the flow of traffic. Ahead, perhaps a hundred yards on the right, was an exit ramp. Lynch made for it as quickly as possible, then sped down the incline and off the highway.

Rush hour was nearing, and traffic was terrible everywhere. Lynch tried to get his bearings, unsure of where he'd actually gotten off the highway. He finally found a street he recognized, turned left, and drove like hell to beat a light. He had a clear shot now, all the way to St. Charles Avenue.

He drummed on the steering wheel nervously, sweat pouring off him soaking his dress shirt a dark gray. He looked at his watch: 4:45. Fifteen minutes, if he was lucky enough to find her there. If she still worked there. If she hadn't gone home early.

What was her name? It was going to be embarrassing looking up an old girlfriend for a favor if you couldn't even remember her name. Christie? No, Christine. Wait, Christina, that's it. Christina, what was it now?

They had met years ago, when she was with the Tulane University Public Information Office and he was with the newspaper. It was during one of his frequent separations from Katherine: Lynch, at a bar, was drunk one night, Christina in a paisley skirt sat next to him. They talked, wound up having a brief but intense affair. It was the first time in his life he'd gotten involved with someone solely for the pleasure of it, aware that the relationship would ultimately go nowhere.

He smiled to himself, one of the few smiles that he allowed himself that day, in memory of the fun they'd had, of the completely and innocently recreational sex they'd enjoyed in her old apartment off Magazine Street. She'd lived in a run-down building decorated in postmodernist hippie style: tie-dyed sheets and bead curtains made from cast-off Mardi Gras necklaces, candles set in wine bottles, mattress directly on the floor next to a Persian rug.

She was a lot of fun, he thought ruefully, and he'd regretted having to break up with her when his wife decided it was time for him to move back. He'd regretted letting her go many times over the years.

And now, he laughed, he was having trouble remembering her last name.

He drove down St. Charles Avenue, the evening rush-hour traffic so thick the streetcar was outrunning the automobiles, past the great homes of the Garden District, toward Audubon Park and the isolated Gothic architecture of the university.

"What was her name, dammit?" he said out loud as he pulled into the Horseshoe, the small parking lot of the main administrative building. He found a parking space near the front door, jumped out of the car, took the steps two at a time.

He entered the building, turned left as memory dictated, and walked down the end of the hall. A small black sign hung from the wall: TULANE UNIVERSITY—PUBLIC INFORMATION OFFICE.

245

Lynch turned smartly left and entered the room, still trying to think of her last name.

A young woman studying a textbook sat at the reception desk, an undergraduate with a scholarship job. She looked up at Lynch curiously. He realized that his hair was frazzled and hung down over his forehead. His tie was pulled halfway down to his belt buckle. He was jacketless and drenched in sweat. The young woman smiled.

"Hot out there, huh?"

"Yeah, really. Listen, I'm looking for Christina," he stammered, "Christina—"

"Daniels?"

Boom, he thought, direct hit the first time. "Yeah, Daniels. Is she still in?"

"I think so. Let me check." The student picked up the phone and dialed three numbers. "Christina? There's a man to see you out here." She looked up at Lynch. "What did you say your name was, sir?"

"Lynch. Jack Lynch." He ran his fingers back over his forehead, then tried to straighten his tie. He realized this was one hell of a way to catch up with an old girlfriend. She'll be glad she's rid of me, he thought.

There was a pause as the receptionist held the phone wordlessly. Finally, she put the phone down, looked up at Lynch in a decidedly different way.

"She'll be right out. Have a seat."

Lynch sat down, wondering what Christina had said to the young woman. He started to light a cigarette, then decided to hold off. In a minute or so, she turned the corner.

Lynch drew in a deep breath; she was better looking than he remembered, taller as well. She was still thin, with blond hair down over her shoulders, a woman of obvious Scandinavian descent. She wore a full, flowered dress with wide lapels and high heels that made her seem even taller.

How'd I ever let her go?

Quit, he thought, no time for that.

"Jack Lynch," she said, holding out her hand. "Long time no see."

"Hi, Christina." He took her hand. "You look great. The years have been good to you."

He felt awkward, the words stupidly corny coming out of his

mouth. He began to wish he hadn't come here, but he needed something and the first thing that came to his mind was her.

"You look good, too, Jack. Kind of rumpled, though."

"I've been in traffic with an overheated car. No air."

"Good heavens. C'mon back to my office. Want coffee? Iced tea?"

"No, no thanks." He followed her past the reception desk to a small office behind the copying-machine room.

"I was surprised to see you're still here," he said. "Pleasantly."

He wedged himself into a seat in front of her desk. There was barely room in the office for a second chair.

"Still cranking out news releases, writing copy for the alumni magazine," she said. "Same old same old. How about you?"

"I got my own company these days," he answered. "Public relations."

"I read all that stuff in the newspapers," she said, hesitating. "It sounded pretty awful. I thought of calling you a few times."

"I've thought of you, too," he said. It was a lie, but he felt like it was the right thing to say. He would have thought of her, too, if he'd thought of it.

"So how are you?" she asked.

"I'm hanging in there. How about you? What, you married or what?"

"Divorced. Got a little girl. She's five. Bought a house out New Orleans East."

"Great," Lynch said. This was the awkward part, the part where two old lovers had to try and establish contact on one level so they could move on to another. "I bet your little girl's pretty."

"She's beautiful," Christina said. "A good girl."

"Great."

"So, Jack, what brings you out here? You suddenly decide you couldn't live without me anymore?" There was an edge of anger coming through in her voice, now that the end of the small talk was in sight.

"Actually, Christina, I need some help."

"Yeah, I figured. What can I do for you?"

"I'm in a spot. I need some information. I remembered how the news bureau here maintains a list of faculty members who're willing to answer questions from the press, to serve as sources, whatever."

"You're not with the press," she said dryly.

"No, but I thought maybe you could turn me on to somebody who'd be willing to help me out."

"Turn on," she said. "Interesting twist of phrase. . . . So what do you need?"

Lynch hesitated. How to tell her what he needed without letting on too much or sounding like a complete wacko? "I'm doing some research for a client. I need to find out more about . . ."

He hesitated. "Well, about radiation."

"Radiation? Okay, let me think. That'd be the physics department." Christina reached across her desk and picked up a small metal box full of index cards. She flipped through the tabs, pulled out a couple.

"Here's two for you. I'll write down their names. School's out of session, so they may or may not be around campus. It's past five now, so they're not likely to be in the physics department anyway. You can try them tomorrow."

"You got their home phone numbers, Chris?"

She looked up at his abbreviation of her name. He was the only one who'd ever called her that. Her family called her Chrissie, but he'd always thought that was too prim and cute.

"It's that important?" she asked.

"Well, just in case I—"

"Okay." she bent down to write again. She looked up when she finished and handed Jack the slip of paper. "This ought to do it. One of these guys should be able to help you."

Jack folded the paper up and slipped it into his shirt pocket. "Thanks, Chris."

"You in a hurry?"

Lynch hesitated. "Kind of."

"No matter," she said, looking away. "I've got to pick up my daughter from day care anyway."

Jack stood. "Can I call you sometime?" He thought of Lois and felt a pang of guilt.

"Sure," she said, her lip curling up in a smile that Lynch couldn't read. He recalled that he'd always had trouble reading her. "Give me a call."

"Okay. Listen, Chris, I got to run. But it's been good seeing you."

"Sure, take off. See you again sometime. You know your way out?"

248

"Yeah, sure." Lynch turned and stepped toward the door. "You always did."

He stopped. "You ever think," she continued, "that if you'd just stayed with me, none of that bad stuff would have happened to you?"

Lynch turned slowly around on one foot to face her. There was an expression of pain on his face that she'd rarely seen on a man.

"Only about a million times," he said, his voice almost a whisper.

"Take care of yourself," she said.

His thoughts faded away, as if his mind had gone blank and he were going through the motions of walking, starting the car, negotiating the traffic like a robot. There was only a dull pain inside him, an ache that he couldn't identify, couldn't name, could only carry like one more weight. When he came to, he was pulling into a gas station on South Carrollton, parking next to a pay phone, fumbling in his pocket for a quarter.

He was vaguely conscious of the jingle of the quarter falling through the pay phone's innards, of the change in the pitch of the dial tone, the change in the tone generator's pitch as he pressed the buttons, then the ringing, and a voice.

"Hello?"

"Hello, Dr. Kuykendall, please."

"Hold on. May I say who's calling?"

"Yes, Jack Lynch. I was referred to Dr. Kuykendall by Christina Daniels in the university public information office."

The traffic passed in an endless stream. Lynch was no longer aware of the heat. Somewhere inside himself, he had finally become focused.

"This is Kuykendall," a masculine, older voice said.

"Dr. Kuykendall, my name is Jack Lynch. Christina Daniels said it was okay to call you. I need some information."

"Okay, shoot."

"Well, this is kind of involved." Lynch struggled with his words. "I'm trying to find out some information about radiation."

"What kind of information?"

"Well, like how do you detect it."

"That's easy. The standard field instrument is a Geiger counter."

Lynch thought for a moment. "That's what I thought. How can I get hold of one?

The voice on the other end laughed. "Well, you can't exactly go down to the U-Rent Center. Not a lot of demand for them."

"Dr. Kuykendall, this might be important. Maybe, maybe not. But if it turns out to be, somebody needs to know."

"What are you talking about?"

Lynch became aware that he sounded like a nut. The last thing he wanted to do was scare this guy off. He forced his voice to become controlled, forced himself to choose his words carefully. Then he thought of something.

"Professor, this would be a lot easier if we could talk face to face. Would you mind terribly if I dropped by."

The voice on the other end fumbled. "Well, I don't know."

"Professor, my name is Jack Lynch. I own my own public relations firm. One of my clients is buying some property, and I have a feeling that things may not be exactly, well, right. And we need to check this out very discreetly. I'd be glad to pay you for your time. My client could afford a healthy consultant's fee."

"That's not the issue. If you're afraid this property's hot, then the authorities are the ones who need to know."

"My client doesn't wish to hold himself up to ridicule by making accusations that may not be true," Lynch said, thinking that he didn't either. "We want to check this out first, before we say anything."

"All right. Come by my house now. My wife and I are leaving for a bridge game in about a half-hour. Can you make it before then?"

"I'm on my way. What's your address?"

Lynch took it down, noting that it was in a fancy old neighborhood just the other side of the park, near the university. He could be there in three minutes.

There was a two-seater Mercedes in the professor's driveway. Obviously, Lynch thought, there's more money in academics than people realize. Maybe his wife has money. . . .

The man who greeted him at the front door was at least six foot four and had a long, gray beard and even longer salt-and-pepper hair. He was dressed straight out of the L.L. Bean catalog. Lynch took an instant liking to the man, who held the screen door open for him.

250

"C'mon in, Mr. Lynch. We'll go back to my office."

"Thanks, Dr. Kuykendall, I really appreciate it."

"Call me Ken," he said. "We'll have to make this kind of quick."

The professor's office was a jumble of books and dark furniture. The smell of vanilla-steamed Black Cavendish pipe tobacco hung in the air.

"Have a seat." Lynch sat down. "Now tell me, what is it you need?"

"First of all, could radiation, like something given off at a nuclear plant, for instance, fog photographic film?"

Dr. Kuykendall rubbed his beard. "Well, first of all, nuclear plants don't give off radiation. Not unless something's gone terribly wrong."

"Say it had."

He thought for a moment. "The answer to your question is yes. Radiation badges, say, like a dental technician or an X-ray lab worker might wear, are a form of photographic film. X rays will fog film, certain parts of the gamma ray spectrum could fog film. It all depends."

"So how do you measure this stuff? I mean, what do you look for?"

"Well," the professor settled back in his chair, preparing the quick lecture, "the basic unit of measure is the roentgen. Actually, we use the milliroentgen, because a roentgen of radiation is quite a big lick. In fact, an atomic blast site, postexplosion, would measure somewhere between five and ten roentgens."

"Which is a lot, right?"

"Lethal. Fry you like a soft-shell crab. A lousy way to die. No, the ambient radiation that occurs normally in the atmosphere exposes us to an average of about 150 milliroentgens a year. That's in a full year. One could take a lot more than that, even that much in an hour, if, say, a radiation worker or X-ray technician made a terrible on-the-job mistake. You could handle that much probably without injury, but you'd want to be careful for a long time afterward."

"So what kinds of levels are dangerous?"

Kuykendall stood up, walked over to a cabinet with closed doors, and opened them. He took out a rectangular metal box, about seven inches by four by three, with a long tube on an extension cord.

251

"This is a Geiger counter," he said. He flipped a switch on the side. "This tube is the counter itself. The box contains the measurement circuitry, a meter, and an audio circuit with loudspeaker. See, when you turn it up—"

He turned a knob. A slow, lazy click came from the loudspeaker. A few seconds later, another.

"The speaker merely serves as an indicator of activity and a warning. You watch the meter for an accurate reading."

"Professor, can I borrow this?"

Kuykendall looked at him as if he'd just landed on the back lawn. "This is a very expensive piece of equipment, son, and it belongs to the university."

"How expensive?"

"You don't want to know."

"I'll be careful with it."

"I don't know. . . . I really should go with you. But my wife and I have this—"

Lynch pulled out a business card and handed it to him. "Here's my office address. My home and work numbers are on the card. If you'll trust me with that for twenty-four hours, I promise I'll have it back to you."

"Okay, I'll take a chance. But I'll need it back tomorrow." Kuykendall handed the box to Lynch. The meter was labeled MR/ HOUR.

"What am I looking for?" Lynch asked.

"It's very simple. You simply hold the tube in front of you, pointed in the direction you suspect. It's not very directional. Just a little. Listen to the speaker. Watch the meter."

"What kinds of levels should I look for?"

"Anything over a slow clicking may be a hot site. If the needle reaches around one hundred, one hundred fifty, then you know it's a hot site. If it gets higher, say up around five hundred or so, then—" He stopped for a second.

"Yes?" Lynch asked.

"I'd get the hell out of there."

Lynch got back in the car, started it, then pulled out into the thinning postdinner-hour traffic. He would have time to get home, change clothes, grab a quick bite, call Lois and tell her he'd be there later, then head out to the Riverbend Studio. It would be better to wait until after dark to poke around out there with a Geiger counter.

252

He reached out and touched the metal box on the front seat in front of him. It was warm to the touch. It was a long drive out there, and he was tired. It had been a long day—

"Oh, no!" he yelled out inside the car. He slapped the steering wheel in frustration.

He'd forgotten that he was supposed to take the rental car back.

30

THE RELATIVE COOL OF THE EVENING HAD FINALLY SETTLED IN BY THE time Lynch got back to his apartment. The red light on the answering machine was blinking. He set the Geiger counter and his briefcase down on the bed, stripped off his shirt, then stretched prone on the bed to listen to the messages.

"Yeah, Jack, this is Maud. The rental car company called. Said you didn't return the car. Your insurance agent called, too. He sounded pretty upset. I'd give him a call."

"Oh, hell," Lynch said out loud.

"Jack, this is Lois. I'm at home. Give me a call. Thinking about you, babe."

He smiled. Two hang-ups followed, then the sound of a voice he didn't recognize immediately.

"Lynch, this is Marco Cerasini. Chrisman's friend. We met the other night. Listen, we're going to be leaving town for a while. I sent a package to your office. It's copies of some stuff. Do what you want to with it."

Lynch sat up in bed, wondered what Teddy's buddy was talking about, then decided not to think about it. He jumped up, walked into the kitchen, fished around in the refrigerator for the scotch and the half-empty bottle of soda, then poured himself a badly needed drink.

He lit a cigarette and took a long pull on the cold glass. He picked up the wall phone in the kitchen, dialed a number.

"Hello?" The sound of her voice made him feel good.

"Hi. What you doing?"

"Hey, there. Where you been all day?"

"Out and about," he answered. "Taking care of biz."

"Well, biz is taking care of me tonight. We go back to River-bend tomorrow morning to shoot that film over again."

Lynch's jaw tightened and he felt a knot in his gut. "Did you find out what happened to the film?"

"We're not sure. X-rayed by mistake, they think, when it was shipped out here from L.A. Jerry Hagan had new stock air-freighted here from Houston. Some guy with the air freight company is going to walk it through security."

"Great," Lynch said. "So you're getting rested up for tomorrow?"

"A little. Actually, I was about to get a workout. Want to join me?"

"Nah," Lynch drawled. "Physical exercise isn't good for you."

"Oh, really. You seemed to enjoy it the other night."

"That's different."

"Yeah, right. Am I going to see you tonight?"

"I got somewhere I got to go tonight, but I'd like to stop by and see you first. Then I'll probably let you get a good night's sleep."

"Where you going?" Her voice was unusually inquisitive.

"Just biz, that's all. Just biz."

"Aren't we secretive tonight?"

"No, it's just that it's nothing important. Listen, though, I got to run, return another call, get in the shower. You know, same old stuff. I'll see you in a bit."

"I'll be here. Bye, love."

"Yeah, lady. See you later."

He hung up the phone, his tired eyes fading out of focus as he stood there holding the glass in his hand. So they thought it was an X-ray machine? Lynch felt like a fool. He probably should just take the Geiger counter back to the doc, then go spend a decent evening with Lois and try to call it an early night.

"What the hell," he said lightly. "It'll be an adventure."

Lois Finlayson sweated and grunted under the heavy iron. She knew better than to try and bench that kind of weight without a spotter, but she was feeling cocky and confident. Things were going well. It was beginning to look as though she were going to come out on top after all.

It had been a long, hard road.

She thought back over the years, all the time she'd waited for this, all the maneuvering and shifting and planning. Meeting Jack and getting involved with him was just icing on the cake, a little something extra, what her mother would have called lagniappe. She settled back into the thick plastic padding of the weight bench and placed her gloved hands on the cold iron bar above her head. The thought of her mother made the muscles in the back of her neck tense. Her arms stretched, then tightened, and with a chest locked full of air, she heaved the bar off its cradle and held it suspended there in midair. Then she exhaled slowly and lowered the bar to her chest. She let the hard metal brush against her sternum, then immediately lifted it off the bone and back up into the air.

She smiled at the ease with which she pressed the weight. She was benching 125 pounds, fifteen pounds over her own body weight. It had taken her years, but she'd finally gotten to where she wanted to be.

Lois Finlayson, despite her size, was incredibly strong.

The doorbell buzzed. She lowered the bar into the pair of metal arms that rose on both sides of her head, then used it to pull herself up. The doorbell went off again before she could get to the door. She opened it to find Lynch standing there in a rumpled white shirt and a pair of jeans, an old pair of running shoes on his feet.

"What, no suit? You don't look right without a coat and tie on," she said brightly, letting herself slide into his open arms. They kissed, the smell of tobacco on his breath as always. He'd had a drink as well, perhaps more than one.

"How are you?" he asked when they pulled apart.

"Hot," she said, brushing a lock of hair off her face. "I've got one more set to do. Come on in and spot me before I get cold."

He followed her into the office, where the bench was set up in the middle of the room.

"I've never seen you work out before," he said, eyeing her. She knew she looked good in the purple spandex workout leotard. She didn't mind his gaping at her; in fact, she was glad to see him loosen up.

"Yeah? So what do you think?"

He got behind the bar. "Hey, babe, this is a lot of weight."

She smiled. "It's really just maintenance. I've maxed a lot more than that."

256

"Jeez," he sighed. "I didn't have any idea you could handle this much weight. Of course, I should have guessed."

"What does that mean?" She smiled at him as she wrapped her hands around the bar.

"With the intensity of your passionate embrace, my dove," he kidded with a very poor W. C. Fields imitation. She laughed as he continued, "It should have been apparent that you were of superior physical attribute."

"God," she said, just before locking her breath down, "you were born to sling it."

"Damn straight," he said as she lifted the bar. It came up with little effort, although in her fourth and last set she was becoming fatigued. She bounced the bar off her chest six times, then struggled with the last rep in the set.

"I'm impressed," he said as he guided the bar back onto its rest for her. "Even intimated. Remind me not to make you angry."

"I will," she said, breathing deeply as she sat up. She stretched her arms, feeling the delicious tightness of her muscles. "Boy, am I glad that's over. You want to take a set?"

"How much is it?"

"One and a quarter."

He plopped onto the bench after she got up. "Sure. Let me see if I can get it up, so to speak."

He placed his hands clumsily on the bar, shifted them around three or four times before he got comfortable, then pulled his knees up and planted his feet on the end of the bench.

"Feet on the floor," Lois said, spotting him.

He did as instructed, clenched his jaw, and lifted. The bar shook in midair, wavering as Lynch struggled to hold it steady. Then he brought it slowly down to his chest, rested it just a moment too long on his sternum, then struggled to raise the weight.

"Holy cow," he stammered. Lois smiled as he dropped the bar to his chest again, then pushed and sputtered to raise it back up. He shakily placed the bar back on its rest and laid there, red-faced, for a moment.

"I'm out of shape."

"Oh," she laughed, picking up a towel and handing it to him, "parts of you work just fine."

She wrapped another towel around her neck, then went into the kitchen and poured herself a glass of club soda. Lynch followed her, making himself a glass of soda with a small slug of scotch included for flavor.

"So where are you off to tonight?"

"Got some business to take care of."

"You seem awfully close mouthed. What is it?"

"Lois, I—"

"Forget it," she interrupted, turning and walking past him into the living room. "I didn't mean to pry."

"You're not prying," he said, following her into the living room. "Honey, I'm just checking out something to do with Pearl Bergeron's . . ."

She stopped cold. "Pearl?"

"Yeah, it's probably nothing," he began.

"I can't believe you!" Her voice rose in anger. "After what happened to me the other day, you're going to keep digging into something that's none of your business!

"You know, Jack," she continued, her tone changing to one of disgust, "if you really cared about me, you'd lay off this."

"What do you mean? Of course I care about you. Part of the reason I'm doing this is because I care about you. I want to find out who's threatening us, to make it all stop."

"It will stop if you just stay out of this. It's too dangerous."

"No, it's not. I'm just—"

"Just what?"

"I'm going to run out to the Riverbend site tonight. There's something I want to check out. It's probably nothing."

Lois sighed. What harm could it do? She thought for a moment, then placed her drink on the table, walked over to Lynch, and wrapped her arms around his waist. She looked at him and smiled tenderly.

"I can't stop you. Do what you have to. Just promise me you'll be careful."

"I will," he said. Then he sipped on the drink hurriedly. "Listen, I need to go. It's a long drive out there."

She raised herself on tiptoe; he bent down to kiss her quickly, then pulled away and set his glass on the kitchen table.

"I'll probably be back late," he said. "I won't call. You get some sleep tonight."

"Oh, I will. Will you be out there tomorrow?"

"If I am, it'll just be to drop by. The press wasn't invited to tomorrow's shooting."

"Good," Lois said. "They just got in the way."

"I'll see you tomorrow, one way or the other."

"I hope so. Please be careful, Jack. I really do, well, I really do care about you."

"Yeah." He smiled. "I care about you, too."

She stood at the window, the perspiration drying on her leotard causing her to shiver slightly as he drove away. She wondered briefly if she should follow him.

But how much trouble could there be in his driving up to Riverbend?

It was the blackest night he'd seen in years. There was no moon; a deep, humid haze made up of a combination of moisture, swamp gas, and refinery pollution had blotted out all but the brightest stars.

He'd driven a little more than an hour, crossed the river, back-tracking now down the state highway to Riverbend. The last street-lights of the last small town had long receded in his rearview mirror. The faint green glow of the dashboard lights reflected off his face, mixing with the pinpoint of orange that hung off the end of his cigarette.

He shook his head to keep himself awake. Besides being tired, the two drinks had relaxed him to that magical point where all he wanted to do was lie on the couch with a magazine and the television going in the background.

That's what I should be doing, he thought. This is silly. But whatever it was that was eating away at him wouldn't let go. And he wasn't going to be able to sleep until he tracked it down. It seemed to him that his whole life had been marked by the struggle to find one elusive truth after another.

A point of light ahead interrupted his thoughts. He slowed, the headlight beams illuminating the gray pavement in front of him, the faded white stripe down the middle barely surviving as a guideline for staying on the road. The small light grew closer; he slowed down even more. Yeah, that's it, he thought.

He turned left, off the road and toward the light. A single security guard in a blue uniform sat inside the booth in a chair, reading a newspaper, a cup of coffee in front of him. Lynch braked and rolled his window down as the man stepped out of the small, white cubicle.

"Hi, I'm Jack Lynch. I work for Mr. Kwang. We left some paperwork over in G Building last Friday. We need it tonight before tomorrow's shooting starts."

The guard looked at him closely, suspiciously. "Nobody told me anything about it."

"We just noticed the file missing tonight. Production meeting. I volunteered to come pick it up." Lynch smiled. "Anything to get out of that damn meeting."

The guard chuckled back. "Yeah, I can imagine. Let me check my list."

He reached inside the door of the guardhouse and picked up a clipboard, flipped through a few pages. "Yeah, you're on the list for last Friday and tomorrow both. Guess it's okay. Can you find your way in the dark?"

"I brought a flashlight."

"Good, you'll need it. I can't turn the lights on from here, and all the other guards are gone for the night. You got a key to the building?"

"Yeah," Lynch lied again. "Miller Taylor gave me one."

"Okay, Mr. Lynch, you're all set. One thing you got to be careful of, though. Don't wander too far from the buildings or off the gravel parking lot. We're surrounded by swamp here. We've had everything from water moccasins to alligators show up in the middle of the night."

"Great," Lynch said. "I'll watch it."

He drove along the road slowly, the gravel crunching under his tires. Ahead of him loomed the great, amorphous shapes of the buildings, their whiteness dulled by the night. He glanced down at his watch; the dial read late.

He looked up just in time to see something with a tail slither off the road ahead of his headlight beams and rustle off into the waist-high grass. He speeded up a bit, to get past the field and into the main area of the complex.

The buildings lay ahead of him. He drove into a parking spot and killed the engine. Reaching across, he switched off the head-lights, throwing everything into nearly total blackness, with only dark shapes in varying shades around him. He sat there for a bit, just

260

listening. The night's deep silence was broken a moment later by the sound of a tugboat's horn on the river perhaps a mile off.

He took a deep, nervous breath through his nostrils. The night's smells were even different, with the baking hot aroma of the sun replaced by the heavy, musty, almost rank smell of decaying swamp and river all around. He reached down and opened his briefcase, feeling around in the charcoal shadows for the pistol. The warm metal felt sticky to the touch, and he realized his hands were sweating. He picked the heavy revolver up and laid it in his lap. Then he reached over and pulled the Geiger counter closer to him. Finally, he felt around in the blackness for his flashlight.

He flicked the chrome flashlight on and pointed the beam out the window. He swept the gravel around the car with the light; Lynch wanted to make sure he didn't step on anything alive getting out. Everything looked clear.

He carefully stuck the barrel of the revolver down his pants and opened the car door. The flashlight beam shook and danced across the lot as he walked. He strode out into the middle of the gray rectangle and stopped, wondering where to start.

"Okay," he said aloud, "here's as good a place as any."

He held the Geiger counter handle in his right hand. He was able to wrap that hand around the flashlight as well. With his free left hand, he flipped the switch to turn the instrument on, then rotated the audio knob. He pulled the counter tube out and extended the hose, pointing it vaguely toward the ground.

Almost immediately the speaker began clicking.

His mouth opened but no words came out. He felt his heart race, his breath coming in short gulps. The speaker was clicking, but not that much faster than it had in the professor's house.

Lynch began walking slowly, the sound of his footsteps crunching on the gravel echoing the clicking of the instrument. He walked across the lot, trying to convince himself that the noise from the counter was normal. In fact, he noted, the clatter from the speaker did seem to be dying off. It was slowing down now to just a few uneven clicks every couple of seconds.

It must have been my imagination, he thought.

He walked aimlessly through the complex, with no pattern or seeming direction to his efforts. He was aware that his time was limited; the last thing he wanted to do was alert the security guard. Even though it was night, and a relatively cool one, Lynch began sweating hard. He wondered which invisible threat he was more frightened of, the clicking of the counter or the creatures in the grass that might drag him off into the swamp for dinner.

Ahead of him stood the cooling tower, so big that its most obvious identifying characteristic was the huge portion of night sky it simply blotted out. He headed toward it, the chattering of the loudspeaker varying in frequency and amplitude. He stopped occasionally, rotating the counter tube in front of him 360 degrees with little change in the clicks. Maybe this is normal, he thought, maybe this is what it's like outside on a moonless night. With no clouds, no structures to shield us, maybe this is what we all get, every day, whenever we go outside.

The tower rose higher in front of him with each step. He came to the edge of the gravel-paved area. In order to get closer to the structure, he'd have to pivot and walk a hundred yards or so to his left, then onto the road that led to the tower itself.

He decided to try his luck cutting across the field. He stepped off the gravel carefully, the light swinging in front of him, checking the grass for unseen creatures. He stared hard in front of him, his eyes straining into the blackness. He wondered if he'd be able to find his way back to the car.

Lynch put a foot out, stepped on bare earth. It was soft, spongy, porous, but there had been little rain lately. The ground held; his feet didn't sink. He took another tentative step, then another. He was concentrating so hard on his own caution that he forgot to notice what was coming from the Geiger counter.

Louder clicks. Faster clicks. He looked down in disbelief. What's with this damn thing, he thought. Then he stepped toward the tower, a little faster this time, a little less carefully.

The clicking and snapping of the loudspeaker increased. It was almost like the static popping of an old tube radio late at night when the station had gone off the air, only louder, fiercer.

He stepped again, then again, and soon he was walking full tilt through the high grass, brushing aside with abandon the rustling weeds. He had to see. And his ears, his senses weren't lying to him. With each step he took toward the cooling tower, the noise from the counter increased. Now it was incessant, continuous. Lynch saw before him now no sky at all, only a huge, dominating monster rising up out of the soft ground and consuming all else, absorbing light and shadow as if it were a giant sponge.

He felt the instrument vibrating in his hand. The chatter of the speaker was so loud now, the sound so great, that he feared he would damage the instrument. He reached over with his left hand and turned the volume knob down, then took two more steps.

He was close enough to the tower to touch it. He bent backward and looked up. The tower was all he could see, straight to the top of the sky. To his right, he saw the dim outline of the tiny stairway that curved around the external surface of the tower all the way to the top.

Lynch was frightened. He felt minuscule now, tiny, threatened. He reached out and laid his hand on the surface of the rough concrete. It was still warm from the day's heat.

He set the Geiger counter on the ground, next to the base of the tower. The access maintenance doors to the tower were in front, where the pavement ran all the way up to the outer concrete lip of the tower's base. He realized that he must be almost in back of the thing. Once again, Lynch was somewhere he wasn't supposed to be.

He was scared now, and began moving quickly. He looked behind him, searching for the telltale blink of a flashlight that would indicate the security guard was looking for him. He felt for the pistol, not that it would be any good in the darkness or against the monolith in front of him. He focused the flashlight on the chattering counter, looking in the darkness for the meter. He bent down to get a closer look, pointing the tube directly at the ground, almost touching it.

The needle on the meter danced hysterically. What was it the professor had said? The needle was dipping and rising so fast that he could barely make it out. He bent even closer to the indicator, closer to the ground.

The indicator was tripping back and forth between 350 and almost 500. Just then, Lynch remembered what the professor had said earlier.

Get the hell out. . . .

He shook during the drive back to the city. Jack Lynch never in his life thought he'd be glad to see bright lights and traffic. It was almost one in the morning. He was exhausted but far too wired to go home. All the way into town, his mind rumbled with questions. What should he do? Who would believe him? How dangerous was it out there, really?

263

One thing was certain: He sure as hell couldn't sleep. He pulled off I-10 near the Superdome, maneuvered over to Poydras Street, then over to his office.

The outside border of New Orleans' Central Business District was a brightly lit ghost town. At one end of the street, a nearly empty bus belched smoke as it made its way through the loneliest part of the night. Two winos sat on the sidewalk a block away, sharing a bottle wrapped in a brown paper sack. Even the usual ambient noise of the jammed city had dissipated to relative silence.

Lynch parked the rental on the street. Then, afraid that someone might break into the car, he placed his pistol inside his briefcase, latched it, and took it and the Geiger counter up to the office with him.

An old black man in overalls was slowly pushing a dirty mop across the tiles of the dimly lit lobby. Jack used his key to enter the building. The man looked up at him suspiciously.

"Left something in my office," Lynch said. "I'll just be there a few minutes."

The old man grunted something as Jack eased past him toward the elevator. Up in his office, Jack turned all the lights on and locked the door securely. He was wound tighter than an alarm clock, his mind racing. Who could he call? What should he do? All those people were heading back to the studio tomorrow, to work there all day bathed in an deadly, unseen fog. He couldn't just let them go. Something had to be done.

Lynch sat at his desk, thinking, smoking one cigarette after another. He raised his feet and planted them on his desk. His right foot hit a shiny piece of paper and slid a few inches. He tried to remember seeing it before and couldn't. It looked like a cheap photocopy or a fax. He reached for it, at that moment remembering that Maud had told him about it and he'd never had a chance to read it.

He picked it up. The phone number and logo at the top was the same as that on the other faxes he'd received from his friend at the *Los Angeles Times*. Lynch scanned the article. It was an extended obituary, an account of the death and funeral of film director Harry McMillan. It was a more or less standard rehash of the articles he'd read before: the murder was still unsolved, the body was being shipped back to the States for burial, Mr. McMillan was survived by a brother, and two daughters blah blah blah. . . .

Lynch stiffened as he absentmindedly scanned the last few paragraphs. His eyes jerked in disbelief. He read the last part of the story again, until the part that caught his eye and made his heart lock up rolled by again:

> McMillan is survived by a brother, Henry McMillan of Milwaukee, Wisconsin, and two daughters: Lorraine Grouse of Denton, Texas, and Lois Finlayson of Los Angeles, California.

Lynch felt sick. Pearl had never had any children; no one had ever said anything about stepchildren.

His head swam. He'd been too long in the heat, smoked too many cigarettes, gone too long without food. He felt the onset of a full-scale blood-sugar crash. Why hadn't she told him?

So Pearl Bergeron was Lois's stepmother, and Lois had been straight with him on one account: She hated her.

"It can't be," he said. "No, this ain't real. I'm tired. None of this shit is real."

He brought his hands up to his face and wrapped them around his forehead, squeezing and pushing until his eyelids pulled back and his eyes burned in the dry air.

His head fell back on the thick padding of the chair. "Hoo, boy," he said out loud, "ain't life just freaking grand."

Carlton. Carlton Smith. That's who he could trust. He was the one man in the world whom Lynch could wake up in the middle of the night with a story like this and not be taken for a lunatic.

Lynch stood up, determined to drive over to Carlton's house. If I have to wake up the dead, he thought, I'm going to make him listen to me. He picked up his briefcase and the Geiger counter, and left the office behind. The janitor downstairs had progressed about ten feet with his mopping.

"Find what you looking for?" he mumbled as Jack walked by.

"Oh, yeah," Lynch blurted out in singsong. "I hit the freaking jackpot!"

He exited the building, both hands full, and walked the half block or so to his car. At the end of the block, two young kids turned the corner, boom box blaring, voices rising above it. Lynch opened his car, slid in, then locked the door behind him. As the two guys approached his car, Lynch, in a fit of paranoia, took the revolver out of the briefcase and laid it on the seat next to him.

The two walked past. Lynch relaxed a bit. He turned on the radio, started the car, and pulled out into the street. Somehow, he'd have to make it back out St. Charles Avenue. Carlton Smith lived in the Garden District.

Lynch pulled into St. Charles and drove away from downtown. He rolled the window down. The cool night air blew over him, taking some of the rawest, roughest edges away. Ahead, a solitary streetcar swayed side to side on its tracks, its long metal arm rising above to make contact with the wires. Lynch was rehearsing what he would say to Carlton, thinking that maybe after all this was over, he finally would leave town, when he saw the blue lights in his rearview mirror.

He sped up a little, looking for a place to pull over and let the police pass. There were too many cars parked on the side of the curb. The squad car was on his bumper now, hanging right off him, the harsh blue lights filling the car and hurting his eyes.

"All right, dammit," Lynch muttered, "I'm trying to get out of your way."

The cop behind him hit the screamer. The electronic whooping caused Lynch to jerk his head around. It was then that it hit him.

"What the—" he said to no one in particular. "They're after *me!*"

He went into a kind of shock, that mental disbelief that descends when the tornado funnel touches down in your next-door neighbor's yard, when the doctor shakes his head and says, "I think you've got a good chance against this," and when you realize the flashing blue lights in your rearview mirror are meant for you, not the idiot in the '65 Chevy who cut you off a mile back and deserves the ticket.

Lynch pulled over and tried to remember what he'd been told about getting stopped by the police: Remain calm, keep your hands on the steering wheel, say "Yes, sir" and "No, sir," and try to remember that he's the one with all the aces.

Two policeman got out of the car. One slowly approached from the passenger side, hanging back like they had taught him in "Car Stopping 101 in the Middle of the Night" back in cop school. The second uniform came up along Jack's side of the car. He saw in the side mirror that the police officer was tremendously overweight, with the kind of paunch that makes you saunter recklessly when you walk, whether you want or not.

266

"May I see your driver's license and registration, please sir?" the officer said politely, leaning down into Jack's window.

Lynch kept his left hand on the steering wheel while slowly pulling out his wallet with his right. As he pulled out his license, he mentally recalculated the number of drinks he'd had. But that was hours ago, seemed like weeks. Was he weaving in traffic? He was pretty sure he could pass a field test.

The cop studied his license. "Your registration, Mr. Lynch?"

"Oh, I don't have any registration, Officer," he said politely. "This is a rental car."

"Apparently that's the problem, Mr. Lynch. You were supposed to turn in this car four or five days ago. The agency has sworn out a warrant against you."

"What?" Lynch said. "You've got to be kidding. Give me a break!"

"I only know what the computer says, sir. May I see your papers on the car?"

"Sure," Lynch said, leaning over. "They're in the glove box."

Out of the corner of his eye, he saw the cop's partner move up on the right side of the car. The partner shone a flashlight inside the car just as Lynch reached for the handle of the glove box, and in doing so, bounced a beam of light off the metal of the .38 caliber Smith & Wesson Secret Service Special that lay in open view on the front seat next to Lynch.

"Gun, partner!" the guy screamed.

Lynch heard a yell to his left to match the one on his right, then a voice was screaming commands. Lynch tried to focus as best he could, but the evening had been so unreal already, and he was so tired.

Lynch felt something slam into the side of his head. He bounced away from the blow and turned to look at what had hit him; it was cold and metal, whatever the hell it was. There were hands on him, and doors flying open, then he seemed to become airborne, with a hand on the nape of his neck, yanking his hair cruelly, painfully. After the terrible, shrieking jets of pain in his shins, the world rotated first 90 degrees, then 180, and he felt himself slamming into the pavement. His knees were on fire and the side of his face was numb and something was scratching the skin off of him. And he felt something in his eyes, it smelled of leather and sweat. He realized it was the cop's boot, heavy and hard. He hurt like hell everywhere.

267

A voice above him was cursing him, calling him "Stupidshit" and "Asshole" and "Fuckhead," and then his arms were yanked behind him so hard, the pain so great through his elbows and his shoulders and ribs, that tears came to his eyes. Something cold and tight and heavy was on his wrists. Time seemed to swing into slow motion, like the gentle rocking of a porch swing, and he was on his feet again. He saw the blue-and-white squad car again, with the lights flashing and the voices crackling on the radio inside. The car seemed to jump at him and hit him in the face, hard, and he saw stars and lights and spangles.

Someone pulled his hair again, and he felt himself coming up off the ground. Then he was thrown into the padded backseat darkness of the squad car. He thought of Lois hanging out of the helicopter. He opened his eyes. He was lying on his side, staring at the back of the front seat, and the car was moving. The voices up front were laughing. Laughing. He thought he saw Sally again, lying next to him in the blackness of the parking lot, and he tried to move toward her. But he couldn't move his arms; the pain in his shoulders was too great.

So he leaned against the seat and breathed in air that smelled of sweat and urine and vomit, and his last thought, before the sweet, cheerless black came and took him away again, was, What in the hell happened to my life?

31

THERE WERE IMAGES, SOUNDS: LOUD, RAUCOUS YELLS, OCCASIONAL screams, bright lights, harsh voices. And smells. If hell had a smell, it was this one, the stink not just of urine and sweat, but the concentrated essence of them, as if the scent had been extracted from some appalling inferno deep in the bowels of the universe and packaged just for this place.

Lynch woke up in a New Orleans jail cell.

When he came to, he was on his haunches, backed into a far corner of the room with his legs curled painfully under him, behind a metal bunk that was bolted to the wall. There were two guys sitting sullenly on each of the two bunks. Lynch didn't know much about jail cells, but he figured that in whatever kind of hierarchy was created in a place like that, the top cats got to perch on the bunks. The middle level guys got to stand by the bars looking out.

And the punks got shoved into corners.

He was cold and dreadfully hungry despite his nausea. He tried to recall last night and what kind of great psychic error had landed him here. He moved to stand up. Instantly, a terrible pain shot through his back, straight up to his head and inside his skull.

He moaned. A deep voice above him said, "Well, look who be awake."

Lynch looked up. It was then that he realized he was one of two whites in the cell. The rest of the men were just a sea of unfocused black faces. He was afraid for an instant, then the pain pushed the fear aside. Something on his face stung: he brought his hand up and touched the right side of his face.

"Jesus," he muttered, pain flashing through his head. Was he burned? he wondered.

Then he remembered. The cop had kicked his legs out from under him, thrown him to the pavement, then mashed his face into the road with his boot.

The night was coming back to him: the Geiger counter, Lois, the pistol on the seat. *How could I have been so stupid?*

He forced himself to raise first his head, then his arms. The concrete floor and walls were wet, clammy with heaven knew what. Lynch was glad he didn't know. He pressed himself up the wall and realized that, yes, he still could stand. He looked out over the cell, trying to make the faces come in clearer. It was then that he discovered that his right eye was swollen nearly shut.

"You look like a truck hit you, man," the voice said again.

Lynch swiveled his head around, a movement that gave him roughly the same sensation in his neck as grinding broken glass in a mortar. There were eight guys in a cell meant for two. The voice came from a large man, deep black, wearing blue jeans and a dirty white undershirt. His bare arms were covered with keloid scars and tattoos. He needed a shave and smelled horribly, although Lynch reckoned that by this time he probably was getting pretty rank himself. From his short time as an inmate, he gathered that city jails had that effect on you.

"Listen, I got to talk to somebody," Lynch said quietly, hoping not to draw attention to himself. Two guys in front of the cell were in a heated discussion about something else. "I don't even know what I've been charged with."

"Of course, you don't. They dragged yo' ass in here about two in the morning and threw you in the corner. Except for some moaning and groaning, you been out all night."

"What time is it?"

"Beats the shit out of me. Nobody got watches in here. You missed breakfast, though."

Lynch felt his stomach flatten in on itself, then a wave of shakiness ran through him. "What's the deal here? You get a phone call, or is that just in the movies?"

The black man smiled at him, showing a gold tooth right in the middle of his uppers. "Naw, man, you gets a call. Say, what's a skinny little white muhfuh like you doing in here? You get caught down in the projects buying dope or what?"

"No, man, I forgot to return a rental car. The agency swore out a warrant on me."

The man stifled a belly laugh, just barely. "If I's you, I wouldn't be telling nobody in here that. You liable to get your white ass stomped. Again. Wha's yo' name?"

"Lynch, Jack Lynch. What's yours?"

"Curtis McEwan," he answered, extending a huge hand. "Anybody takes a ass-whipping from the Man like you took's okay by me."

"Glad to meet you, Curtis." Lynch shook the man's hand gingerly. Something in his shoulder wasn't right. He wondered if it was broken or dislocated or something. Maybe they ripped it clean out of the socket, and he just didn't know it yet.

"Say, Curtis, what's the program here? How do you get anybody's attention?"

"Best way's to make your way up to the front of the cell, then try to get one of the guards' attention. Be polite, but not *too* polite."

"Gotcha," Lynch said. He took a step away from the bed. There was maybe a foot or two of open space in the whole cell. He stepped over the other white guy in the cell, a young, skinny kid with bad acne who'd nodded out against the opposite wall, and moved up to the layer of flesh between himself and the door.

"Excuse me, guys, I got to get up here."

Nobody moved. Lynch cleared his throat. The guy to his right chuckled.

"Excuse me," he said again.

Nobody moved. Lynch scanned the three guys who were standing against the bars now, picked one, and tapped him on the shoulder.

"Excuse me, can I move up there for a second."

The man turned. Lynch did a quick audit: early twenties, good shape, mean. That's all he needed to know.

"Excuse yo' ass, muhfug," the man said.

"Listen, I just want to get the guy's attention so I can make my phone call, that's all."

A hand shot out, punched Jack in the right shoulder. His face screwed into a silent whorl of hot pain. His legs buckled and he started down. The room spun around, then a pair of arms grabbed him.

"Let him go, chump," a voice growled. Lynch tried to stiffen his legs, make his eyes work. Curtis was holding him up.

"I'm okay, man," Lynch said, straightening. "Thanks."

"What you doing rabbi'ing for this honkie muhfug? He gone be yo' pretty boy?"

Curtis stared at the young man. The cell went dead silent. Maybe five seconds passed. The younger man averted his eyes, stepped away from the door.

"Don't make a fug to me, man, shit, let the honkie up there."

"Thanks, man," Lynch whispered.

"Just get outta here 'fore you cause any more trouble," Curtis said, turning back to his perch on the bunk.

Lynch walked up to the cell door, looked out into the dingy hallway. Rows of harsh fluorescent lights hung from the ceiling. As he got closer to the door, the noise outside became even louder, until it was an incessant din of metallic banging and voices that melted into an audio blur. He looked as far as he could see down the hall in each direction. A uniformed deputy was strolling down the hallway toward the cell.

"Officer," Lynch called when the man got even with the cell door. The man ignored him, kept walking. Lynch had tried this politeness shit before and it had gotten him nowhere.

"Hey, you!" he barked.

The man stopped.

"Yeah, you! Listen, I ain't got to call my lawyer yet. I don't even know what I'm charged with."

The uniform turned, walked two steps closer. "Step back from the bars," he ordered. Lynch spotted the long nightstick that hung from his belt, pulled his arms from the bars and stepped back. The uniform took one step forward. "Name?"

"Lynch. Jack Lynch."

"Sit quietly, Lynch Jack Lynch. I'll be back."

A half-hour later, another uniform came, handcuffed him, and escorted him to the booking room. The building was filled with a continuous parade of haggard people, stressed khaki officers, sweaty patrolmen in off the streets in their rumpled blues; people crying, swearing, laughing, threatening. Lynch was led up to a counter, his hands behind him.

"I haven't had a chance to call my lawyer," he said. "What am I charged with?"

A tired-looking desk officer flipped through a stack of papers on a clipboard. "Okay, here we are: grand theft auto, carrying a concealed weapon, resisting arrest, assaulting an officer. Arraignment's at two this afternoon."

"Resisting arrest, assaulting an officer," Lynch squealed, his voice breaking. "Jesus, those guys beat the shit out of me!" His jaw ached with the effort of yelling.

"Lower your voice, bud," the officer said.

"Okay, okay." Lynch took a deep breath, tried to get himself under control. "Can I call my lawyer?"

"Yeah, c'mon around the counter." Lynch walked around. The uniform led him to a desk, empty except for a black rotary telephone that looked like something out of the 1940s.

The uniform reached behind, unlatched the handcuffs, pointed at the chair.

"Don't be stupid," the man said. "Be here when I get back."

Lynch sat down, grateful that the seat was padded. He stuck a finger in the rotary dial, dialed the bank. A switchboard and a departmental secretary later, he had Carlton Smith's office. His personal secretary answered.

"I'm sorry, Mr. Lynch, Mr. Smith is up at the Riverbend Studio with Mr. Kwang today."

"Listen, can you get word to him? I'm supposed to be there too, but I've had a little problem. I've been arrested."

"Arrested?" the feminine voice said. "You?"

Lynch almost laughed. "Yeah, me. And I need him, bad. Can you get him for me?"

"I'll try to get word up there," she said. "I'm not sure the telephones are connected yet."

"Great," Lynch said. "Do what you can, will you?"

He hung up the phone just as the desk officer came back in. Lynch stood up, put his hands behind his back without even being asked. As the handcuffs clicked on, he tried frantically to think of something to get himself out of this mess. Then it hit him.

"Wait, Officer, before I go back to the cell."

"Yeah?"

"I want to see Lieutenant Frontiere. It's important."

The man eyed him suspiciously. "What you want with him?"

"He'll want to see me. Tell him I have information he needs about a murder."

273

"A murder? Yeah, right."

"I'm serious. I know something about a murder he's investigating. If you'll tell him who I am, he's going to want to see me."

"Right, John Dillinger. Back to the cell." The uniform snapped the cuffs on, grabbed Lynch's upper right arm. Pain shot through him like someone driving nails into his bones.

Lynch was mad now, had nothing to lose. "Listen, you idiot! I get pulled over for a stupid misunderstanding about a rental car and the next thing I know two gorillas are mopping St. Charles Avenue with my face!

"You can do any goddamn thing you want to me," he continued, "but sooner or later you're going to have to let me out of here. And when you do, I'm going to file the biggest goddamn police-brutality lawsuit you've ever seen. I know every reporter in this town, and I'm going to personally see that this shithole gets opened up like a bag of fertilizer. And when Carl Frontiere finds out what I know and that you wouldn't let me see him, he's going to ream you a new asshole so big a 747 could fly through it on autopilot!"

The officer gazed at him in an awful, stony silence. Lynch had the distinct impression he'd just sucked in his last, painful breath. He braced himself, ready to hit the floor again, when the officer broke a smile.

"Chill out, man. I'll get him for you. Sit down over there. You know something, Mr. Lynch, you ought to clean up that mouth of yours."

Lynch's dirty mouth opened in shock. "I'm sorry," he stammered. "It's— It's just been a long day."

It was ten o'clock by the time Lynch stood at the booking window, Carl Frontiere behind him. The booking officer pulled a wire basket out of a rack and removed its contents. He handed Jack a manila envelope containing his watch, wallet, keys, and change. Then the officer handed Lynch his briefcase through the window.

"I don't want to make an issue out of this or anything," Lynch said through the window, "but what happens with my pistol?"

"Impounded as evidence," the officer said.

"Let that one go," Frontiere said. "Forget it, let's move."

"Okay, but where's my Geiger counter?"

"Your what?" the window officer asked.

"That piece of equipment that was in my car when the cops stopped me."

"I don't have it here, sir. It may still be in the car."

"Where's the car?"

"At the auto impound lot," the officer explained.

"The Geiger counter belongs to somebody else," Lynch, frustrated, said to Frontiere. "I got to return it to him."

"We'll worry about that later. C'mon, let's go."

Lynch was never so glad to get out of a place in his life. Even the searing brightness of the sun and the overpowering stench of car exhaust in the parking lot felt great. Frontiere led the way over to his car and opened the door on the driver's side as Lynch stood leaning against the passenger door. He started to get into the car, then hesitated.

"Lynch, I just want one thing made clear, okay?"

"Sure, Lieutenant. What?"

"You're not going to do anything stupid like try to escape or run or anything like that, are you?"

"Oh, Jesus, Carl, can we just get going?"

"I just wanted to check. Technically, you're in my custody. I've gotten used to having you around. I'd hate to have to shoot you in the back." He opened the door and eased into the sweltering car.

Lynch climbed in next to him. Frontiere turned the car's massive air conditioner to high and pulled out into the traffic.

"So what's this about radiation?"

"I hope I'm wrong," Lynch said. He leaned his head against the padded headrest, closing his eyes, trying to relax. Every bone in his body ached. His hands shook from fatigue and hunger. He kept thinking about Lois, about her being Harry McMillan's daughter, about how she hated Pearl.

Frontiere flicked on the blue lights located behind the grill of the car, hit the siren for a single blast, and sped through a red light and onto the entrance ramp of the highway. He quickly ran the car up to eighty, barely keeping up with the stream of civilian traffic lawbreakers.

"It was a hunch, really. They kept talking about the film getting screwed up and nobody could figure out why. Then I remembered somebody on the crew mentioning that the film had been sent up to the studio a couple of days before the shoot."

"How bad is it?"

"I don't know," Lynch said wearily. "I'm no physicist. I do know the place is not real hot until you get close to that cooling tower. The ground around the tower is practically on fire with it."

"Great," Frontiere muttered.

They drove on a minute or so in silence. The inside of the car was cold enough now to hang meat in. Lynch shifted in his sweaty, dirty clothes and felt himself shiver.

"You cold?" Frontiere asked.

"Little."

"Say, you look awful. When's the last time you ate?"

"Lunch yesterday, I think."

"Let's stop and get you a bite."

"No time. We got to get up to Riverbend. All those people are up there working in that stuff. We got to get them out."

"Lynch, we aren't going up there and cause a panic. I want to see the place, not that it'll do much good. We'll get the people out of there, but we'll do it quietly. We'll tell Kwang what you found out. Nobody else."

Lynch's eyes were closed. He slid down a little in the seat, leaned his body against the door.

"Your eye still hurting?"

"No," Lynch said, sitting up. "Hey, how come those guys get away with working over people like that."

Frontiere laughed. "You sit there talking to a New Orleans street cop with a loaded pistol on the seat next to you. Hell, you're lucky he didn't blow you away."

"Oh, great."

"I know Pignoli," Frontiere said, "the guy who popped you. A real hardass. If he'd really wanted to hurt you—or if you'd been a black guy—you'd be lying up in the security ward at Charity Hospital right now."

"So I should be grateful to the S.O.B., right?"

Frontiere laughed again, and mashed on the accelerator to get past a slow-moving semi.

Frontiere's driving habits, and his ability to get past unpleasant traffic situations with a blast of his siren, cut fifteen minutes off the driving time to Riverbend. The police lieutenant slowed at the security guard's booth just long enough to flash his badge at him, then sped past without stopping. Lynch looked out the back window, a cloud of gray gravel dust obscuring the hapless guard.

276

It was close to noon. Lynch figured the crew would be breaking for lunch soon. Somewhere, deep in his fatigued brain, it occurred to him that this was the third time he'd been up here. He'd have to remind his dentist to skip the X rays for the next couple of years.

"Which way?"

"Up here," Lynch pointed, his empty gut knotting up. "Bear to the left, then head straight up there to that block building."

Frontiere maneuvered the car up to the parking lot, then skittered to a halt in the loose gravel. Both men jumped out. Lynch headed toward the door. He opened it to confront the young woman security guard, who stood there, legs apart, left hand on her hip, right hand holding a walkie-talkie.

"What's going on here?" she demanded. "The front gate said you two just drove by without stopping."

"Where's Kwang?" Lynch asked. "We need to see him, fast."

"Just a minute, what's going on here?" Lynch pushed past her, with Frontiere behind.

"Stop!" the woman cried. Frontiere stopped, pulled out his badge again in one swift, practiced motion.

"Lieutenant Frontiere, New Orleans Police Department, homicide."

"This isn't your jurisdiction," the woman said, her voice quavering.

"Lady, if you don't sit down in that chair and behave yourself, I'm going to have you tied and gagged. This gentleman asked you a question. Answer it."

"I don't know. He came in about ten minutes ago, headed that way." She pointed down the hall.

Lynch turned quickly and went down the hall, toward the room where the newspaper reporters and crew had gathered the previous Friday. He opened the door: Andrew Kwang was inside, sipping a cup of tea, with Sheldon Taplinger taking notes as he dictated.

"Carl," Lynch turned. "Can I talk to him alone?"

"Why alone?"

"He's my client. I can handle this best alone."

Frontiere stared for a moment, then decided, perhaps against his better judgment, to extend his trust one notch further.

Lynch walked in. Kwang glanced up at him, confused.

"Sheldon," Lynch ordered. "Step outside. I need to talk to Andrew alone."

Taplinger stood up, face flushed. "Who are you to order me around—"

Lynch took two quick steps toward the young man, then had him by the lapels. "Out," he snarled. "Now."

"There's no need for that, Mr. Lynch," Kwang said, his voice as steady and calm as always. "Sheldon, leave us alone."

Lynch eased his grip. Taplinger was shaken, embarrassed, angry. "Are you sure that's a good idea, Andy?"

"Go."

Taplinger left the room, opened the door angrily, slammed it behind him. Outside, Frontiere leaned against the closed door, blocking it. Lynch walked over to the table, sat down across from Kwang.

"Tea, Jack?"

"No time, Andrew. We've got to talk. Quick."

"About what?"

"I think there's something terribly wrong here. I think the Riverbend plant is contaminated."

"Contaminated with what?" Kwang asked, the expression on his face as close as he could allow himself to incredulity.

"Radiation," Lynch said.

"That's impossible," Kwang insisted. "This plant was never functional. That was guaranteed."

"The fogged film, Andrew. I sneaked onto the grounds last night. I had a Geiger counter. The place is hot, especially around the tower."

Kwang read Lynch's eyes for what seemed like an eternity. "Are you sure?"

"As sure as I can be. I'm no scientist. But we need to get these people out of here. Get somebody in to check for sure. Quietly."

"I don't want any more scandal."

"Me, either."

Kwang stood up, paced around the table nervously, hands in pockets. Finally, he turned. "Okay, I'll get Taylor. Tell him there's a problem with the licensing or something. Anything. Tell him to clear the crew out as quickly as possible."

"Good," Lynch said. He let out a deep breath. "Andrew?"

"Yes?"

"What happened the night you went to Pearl's? Why did you go there."

"I did not kill Ms. Bergeron," he said, stone-faced.

"I never thought you did. But you were there."

"I went there because I thought it might help. I felt certain there was some other reason she didn't want me to have this facility."

"I think we know why now. But it didn't have anything to do with you. What happened when you got there?"

"I rang the bell. There was no answer. I don't know why, but I turned the doorknob on the security gate. It was unlocked, which I thought very unusual. So I opened it, pushed the door just a bit. That's when I saw her."

"Pearl?"

"Yes. I went in. She was lying head first at the bottom of the flight of stairs. It seemed obvious to me that, given her condition, she was almost certainly dead. I felt for a pulse, turned her over. I got a smear of blood on the wall. She was beaten very badly."

"You never went upstairs?"

"No."

"Did you hear anything?"

"No, not that I can remember. I was in some distress. I remembered our altercation in the restaurant. I am ashamed to say I panicked. I wandered around frightened, thinking. When I got back to the hotel, I came in through a back entrance and found my way to a service elevator. No one in the lobby saw me come in. Sheldon agreed to lie and say that I was in the hotel all night."

Lynch was staring off deep in thought, trying to visualize what Kwang had described, comparing Kwang's description with the pictures he'd seen. Pearl's body had been moved, just as Kwang described. Everything else had the ring of truth to it as well, which sickened Lynch even more.

Suddenly, his head swam. Carl Frontiere was looking for a left-handed killer. He saw Lois moving the Steadicam back and forth, left to right, so fluidly and so smoothly. She touched him first with one hand, then with the other. She took him in her left hand at one time, with her right at another. The tremors that went through his body left his mind in fog.

"Where's Lois Finlayson?" Jack asked.

"The young woman?" Kwang asked. "I believe she's with A crew, over by the cooling tower. Hagan decided to do location shots from the top."

Lynch bolted out the door, nearly knocking Frontiere over. "C'mon!" he yelled.

Lynch forgot about the car, shielding his eyes against the sun as he led Frontiere at a dead run across the compound, between two buildings and down the gravel road that led to the area in front of the tower. It loomed before them now like an enormous white tombstone. Lynch ran ahead on nervous energy, the pain in his shoulder crunching nerves with each pounding step, each sharp intake of air a burst of flame in his chest.

The crew was gathered around the base of the tower, in the shadow created by the gigantic concrete monument. Jerry Hagan stood on the edge of the crowd, a pair of binoculars to his eyes, looking up.

Lynch ran up to him. Breathless, he struggled to get his words out as Frontiere caught up with him from behind.

"Where's Lois?"

Hagan turned, looked at him in surprise. "What in the hell happened to you? You look like somebody stuffed you in a Coke bottle, then yanked you back out."

Lynch put his hand out and grabbed Hagan's shoulder, partially to steady himself, partially to get the man's attention. "Where's Lois?"

"She's up there." He pointed. "She took the shoulder mount rig up to the top. She's doing some vantage shots from the top of the tower and one shot straight down the throat."

Lynch panted. "Has she got a walkie-talkie?"

"Man, she's only going to be up there a half-hour, plus the fifteen minutes or so it takes to get there."

"Fifteen minutes?"

"That's a long walk up that staircase, buddy. Close to a quarter-mile of steps, I'd say."

Lynch turned to Frontiere. "I'm going up after her."

"What the hell is going on here?" Hagan demanded.

Lynch turned back to him. "In a few minutes, Miller Taylor and Kwang are going to be here. Everybody has to leave this place. Now. Have the crew start getting their gear together."

"You're crazy," Hagan snapped. "We ain't going nowhere."

Frontiere flipped out his badge again, flashed it at Hagan. "Oh, yes you are. Get moving."

Hagan sputtered something in reply, but Lynch was no longer

listening. Ahead of him, perhaps twenty feet away, the metal stairway that ran in a slow, lazy circle around and up the side of the cooling tower shimmered in the sun. It was painted green, almost the color of the grass and trees in the distance, or of the algae that floated on the surface of a standing pool of stagnant water.

Lynch ran to the stairs and jumped the first three, his full weight hitting hard. The flimsy railing shook and vibrated all around him. A spray of concrete dust erupted to his right. He slowed, took a few more tentative steps on the light metal, then began the climb to the top.

He had always been slightly acrophobic. The combination of heat, sleeplessness, fatigue, pain, and hunger made him light-headed, dizzy. The ground below receded as he ascended higher with each rickety step. How Lois had climbed those steps with all that gear astounded him; then again, he thought, many of the things she seemed capable of were astounding.

He focused on each step in front of him, the diamond pattern stamped in the steel a visual rhythm to match his movements. His right hand dragged along the rail, his left remained firmly on the hot concrete. He looked to his right, away from the tower, and paused to take in the incredible view. Below him, wandering lazily through the lush growth, was the broad expanse of the Mississippi River.

He thought of Lois hauling all that equipment to the top of the tower. He heard Frontiere's words like a continuous tape stuck on "Play."

"Strong," he'd said. "But not necessarily an Olympic athlete. Maybe young and agile."

He saw her in his mind's eye, benching her own body weight, swinging the sixty-pound camera harness around like it was a cape. She didn't *look* that strong, but he'd seen so often how looks can lie, how what seems may not necessarily be what is.

"You got to be in pretty good shape to beat somebody to death with your bare hands," Frontiere had said, "but you ain't got to be Arnold Schwarzenegger."

"Oh God," Lynch muttered, breathless, as he began to climb again.

She'd held his hand tightly, passionately, with an intensity he'd never felt in a woman before. "Jack," she'd said, "I don't ever want to talk about Pearl Bergeron anymore. I don't ever want to hear her

281

name mentioned. I want to get on with my life. I want to forget Pearl Bergeron ever existed. Will you help me do that?"

To Lynch's right, a solitary tugboat pushed a line of barges ahead of it against the current. Pain wracked his shoulder, but he no longer seemed to care.

Finally, the concrete began to constrict inward, and the angle of the steps increased. He was ascending the throat now—near the top, near Lois.

Then he saw her.

She was at the top of the stairway on a small platform that extended from the very top of the tower, next to the lip that surrounded the black abyss. She stood straight and tall, with the camera rigged on her shoulder. A fanny pack was strapped around her waist. A taped, used film magazine lay to the left of a metal case at her feet. She was panning slowly, filming the same view that had left him in starstruck awe. He sucked in a breath. She was beautiful. And he understood at that moment that he loved her more than he had realized. Even in his weariness he ached for her.

"Lois," he said, trying to keep his voice as calm as possible.

She pressed a button on the side of the camera to stop the motor. She pulled the camera away from her face and off her shoulder. She turned, and in her eyes was a coldness he had never seen before. She set the camera down on the platform.

"What are you doing here?"

"Lois, they're evacuating the facility. There's something terribly wrong here."

"All right. Let's go." She leaned down and opened the lid of the metal case.

"Lois," Jack interrupted her motion. He climbed a few steps closer to her. The metal stairway squealed under the strain. "Why didn't you tell me your father was Harry McMillan?"

She froze, her hand on the case. She didn't move for perhaps ten seconds.

"Lois?"

"How did you find out?"

Her damp hair hung down over her shoulders. He saw in her arms the hardness of muscle, in her eyes the determination of something he suddenly realized was hate.

"One obit, Lois. One short, tiny, goddamn little obituary."

"Probably the only one," she said.

282

"It took me a while to put it together."

"And now you got it figured out, huh?" Lois said. "I was fourteen when my father left us for that bitch. Do you know what that did to my mother?"

"No," Lynch said sadly. "I don't."

"She went crazy after that, was never really the same. She married this bastard, this sadistic piece of shit who adopted us, changed our names. Did things to us my father would have killed him for if he'd cared enough to find out.

"My sister tried to commit suicide when she was seventeen," Lois continued. "Slashed her wrists. I found her."

"God, Lois. I'm so sorry."

"Pearl was the coldest person I've ever met in my life. She pulled my father away from us. He made a ton of money, but we never saw it. While they were off in Europe, my sister and I were struggling through school on scholarships and loans, waiting tables."

She paused for a second, looked away from Jack toward the horizon. "My stepfather disappeared one night. My mother was on welfare the year she died."

"Jesus, honey, I'm—"

"Pearl hated me. I don't even know why. She drove my father to drink. She divorced him when she was through with him. They never found out who killed him. But if she didn't do it, she may as well have."

"Lois," Lynch said slowly. "Did you go to her apartment that night?"

"Yes," she said, her voice dead. "The night of the press conference."

"You wanted to try and talk to her, didn't you? You wanted to try and get her to give you this one last chance."

Lois tightened, her body tensed, her fists clenched.

"And she wouldn't talk to you, would she?" Lynch continued. "She probably laughed at you. Was at least her usual bitchy self, right?"

Lois went ashen pale. Even in the glaring sunlight reflecting off the concrete, bathing them both in a white light that was almost spiritual, he could see her lose color.

"Yes," she said, her voice low, barely perceptible above the whistle of the steady wind that blew past them.

"She pushed you, didn't she? You didn't want to do it, did you?"

Her silence was like a roar in his ears. *C'mon, dammit, deny it! Tell me I'm wrong! Throw something at me, spit at me, scream at me! Do something!*

"Lois, you killed her, didn't you? And you tried to scare me off, to keep me from poking around. You cut your own safety belt in the chopper, didn't you?"

Her eyes narrowed. Hate came back into her eyes, a hate that had kept her alive all these years, through all the struggling, through all the suffering.

"Of course I killed her, you idiot. I didn't go over there with the intention of killing her. But once I started, I went after it with as much passion as I could muster. . . ."

Every muscle in his body melted, and Lynch found himself falling against the concrete of the tower and sliding down onto the step.

"Oh, Lois. My God . . ."

She squatted down and looked at him. "Jack, I was only trying to scare you off the—the murder—so we could be together. This doesn't have to be the end of anything. Nobody knows but us. Kwang will go on trial, he'll be acquitted. That'll be it."

"That won't be it. You killed Pearl. She's never coming back, and that won't go away."

"It'll go away if we make it go away."

"No, it won't!" he yelled, with as much energy as he could muster. "You killed somebody, Lois!"

"Somebody that needed killing, Jack! She *needed* killing!" Lois jerked against the railing of the platform. A tiny, sparkling cloud of concrete dust erupted above Lynch's left ear.

He flashed back on his first conversation with Frontiere. He remembered the excuse Frontiere's other murderer had given.

"Nobody *needs* killing, dammit! Nobody!" he screamed. He was back on his feet now, hands locked on the railing.

"She did," Lois sniffed. "You didn't know her like I did." Then her tone changed. She was sweet now, supplicating. "Jack, we can go away together. We can be happy, we really can."

"Lois, the police are already here," he said slowly.

She screamed, a cry of anger, fear, frustration. "I don't believe you did that!"

284

"Goddammit," he yelled again, "this isn't the movies anymore, Lois! It isn't the goddamn *Maltese Falcon,* and I'm not goddamn Sam Spade, and you're not goddamn Mary Astor! This is real, Lois. Real. You snuffed out a human life!"

Then, almost in a daze, she said, "I won't go to jail, Jack. I won't."

"Maybe you don't have to. I know a good lawyer. We can fight this. We can fight it together.

"But not by running," he added after a moment. Anything to get her off that tower . . .

She reached behind and unzipped the fanny pack. When her left hand came back, it held a small, silver automatic pistol.

"I won't go to jail, Jack. I mean it."

"Lois," he whispered. "Don't . . ."

Behind them, from far away, came the faint wail of police sirens. Lynch looked around. He could see far to the northeast the highway to Norco. Faint blue lights flashed in tiny pinpoints, growing larger by the second. Frontiere must have called for backup, he thought.

Lois heard the sirens as well. Her lower lip began to tremble, an almost inperceptible motion. "Jack, no."

The sirens became louder, just a bit at first, but rising with each heartbeat.

"Lois, let's get down from here," he said.

"I won't go down there," she said, her face screwed up in fear and rage. It was the first time he'd seen the smooth lines of her face break. She raised the gun to him.

"I won't go," she said again.

Jack studied the gun, wondering if she'd really use it. "You don't want to shoot me, Lois. You and I love each other. We care. We can get through this together."

His leg cramped. He shifted his weight from one side to the other; the metal shook beneath him. He took a step up. Something creaked. He thought for a second it was his imagination, then he saw a puff of dust at the point where the stairway was bolted onto the concrete. His heart jumped in his chest.

"Lois, I think we'd better go. It's not safe."

"Don't tell me what to do!" She stamped her foot and the platform vibrated. Little puffs of dust appeared in several places.

"Be still!" he shouted. "We've got to get down from here."

"Damn you!" she yelled, stamping her foot again. "This is all your fault! None of this would have happened if you hadn't stuck your nose in where it didn't belong!"

The gun wavered in her hand. Lynch took a step toward her. A pair of bolts under Lois's right foot popped and bounced off the side of the tower like pebbles off a mountain as they fell the hundreds of feet to the ground. A metal support below her feet came loose and followed the bolts down.

The platform began to sway.

"Ohmigod!" he yelled. Lois looked down, the metal grid underneath her shaking in the wind.

"Jack, help me!"

"Don't move."

He took a step toward her. Behind him, the sirens blared. "Lois, set the gun down and hold onto something," he said, trying to muster as much calm as possible.

"No! This gun is getting us out of here, Jack."

Lynch moved again. There was an horrendous tearing sound, the sound of metal twisting and ripping. The platform above him came completely loose from the top of the tower and dangled in midair, attached now only to the stairs. Lois screamed, and the camera and the metal case slid on the tilted platform toward the tower, then dropped into the gap and down the concrete side. As she grabbed for them, the platform lurched farther away from the concrete.

Lois jumped for the safety of the concrete ledge at the very top of the tower. She miscalculated, jumped too far. Her legs caught the lip of the tower, her torso already too far over the edge.

Lynch yelled and hopped up the last three steps in a split second, then pounced for her feet. His fingertips brushed the bottom of her shoes as they went up in the air.

With a ghastly shriek, she went over the side, into the gaping maw of the tower. Her scream echoed in his ears all the way into her own last silence.

Lynch's eyes locked shut, and he let loose a howl of anguish. He collapsed onto the stairway, which still bounced and dangled, barely attached to the concrete. He rolled his fists into tight balls, then slammed them into the tower as hard as he could. He pounded the rough, unforgiving concrete again and again and again, until the blood came and his bones broke, and the sound of his own pain drowned out everything else.

286

32

AS LYNCH DROVE HIS BATTERED EIGHTEEN-YEAR-OLD FIAT SPYDER through the parking lot of the state capitol in Baton Rouge, he remembered his one semester of graduate school, before he'd dropped out to take the newspaper job and marry Katherine. In one course, he'd read T. Harry Williams's wonderful biography of Huey Long. He had read it with delight, and it was where he first discovered his passion for observing the nuances of power, his fascination with deal making, the dynamics of politics. He had spent his life since then on the fringes of power.

In the month since Lois's death, he'd read the book again. The complexity of the man, the strange mix of good and evil, the fatal disregard for his enemies fascinated Lynch as it always had. Nothing had changed. He was just mortally weary.

He had holed up in his apartment, refusing to go to his office or take calls, his wounds slowly healing. Maud Pelletier came by twice a week with groceries. She was still going into the office every day, despite his inability to pay her. Carlton phoned periodically with updates on his legal problems. A package arrived in the office mail. Maud brought it over. It sat unopened on the kitchen table for three weeks. Lynch slept and read books and stared at the television, then read some more.

During the fourth week, he finally opened the thick manila envelope. An unsigned note instructed him to read the documents and do whatever he felt he should with them. He remembered the message on his answering machine, the night before all hell broke loose.

The package contained copies of documents dating clear back

to the 1950s that explained the mystery of Riverbend. The Louisiana Public Service Commission had given the army permission to use a stretch of desolate, bleak swampland as an experimental dumping ground for the effluent from nuclear weapons plants. Waste would come in from all over the country and be buried there in specially designed drums deep in the ground.

One document in particular caught Lynch's attention: a memo outlining the physical boundaries of the area. It was signed by LaMar Bergeron, Commissioner, Louisiana Public Service Commission. Pearl, it seemed, had been taking care of Daddy as well as Daddy took care of her.

It was an experiment doomed to failure. The drums rusted through in the soggy swampland within two years, and the project was abandoned. No one cared that the land was poisoned. It wasn't fit for anything except the livelihoods of a few Cajun trappers and fishermen. The last shipment had been buried in 1956. The remaining nuclear sludge gradually soaked over generations and through history deeper into the mud. Cleaning it up was hopeless. The best that could be done was to keep people away for the next hundred years.

The charges against Kwang had been dropped, and he had long since left town without a word. The State of Louisiana had filed an injunction against the studio, based on substandard-concrete, prohibiting it from going ahead with its plans. Shortly after that, Lynch received the first phone call from Baton Rouge.

He'd been letting the answering machine take his calls these days. Robert Brewster left a number, said he was with the governor's office, and Lynch could return the call collect. He never did.

A few days later, Brewster called again. Lynch didn't pick up the phone, didn't call back. The third time, Brewster said he'd send a state trooper down there to knock on Lynch's door.

Lynch returned the call.

Brewster, it seemed, was a nice enough fellow. Could Lynch drive up to the capitol for a meeting with the governor? A private, friendly meeting?

Jack Lynch had been around long enough to know that when the governor asked you to visit, you bloody well better show up. He picked up his phone and called a number out in Jefferson Parish, then left his apartment for the first time in a month.

The man was willing to knock a hundred off the price of the car.

It needed new tires; the seats were ripped, and a thin stripe of brown rust ran around the lowest four inches of the body. But the Fiat ran, and he could have it for eleven hundred. Cash please, no checks. It took the last of Kwang's advance to pay him.

The car made it to Baton Rouge, although whether it would make it back was speculation. It was early October now, and school was back in session. Lynch got lost looking for the capitol, then wound up driving through Tigertown, marvelling at the youth and exuberance of the LSU students. He felt old.

He finally found a parking space near the capitol building. His appointment was for two in the afternoon. He looked at his watch: 1:45. He walked up the steps of the towering, twenty-four-story limestone building. The house that Huey built. . . .

He walked down the high-columned marble hallway, past the legislative chambers, into the rotunda, and down the corridor. He stopped in front of the massive door to the governor's office and tried to remember Williams's description of the place where the Kingfish had bought it. A tiny man, a doctor, had stepped from behind a pillar and put a bullet in Huey's gut. The troopers and bodyguards let loose with a fusillade that had scarred the marble for years. Huey, operated on by an incompetent doctor who forgot to check for blood in his urine, went to his reward.

"Yes, Governor Bergeron is expecting you, Mr. Lynch, but he's in his private quarters. Take the elevator to the twenty-fourth floor." The young secretary pointed with a long, polished fingernail.

A few minutes later Lynch found himself being led into the governor's private sitting room by a man who introduced himself as Robert Brewster. Governor LaMar Bergeron's taste, Lynch observed, ran to eighteenth-century cathouse. A man out of his time.

Bergeron got up from his red-velvet chair and walked across the Persian rug to shake Lynch's hand. He was a big man, and wore a gray pin-striped suit and an off-white shirt with an expensive silk tie. He had a huge head of white hair, stylishly cut, perfectly combed. His complexion was ruddy yet gave the appearance of being so from time spent outdoors rather than in other indoor pursuits. Lynch felt self-conscious in his own threadbare, windblown suit.

He found himself strangely calm, as if even in the company of powerful men he was now untouchable. He shook Bergeron's hand in a noncommittal manner and took a seat on the sofa where the

289

governor pointed. Brewster sat in a chair opposite, unbuttoning his suit coat and pushing the sides behind him as he did so.

"Thank you so much for joining us today, Mr. Lynch," Governor Bergeron said, his voice devoid of the slight Cajun lilt he adopted in his speeches. "As we used to say in the service, smoke 'em if you got 'em."

"No thanks," Lynch said. "I'm trying to quit."

"Good for you," Bergeron said jovially. "Drink?" Lynch shook his head.

"We asked you here today because there are some things we're trying to wrap up in regards to the Riverbend site. We understand you've been privy to some information. We'd like to have your thoughts on it."

"What do you mean? What information?"

"Now, now," the governor said. "There's no need to be coy. We know that you were scouting around the facility with a Geiger counter the night before the facility was closed down."

"You guys wouldn't happen to know where that thing is, would you?" Lynch asked. "I got a letter from the university physics department wanting me to pay for it. There ain't no way I've got that kind of money."

The governor smiled. Brewster spoke up. "We might be able to help you out on that account. Why don't you send me a copy of the letter?"

"So you obviously know what kinds of problems we've got down there," Bergeron said.

"I know there are problems," he said. "I don't know where they came from, how it got to be that way." Lynch was no poker player, but he had sense enough not to show all his cards.

The governor sat forward in his chair, folded his hands together as if praying, and put on his earnest mask. "I want to speak frankly with you, Mr. Lynch, and candidly."

Lynch winced. Whenever a politician wanted to speak frankly and candidly, it was a pretty good bet that a wagonload of horse manure was about to show up on your front porch.

"Despite my daughter's personality . . . quirks, shall we say, her objection to Kwang's purchase of the Riverbend site was a noble one. She was trying to protect me. I was entirely innocent in this situation. The problems at the Riverbend site have been around for years, long before I became governor. But she knew that if the problems were discovered, it would be the present governor who would pay the price. It was a no-win situation, Mr. Lynch. She knew that."

Lynch fought back a smile at the governor's lie. Entirely innocent, my ass. "Why didn't somebody just come out and say what happened, let the truth out?"

"Mr. Lynch, are you aware of the condition that this state's government is in? First of all, Louisiana has been in an oil-bust recession for nearly ten years. We are broke. We can't afford schools, we can't afford roads. Our unemployment rate is off the wall. Tax revenues are down the toilet. The state can't afford to clean that place up, even with federal help, which the feds can't afford either.

"Secondly," the governor said solemnly, "the people of this state can't take another blow. They've had enough. I know what's best for my people. And this is one issue that is going to stay buried."

Aren't the people lucky, Lynch thought, to have you to know what's best for them. . . .

"You're going to have a hard time covering this up," Lynch said. "Whenever you get more than two people in on a secret, sooner or later the word's going to get out."

"No one's going to believe that story without proof, Lynch," the governor said, dropping all pretense of formality. "And there's only two ways to prove it. You got to have a paper trail or somebody else has got to get out there and measure it. Neither of those two things is going to happen."

"Maybe you've got the paper trail covered," Lynch said. "But how are you going to keep people off that property for the next ten generations?"

"The State of Louisiana has seized the property as unsafe," Brewster said. "We've made Kwang an offer, and he has accepted it. Which is exactly what we planned two years ago when we couldn't stop the Louisiana Power and Light Company from putting it on the block."

"Why the hell did you guys let LP & L build the plant in the first place?" Lynch asked.

"Can you think of a better way to cover up a nuclear waste site? We thought the concrete would seal everything up. It didn't work that way. In typical fashion, the contractor used substandard concrete. . . ."

"All those workers," Lynch sighed. "Jesus Christ."

291

"This is the real world, Lynch. I'm afraid Jesus doesn't have much to do with it," Bergeron said.

"If you're going to condemn it, you've got to make it public why," Lynch said. "That queers the deal right there."

"Not at all. The concrete is deteriorating like hell. The death of your girlfriend proves it. The place is a safety hazard. We've shut it down until the state can pay for its destruction. And that will be quite a long time."

"Did you know up front that Lois killed Pearl?" Lynch asked quietly.

"No, we didn't know that. If we had, though, we would have taken care of her later. The important thing was to get Kwang out of the way and get control of that property."

"Now all you have to do is shut everybody up," Lynch said, "including me."

"Basically," Brewster said cheerfully, "you're right."

"We had a couple of gentlemen even try to blackmail us," the governor added, smiling at his aide.

"What'd you do?" Lynch snapped. "Have them bumped off?"

Bergeron laughed, a raucous politician's belly laugh. "I'm the governor, Lynch, not some Desire Project crack dealer. You don't bump people off in politics, you either ruin them or you buy them. Both of those gentlemen now have obscure but high-paying jobs in state government. They're quite well, and quite happy."

"I thought we were broke," Lynch said.

"And the police officer to whom you so injudiciously told this fabrication has just received a rather significant promotion," Brewster added.

Bergeron nodded. "And Kwang's not going to say anything. He wants his money from the state, and then he never wants to hear from us again."

"Which leaves me," Lynch said.

"Which leaves you," LaMar Bergeron agreed. "We've both lost a lot, Lynch. Why should either of us lose anything else?"

"You have a great deal to gain by joining the team, Jack," Brewster said. "And a great deal to lose by bucking us. I understand you have some outstanding legal problems down in New Orleans. Did you *really* assault an officer and resist arrest? You don't seem the type."

"Grand theft auto, carrying a concealed weapon," the governor interrupted. "It's not much, but it could get you a couple in Angola. You ever been to Angola, Lynch? I could arrange for a tour."

Lynch stared at the two men in stony silence. If he were capable of rage or revulsion anymore, it would have gone through him like a firestorm. Instead, he settled back on the sofa and let the two men wonder about him for a moment longer.

He thought of the documents. They were safe in his locked box at the bank. They might be useful someday. Not today.

"You have my silence," he said finally. "But that's all. I want nothing from you. I'm not on your goddamn team. I'm just smart enough to know when to keep fighting and when to cut my losses."

Bergeron smiled. "That makes you a wise man indeed."

He clapped his hands together one time, firmly. "Gentlemen, I believe that concludes our business."

Lynch kept the top down all the way back to the city. A front had come in overnight, as mean and as early a blast of cold air as Lynch could remember. There was no kind of cold like the rare and intense New Orleans cold; the humidity made it seep through your bones as if they were made of sponge, and no amount of clothing could warm you up once it set in.

What he needed was a drink. He felt as though his pilot light had gone out, and it would take nothing less than a high-octane jolt to get it going again. As he blasted down the highway at seventy miles an hour the tears in his watering eyes blew dry, and he pulled his coat close around him with one hand. His hands still ached from his losing battle with the concrete tower. Awkwardly, he folded his coat collar around his neck. He drove on alone into the oncoming night, toward the warmth and safety and escape of his apartment.

Lynch was glad he hadn't really fallen in love with her.